THE SIZZLING NOVELS
OF
MARCIA MARTIN . . .

SOUTHERN NIGHTS

It was every woman's dream come true . . . a dazzling inheritance, a sprawling family estate, and a seductive, irresistible man. But Maggie Hastings longed to uncover the secret of her heritage—even if it threatened her newfound love.

"FOUR STARS . . . Romance fans be on the lookout for this wonderfully entertaining novel by a fresh and exciting talent . . . Ms. Martin demonstrates fine craftsmanship and a perceptive eye . . . MARVELOUS READING."

—*Rave Reviews*

"MARTIN MAINTAINS THE MOMENTUM in this steamy contemporary romance."

—*Publishers Weekly*

"PASSIONATE . . . compelling . . . *Southern Nights* is truly a great book!"

—*Rendezvous*

SOUTHERN SECRETS

Marcia Martin's enthralling new novel brings together a woman born to a privileged family . . . and a man raised on the wrong side of the tracks. Tragedy and scandal all but ruin their lives—until, together, they forge a new beginning.

Jove books by
Marcia Martin

SOUTHERN NIGHTS
SOUTHERN SECRETS

SOUTHERN SECRETS

MARCIA MARTIN

J

JOVE BOOKS, NEW YORK

SOUTHERN SECRETS

A Jove Book / published by arrangement with
the author

PRINTING HISTORY
Jove edition / September 1991

ISBN: 0-515-10661-5

PRINTED IN THE UNITED STATES OF AMERICA

10 9 8 7 6 5 4 3 2 1

For you, Dad.

Acknowledgment and thanks to
Kenneth T. Davies, Attorney-at-Law
and
Lenore Jones Deutsch, Psychologist

SOUTHERN SECRETS

Part One

❀

Kings are like stars—they rise and set.

They have the worship of the world, but no repose.

—Percy Bysshe Shelley

The Kingsport Legend

In 1770, on the very day the colonists arrived, a colossal storm hit the North Carolina coast, ravaging crops and swelling the life-giving river until it overflowed its banks and flooded a sacred burial ground. The Sapona tribe who had ruled the river mouth for centuries took it as a sign. The white interlopers were to be annihilated.

The tempest provided cover as the warriors crept through the forest and encircled the covered wagons. Unknown to Chief Watcoosa, his only son followed. Filled with the curiosity of a child, the boy climbed a tall oak to observe the coming battle.

Rain poured down. Thunder rolled. Colonist Josiah King darted across camp to check on the prized printing press he'd brought all the way from Massachusetts. Suddenly a bolt of lightning shafted from the clouds, smiting a nearby oak like a blinding scythe.

The chief's son screamed as the jolt shook him from his perch. He plunged to the ground, and more slowly the giant tree began to fall above him. Josiah ran forward and leapt, stretching his body as a diver might. He landed solidly across the boy just as the oak crashed around them.

The colonials grabbed axes and began to chop at the imprisoning limbs, failing to notice the silent Saponas until they'd surrounded the fallen tree. As the trembling whites stopped to stare at the red men, Chief Watcoosa stepped forward, tears mixing with the rain streaming down his face. With a mighty wail, he fell to his knees and began pulling at the branches. Suddenly the braves and the settlers were working together—cutting and heaving until the battered captives were freed.

Though cut and bruised, the young prince was alive. So was the hero, though he would walk with a limp the rest of his life.

It was said that Chief Watcoosa became blood brother to Josiah King that night . . . that he later provided food, materials, and even labor so the fledgling white settlement could be built.

It was said that the chief invoked the ancient spirits. So long as a single member of the King bloodline survived, the town would be blessed—safeguarded by the powerful gods of wind and storm.

Centuries passed. The coastal city remained unscathed by destructive hurricanes that struck nearby shores only to skirt miraculously around its boundaries.

Outsiders claimed that it was purely the geological formation of the cape that fended off the brutal storms.

But in Kingsport, all who knew the legend believed.

Chapter One

May 29, 1967

It seemed he'd always looked at her from over fences.

The first time Danny set eyes on Savannah, he was nine years old and she only seven. It was a warm day, too warm for the brown suit and boots, but Ma insisted he wear his best as they made their entrance at Kings Crossing. Pa had just died, and she said she was lucky to find a housekeeping job in such a fine place.

Everyone in Clancytown knew of the Kings, the distinguished family for whom nearby Kingsport was named. In addition to a gas station, hardware store, and "who knows what all," they owned *The River Watch* and lived in a palace. Everyone had heard of the Crossing; few had seen it. And the news that Edna Sawyer landed a position there flashed through the mill town like a comet. Danny could feel the jealous eyes peering from sagging porches as they loaded the pickup—eyes staring from dusty street corners as the Sawyers left behind the clutter of shanties and smokestacks and lumberyards that were Clancytown.

His excitement mounted as they journeyed alongside the Cape Fear River toward the sea. Each mile brought a prettier view. Now the old river road was lined with a profusion of willow and wild flowers, palmetto, cypress, and Spanish moss. Just ahead was the city—rich, refined, historic Kingsport, the seaside aristocrat of which Clancytown was a poor relation.

The rough road was transformed into a smooth avenue, the wilds to a sedate row of Royal palms. The air took on the mellow tang of the ocean. Sidewalks appeared, and then the big old dignified houses with crisp fencing and trimmed lawns. The pickup turned on Bonaventure Street, eventually crossing a bridge to the elite "south side."

Danny had never been on the oak-lined drive, but he knew it led through The Cloisters. Here lived the truly wealthy of Kingsport, the bluebloods—separated from the city by a discriminating branch of the Cape Fear, settled in the lee of prestigious Kings Crossing. The truck chugged along, and Danny stared at the succession of stately mansions sitting back off the road—all the while remembering that the plantation-style Crossing was reputed to put The Cloisters to shame.

His expectations were high, but as they drove through curving brick markers with a tall iron gate, he realized he'd been unprepared for anything quite so grand—something that looked like a city park of magnolia and oak and clusters of palm, with lawns swelling up a slow hill to a huge red-brick house with white columns and porches. His head was out the window, his eyes wide, as Pa's old pickup rattled to a stop amidst the overwhelming fragrance of roses. Danny's gaze fell from the columns of the house to the bright flowers in the courtyard.

And there in the rose garden beyond a wrought-iron fence was the most exquisite creature he'd ever seen. A princess in a lacy dress, with hair the color of sunlit wheat and eyes as blue as robin's eggs. She smiled, and his heart melted, running down to collect like a pool of butter in his hot, sticky boots.

At that moment a lady in a yellow dress came hurrying across the veranda and down the stairs. She was wearing a sunhat, but Danny could see blond curls dancing around her shoulders.

"Mrs. Sawyer? Thank heaven you've *finally* arrived! I expected you an hour ago, and we're having guests for dinner. Your uniform and rooms are all ready. Now, please put your truck out of sight by the pool house out back. And do hurry. Time is of the essence!"

The lady's voice managed to be both melodiously refined and authoritatively clipped. Danny picked up on the word "pool," but his focus was on the princess who moved to the fence, put a hand on the wrought iron, and looked curiously through the ornate metal.

"Savannah!" the lady snapped, suddenly noticing where the girl had strayed. "Get your hand off that dirty fence. You come inside right now, young lady. I don't want you getting soiled before the Andrews arrive."

The princess backed away with a parting smile, and Danny ogled until the old truck moved in reverse and he could no

longer see her. *Savannah*, he repeated to himself, and thought
no other name could possibly have done her justice.

That night he learned a lot about his new home. There was a
maid, a cook, and a butler, but they had weekends off. His
mother was expected to wear a crisp uniform and work well beyond the supper hour; he was expected to eat in the kitchen and
stay out of sight. It didn't bother him that he could hear other
children in the candlelit dining room beyond the swinging
door—*privileged* children, of which Savannah was one. Danny
was in a state of awe. The kitchen was as large as their entire
house in Clancytown.

The evening rolled on. Danny caught gusts of chatter and
laughter as his mother dashed in and out of the dining room,
serving first a course of cold potato soup she called "vishy-"
something, and then a preponderance of glazed ham with pine-
apple topping, candied yams, green beans, tiny buttered potatoes, and golden biscuits, all to be followed by a peach cobbler,
the aroma of which made his mouth water.

In between her entrances and exits, his mother prepared him
a plate of the delicious fare. Danny nested in a breakfast nook
with a bay window, savoring the food and well content to stay
out of his mother's frenzied way. They were both surprised
when Mr. King walked nonchalantly into the kitchen and proceeded to help himself to a cup of coffee from the urn.

Danny peered across the lengthy room, took in the man's tall
physique, shining black hair, and chic dinner jacket. He'd seen
Mr. King from a distance several times, but never this close.
The man turned to lean casually against the counter. Danny saw
his mother's head bob respectfully, her hands clenched ner-
vously.

"Should I refill the silver service, Mr. King?" she asked,
wondering how in the world the group had managed to drain the
coffee she'd just delivered to the dining table.

He smiled. "No need for that, Mrs. Sawyer. I just came in to
tell you it was an elegant supper. Truly elegant."

"I can't take any credit for the food, Mr. King. I got here too
late to do any of the preparin'."

"We have a cook for that," he said with a note of surprise.

"But Mrs. King said . . ."

He held up an indulgent palm. "Whatever my wife said, I'm
sure she didn't mean to imply you're expected to fulfill the du-

ties of the staff. Ophelia gets a bit flustered when we have company."

The way he said her name was like music. Danny was struck with the notion that he adored the pretty lady in the yellow dress.

"Besides," Mr. King went on, "the way a supper is served makes all the difference—like the way a present is gift-wrapped, for instance. Elegant, Mrs. Sawyer," he repeated. "Truly elegant."

Jim King glanced across the room and noticed the boy. His heart skipped as it always did when he saw a boy the age his own son would have been. He strolled over, and the lad leapt from his seat.

"Hello, Mr. King," he said in a strong, young voice and extended a hand.

Jim joined him in a friendly shake. "Well! Hello to you, too. You must be Danny."

"Yes, sir, and proud as punch to meet you, sir."

Jim's blue eyes lit up, the smile lines deepening around their corners. "I'm proud to meet you too, son. It'll be nice to have another male around the house. I trust you're finding the Crossing comfortable so far?"

"Oh, yes, sir! Far more than comfortable, sir!"

Jim nodded, his gaze settling on the boy's clear, hazel eyes. "Good," he murmured. "Good . . . Well, I'd best be getting back to my dinner party."

"Yes, sir!"

Jim looked back over his shoulder, smiled once more, and Danny knew he'd never met a finer gentleman in all his life. A proper father for the princess . . . a proper man to wear the name King.

Danny had a second helping of cobbler as his mother did the dishes. Looking through the bay window, he scanned the darkening grounds of Kings Crossing and thought there was surely no grander place on earth. Later that night, when he climbed into a poster bed in *his own room*, he was sure of it. He was sorry Pa had died of the dreaded "brown lung" that claimed so many folks who worked in the textile mills; but if anything good had come out of it, Danny was certain it was the fact that he and Ma had ended up at the Crossing.

* * *

The next day was Sunday. As Danny donned the brown suit again, he thought about all the great things he would tell the guys at church. Ma stopped by his room wearing her Sunday best, and as they went out back to the truck, it never occurred to Danny that they wouldn't be driving back to Clancytown, to the old frame meetinghouse he'd attended all his life. He was surprised when his mother pulled to a stop behind the long black Lincoln parked in front of the house.

"From now on we'll be attending First Baptist with the Kings," she explained, and went on to recite what Mrs. King had told her just that morning.

When the family built the church more than a century ago, the grateful congregation set aside the front pews for their use. It had remained that way through the years. Time and war had reduced the clan. There were now only three Kings left. But it didn't matter—the tradition stood. The family sat at the front; their servants, one row back. No one would have dared presume to sit in the empty King pew on the right of the aisle . . .

His mother went on with the recitation, but Danny glanced away distractedly. The morning sun was hot, the smell of the nearby roses overwhelming. He began to perspire, put a finger inside his collar and pulled it away from his damp neck. If the almighty Kings were coming, he wished they'd danged well get on out here!

Then they appeared, and he forgot all about the heat. Bypassing the elegant adults, Danny's eyes zeroed in on the princess. Her pale hair, which was pulled up on the sides and fell to her waist, was dazzling in the sunshine. She had on little white gloves, lacy socks, and a pink dress with a sash around the waist. A spray of rosebuds was pinned near her shoulder.

He remembered the way he'd first seen her in the rose garden, took a deep breath of flowery air, and thought that from then on whenever he caught the scent of roses, he'd think of her. She strolled up to the limousine, finally seemed to notice the truck, and without hesitation put up a gloved hand and waved. Danny thought his face would catch fire as he raised an answering hand.

First Baptist Church sat on Providence Street—a tall, brick building with a white steeple. There was the buzz of whispering voices as they stepped inside the cool sanctuary, but Danny noticed that a hush fell as the Kings made their way down the aisle, acknowledging with a nod the admiring faces turned their way. When they reached the front of the church, Mr. King stepped aside to allow his wife and daughter to precede him. Mrs. King took the opportunity to motion sharply to the second row.

There was plenty of room in the front pew, but Edna Sawyer slipped dutifully into the second. Danny followed. It didn't occur to him that the setup was insulting. There was too much to take in. He'd never seen the likes of such a church—immense stained glass windows, so brilliant with sunlight that the white robes of the choir virtually glowed . . . a tiered altar with a shining cross and dozens of candles . . . a bank of brass organ pipes towering to a ceiling lit by suspended chandeliers. The organist boomed an introduction to the first hymn, everyone stood, and the stirring sound of the entire church launching into song brought goose bumps to Danny's flesh. He joined in the familiar "Nearer My God To Thee," fighting the urge to crane his neck and take a better look at the illustrious congregation.

As the sermon got underway, his gaze drifted stealthily over his shoulder. A man and a little girl sat alone in the third pew across the aisle. The man had sparse brown hair, a hooked nose, and a protruding Adam's apple that bobbed up and down, up and down. The girl looked about Savannah's size, had curly hair somewhere between red and brown, and— Suddenly Danny realized she was looking at him. And then she winked!

His gaze fled to the next row up and landed smack on the pale eyes of a boy about his own age. His hair was blond, his seersucker jacket fashionable, his smirk of superiority instantly annoying. Danny felt suddenly laughable in his outdated clothes.

Raising his chin, he looked past the boy and saw the unmistakable white suit and blond head of Big Ed McKenna. *I should have known*, Danny thought. Naturally, it would be the McKennas who sat directly across the aisle—as close as they could get to the front without infringing on the King pew. Beyond Big Ed's shoulder was the outline of his wife's dark hair, and beside her the similarly dark head of a small boy. Danny went back to studying the big man's wavy, yellow hair and figured church was one of the few times he could be caught without the Panama hat that gave him the look of a fine Southern gentleman.

Well, he was no such thing. Pa used to say McKenna might be rich as sin, but he wasn't a gentleman like old Mr. Clancy, and he wasn't one of Kingsport's own. He'd simply shown up years ago and bought his way in—into the city with a steady flow of cash, and into society with a marriage to Margaret Clancy.

Danny slouched back in the pew, remembering. Ma said it wasn't right to blame anybody for the way Pa died. People who worked in the mills knew the risks and took their chances. But Danny didn't accept that. Pa had been respected as one of the smartest men in town, and Danny recalled his father's explanations of the way conditions had changed since old Mr. Clancy sold out to McKenna.

Everyone in Clancytown revered him, but it was a reverence based on fear. He was a large man, a powerful man, and folks whispered about the deadly look that came to his eye when anyone tried to buck him. No one in Clancytown was about to question Big Ed McKenna, much less make a fuss about worsening conditions in the mills—even if the boss's neglect made a hard job harder . . . even if they had to watch their loved ones drop like flies.

The elaborate church service continued, but Danny's initial enjoyment of it was gone.

On the way back to the Crossing, it was all Savannah could do to keep from twisting in her seat and peering out the back window in a most unladylike fashion. The pickup truck was right behind them, and ever since the new boy arrived, she'd been prickling with curiosity.

"After lunch, can I play with Danny?" she asked the back of her mother's head.

"He is *not* a new playmate, Savannah. He's merely the son of our housekeeper."

"What can it hurt?" came the resonant voice of her father. In the discreet recesses of the back seat, Savannah grinned. She could always depend on him.

"Jim, honey," her mother chided with a sidelong glance, "she already spends far too much time with that Libby Parker from the McKenna house. Too much mixing with the servant element isn't seemly for a young lady like Savannah. She's at an impressionable age. She needs to consort with people of her own class."

Her mother looked ahead, and her father said nothing more.

But Savannah caught his eye in the rearview mirror. She knew that look.

Keep your mouth shut, it warned, *then do as you please.*

The limousine pulled smoothly into the courtyard, and Savannah saw the truck turn along the side drive to the pool house. Her mother and father started up the front steps as she tarried in the garden, seemingly examining the roses that were Ophelia King's pride and joy. After her mother was safely inside, Savannah waited a few long minutes, then skirted around the side of the house. Mrs. Sawyer must have gone directly in to make lunch, for Savannah found the boy standing alone on the patio, twirling a stick in his hands as he looked out across the back lawns.

"Would you like a tour?" she asked.

He spun around. Savannah came closer. Danny Sawyer was older and bigger than she, but he had pretty greenish eyes, pink cheeks, shiny golden-brown hair. She liked him instantly.

"Hi. I'm Savannah."

"Hi," he returned woodenly.

"Your name is Danny, right?"

"Right."

"Short for Daniel."

"Nope. Long for Dan."

She squinted up at him in the bright sunlight. "It's all the same. I looked it up in Daddy's book last night. Daniel comes from the Hebrew meaning 'judge,' you know."

No . . . he didn't know. "What about Savannah? What does that mean?"

"Oh, I was named for the city where my mother was born. She was a Benton before she married, and the Bentons have always been a leading family in Savannah. It's in Georgia."

She related these things without conceit, as though they were merely a matter of fact, and Danny became more enthralled by the minute. She wasn't at all like the girls in Clancytown. In fact, she wasn't at all like anyone. She was Savannah King.

"Well?" she said.

"Well, what?"

"I asked if you'd like a tour. You're new here, and the Crossing has lots of things to see. Lunch won't be ready for a while. Would you like me to show you around?"

He nodded dumbly, and the princess reached out a gloved hand. Danny stared in horror. He would no more have touched the girl's fingers than a snake that was rearing to strike. Dropping the stick, he stuffed his hands in his pockets and walked briskly past, slowing only as he reached the steps to the back lawns. He turned to find her just behind him, looking up with a smile that was both charming and alarming.

It was at that moment that Ophelia and Jim King strolled out of the drawing room and onto the patio. Spotting the two children, Ophelia took an immediate step in their direction, her mouth opening to call them back. Jim's hand flashed out.

"Let them be, Ophelia," he said, gently grasping her arm. "He's a nice boy, and Savannah spends too much time with us grown-ups. It will be good for her to have another child about the place."

Ophelia turned him a doubtful eye, but her husband was, after all, the master of the family, the master of the Crossing, the master of her life. Shielding her eyes, Ophelia watched her daughter walk away with the Sawyer boy. The sun was hot; nevertheless, a frosty shiver raced up her spine.

Savannah led a leisurely path across the Crossing grounds. Though the roses in front were the pride of the house, there were other pretty gardens and a waist-high boxwood hedge that bordered the formal lawns against a backdrop of fields stretching in one direction and forest in the other. They stopped by the garage, a rambling building with a weather vane on the roof and a half dozen bays inside. A flashy new truck was in one, a white sedan in another. Danny supposed the black Lincoln resided in one of the four remaining stalls, and it struck him that there was plenty of room for Pa's pickup. But then again, the rusty old thing wouldn't have fit in anyway.

"This used to be a carriage house," Savannah said, and to prove her point, motioned to a black, horse-drawn carriage sitting at the far end of the building. It must have been very old, but its spoked wheels and leather seat were shining, obviously kept up in the same painstaking fashion as the rest of Kings Crossing.

They moved on to the pool which was built half below ground and half above. Redwood panels surrounded the elevated structure and provided a wide deck sporting a diving board, a collection of reclining lounges, and a striped umbrella shading a white table and chairs.

"Daddy had this built a few years ago," Savannah said.

She climbed the steps, Danny followed, and they looked into

the shimmering depths. The pool floor was covered with a blue liner that made the water look like a tropical sea, so cool and inviting. If Danny were anywhere but Kings Crossing, with anyone but Savannah King, he'd strip off his hot clothes and dive in. The brash thought made him grin, and she caught him at it.

"What is it?" she asked, an answering smile on her lips.

"I was just wondering," he began in the first unguarded words of his two-day stay, "what your mother would say if she caught me skinny-dipping in here."

Savannah's eyes went wide, and then she broke into bright laughter. "It isn't what she'd *say*, it's what she'd *do*! She'd jump right in, clothes and all, and yank you out by the hair!"

Danny chuckled, the sound fading as he took another look at the grandeur of the poolside. Lanterns were positioned in intervals about the deck railing, and he had a quick image of how the place must look at night—the water shining from an underwater spotlight, the lanterns glowing against the darkness.

He turned back to the girl and cocked his head to one side. "Do you know how lucky you are?" he asked.

"Lucky?" she repeated with a puzzled look.

Danny knew then that she had no idea . . . absolutely no idea at all. "Do you think *everyone* lives like this?" he thought of saying. But as he gazed into her eyes, the moment of closeness escaped. All he could bring himself to do was back away from the pool's edge and retreat into silence, once more the self-conscious country boy come to town.

After a moment Savannah turned and led the way along a walk lined with bursts of hydrangea blossoms, ranging from purplish blue to pale pink. Danny was familiar with what the Kings called a "pool house"—after all, Ma parked the truck just behind it. He'd looked curiously at the white frame structure with redwood trim, wondering just exactly what a pool house was supposed to do, figuring that it housed tools and equipment and such. Instead, the inside looked like a miniature beach house with woven rugs on the floor and fishnets draped about the walls. There was a lounging area and bar, a side room with changing booths, and another with a shower.

Savannah sensed his perplexity. "This is for guests," she said. "When people come over to swim, they come in here to change or maybe to get something to drink." The boy just looked around, said nothing, and she wondered if maybe he was getting bored. "Come on," she added. "We haven't gotten to any of the good stuff yet."

From the pool area, they walked toward a stand of live oak. The trees were ancient and huge, their black limbs reaching out to each other, twisting in near embraces, dripping Spanish moss like a thick gray curtain. Danny had no reason to suspect there was anything behind the concealing copse, but as they circled around, he discovered the surprising presence of a tennis court.

"Daddy was a champion at the university in Chapel Hill," Savannah commented. "He's teaching me. Do you play?"

Danny shook his head, his gaze lingering on the court.

"Would you like to learn?"

He looked quickly over, nodded once, and Savannah saw the excited sparkle in his eyes. He wasn't bored after all, she thought, and was pleased.

On they went along the edge of a pine forest, beyond which, she said, was the beginning of The Cloisters. A little farther on they stopped at a stone springhouse. It was cool and dark inside, the spring gurgling pleasantly against mossy rocks.

"This is where they kept butter and milk and things in the old days," Savannah explained. Beyond the springhouse were the picturesque remains of a building she said was once a dairy.

The two of them continued past the grounds that could be seen from the house to the fields that sloped gracefully toward a line of cypress edging the river. What Savannah didn't show Danny, she told him about. Kings Crossing was a couple of hundred years old and spanned a hundred acres. The legendary Josiah King had built the springhouse, dairy, and original house of stone, which later generations replaced with the brick mansion.

The house and grounds sat on the prime hilltop acres near the point, where the meeting of river and sea kicked up cooling breezes. The rest of the land was a buffer of privacy, field and forest that had long ago been allowed to grow wild, dunes that stretched south along undeveloped coastline. The beach was fun to explore, but the ocean, where it swirled in reckless welcome of the river, was too rough to swim in. Another boundary was the Cape Fear tributary, which at its narrowest point separated the Crossing from the Kingsport peninsula by the mere breadth of a football field.

"That's how the Crossing got its name," Savannah explained. "Years ago, the family went back and forth to town mostly by ferry. The old landing is still there, but it's falling apart. There's quickmud, too. I'm forbidden to go there." Her eyes took on a mischievous sheen. "But you know what?"

"What?" Danny asked.

"Sometimes I go anyway. There are old boats, an old dock, and all kinds of hooks and ropes and things. And there are oyster beds all up and down the bank. Sometimes I just go there and sit and make up stories. You know?"

He didn't know, but he nodded anyway. In most ways Savannah was a little girl; in others—the way she talked, for instance—she seemed all grown up. It made him nervous.

They were on their way back to the house when a young voice called her name from the pine forest.

"That's Libby," Savannah said, and came to a halt. "She lives over at the McKenna house behind the woods. She's my best friend."

At the name of McKenna, Danny felt a chill—a sensation that repeated as he saw two boys follow the little girl out of the pines. The bigger one was fair-haired; the other, dark. Danny immediately recognized them from church. So, the McKennas lived just across the woods.

"This is Libby and Clayton and Rory," Savannah was saying pleasantly. "And *this*," she announced with a flourish of her hand, "is Danny. He lives here now."

Danny was sizing up the blond boy who was maybe an inch taller than himself, though not as filled out. Rory was spit-and-polished from head to toe and wore an irritating look of superiority as he returned Danny's examination.

"Nice suit," he commented with a snicker.

Suddenly remembering his dowdy clothes, Danny felt searing heat rush to his face. Big Ed McKenna's son! Now, he had *two* reasons to hate him! He took a quick angry step toward the boy but had no chance to do more as Savannah took up the challenge.

"Yes, it *is* a nice suit," she said smoothly. "But it really doesn't matter what people wear. Daddy was telling me just the other day—it isn't what's on the outside that counts, but what's on the inside."

Libby giggled. "That's easy for you to say, Savannah! You've always got something new and pretty to wear!"

Danny thought the comment was entirely off the point, but it helped to clear the air. Savannah joined her girlfriend in a giggle. Rory took on a more tolerable look. Clayton, who'd yet to say a word, ventured a timid smile. And somehow or other, the five of them ended up agreeing to meet after supper for a game of tag. As the others disappeared into the pines, he and Savannah continued toward the house.

"What's *his* problem?" Danny asked as they walked along.

She looked up with those peacock-blue eyes. "Rory? He's always like that. My mother and his have been best friends for years, but if you ask me, he's really icky!"

Danny slipped into a grin. "Icky, huh? I could come up with a better word than that, but I reckon I shouldn't use it." They walked the rest of the way to the house laughing together.

As the month of June passed, the clique of five became a common sight trooping about the grounds. Savannah and Libby, Clayton and Rory—Danny often thought how different they were from the kids in Clancytown. There, the main activities had been kick-the-can, stickball, and on summer nights sneaking out to go frog-gigging, or just to spy on the teenagers. Here, there were strictly chaperoned dips in the Kings' pool, roaming explorations of the beach and forest, and forbidden treks to the old landing at the river. At night, when summer twilight lingered until nine, the fields rang with calls of "Red Rover" and "Run, Sheep, Run" and—Danny's contribution—"Ain't No Boogers Out Tonight." The five of them might have their differences, but the common bond of childhood held them together.

By the time July rolled around, Danny knew his cohorts as well as if he'd grown up with them. Libby was a tease, a mischief-maker who sometimes behaved outrageously just to irk her straight-laced father, the butler of the McKenna house. Clayton was a somber boy about the size of the girls, who tagged along with everyone else and ran home to "Mommy" when his big brother became too much to take. Rory was a cruel one. His mean streak came out most blatantly against his brother, but occasionally rippled to touch one of the others, particularly in scoffing challenges to Danny.

Danny often clenched his fists in instinctive readiness for a scrap. He'd grown up fighting in Clancytown and wasn't the least bit afraid to get into it with Rory. But somehow it didn't seem to be the thing to do out here at the Crossing. So far he'd held his temper, settling for stony up-and-down looks meant to remind Rory of their equal size and intimidate him with the threat of superior prowess. *Come on, hit me!* Danny would rage silently, his eyes blazing, his hands balling into fists. The blond would take it for a minute or two, then smirk and walk away, leaving Danny with the minor victory of having made him back down.

Clayton was completely cowed by Rory; Libby was all-forgiving. Among the group, Rory's other adversary was Savannah. Just thinking about it made Danny smile. Even if she was tall for her age, she was still only seven years old. But with a simple well-turned phrase, she could put Rory in his place and make him look like a clod. The McKennas might be well-to-do, but Savannah had the advantage of generations of breeding behind her. When it came to class, there was no contest.

On the Fourth of July, the parade in town was followed by an annual barbecue at Kings Crossing. Danny helped his mother with a few things in the kitchen, then wandered out across the back lawns to the barbecue pit. A black man dressed like a chef was there. Mr. King was watching him baste a giant pig on the spit.

"Hello there," Mr. King said as Danny walked up. "Doesn't this smell great? I'll have you know, Jacob here turns the best pig in the county!"

The three of them were still out there together when people started arriving. Danny was flattered when Mr. King put a light arm about his shoulders and presented him to a few of the guests: Mr. and Mrs. Gibbons, a round-faced couple who owned Providence Sundries in town and Dr. Leo Crane, a tall, skinny, amiable man Mr. King introduced as a psychiatrist and "die-hard bachelor." Danny's face fell when Big Ed McKenna stepped up.

"This is Danny Sawyer," Mr. King said.

Big Ed nodded carelessly, then went on talking as if Danny wasn't there. There was no recognition of the name Sawyer—no recollection that a man who'd worked for him for ten years had just *died* from his blasted mills! Bitterness hardened Danny's features as he looked from the white suit to the Panama hat to the ruddy face with eyes the color of Rory's. Big Ed made a remark that was meant to be funny, guffawed at his own joke, and moved away. Danny's gaze followed, his back as stiff as a board.

"You don't like him much, do you?" Mr. King asked.

Danny looked up in surprise. He didn't know quite what to

say. "Well, I . . . no. I *don't* like him. Didn't know it showed though."

Mr. King laughed. "Only as plain as the nose on your face."

The crowd had started to swell. Mr. King laughed once more, patted Danny on the back, then excused himself and went off to circulate among the guests.

By six o'clock the back lawns were covered with people—all the best people. The Cochranes, Taylors, and Harrisons, Mr. Harrison being the mayor of Kingsport. The Todds, the Andrews, who owned the biggest department store chain in two states. And of course, the McKennas—Rory in crisp slacks and a shirt that made him look about thirteen, Clayton in knickers and a ridiculous straw hat that made him appear all of five.

Danny hung on the sidelines with Libby and watched as the rich mothers shooed their children together like sheepdogs tending a fold. Mrs. King seemed particularly adept at throwing Savannah together with Clifford Andrews. She tried several times with Rory, but Savannah always managed to slip away. Danny was annoyed to see she didn't do much dodging when it came to Clifford, a slick-haired boy in a navy blazer that made him look as though he belonged on a yacht somewhere.

"Doesn't Savannah look pretty?" Libby murmured. "That's a new dress. It's made of the palest green linen, embroidered all over with tiny rosebuds."

Libby sighed while Danny cut his eyes across the lawns.

"It matches her mother's," he said shortly.

The wistful look faded from Libby's face as her gaze leapt to Mrs. King. The woman didn't like her, never had. Sure enough, the dress she was wearing was a grown-up version of Savannah's frock.

"Yeah, I guess it *does* match," Libby agreed. "You know, now that I look at it, that dress isn't so nice after all."

Danny gave the girl a silent look of understanding. Mrs. King was a pretty lady, but her snobby ways were hard to swallow. She'd never said anything to him outright, but Danny sensed her disapproval. So did Libby; they'd talked about it before. Whether she said so or not, Ophelia King didn't think either of them was good enough to mix with her daughter.

Danny meandered off by himself. It wasn't until after the barbecue was served and everyone settled down to eat that Savannah came running over to where he was sitting under a live oak.

"Let's get out of here," she said, looking over her shoulder for signs of her mother.

"It's almost time for the ice cream," he replied noncommittally.

"We'll be back in time for that."

"Back from where?"

"There's something down by the landing I want to show you."

"What have you seen that *I* haven't?" Danny asked, still in a sullen mood.

Her eyes lit up. "Remember the nest we found last week? The eggs are hatching! I went out there this afternoon while you were with Daddy at the barbecue pit. One of the ducklings is already out!"

He was on his feet in an instant, his earlier sourness forgotten. It was nearly eight o'clock, the dying light lying on the fields in a soft haze. They were still a short distance from the landing when they heard the scream.

"Help!" came the shrill cry. "Help me!"

"That's Clayton," Savannah said, and darted in the direction of the sound.

"Be careful!" Danny commanded as he easily overtook her and sprinted ahead. "There's quickmud over here!"

They found Clayton struggling in a swamp of quickmud, on the verge of hysteria. The thick, sucking mire was up to his hips, and just beyond his reach, lying lightly on the surface, was his little straw hat. He must have been running to have stumbled so far into the stuff before he realized what it was.

"Help me!" he screamed again, his voice hoarse and high-pitched, his eyes bulging.

"How in the world did you get stuck out there?" Savannah called.

"R-Rory . . ." was all the boy could manage, but Danny shot a look at the straw hat and formed a quick picture of what must have happened. The damn bully threw his brother's hat out there in the quickmud, and Clayton had tried to retrieve it.

Clayton dissolved into loud, racking sobs. Danny looked swiftly around. The pool of orangey-brown quickmud was surrounded by tall cypress with no low branches, and Clayton was several yards into the slow but dangerous muck. Danny started searching for a fallen limb—anything he could stretch out to the boy.

"Give me your hand, Danny," came Savannah's brisk command.

He whirled around and saw the determined look on her face. "What?"

"I said give me your hand. You stand at the edge, and I'll wade in. You're strong. You can pull us out."

Danny's wide eyes followed her movements as she removed her sandals. His gaze swept from the frilly dress with roses all over it to the ribbon binding her shining hair in a ponytail. She moved to the edge of the quickmud, looked back, and held out a hand.

"No," Danny said. "I'll find another way."

Clayton wailed, and she stepped into the muddy patch. "Come *on*, Danny! This will be quicker!"

Against his better judgment, he pulled off his shoes and joined her. Clayton's sobbing ebbed as he watched them make a chain. Danny went in a few feet and latched onto Savannah's arm as if he expected her to be wrenched out of his grasp by some fierce quickmud monster. He shook his head anxiously as she waded in up to her thighs, her skirt billowing out around her like a lily pad. But she was right. It took only a minute to pull Clayton out. When it was over, the three of them sank to safe ground, equally covered in sticky grime.

"You know better than that, Clayton," Savannah eventually scolded. "It's a good thing we came along. What happened?"

Clayton's dark eyes looked everywhere but at her. "Rory took my hat . . . I . . . it doesn't matter." He came to his feet, finally meeting the questioning looks of his saviors. "Thank you," he said, then sniffled and looked as though he was about to burst into tears once more. He turned and took a step toward the path through the trees. "I . . . I'm going home."

Danny nodded. Clayton was a muddy mess. He couldn't possibly go back to the party looking like that. For that matter, neither could he and Savannah.

"I'll tell your mother—" Savannah began.

"No!" Clayton cried, spinning around. "I can't tell on Rory! Not ever! Promise me you won't say anything to *anyone*! Please! Promise you'll never tell!"

His look of terror convinced them both. They promised, but as Danny watched Clayton stumble away—his muddy legs spraddled, shoulders slumping—he knew he'd be hard-pressed not to haul off and clobber Rory the next time he saw his cocky face. He looked over at Savannah and his feeling of awe returned in full force. The way she took over and marched right into that muck—new rosebud dress and all! Cocking his head, he studied her profile and thought she was the damnedest thing he'd ever seen.

"Well," she said with a sigh. Getting to her feet, she took a critical look down at her ruined dress and mud-caked legs. "They must have served the ice cream by now. Mother's going to kill me."

Danny climbed up, his gaze roving over her. He, too, was a mess. But it didn't matter about him. Savannah was the one who would be crucified if caught looking this way.

"She doesn't *have* to see you," he suggested. "Just slip in the side door and go on up to your room."

"That's easier said than done. You don't know Mother."

Oh, but I do, he thought, and could just picture Mrs. King's outrage if she caught sight of her daughter's current state . . . particularly on the night of the Fourth of July barbecue!

"Well," he began with a gleam in his eye. "You could always swim the river and catch the last train out of town."

Her rippling laugh echoed through the cypress. "Oh, Danny! You can always make me laugh at the most awful times!"

Flushing with pleasure, Danny jumped to his feet and started briskly toward the darkening path. "Come on. Let's get going. Maybe we'll be lucky." But it was not to be. Just when he thought they'd made it, Mrs. King wandered out on the patio and caught them making for the kitchen door.

"Savannah?" she called. Danny looked up. A few dressed-up ladies were with her. One of them was Mrs. McKenna. He stepped in front of Savannah, managing to hide her to a degree in the shadows.

"Savannah?" Mrs. King called again, this time in a sharp tone.

Danny didn't move, but Savannah stepped around him and moved toward the light of the patio. He heard her mother's hissing intake of breath, saw Savannah's chin drift toward her chest. The other ladies stopped their chatter, glanced over, then stared openly. Mrs. McKenna was the one to break the silence.

"I'd best be going, Ophelia," she said, and swept her hostess's cheek with a kiss. "It's time for me to find Clayton and head on home."

Good luck! Danny thought. Mrs. King's companions drifted

away, leaving her standing alone above them like some dreadful judge who at any moment might shriek: "Off with their heads!"

"Savannah," she said, the name like a blade. "As the daughter of this house, you have social responsibilities. Clifford Andrews wanted to say good-bye. I've been looking for you for nearly an hour, and you show up looking like *this*! I'd like an explanation and a good one! What could *possibly* have led you to get yourself is such a state . . . tonight of all nights?"

Savannah glanced aside, and Danny's heart went out to her. Sure, she was a mess, but what she'd done for Clayton was downright heroic. She didn't deserve to be roasted over the coals. Before he had a chance to change his mind, he stepped quickly forward.

"It was my fault, Mrs. King. I wanted to show Savannah something out near the old landing. We—uh—got stuck in the mud."

"No . . ." Savannah protested.

"The *landing*!" Mrs. King exclaimed. "Savannah is forbidden to go there, as are *all* you children!"

"Yes ma'am, I know. I'm sorry."

"Well! I should think you would be sorry!" She whirled on Savannah. "And *you*, young lady! Get up to your room this instant. You look positively disgraceful! I don't want anyone catching so much as a *glimpse* of you!"

Savannah turned tearing eyes from her mother to Danny, her mouth opening as if she would try a further explanation. Danny gave her a stern look and jerked his head toward the house. She backed slowly away as Mrs. King lit into him.

"You're older than she is, Danny. You should have better sense. The landing is no place for children, and although you might be tempted to go there, I would very much appreciate your refraining from enticing my daughter. She did not grow up in Clancytown, where perhaps the little girls run rampant in the mud. This was a very important night. All our friends are here . . ."

His gaze dropped to the broken tile of the patio floor, and by the time she finished, Danny was crimson from the tips of his ears to the bottoms of his feet.

"Now that I think of it," she concluded huffily, "you can come into the kitchen with me right now. I intend to have a word with your mother!"

While they were there, Mrs. King spitting quick, sharp remonstrations in his mother's wide-eyed face, Mr. King strolled in. "What's this, Ophelia?" he asked mildly. "I can see the boy could use a bath. That's really all there is to it, isn't it?"

"No, Jim! It isn't!" Mrs. King retorted. "Savannah came back looking like an absolute ragamuffin—covered with mud from head to toe. And it was *his* doing! I told you she was at an impressionable age!"

"Savannah is a child," Mr. King said. "This is the one time in her life she should be free to get dirty now and then." He took a step in Danny's direction. "Why don't you go on and get cleaned up, son?"

"Jim, really!"

"Now, calm down, Ophelia," Danny heard him reply as he fled the room. "It isn't the end of the world."

Danny pretended to be asleep when his mother looked in, and took special care to stay out of the way of both her and Mrs. King the next morning. After lunch he found a shaded spot on the patio and settled down near the music room. Savannah was having a piano lesson, and he didn't know what she was playing, but Danny thought it was a pretty tune. He was lolling there against the wall, listening with his lids half-closed, when he became aware of a shadow. At the alarming thought of Mrs. King, his eyes flew open.

"Hello there."

Danny was flooded with relief. "Afternoon, Mr. King," he replied, scrambling to his feet.

"Savannah told me what really happened last night, Danny. It wasn't your suggestion to go to the landing, but hers. You must think a lot of her to take the blame on yourself and come to her defense the way you did."

The boy looked away uncomfortably. Jim leaned against the wall and studied him. "You don't have any brothers or sisters?"

"I had a brother. He was a lot older than me . . ."

"Than *I*," Jim corrected gently.

"Huh?"

"He was a lot older than I."

Danny's cheeks colored, but the kindly look of Mr. King's face put him at ease. "Yes, sir, a lot older. I came along late, kinda unexpected, I guess. Anyway, I can hardly remember him. He died in a car crash when I was four."

"I'm sorry. It's hard to lose family. I had a son once—for a very short time. He was born too early and just couldn't make it."

The man's face turned so sad that something wrenched inside of Danny. "I'm sorry, sir."

"It was a long time ago. Time tends to heal. Or maybe you just learn to live with things. But you—you've had a *recent* loss."

And somehow it all came out, the way Pa had started working in the mills right after he and Ma got married, all the good things he'd said about old Mr. Clancy, all the bad about Big Ed McKenna, right up to the way Pa died—shriveling to nothing as the "brown lung" of Clancytown claimed one more. Ever since it happened, Danny hadn't talked about Pa . . . not to anyone. His voice trailed off, and he looked away, embarrassed.

"Sometimes it helps to talk," Mr. King said, placing a warm hand on his shoulder. "I'm truly sorry about your father."

"*That's* why I don't like Big Ed McKenna," Danny stated, the name gritting from between his teeth.

Jim gave the boy a long, probing look. "Is there something he could have done to prevent it?"

"Pa said there were inventions that could clean up the air, things that could be installed at the mills. He got some men together one time and talked to the foreman about it. The next day Big Ed himself came down and gave a speech about rising costs and maybe having to lay some people off. Nobody ever brought up the idea again." When Danny finished, he saw that Mr. King's face had taken on a hard cast he'd never seen before.

"Is that a fact?" Jim said, his voice slow and measured. "I thought such safety precautions were required by law." The more he considered what the boy had said, the more the idea gelled. "That's an interesting story, Danny," he added. "Very interesting indeed. So much so, I figure, that the public would be greatly interested in reading it."

"Reading about Pa?"

"And others like him." Jim pushed away from the terrace wall. "You're an inspiration, Danny. I think I'll go inside and make a phone call or two." He walked across the patio, then turned suddenly. "I have an idea," he called. "I'm going to give Savannah a tennis lesson in a little while. Would you like to join us?"

The boy's eyes lit up like a pair of candles. "Yes, sir!"

"All right, then. Be at the court in an hour." Mr. King smiled and passed a hand by his brow in a comradely salute. "See you there, Danny-Buck!"

It was a fond nickname that stuck, as did his practice of including Danny in activities with Savannah. Mr. King went to *The River Watch* each morning but was usually back by early afternoon, rounding them up for lessons in tennis, swimming, badminton, or croquet. "Mrs. King will see to it that Savannah grows into a lady," he sometimes said. "I intend to see she has some fun along the way." And as if to prove it, he introduced Savannah to softball and football, and even raised a basketball hoop out behind the garage. Danny excelled at all three sports, and he beamed when Mr. King declared him a "gifted athlete."

Even rainy days became a treat when the three of them gathered in Mr. King's study, and he read from a wonderful collection of stories he called classics. Occasionally Danny caught sight of Mrs. King watching them with a sour look on her face. One morning in mid-August, she called him aside after breakfast.

"You're a big boy, Danny," she said. "There are many ways you could help out around here. After all, you're getting free room and board and all the privileges of living at the Crossing. It's only right that you pitch in and learn a sense of value."

Danny suspected her concern was less with his values than with the time he spent with Savannah. As for the Crossing, a staff of six kept it shined up and running like a top. His mother ran the household like a tight ship. Loretta, a jolly old black woman, did the cooking. Her husband, Cletus, doubled as butler and chauffeur; their daughter, Amaryllis, was the maid. The Ratoni brothers took care of the grounds and any handiwork that needed doing. Even so, Mrs. King managed to find a need for Danny's "pitching in" nearly every day—cleaning the pool, sweeping the tennis court, assisting the Ratonis. Luckily, Danny was a fast worker, and she was too preoccupied with her bridge clubs and garden shows and society goings-on to be very effective at keeping up with his whereabouts.

She kept a tighter rein on Savannah, however. She took piano and dance lessons, spending "quality time with quality people." But Mrs. King was a busy lady, and most days she was away from the house some time or another, all dressed up and getting old Cletus to chauffeur her in the Lincoln. It was then that Savannah escaped to run wild with Danny and the other kids. He

liked to think she had far more in her of her father than her
uppity mother.

It was a happy summer, despite the shadow of Mrs. King, despite the fact that his own mother hardly had time for him anymore, despite the loss of old friends left behind in a town that
might as well have been on the other side of the world. The new
gang filled the gap, and although Rory and Clayton and Libby
had their shortcomings, there were more interesting things to do
around the Crossing than there ever had been in Clancytown.

But of all the new and wondrous times that filled his ninth
summer, Danny's favorites were those spent with Savannah and
her father. If his buddies in Clancytown had known how much
he looked forward to spending time with a girl, he'd have been
the laughingstock of the whole place. But it wasn't just Savannah; it was her father, too. Danny treasured all the things he was
learning from Mr. King and loved hearing the familiar "Danny-
Buck" roll out of the man's smiling mouth. Each time Danny
heard it he felt special, almost like one of the family. And nothing could have made him more proud than to stand in for the
son Jim King had lost.

It was the first night of September. A full moon was just coming up over the pines, adding the luster of daylight to the summer darkness. Clayton and Rory and Libby had left the
Crossing. Savannah leaned back on her elbows, stretched her
legs out on the cool grass, and closed her eyes. A few feet away,
Danny lay on his side, absently picking stones out of the earth
and sailing them toward the trees.

There was a sweet taste in Savannah's mouth, a pungent floral smell all around her. After the others left, Danny had collected lengths of honeysuckle, then shown her how to select the
best flowers and pull the stems so she could get every drop of
nectar.

She smiled dreamily. He knew so much! All about caterpil-
lars and cocoons and when to watch for the butterflies . . . about
wild flowers and how to weave them into a chain she could
wear around her neck . . . about oysters and clams and how to
tell when they were ripe for the picking. One night he'd asked
her to bring a pair of work gloves to the landing. When she got
there, she saw that he'd already dug up a pile of oysters. She
helped him gather brush, then sat in the sand as he built a forbidden fire, roasted the devils in a wire basket he'd stolen from

the kitchen, then pried them open with his jackknife. They were delicious! And as usual, Savannah had ended up sitting back and watching him with awe. In her little girl's mind, he was the best big brother she ever could have hoped for.

Danny glanced over. "What are you smiling about?"

"Oh, nothing," she murmured. "It's just awfully nice out tonight."

Danny's brows drew together. The summer was coming to an end. He had the sinking feeling that other things were, too.

"School starts next week," he said.

"I know."

Danny shifted the stones in his palm, picked one, and sent it skimming into the moonlit pines. "Ma says I'll be going to Eastover. You'll be going to that fancy school near the Heights. We won't be seeing much of each other."

The summer evening was warm, making Savannah feel drowsy. She rolled her head lazily toward him. "We still live in the same house. We'll still see each other every day."

"Yeah, but it won't be the same."

"Why not?"

"It just *won't!*" Danny sent another stone flying, then looked quickly at her, his expression brightening. "Hey! I've got an idea. Let's be blood brothers."

She giggled. "You're funny, Danny. We can't be *brothers.* I'm not a boy, you know."

Danny rolled his eyes. "That doesn't matter. That's just what it's called, that's all. It's an old Indian custom. It means you're friends for life."

"Oh. How do you do it?"

"We cut our fingers, and when they bleed, we press them together so the blood gets all mixed up."

Savannah's eyes snapped open. "We *cut* our *fingers?*"

Danny broke into a tolerant grin. "All right, then. We'll sterilize a needle and just prick them a little bit. You won't feel a thing. Then each of us swears we'll always be friends, no matter what."

"Mother says it isn't ladylike to swear."

Danny fought to keep his mouth from pinching up. "Guess not. Guess it's more gentleman-like. When a gentleman swears, it means he gives his word and sticks by it. You can do *that,* can't you? Give your word and stick by it?"

"Of course I can!" Savannah returned huffily.

It took a half hour to get back in the house, procure a needle, sterilize it, and sneak back out without being caught. By the time they sank to the ground once again behind the cover of the pool house, the last trace of twilight was gone, the moon high in a clear sky.

Danny went first. Pricking his thumb, he drew a dot of blood, looked across the brief distance between him and Savannah, and found her shining eyes.

"I am your friend for life," he said. "My blood is my word."

He handed the needle to Savannah, then heard a quick gasp as she repeated his actions on her own small finger.

"I am your friend for life," came the girlish voice. "My blood is my word."

"I swear," he said.

"I swear," she repeated firmly.

He held out his hand in the darkness. She met it, and there in the late summer moonlight, amid the songs of katydids and the smell of honeysuckle, Savannah King pressed her bloody thumb to that of Danny Sawyer . . . and smiled.

Chapter Two

July 4, 1972

THE FENCE had tall iron bars with tips like spearheads—
forbidding, perhaps, to a stranger. But Danny had known the
fence and the illustrious building it surrounded since he was
knee-high. He grabbed hold of two of the bars, hauled himself
onto the brick foundation, and glanced over his shoulder.

The city was drenched in sunlight—its white buildings were
blinding, and its sidewalks buzzed with the throngs that had
turned out to celebrate the Fourth of July. Across the way,
where a stage was draped with red, white, and blue bunting, the
commons were crowded with spectators waiting for the parade.
Three feet below, normally sedate Providence Street was noisy
and bustling.

Danny's perch lifted him above some of the heat, and he was
wearing only scant gym shorts and a T-shirt. Still, the noonday
sun burned like fire. Patches of sweat broke out under his arms
and trickled down his sides. He looked again in *her* direction—
over the spears, beyond the statue of Josiah King, up the clock
tower to the balcony. The family was at their post above the
masses, looking down from *The River Watch* building like gods.

Mrs. King waved to someone below as Mr. King stretched an
arm around his daughter's shoulders. She looked up, the movement stirring hair that shone in the sun—more like platinum
than gold. A familiar lump rose to his throat, and Danny looked
away.

Only in the deepest part of himself did he admit that he
missed Savannah. Everything used to be so different, so easy.
He used to love to make her laugh, to watch her eyes light up
when he managed to catch a butterfly, or do some other ordi-
nary thing she viewed as wondrous. On those golden after-

noons, it was easy to forget that Kings Crossing was anything but home, just like it was for her.

But last summer, everything changed. He'd been the thirteen-year-old who shot up like a weed, but it was Savannah who turned into a different person. Instead of hanging around the landing, she "preferred" to garden. Instead of racing barefoot through the woods, she dressed up and went shopping or visiting.

Then Mrs. King caught him watching her daughter at the pool. Danny had been looking over the hedge, studying Savannah in a bathing suit, thinking that her stringbean body was changing . . . when suddenly he was grasped from behind and twirled around. Mrs. King's face had been red as a beet.

He still remembered how he'd felt—embarrassed and ashamed without really knowing why. When Mrs. King announced there was to be "no more playtime with Danny Sawyer," he expected Savannah to buck the order. But she didn't. In the space of a few short months, she'd become a stranger, a lady who knew her place . . . and his.

Danny had put on a tough act, but beneath it he throbbed with the ache of betrayal, the sting of inferiority—hurts that only aggravated the tumultuous hormones erupting in his body. He felt dirty, worthless. For a couple of hot, sweaty months he barely slept, spending most steamy nights down by the river, feeling as though he wasn't fit to inhabit the same planet with anyone else.

A year had passed since then. Now, at a big strapping fourteen, he realized that the most miserable summer of his life had something to do with the fact that he'd begun to change from boy to man, and that the change must have shown in his eyes the day Mrs. King caught him looking.

Now he knew the meaning of one's station in life. "There are folks like us," Ma had explained, "and there are folks like the Kings. The sooner you get it in your head, the better."

Now Savannah kept her distance. She was the young lady of the house, Danny a servant. It was understood the two were not to mix.

A sea breeze whistled by. But it was hot and short-lived, half-heartedly rustling the palms that lined the sidewalk.

Danny fired a last look at Savannah's head and jumped down from the fence with a snort. He was a basketball star in a part of the country that worshiped the sport. He could have just about any girl at school, and some had breasts that made his pulse race. Why moon over some twelve-year-old who was straight as a stick?

Crossing the street, he carved his way through the crowd milling about the parklike Kingsport commons. Roberta Sikes strolled by in skin-tight shorts, and without realizing it, Danny turned clear around to watch her. When he caught her eye, she smiled provocatively. He backed away with a silly grin, bumped into the Reverend Lowder, and was awarded a sermon on courtesy before he could escape into the crowd.

Finding a group of basketball buddies at the old Civil War cannon, Danny joined in as they hawked the girls, whistling and hooting and punching each other if they got a reaction. After a while, he hoisted himself onto the cannon platform. It was a little cooler there, and he had a better view of the crowd. That was when Roberta walked over, rolling her hips and thrusting her breasts forward so he couldn't help but stare at the thin blouse where he could swear he saw the shifting darkness of nipples.

Roberta climbed onto the platform and settled herself so that her legs dangled off the edge next to Danny's. She leaned back on her palms and took a good look. Just as she thought, Danny Sawyer had grown up. He was tall and wasn't skinny like the other guys. Muscles showed in his sun-bronzed arms and legs. Her gaze rose to his face. Danny had always been a pretty boy, with that chestnut hair and flashing smile, those hazel eyes with the thick, dark lashes. Now there was an added appeal. He was filled out, manly.

"Hot day," she said, bouncing a leg on the platform so that it brushed rhythmically against him.

Danny looked into her big, brown eyes. Roberta was fifteen, but she seemed older.

"Yeah," he managed from a dry throat.

"So, what are you doin' tonight?"

Roberta didn't mess around. "Nothing much. What are you doing?"

"There's a party after the fireworks."

"Where?"

Roberta shifted to face him more fully, the line of a breast swelling against her neckline. "Clancytown," she said. "After the fireworks over at the old docks."

Her gaze dropped to his lap, and Danny was mortified when she seemed to look directly at the bulge between his legs.

Roberta returned her eyes to his flushed face. "Some of us

kids have fixed up one of the warehouses at the river. We got a stereo and some couches. A keg of beer." She reached over to trail a forefinger along his arm. "It can be *very* dark there at night. *Very* private."

An image of what might take place sprang to Danny's mind, and the nervousness within him evaporated—overpowered suddenly, thankfully, by the drives that were prone to swell within him these days. An instinct for conquest took over, and he met Roberta's eyes squarely, shifting his leg so that it pressed against her sun-warmed flesh.

"What time is the party?" he asked.

"Nine o'clock."

"Nine sounds good."

"It's settled then," Roberta murmured, a delicious feeling of anticipation washing through her. "I'll see you at the docks."

"You sure will."

There was a sparkle in Danny's eye. It died when he looked beyond Roberta's shoulder and saw the McKenna household making its way through the crowd. Mrs. McKenna and Clayton were in the lead, then came Mr. Parker and Libby. Big Ed and Rory brought up the rear.

Danny's vision narrowed to Rory. The sandy blond head reached to his father's jaw. Big Ed was probably six-foot-three, which put Rory at close to six feet. He'd gained an inch since basketball season, Danny mused. He hadn't seen Rory since then.

His thoughts shot into the past, when the kids of the two estates had seen each other nearly every day. They'd been a sort of gang, with Rory and Danny—the "big boys"—battling sullenly, continually, for the position of leader. But those days were long gone. As children, they'd played together as equals. Now they all knew there was no equality. The McKennas and Kings were heirs to fortunes; the Sawyers and Parkers were offspring of servants. The stand-off between himself and Rory had never ended—it had simply been postponed when the childhood gang dissolved, a victim of newly matured social consciousness.

The battle resumed when they met on the basketball court. Like all the other "richies" from The Cloisters, Rory went to Pine View Heights, arch rival of the Eastway Junior High Jets and later the Senior High Rockets. In the two years they'd played forward against each other, Danny had gone home with black eyes, bruised ribs, and bloody lips. By now he'd learned most of Rory's tricks and had developed a few of his own. Last season, he'd managed to deal a swift, undetected blow that loosened one of his adversary's teeth. Still, it galled him that Rory McKenna played dirty, and more often than not, the refs let him get away with it. But after all, he *was* from Pine View Heights—the snob school, envied and despised by the masses who had long ago dubbed the Panthers the "Pine View Pussies."

Rory drew near. When he noticed Danny, he slowed his pace, allowing his family to go ahead. Danny hated himself for feeling inferior as he noted the guy's expensive polo shirt, the light sweater knotted about his shoulders, and the gleam of a gold watch as he lifted a hand to expensive sunglasses, slid them down his nose, and smirked. Years had passed, they'd both changed, but it was the same infuriatingly superior look Rory had given him the first time they laid eyes on each other . . . all those years ago in the sanctuary of First Baptist Church. Danny stiffened.

"Pine View Pussy," he muttered as Rory moved on. He hadn't really meant to be heard, but Roberta giggled, and the guys below caught the phrase and picked it up.

"Pine View Pussy," they chanted. "Pine View Pussy."

From several yards away, Rory glared over his shoulder. Danny grinned tauntingly. Still, Rory seemed to have the last word as he turned away, raising his nose as if he suddenly smelled something putrid.

The crowd parted before the McKennas like a biblical sea. There was much hat-tipping as Mrs. McKenna passed and respectful handshakes for Big Ed. Rory swaggered off in his father's wake, and as Danny watched, he caught the initials on the sweater. PVH.

Pine View Heights. Danny's lips curled in disgust. He hated everything about the school, but most of all he hated the way the kids thought they were so damn much better than everyone else. Pine View Heights . . . where Savannah would be going in the fall.

The warm body of Roberta Sikes was against him, but Danny's gaze darted helplessly to Providence Street, where it climbed the iron fence of *The River Watch* building. Savannah was still there on the balcony.

It seemed he'd always looked at her from over fences.

* * *

Savannah sensed that she was being watched. She scanned the commons but could single out no one looking her way. In the haze of the hot July day, the distant crowd melted into itself, ebbing and flowing in an anonymous stream.

Her gaze swept the familiar streets—Bonaventure, Cape Fear, Clancy. Joined with Providence Street, they formed a respectful square around the Kingsport commons that had been a meeting place since Revolutionary times. She looked back to the greens, and a tingling sensation flashed up her spine. Whoever he was, he was still watching.

Savannah reminded herself of the solid presence of her parents—her mother, pretty and vivacious in a cherry-red dress that accented her blondness; her father, dark and handsome in a tailored suit. The eerie feeling subsided. It was silly to feel threatened on such a bright day. Besides, people often watched the Kings. Jim King was one of the most revered men in town, his wife one of its most gracious ladies. The Kings were accustomed to being stared at . . . and envied.

Hoping the voyeur still had his eyes on her, Savannah tossed her head contemptuously and turned to look across the skyline to the sea. As usual, the sight both calmed and lifted her spirit. She never tired of the tower view, the patchwork of rooftops—some black, some red, some copper turned metallic green—stretching like a crazy quilt to a fringe of live oak and palms bordering a white beach. Beyond, the blue ocean swept to the horizon, forming a dark line against the pale sky. A warm, salty wind puffed against her face. Savannah took a deep breath and smiled. If ever she had a problem, she need only climb the tower and face the wind. It always managed to sweep the cobwebs away.

Ever since she could remember, she'd loved visiting her father at *The Watch*, standing with him on this very balcony, soaking up the feeling of permanence that emanated from the old stone tower. It was centuries old—fortified over the years, but built during the American Revolution. From the widow's walk above, one had a clear view of the point where the Cape Fear River met the Atlantic, an invaluable vantage point for the Patriots who had kept watch against British ships.

Savannah's own famous ancestor, Josiah King, had founded the newspaper and built the tower back in the 1770's. A statue in his honor stood below in the fenced courtyard. Savannah knew the stories by heart—how Josiah had worked late into the

night with only the light of a candle . . . how he'd taken dangerous, midnight rides to deliver news of the revolution . . . how
colonial Kingsport had cheered when a Redcoat colonel was reported to have thrown down a copy of *The Watch*, angrily
terming it "a hotbed of sedition."

Her father said such Patriot newspapers had laid the foundation for the freedom of the American press.

Now, of course, all that remained of the original newspaper
building was the clock tower. The rest had been modernized and
expanded, making way for giant presses, expansive mail equipment, and rows of offices. With nearly three hundred employees, *The Watch* was one of the largest employers in Brunswick
County, as well as one of the most respected newspapers in the
Carolinas.

Everybody said Jim King was responsible for that. *The Watch*
had always been well thought of, but it was *his* influence, *his*
dedication to the public well-being, that had prompted an inves-
tigation of Clancytown a few years ago. The target was "brown
lung," how it could be diminished with modern safety regula-
tions and how it had been ignored by the powers at Clancytown
Mills. These issues were highly sensitive ones—not only did
the mills feed and clothe hundreds, but also they were owned by
powerful Big Ed McKenna. Most men would have let things go
along the way they always had, but not Jim King. He sent undercover reporters into the mills. The resulting exposé of unhealthy working conditions led to expansive renovations. It also
netted *The Watch* a Pulitzer for public service. People said Jim
King ran the paper the way he ran his life—"like a Southern
gentleman."

Savannah looked up at her father and caught his eye. He
winked. She winked back, and they shared a smile before turning back to the balcony and the crowds below. That was when
she noticed Mr. Parker and Libby, whom she hadn't seen in a
week. Lately it seemed Libby always had chores to do over at
the McKennas'.

"Libby!" she called, waving when the girl looked up.

"Hush now, Savannah," her mother scolded. "It isn't seemly
for a young lady to hoot like a fisherman's wife!"

"See you later at the barbecue!" Savannah called in rare dis-
obedience. The Fourth of July barbecue at Kings Crossing was
a tradition. Everyone came.

Ophelia King snatched her daughter's gloved hand out of the air. "You most certainly will *not* see her, Savannah!"

At her daughter's stricken expression, Ophelia's heart grew tender. "Dear, dear," she said softly. "Whatever am I going to do with you? I thought you finally understood. You're a young lady now. You have a place in society. You should be cultivating friendships among young ladies and gentlemen, people like Hillary Cochrane and Clifford Andrews, Clayton and Rory McKenna."

Savannah fought the urge to shiver. Clayton was likable in a pitiful sort of way, but there was something creepy about Rory. Sometimes, when she caught him looking at her, her skin positively crawled.

"The Parker girl is, after all, of the serving class," Ophelia went on. "And that mother of hers ran off with . . . well, never you mind. Now that you're growing up, you must be more selective. Like your Grandmother Benton always said, a lady is known by the company she keeps."

Savannah held her breath, expecting the familiar recitation on the "blue" blood that ran in her veins. Her mother's aristocratic family had lost a fortune in the War Between the States, but they'd retained the pride and refinement of the upper class. Ophelia Benton King carried on the traditions of good breeding. Savannah was expected to do the same.

Thank goodness her mother only smiled, and Savannah turned away. She believed in her mother as she believed in her father. They were beautiful and perfect and all-knowing. Still, her expression was troubled as she sought out the bouncing, auburn curls of Libby Parker where she followed her austere father along the street.

A drum cadence rolled out, followed by the brassy sounds of a high school band playing "Seventy-Six Trombones." Red and white uniforms marched into view, and the parade of bands and floats and convertibles began a colorful trail around the commons. In the midst of the noisy spectacle, Savannah forgot about Libby.

When the parade was over, the Kings stepped inside the office of the publisher. As they walked through, Savannah looked lovingly at some of the furnishings—polished antiques, sporting prints, and beyond her father's oak desk the antique globe she'd studied for tireless hours. The place smelled pleasantly of

leather and books and the lingering scent of her father's cherry
blend pipe tobacco. It was her favorite room in the world.

One day it would be her office, she thought. She was the last
of the Kings, and she knew more about newpapering than most
people twice her age. *The Watch* was in her blood, and she had
no doubt of her future there, though her mother discouraged
such aspirations, intent on the image of her daughter as a matri-
arch of society, "not a smut-fingered newspaperwoman." Savannah's dream was unfaltering, but she didn't speak of it
anymore. Ophelia King lived for her bridge clubs and charities
and social seasons. She never could have understood the urge
for any career other than that of a genteel Southern lady.

They exited the penthouse office and moved along the spacious hall through Editorial. Because of the holiday there was
only a skeleton crew, but everyone who was there turned out to
salute Jim King as he passed. Henry Yates, who'd been with
The Watch for decades. Timothy Martin, who'd been there
scarcely a year. Even pinch-faced Jack Doggett, whose heavy-
handed sensationalism her father disliked.

"Afternoon, Mr. and Mrs. King. Miss Savannah . . ." "Miss
Savannah," the greetings echoed. "Miss Savannah . . ." It was
like that all the way down the escalator from the fourth floor.
Savannah stepped into the sunshine, a bright smile on her face.
Life was so perfect!

Danny was outside the entrance, admiring the expansive
glass doors with the chrome masthead of *The River Watch*,
thinking that it was the most fascinating place in the world. He
was working part-time maintenance there this summer, and he
loved it—didn't mind the way his fingers stayed black from the
newsprint, or the way the smell of ink lingered in his nostrils
long after he'd left the building. Next summer, Mr. King promised, he could be a copy runner. Danny couldn't wait. Like most
folks, he took pride in *The Watch*. The newspaper was nearly as
old as Kingsport, as much a part of it as the river or the sea.

He'd been leaning against a parking meter, but as the King
family emerged, he quickly straightened.

"Hello, Danny-Buck," Jim said cheerfully.

Savannah's smile faded as she looked up at Danny. He was
awfully big, not at all like the boy she used to know. Plus, he
seemed to be so blistering mad at her all the time. Only a few
nights ago he'd thrown her a wild invitation to sneak out with

him to the old landing, calling her "chicken shit" when she refused. *Chicken shit!* The memory made her blood boil.

"What are you doing hanging around out here instead of having a good time over at the commons?" her father asked.

"I was waiting for you," Danny returned. "Thought maybe I could hitch a ride home."

"Aren't you going to stay for the town picnic?"

"No, sir. Ma said she wanted me back in time to help get things ready for the pig-pickin'."

"Barbecue," Ophelia corrected with a bob of her head. "They might have *pig-pickin's* out at Clancytown, but we're a bit more refined at Kings Crossing. Come along, Savannah."

Mrs. King proceeded briskly in the direction of the black Lincoln parked in the publisher's private space. Her nose in the air, Savannah followed. Mr. King looked fondly after them, and Danny found himself wondering why the hell the man was so enamored of his wife. True, she was pretty, but she was also snobby, prissy . . . and turning Savannah into someone just like herself!

"The pigs have been in the pit since yesterday," Jim commented. "What else is there to do?"

"Lots," Danny replied succinctly. Mr. King was a gentleman and a sportsman, but he didn't know the first thing about real work.

Jim studied the boy's face. Danny was growing into a good-looking young man. He was a bit high-spirited, perhaps, but strong and bright—the kind of boy he'd have liked for a son.

"Come on then, Danny-Buck," he said, "if you're bound and determined to do yourself out of a proper Fourth of July."

They walked to the Lincoln where Mrs. King and Savannah were waiting in the hot afternoon sun. Heaven forbid that they should get in the car all by themselves! Danny thought. When Mr. King opened the front passenger door for his wife, Danny took the cue and performed the service for Savannah.

Sweeping the door open, he bowed before her like a dutiful servant. *"Miss* Savannah," he said in the most lilting, mocking voice he could manage. Raising her chin, she slid into the back seat and smoothed her skirt over her knees.

She grew prettier by the day, Danny thought, and wished it were otherwise. Someone who'd turned out so snooty had no right to look so pretty. He treated himself to a slam of the door that made her jump, and as he went round to the other side of the car, he tried to remember the many things he'd come to dislike about Savannah King. Instead, he found himself picturing her blue eyes.

When he climbed into the back, Savannah gave him an angry look, then turned to peer out the window. Danny pressed himself so tightly against the door, he felt the handle in his ribs.

All the way back to Kings Crossing, the proper distance of the car's breadth remained steadfastly between them.

Margaret McKenna secured the lavender scarf about her throat in a fashionable knot. The bruises that once marred her flesh had faded long ago, but each time she looked in the mirror, she saw them still. A scarf tied rakishly about her neck had become rather a trademark. No one knew that she couldn't bear to go without it, that somehow her throat—bare and unadorned— seemed far too vulnerable.

A shot rang out. Then Clayton's high-pitched scream. Margaret snatched aside the curtain to peer across the back lawns. Clayton stumbled more than ran across the grass. Then he fell.

Margaret dashed to the curving staircase in a flurry of organdy, her heels clicking down the polished hardwood steps. Through the dining room, out the French doors, across the patio. She was at Clayton's side in under two minutes, her heart stopping as she took in the scene.

The boy was lying facedown, and blood was everywhere. It wasn't until she dropped to her knees and swiftly turned him over that Margaret saw the source. The pet rabbit's head had been blown clean off, and Clayton was holding onto the bloody thing for dear life. Mindless of the new dress she'd donned for the Kings' barbecue, she pressed close until she could gather the boy, the rabbit, and the whole mess onto her lap. She smoothed Clayton's hair, talking to him in low, soothing tones.

As she comforted her youngest, Margaret's gaze lifted to the patio and settled on the fair-haired figure of her firstborn. He still held the rifle his father had given him that morning. As she watched, Ed walked out of the house, joined the son who was his very image, and planted a comradely hand on his shoulder. The simple gesture spoke volumes of his allegiance to Rory.

Margaret's expression shifted from disbelief to outrage. But beneath it all was the familiar, smothering blanket of fear.

* * *

It was nearly nine o'clock, but just turning dark—a soft, summer dark with flowers on the breeze and fireflies in the air. Libby leaned against an oak at the edge of the Crossing grounds. Torches glowed in even increments along the back lawns, leading to a point at the barbecue pit, flickering off the party guests who strolled within their borders. The gay sounds of music and laughter drifted her way, and she'd never felt so alone.

She'd been watching Rory from the shelter of the trees for a half hour. He was so fair. So beautiful. She never tired of looking at him. Just now, he'd left the patio and gone inside the house with Laura Kimberly, daughter of a tobacco magnate, suitable companion for the son of Big Ed McKenna.

Libby's gaze lingered where Rory had disappeared—the Kings Crossing house, the most beautiful place in the world to her way of thinking. Although she could see only the back, she imagined the whole of it—the black shutters turned crisply back against brick walls, the white columns that gave the place the look of a plantation, the delicately railed verandas that encircled the house like petticoats on two floors. Gabled windows faced in all four directions from the roof—a "tiled monstrosity worth the price of a sensible house," her father was fond of saying.

Although the McKenna house was bigger, it seemed raw and gaudy in comparison. There were no sculptured gardens or hedges, no ancient fields sweeping to the river. It was obvious to Libby that her home was a relative newcomer, just like all the other ritzy houses in The Cloisters. Kings Crossing had the distinction of being first, and its superiority showed in everything from its extensive acreage to the prize-winning roses in Mrs. King's garden. As Libby looked up at the house from the torch-lit patio, past the verandas, to the peaked roof, she thought it a proper setting for Savannah.

She was a lady, just like Rory was a gentleman. They were at home in a place like the Crossing. As for Libby, whenever she set foot inside the house, she felt that her dress was inappropriate, her shoes too scuffed, or her hair mussed. Mrs. King was responsible for a lot of that feeling. Ever since Libby could remember, the woman had been looking down her nose. A raised brow here, a cut of the eyes there—Ophelia King was a genius at making her feel like dirt without saying a word.

Libby turned hurriedly away as the argument with her father came to mind.

"You're not going!" he'd yelled.

"I am, too! Savannah is expecting me!"

"It's her mother who said you weren't to come!"

"I don't believe you!" Libby had retorted. She wouldn't give her father the satisfaction of admitting it, but she knew very well that it must be true. Mrs. King had seen to it that she was excluded from the most important annual event at the Crossing.

"Get in your room, you common girl!" her father had cried, his sharp-featured face all red and splotchy above the ever-present, starched white collar. "You're a disgrace to your name. *Libby!* Don't you remember what that means? 'Consecrated to God,' that's what! I gave you the name myself, hoping the Lord would keep you on the straight and narrow. But I can see the Devil has his hand on you! Only twelve years old and just like your mother! Always fretting about parties! You'd do better to get down on your knees and pray you don't follow *her* path! Get on in there, now!"

Get down on your knees and pray! That was her father's solution to everything. Libby often wondered why her mother had ever married him, and couldn't blame her for leaving. From what she could remember, the woman had laughed a lot, and Libby could only assume she'd found it intolerable to live with a solemn-faced, religious fanatic who seemed to find more pleasure in pronouncing judgment than anything else.

After tonight's red-faced lecture, he'd shoved Libby into her room and locked the door. She'd waited an hour before climbing out the window and sneaking over to the Crossing. Now the barbecue was breaking up, and she hadn't caught even a glimpse of Savannah.

Crickets serenaded Libby from the wood as she traipsed along its edge, skirting the pool house, moving aimlessly in the direction of the courtyard. From the shelter of a giant magnolia, she watched a few fancy cars wheel out of the drive before she spotted Savannah emerging from the pool area—holding hands with Clifford Andrews! Libby clapped a hand over her mouth, her dark eyes shining over the tops of her fingers. She was just far enough away to remain concealed, just close enough to catch their words as they came to a stop in the courtyard.

"I'll be by on Friday night to pick you up for the Teen Cotillion Dance," Clifford said.

His voice was changing. It seesawed between tenor and baritone.

"That's fine, Clifford," Savannah replied.

"Mother says you should be ready by seven. After all, we don't want to be late."

"Oh, I'm sure we'll have plenty of time," Savannah assured him. "The dance doesn't start until eight, does it?"

"Yes, but Mother says you can never be too careful . . . or too punctual."

"Of course. Certainly, Clifford. Whatever your mother says."

He dropped her hand, and Savannah watched as he made quick progress to the sleek Cadillac waiting in the drive. The car rolled away, she turned . . .

"Certainly, Clifford! Whatever your mother says!" came a mocking voice from the darkness of the rose garden.

Savannah spun in the shadows as Libby's gaze leapt to the figure moving toward her friend.

"I *swear*, Savannah!" Danny scoffed. "Do you think Clifford Andrews would dress up in a chicken suit and parade through town tar and feathered if *his mother* said he should?"

"Danny!" Savannah huffed. "I should have known it was you! What are you doing out here in the bushes? Spying on me?"

"Ha! I have better things to do than that! Just happened to be here, that's all, when you and your boyfriend strolled into the courtyard."

"A gentleman wouldn't have stayed around to eavesdrop!"

Danny grinned in the darkness, an expression that was lost on Savannah. "Couldn't resist," he said. "Once I heard Clifford start talking about his mommy."

"Clifford is a nice boy! There's nothing wrong with having respect for one's mother."

Danny ambled closer. "Respect for one's mother is one thing. Being tied to her apron strings is another."

"What would you know about it? From what *I* hear, you give your mother nothing but trouble."

He laughed. "Didn't know you cared enough to listen to any gossip about me."

Savannah tossed her head. "I don't! But one can't help but be aware of common knowledge—like the time three weekends ago when the police brought you home roaring drunk!"

Danny brought a concealed beer from behind his back, hoisted it to his lips, and took a healthy swig. His eyes glinted as he gave Savannah a challenging look.

"It's summertime," he said. "So what if I had a few beers? At least I don't pussyfoot around like some wimp waiting for my mother to tell me every move I should make! *Mother* says you should be ready by seven," he mimicked in a singsong voice. "*Mother* says you can never be too punctual."

Savannah sprang to Clifford's defense. "There's nothing wrong with that! Punctuality is a virtue! Mother says so!"

"Oh, God!" Danny rolled his eyes. "Now he's got you doing it!"

Savannah's arms fell to her sides, her hands making fists as she strained to see her tormentor in the summer darkness. She'd never let him know it, but his taunts were hitting home.

"You don't know anything, Danny Sawyer!" she cried. "Nice people have certain responsibilities, and punctuality is one of them!"

"Oh, well, forgive me!" he retorted with a short bow. "I guess if I was one of the 'nice people,' I'd know all these things! Tell me, Savannah! What else do 'nice people' know?"

She glared up at him, and then—out of the blue—unexpected memories bolted through her mind. Danny . . . letting a caterpillar crawl across his palm as she watched in a state of awe. Danny . . . pulling her out of the quickmud, stepping up and taking the brunt of her mother's wrath when she came home in disgrace. Like air from a punctured balloon, Savannah's anger deserted her.

"Danny," she said softly, "what's wrong? Why are you so mad at me all the time?"

Danny halted in the midst of raising the beer to his lips. Memories assaulted him as well, culminating in the picture of Savannah turning her back on him and flouncing into the house to receive a group of "nice people" who'd come to call. With a swift move, he drained the can and crumpled it in one strong hand.

"Nothing's wrong, Savannah," he said curtly. "You have your place, and I have mine. Just so long as we remember which is which, we ought to be okay. Right?"

He stared down at her, and she could feel more than see the contempt in his eyes. Her temper flared anew.

"That's right, Danny," she replied in her most grown-up voice. "And your place is not to spy on me. Is that clear?"

He would have died before he showed that she'd hurt him. "Perfectly clear . . . *Miss* Savannah!"

Savannah watched him stalk away—her feelings tumbling between anger, uncertainty, and a troubling sense of sadness.

Libby hurried out from the cover of the magnolia. "Savannah!" she hissed.

Savannah whirled, her hand flying to her throat. "Good heavens, Libby! You nearly scared the life out of me!"

"Sorry. Didn't mean to."

Savannah's wide eyes searched her friend, took in the casual shorts and shirt Libby would never have worn to a Kings Crossing barbecue. "Where on earth have you been?" she asked.

"Daddy wouldn't let me out," Libby admitted. "Said we weren't invited."

"Ridiculous! When *haven't* you been invited?"

Libby was tempted to cry: "Ever since your mother said so!" But it wouldn't do any good. A person simply couldn't come between a daughter and her mother—but that was an odd thought for a girl whose mother had deserted her years ago for the charms of a bootlegger.

"Libby?" Savannah prompted.

Once, when she was tiny, Libby had even fantasized about pretty Mrs. King being her mother. Now the outrageous thought made her want to laugh and cry at the same time.

"Libby! Who said you weren't invited? Tell me!"

Libby mustered a smile. "My father. You know him. Since when have I been able to tell him anything?"

Savannah sighed in relief. For a moment, she'd thought maybe Mother . . . "Listen," she suggested. "There's plenty of barbecue left. Want to go get some?"

Her words were directed at Libby, but Savannah's eyes turned in the direction in which Danny had disappeared.

"You like him, don't you?" Libby asked.

"Who?"

"Danny Sawyer."

Savannah's head snapped around. "Don't be absurd!" *Absurd.* It as her new word, one she enjoyed using. "Danny's the craziest boy I've ever known."

"Crazy is right," Libby observed. "Crazy about *you!*"

"What are you talking about, Libby Parker?"

Libby took a deep breath, the movement causing her light blouse to press against her developing bosom. "We're turning into women, Savannah. Haven't you noticed? Pretty soon you're going to have to realize that we attract boys—and not just boys like Clifford Andrews! *All* boys!"

Libby's dark eyes were now sparkling with excitement. Savannah studied her shorter companion who was already showing signs of the womanhood she had yet to fathom.

"Come on," she said, linking her arm with Libby's. "Let's go get something to eat."

It took Danny an hour to hitch a ride to Clancytown, another fifteen minutes to get to the old docks and find the warehouse Roberta had described. When he walked in, his first impression was of a candlelit barn that reeked like a brewery. A dozen teen-aged couples were locked in forbidden embraces on a scattering of couches. Blaring music came from the corner where a few others hovered. Roberta was one of them. She saw him and sauntered over.

"I was beginning to think you weren't coming," she said.

"It was hard to get away from Kings Crossing."

She stepped close and rubbed her breasts against his chest. "Speaking of hard . . . all the couches are taken. But there's a little beer left, and I just happened to bring a blanket."

They found a secluded spot in the shadows. Down below, between cracks in the boards, Danny could see the waves come and go around the old Clancytown docks. He closed his eyes and kissed Roberta's open mouth. It was warm and wet, practiced and exciting. He moved a hand to her full breast.

A new song came on the radio, the music resounding through the old warehouse, pulsing through Danny's body like his own racing blood. The singer wailed something about love and dreams coming true, and the image of Savannah exploded in his mind. Danny's eyes flew open. Roberta looked up as he raised his head.

"Don't stop," she mumbled breathlessly.

With a sudden roughness Roberta misread as ardor, he tore open her blouse so that buttons flew across the rough planks. And there on a scratchy blanket, in the flea-bitten mill town he thought he'd left behind, Danny lost his virginity among the aromas of candlewax, river mud, and woman.

Margaret sat in the dark, rocking gently beside her son's bed. Clayton had fallen asleep, exhausted, a couple of hours ago, and it had been maybe an hour since she heard Ed and Rory return.

She remained in the darkness, savoring the quiet for as long as it would last, remembering things she hadn't thought of in years.

Ed, the way he'd looked when he first came to Kingsport—big, tall, fair-haired, like a Viking—a fine specimen of a man, with a hungry look in his pale blue eyes. There had been a mystery about him that piqued her interest, the way he swept into town with all that money.

Some folks whispered he'd made a fortune smuggling drugs on shrimp boats up the coast—it wouldn't be the first time the dangerous North Carolina coast had screened such a purpose. The whispers stopped when Ed started making investments around town.

Now Margaret saw that he'd gained pieces of lots of folks that way. But none more than the Clancys. The proud, aristocratic Clancys. One of the fine families of Kingsport. Owners of the textile mills and lumberyards that made up Clancytown.

A series of disasters had struck. A fire at a lumberyard. An explosion at the mill, then a terrible accident that killed three people. After that, it seemed Margaret's father had no stomach for Clancytown. He sold it lock, stock and barrel to Big Ed McKenna. And when Ed started courting his daughter, he could hardly refuse.

Margaret married Ed in the spring. Her father died that summer.

It wasn't until later that Margaret realized her role. She was Ed's legitimacy, his ticket into the staunch, Southern aristocracy that would turn up its nose at the vulgar money of a newcomer, but never at a Clancy.

Now, she supposed, Ed had everything he wanted—acceptance by society and a house in The Cloisters. He was one of the most powerful men in Kingsport, but Margaret had the feeling he wasn't satisfied yet. There was something about *The River Watch* that obsessed him, and she knew he'd never forgiven Jim King for that business about the mills. On the surface, Ed was friendly to the Kings, but behind the false front, Margaret knew he was plotting.

She sometimes thought of warning her friend. "Beware, Ophelia," she would say. "I have a feeling Ed might come after you."

But if she broke her silence, the image would shatter. And image was all Margaret had left, that and Clayton. It took all her strength to protect him and keep up appearances. Her friend's family would have to fend for themselves.

Her thoughts returned to Ed and the first time he'd raised a hand to her, the time she'd drawn her first terrified breath. He'd been drinking, and it was only a slap. But Ed was a big man. His casual slap had spun her around, nearly throwing her off her feet. He'd apologized, but once they started, the secret blows became increasingly frequent and severe. The proverbial can of worms had been opened. There was no putting the lid back on.

The outbursts happened only when he'd been drinking. With a growing sense of horror, Margaret had realized that that was when the real Ed showed himself—like a thief stealing from behind a curtain. The worst episode had occurred two years ago after the barbecue at Kings Crossing. He'd started in about the Kings again, how uppity they were, how Jim King had inherited everything he owned, how they didn't deserve what they had. Margaret had tried to stand up to him, which led to a violent quarrel. That Fourth of July night she'd nearly lost her life before Ed came to his senses and took his hands from her throat.

Her most peaceful times had been when Ed was away on one of his hunting trips. Once, Margaret had thought the hungry look in his eyes was simply ambition. But it was more than that. He was a hunter through and through. A predator.

As years went by, his trips had turned into expeditions, his quarry into the exotic. His last trip had been a safari to Africa, and he'd taken Rory . . . Rory, whose pale blue eyes held the same icy glaze as his sire's. His first kill, a beautiful gazelle, hung with his father's numerous trophies in the game room below.

His *first* kill—only his first. In the past year, Rory had shot all manner of local fowl and animal. And today, he'd killed Clayton's pet rabbit. Margaret shuddered in the darkness. Rory was her firstborn. She'd carried him in her womb. Nurtured him. Loved him. But there was no escaping the truth. There was something wrong—*dead* wrong—with a fourteen-year-old who so enjoyed killing.

Big Ed McKenna sat in the fashionable game room of his fashionable house. His family and servants were abed and all was quiet. Lifting his considerable girth from the leather chair, he crossed to the bar and poured himself another bourbon. He swirled the brown liquid in the glass, scrutinizing it in the lamp-light. It was the finest liquor. That as all he drank nowadays.

With an amused snort, he sank back into his char. What a difference seventeen years had made. Then, he'd been wearing uncomfortable clothes on an uncomfortably pitching ship that made its way into an unlit harbor. The scourge of the coast had unloaded their cargo. Tonight, he sat in the luxurious home of a wealthy man. What a difference.

His eyes scanned the game room—the walls of knotty pine, the tiger and bear rugs that cost thousands, the trophies that showed the skill and cunning of a hunter. He'd gotten the elk at an exclusive resort in New Hampshire, the boar at a retreat in Tennessee. The gazelle was Rory's, bagged on that mosquito-infested safari last year.

Of course, the real prize was upstairs, secluded in Clayton's bedroom. Ed tossed down the contents of his glass. Margaret was a thoroughbred. Nothing matched the thrill of her well-bred voice reduced to pleading.

He weaved as he made his way once more to the bar. What right did she have making a scene out on the lawns? A damn rabbit, for God's sake! A little girl's pet! And then, to insist on staying home, forcing him to make her excuses at Kings Crossing.

One more bourbon, and he was ripe for the trip upstairs.

Margaret ceased her rocking. Like prey sensing its doom, she knew he was coming. Clayton, too, seemed to know. He lurched up with a sudden cry.

"It's all right," she whispered. "Mommy is going to step outside, and then I'll be right back."

Clayton sank back to the pillows, his tortured dreams put momentarily at bay by his mother's calming voice. Margaret pulled the door quietly shut, took a few steps across the landing, and watched her husband climb the stairs . . . reach the top . . . spot her just down the way. He took lopsided steps toward her. Margaret recognized the signal.

"Everyone asked after you at the barbecue," he said.

"Oh?"

"Clayton, too."

"Clayton was in no shape to attend a barbecue."

"Come on, Margaret. The boy must be made to understand his responsibilities. I don't intend to make a habit of making excuses for him . . . or you."

"He's only a boy, Ed."

"He's two years younger than Rory—though you seem to have it in your head that he's just a child."

"His pet was killed brutally, purposely. Can't you understand . . ."

"I understand *one* thing. You've turned Clayton into a mama's boy."

Margaret's heart began to pound. "He's my *son*, Ed."

"So is Rory."

"No," she murmured. "Rory is *your* son."

Ed gave her a sloppy, one-sided, malevolent grin. "So *that's* it. You're afraid of your own son. Admit it!"

Margaret swallowed hard as she took a step forward. There was no way Ed was going to come anywhere near Clayton's door.

"All right, then," she said. "I *am* afraid—afraid of what your blood has passed on to him."

Ed leaned casually against the railing. "My blood? And what, dear wife, could my blood possibly pass on to him?"

"You know."

"No, I don't," he returned loudly. "Why don't you tell me?"

"Keep your voice down, Ed."

"I don't care to, *Miss Blue Blood*! What genes have I passed to Rory that aren't fit for a Clancy?"

Margaret stepped closer, her eyes blazing. For once, this man would not intimidate her!

"Cruel genes, Ed McKenna! Cruel, sadistic, *killing* genes! You think I don't see him for what he is? A replica of you, that's what! There's something wrong, Ed. Don't you see it? Or are you too blinded by your own brutal urges?!"

Ed's expression turned murderous. "Just because you deserved being slapped around a few times, you think Rory has bad blood. Is that it?"

His voice boomed with anger, and inside Margaret cringed. But the controlling force in her actions was the protection of Clayton—poor innocent Clayton, who had no stomach to fight the predatorial beings who were his brother and his father.

"That's right!" she cried. "If blue eyes and blond hair can be passed on to a child, why not cruelty?! You'll not get your hands on Clayton! Not as long as I live!"

Ed lunged for her, but Margaret dodged him and turned. He was twice her size, but she was sober. She began backing up—

forgetting that only the treacherous staircase loomed behind her.

Within the safe recesses of his room, Clayton came awake with a start, his hackles rising as he sensed the danger barreling toward his protector.

Down below in the servants' quarters, Libby stared up at the ceiling a second more and crawled out of bed. Knowing her father would have her hide if he knew, she sneaked out of her room and into the foyer to see what was going on.

Rory had never been asleep. He made for his bedroom door, opening it just as his mother reached the doorway.

Their eyes met, and Margaret's concentration disintegrated. By the time she looked back to her husband, she had only an instant to catch sight of Ed's long arm swinging in her direction . . . and behind him, the horrified face of her younger son.

Ed's hand connected with her cheek. She spun a few feet like a crazed ballerina and went down the stairs—now a tumbler somersaulting along the punishing edges of the hardwood steps, landing at the bottom in a sprawl. Her head thudded once on the floor, and she was still—the housedress settling softly across her thighs, the inseparable scarf trailing from her neck, a streak of blood forming a red line from her hairline to her left brow.

The whole thing happened in under a minute. Libby's eyes stretched open until she thought they would pop. She couldn't move, couldn't utter a sound.

Clayton's breath stopped in his lungs. He looked woodenly at his brother and father, then turned back to the sight of his mother's body. Of their own volition, his eyelids slammed shut. But it didn't matter. The scene was emblazoned on his brain.

Rory's pale eyes gleamed. It was an instinctive response. He had no more control of it than his father had of his temper.

Suddenly sober, Big Ed was the first to move. Lumbering down the stairs, he dropped to a crouch by his wife.

"Margaret?" he said. "Margaret?!" He didn't touch her, merely looked long and hard at her staring eyes. Coming to his feet, he planted fists on his hips and studied her with irritation.

Libby found her voice and screamed just as her father came bounding into the foyer, his housecoat flapping behind him.

Ed became aware of Libby's presence for the first time. Stepping quickly over to the girl, he grabbed her by the chin.

"How long have you been standing here?" he demanded.

Libby only stared.

"How long?" he yelled.

"I . . . I just got here," she whimpered.

Big Ed released her and glanced at Parker. "Get this girl out of here," he ordered.

As Libby was virtually dragged away by her father, Ed looked up the stairs at his two sons.

"Call an ambulance, Rory," he commanded. "There's been an accident."

Suddenly, Clayton let loose a shriek that caused Big Ed's hair to stand on end. He hurried up the stairs.

"I thought I told you to call an ambulance!" he barked at Rory. As his eldest disappeared, Ed took Clayton by the shoulders and shook him once. It did nothing to change his younger son's fixed expression of horror.

"Clayton, look at me!" Big Ed commanded. He looked into the vacant brown eyes that would remind him forever of Margaret. "It was an accident," he said.

No response. Clayton didn't even seem to be breathing. Ed shook him once more, finally eliciting a hoarse moan.

"Go to your room," Ed said, releasing the boy with a shove.

Clayton moved in the direction of his bedroom purely because he was conditioned to obey his father's orders. He hadn't the capacity to think.

When Rory returned from the phone, he saw his father come out of his mother's room. He was carrying her bloody dress from earlier in the day.

Ed glanced up with a start, then looked squarely into the ice blue eyes so like his own. "No sense muddying up the issue," he said, "with talk of dead rabbits or private family business."

By the time the officials arrived, the bloodied organdy dress was a smoky memory in the bowels of the furnace.

Dr. Leo Crane sat in the drab recliner of his drab living room, having a midnight snack while the police radio crackled in the corner. It was his only companion on such insomnia-ridden nights.

He was an odd-looking bird—tall, gangly, with a beaklike nose that did his name justice. Plus he was a psychiatrist in a city that guarded its secrets as closely as old family recipes. He'd long ago been drawn into the general practice that Kingsport called for most frequently. It was during such calls that a need for psychological services occasionally surfaced. His other source was the police.

Dr. Crane was sitting there, feeling like a lonely old bachelor who didn't fit in anywhere, when the announcement about Margaret McKenna came over the radio. He halted in the midst of popping a dill spear into his mouth.

Margaret? . . . What did they say? . . . *Margaret?*

Images flew through his mind. The church picnic . . . the Christmas pageant . . . the Easter parade. First Baptist Church had been the only common ground between him and Margaret Clancy. "Birdie," she'd always called him. "Birdie."

Leo had loved her from afar since he was a kid. But by the time he finished medical school and returned to Kingsport with the credentials that would have allowed him to court a Clancy, she was long married to Ed McKenna.

God! Only a moment ago he'd been feeling old. But Margaret was his age, and she was dead. Suddenly, forty-one seemed young.

By the time he reached the McKenna mansion, the drive was crowded with vehicles—medics, police, the coroner. After all, this wasn't a nobody, this was Margaret Clancy McKenna. He walked in just as the police photographer took a shot of the body. The flash went off, illuminating Margaret's death mask in vivid detail.

"Is that absolutely necessary?" Big Ed growled as Leo felt his stomach turn over.

"Just part of the job, Mr. McKenna," the officer replied.

Nevertheless, he put the camera away. After a moment Leo swallowed the gorge in his throat and stepped up. He was nearly as tall as Big Ed, though the man outweighed him by fifty pounds.

"Hello, Ed," he said. "I'm so sorry."

Big Ed turned and looked him over casually. "Crane. What are you doing here?"

"I often listen to the police radio," he answered. "I came as soon as I heard. Is there anything I can do?"

Ed tilted his head in the direction of Margaret's body. "I'd say your offer is a little late, wouldn't you?"

The man's eyes were bloodshot, but he was cool as a cucumber—*too* cool, Leo thought. "Where are the boys?" he asked.

"In bed."

"Do they know?"

Big Ed folded his arms across his barrel chest. "They know."

"How are they taking it?"

"How do you think?"

"I'd be happy to talk with them if you think it might help."

Ed gave him a contemptuous look. "My sons are from strong stock, Crane. They don't need mollycoddling." With that, he turned his back and walked over to one of the police officers. "How long before you get the hell out of my house?" he demanded.

Leo shrugged. He hadn't expected much from Ed McKenna anyway. There was no love lost between them.

He stepped carefully around Margaret, avoiding looking at her by focusing his attention on the staircase that had been her executioner. Granted, it was steep and the steps were uncarpeted. But what would lead Margaret to fall after the thousands of times she must have gone safely up and down those stairs?

He examined the staircase a moment more, then tortured himself with a parting look in her direction. The police were putting her into a body bag, and—horrendously enough—as one of her lifeless legs fell askew and had to be replaced, all Leo could think of was the one dance he'd shared with Margaret at a Valentine's party twenty-five years ago.

He left the mansion feeling sick, wondering about the circumstances that had led to her death. The next day he phoned a friend at the police department.

"I knew Margaret for many years," Leo said. "Has anything come to light from the medical examiner? Any details you can share?"

"No details at all," his friend replied. "Word came down from the chief's office this morning. The file on Margaret McKenna is closed. She died of a broken neck sustained in an accident. Plain and simple."

There was no inquest.

For a solid year, Big Ed wore a black band on his sleeve, and every Sunday the flowers on the altar of First Baptist were donated in memory of Margaret Clancy McKenna.

Everyone in Kingsport knew how much he'd loved her.

Chapter Three

December 31, 1975

It was the third New Year's Eve gala at the McKenna house, and as the hour approached twelve, the party grew loud.

Libby moved discreetly through the crowd, her eyes turning to Big Ed as his laughter boomed from nearby. He was certainly enjoying himself, but then he always enjoyed showing off. Libby was of the opinion that he'd started hosting an annual New Year's Eve bash purely to compete with the Fourth of July barbecue at the Crossing. He certainly pulled out all the stops to make his party the most posh event on the social calendar.

The staff had been working for days—every piece of silver on the elaborate hors d'oeuvres tables was gleaming, and every furniture surface shone. A giant Christmas tree twinkled in the foyer. The lamps glowed. From the terrace room came the music of an orchestra, and through the whole of the downstairs the most socially prominent of Kingsport's citizenry paraded.

The mayor, city council members, county commissioners . . . the Kimberlys, Cochranes, Andrews, Kings. Everyone who was anyone was there, and although Libby was prohibited from mixing with them, she was allowed to attend. "As long as you stay on the sidelines," her father warned. The only reason she was afforded even that privilege was because Big Ed had said she might come to the party. Libby was grateful, though most times when she looked at the man, she was chilled by the memory of his striking Mrs. McKenna and her subsequent tumble down the stairs.

Three and a half years had passed since then, but for Libby the image remained vibrant. No one knew how much she'd seen that night. Not Big Ed, not Rory, not Clayton—and especially not her father. They all treated Mrs. McKenna's death as an accident. Libby knew it wasn't as simple as that, although she had no doubt that to say so would be the end of her.

Shaking off the morbid subject, she returned her attention to the party and moved into the terrace gallery. The orchestra was playing a slow love song, and a lot of couples were dancing. Across the way she caught sight of Clayton, leaning against a doorframe and looking like the proverbial wall flower. He was attractive, she thought. But since his mother's death, he'd developed a perpetual, wide-eyed look and stuttering shyness that made him seem younger than sixteen . . . unlike Rory, whose good looks were enhanced by the air of a full-grown man.

Libby's gaze moved through the dancers and found him with Hillary Cochrane. Lately Libby had caught his eyes on her a few times. It sent her pulse racing to think that finally, after all these years, Rory might notice her. She knew she'd filled out. "Bosomy, just like your mother!" her father accused, and insisted on selecting all the clothes in her wardrobe, each outfit more dismally concealing than the last.

Libby smiled to herself as she glanced at her father who was tending bar across the room. She'd outfoxed him this time. Savannah had given her a dress out of her vast collection. Libby had taken up the hem, but otherwise the elegant taffeta fit beautifully. The scoop neckline hinted at her high bosom, and the emerald color accentuated her auburn hair. Sweet Savannah.

Libby surveyed the crowd, saw her friend dancing with Clifford Andrews, and thought once again that the guy wasn't right for Savannah. She was in an ivory dress trimmed with ecru lace, and with that long blond hair falling down to her waist, she looked like an angel. Clifford, as dark as she was fair, was wearing a tuxedo. He was attractive, Libby supposed, in a dandified way. But he was a snob, and she didn't like him.

She pictured Savannah with someone like Danny Sawyer. All the girls in school had a crush on him, and every time he looked at Savannah his feelings were plain to see. But she was blind to it, and whenever Libby mentioned Danny, Savannah called her "a hopeless romantic."

"Really, Libby," she would say. "Why bring *him* up? You know I'm practically engaged to Clifford. Everyone in the two families knows it. We're a perfect match!"

Libby sighed as she glanced again at Rory. Dressed in a flawless white dinner jacket, he was still holding Hillary Cochrane, daughter of the president of Waccamaw Bank. Another "perfect match." He was too far away for her to make out his features, but she pictured the lines of his face, the pale blue of his eyes.

Libby supposed she was a hopeless romantic. She'd managed to kiss four boys in her sheltered sixteen years, and although she found their attentions exciting, she'd never felt the thrill she read about in forbidden books. She was sure it would be different with Rory. When she imagined kissing that beautiful mouth, touching that fair hair, she felt a warm tingling deep inside.

The dance ended. It was nearly midnight, and when Clifford went off to get champagne to toast the new year, Savannah spotted Libby and joined her at the edge of the crowd.

"Doesn't everyone look beautiful?" Libby asked dreamily.

Savannah followed her line of vision to Rory McKenna. "Everyone?" she repeated. "Or just Rory?"

Libby smiled. "Rory, of course."

Savannah's face took on a sober look as she studied his model-perfect form. The disgust she felt for Rory McKenna had only grown through the years, particularly since she started school at the Heights. There, he'd made a habit of catching up to her in the halls or at her locker, startling her with whispered hellos or an abrupt, familiar touch. Each time she jumped, he laughed as though he'd gotten away with something enormously funny.

Rory was a senior, a basketball player, and a leader of the elite "in" crowd. Many of the girls at the Heights were dying to go out with him, but Savannah's aversion remained stalwart. Thank heaven for Clifford, who had made a name for himself as president of the junior class and provided a constant reminder that Savannah King was spoken for. Otherwise she could have sworn Rory would have been downright blatant in his pursuit. Savannah had never slipped a word of her suspicions to Libby, who continued to adore him.

"Come on!" Libby whispered. "Haven't you ever fantasized about being with a man?"

Savannah flashed her a look of mortification.

"Oh, I don't mean being with a man *that* way! I just mean kissing him, for heaven's sake. Haven't you ever kissed a guy or just thought about it and felt warm all over?"

Savannah thought of Clifford's lips, soft and unmoving on her own. "No," she answered truthfully.

Libby rolled her eyes. "Honestly, Savannah. You're no fun."

Savannah put her hands on her hips. "Honestly, Libby. All you ever think about is boys!"

Libby grinned impishly. "I know. I'm awful, aren't I?"

"Just terrible!" Savannah agreed teasingly.

About that time, Clifford showed up with the champagne. "Good evening, Miss Parker," he said with a short bow.

Libby despised his formal manners, the way he looked down his aristocratic nose. She curtsied mockingly.

"Evenin', Mr. Andrews," she said in an exaggerated Southern accent.

Clifford glanced back at her curiously. Was the chit making fun of him? It wasn't even worth thinking about. With a quick snort, he turned to Savannah.

"Come along, my dear. It's almost time. We don't want to miss everything by secluding ourselves in the corner." With a last, disapproving glance at Libby, he steered Savannah away.

Noisemakers and champagne were passed out. The countdown began, the crowd joining in as the last seconds of 1975 ticked away. A crash of noise exploded when midnight struck, and then the orchestra launched into "Auld Lang Syne" as everyone embraced.

Clayton watched from the sidelines as Savannah raised her face to Clifford Andrews. She was such a lady—so proper, so refined . . . just like Mother. He'd idolized Savannah King since they were nothing but kids, ever since that time she and Danny Sawyer rescued him from the quickmud down by the river. Since then, Savannah had made it a point to be nice to him— sending cards on his birthday, greeting him warmly whenever they turned up in the same place. She had no way of knowing how much it meant, that she should single *him* out and virtually snub his popular brother. Savannah was the closest thing to a girlfriend Clayton had known in his miserably shy lifetime, and as he watched her being kissed, he felt a mixture of pride and envy.

At the opposite end of the room, Libby was peering through the crowd, her eyes glued to the handsome blond in the white jacket. Rory's fingers reached out to cup Hillary's chin. He tilted her face up and gently pressed his mouth to hers.

Libby quivered. He was just as she had dreamed he would be.

Danny sat alone on the veranda outside his room. Ma had gone to bed long ago—never mind that it was New Year's Eve, and there might be a reason for staying up. She looked old these days, he thought. Despite the fact that the staff did most of the heavy work, his mother seemed to be constantly busy, continually tired. Getting a good night's sleep took precedence over any holiday.

The night was clear and cold and quiet, just what Danny needed after that smoky excuse for a party. Liquor had flowed in a secret stream outside the school gymnasium. Loud music had rocked the interior, which was decorated with crepe paper and tacky stars. The whole thing had been uncomfortable, particularly when Roberta Sikes had shown up.

Ever since their fling years ago, Danny hadn't been able to look her in the eye. Forget that she was one of the most popular numbers around. Forget that *she* was the one who seduced *him*. There had been other girls since, but when he looked at Roberta, he saw a low point in his life. And he couldn't bear to look anymore, not since she turned up pregnant. Hell, Pete Ryan was even taking bets on who the father might be, since Roberta refused to tell.

There but for the grace of God . . . Danny shivered. That kind of thing could wreck a guy's life before it even got started. He thought of his own dreams, the urge to get out of Kingsport. Maybe then he could shed the feeling of being second best. Things were too structured here, too rigid. Either you were born to the high life, or you weren't. It was frustrating to live in it but never be part of it. At Kings Crossing, there was always that line between enjoying the privileges and remembering one's place.

And Danny was sick of remembering. He was strong and smart, his body tough, his instincts quick. But those distinctions carried no weight on the social scale, only on the basketball court—the one place he felt good enough. His one ticket out.

The only other time he felt like somebody was at *The Watch*. The past few years he'd been a copy runner—reading everything he could get his hands on, picking up tips from editors. Some months ago, he'd worked up the courage to ask Mr. King to look at one of his own reports—a scathing comment on substandard cafeteria practices in the public schools. The memory of the man's reaction would be with him forever.

"Danny-Buck!" he'd exclaimed with wide eyes. "You're a natural!"

With a few minor changes, the story ran on the editorial page the following Sunday. His mother collected a dozen copies. As for Danny, as soon as he saw his name in print, he knew he'd never be satisfied unless he could become a reporter. But that meant going to college, and *that* hung on basketball.

He peered into the night, longing to push aside the curtain of time and see into the future. But there was only darkness and the occasional whistle of wind in the rafters. Huddling in his old sheepskin jacket, he raised the bottle to his lips.

He'd found the champagne in the kitchen when he got home—barely three glasses gone, and just on the point of going flat. What a waste, he'd thought. But then Mr. and Mrs. King weren't the type to worry about such things. They'd shared a single toast before they left for the McKennas' and thought no more about it. Even Savannah had joined in with a few small sips.

Danny grimaced and took a long pull on the bottle. *Savannah . . .* pure, perfect Savannah who'd never let a curse word, a shot of booze, or a guy's tongue cross her lips. He'd watched her tonight, waiting for Clifford Andrews in her virginal white dress, greeting him with her virginial white smile. Almost sixteen years old and innocent as a baby. Danny was sure he was right—no one could put on such a perfect act!

He was experienced; she was a babe in the woods. He was a senior at Eastway; she was a sophomore at Pine View Heights. He dated around; she belonged to the heir of the Andrews fortune, and as far as Danny knew, she had never even been touched by anyone else.

The distance between them had swelled like the Cape Fear in springtime, he thought. Only there was never any change of seasons. The rain just kept coming down, day after day, adding to a whirlpool of provoking remarks, biting retaliations—back and forth, on and on. His relationship with Savannah had all the appearances of pure and simple mutual contempt—a condition that distressed Mr. King while it left the Mrs. openly pleased. But in reality, there was nothing pure or simple about Danny's feelings. His baiting sprang from a variety of sources, not the least of which was a hunger for Savannah he just couldn't shake.

But damn! She'd grown into a beauty with the face of a doll and a tall slender body that looked older than its years. What the hell was he supposed to do—ignore the fact that she lived and slept under the same roof? No eighteen-year-old male with nor-

mal drives could, and yet everyone seemed to expect it of him
. . . particularly Savannah.

What the hell does it matter? Danny thought finally. He was
going to land a scholarship and be long gone from here by fall.

Leaning back in the rocker, he propped his boots on the railing, drew the jacket a little closer, and continued drinking.

Savannah let herself quietly into the dark house. It would be a
couple of hours before her parents came home. Most people
stayed a while to celebrate New Year's Eve, but not Clifford.
Since he'd been given a car, he abided by his parents' curfew to
the minute.

She thought about him as she climbed the stairs, recalling
how dashing he'd looked in his tuxedo. Clifford was a year
older than she and decidedly attractive with his raven hair and
dark eyes. But New Year's Eve was no different from any other
night. He didn't come in, didn't press. Sometimes Savannah
wished he would. Maybe then she'd understand what Libby
was talking about when she mentioned feeling "warm and tin-
gly."

Savannah entered her bedroom, flipped on the light, and
closed the door behind her. Stepping out of ivory-tinted, *peau
de soie* pumps, she proceeded to the vanity where she took the
pearls from her throat, unzipped the lacy dress, and let it fall to
the floor.

Her gaze dropped to the foreign object on her left hand.

"A pre-engagement ring," Clifford had said. "I was planning
to save it for your sixteenth birthday, but Mother said I might
give it to you tonight. Start the year off right, and all that sort of
thing." Then he'd slipped the thing on her finger and kissed her.

Savannah had never questioned her future with Clifford, had
always looked forward to making her parents proud by joining
two of the most powerful families in Kingsport. Tonight she'd
scurried up to her mother just before leaving the McKennas'.

"It's a pre-engagement ring," she announced, and watched
Ophelia King's face light up.

It should have been one of the most fulfilling moments of her
life, yet all Savannah had felt was a surprising sense of disappointment. Then worry flooded her mind so that she barely remembered Clifford driving her home. Why hadn't she thought
of it before? She'd been submitting stories to her father the past
year or so, labors of love written in the privacy of her room,

shared with him in the privacy of his study. He was a wonderful teacher, and she'd gained years of experience on those quiet evenings hidden away from her mother's watchful eye. Savannah relished those times with her father more than any—except for the few occasions he spoiled by bringing up the "natural gift for reporting" Danny Sawyer was supposed to have.

All those nights had been spent in secret preparation for the time when she would take her rightful place at *The Watch*. But Clifford Andrews wasn't the sort to have a working wife. What would he think of a bride who wanted to be a newspaperwoman? What would his mother think? Savannah focused once more on the ring. The diamond wasn't ostentatious, but its meaning was clear. Its presence on her hand meant that she would one day be an Andrews—no worries, no responsibilities . . . no choices.

The ring was suddenly heavy, the spacious room suffocating. Savannah donned a prim nightgown and robe, and stepped onto the veranda in search of fresh air.

Danny noticed as soon as the light went on. His quarters were clear at the other end of the house, but the porch was unbroken around the entire second story—a small, inconsequential bridge between the lives of Savannah King and Danny Sawyer. He stopped rocking and stared along the dark floor where the light from her bedroom spilled out like a golden beacon. And then—of all incredible things!—she stepped outside and moved to the rail.

Dressed in a long white robe, outlined by winter moonlight, she virtually glowed. A lump of conflicting feelings rose to Danny's throat. He washed it down with champagne, but only a moment later his eyes were cutting rebelliously in her direction. Danny deposited the bottle on the floor with a clunk and rose from the rocker, just drunk enough to be foolhardy.

There was a distant creaking noise, followed by the rhythmic thump of approaching footsteps. Savannah whirled, straining to see through the darkness. When Danny emerged from the shadows, she pulled the neck of the robe close about her throat.

There was something about him that threatened her these days. Or maybe it was something about herself. Lately she'd found herself watching him when he was unaware—sitting in the breakfast nook, his head bent over his books . . . tuning the ridiculous old pickup he kept running through some mechanical magic. A few weeks ago, when the Eastway High team came to the Heights, she couldn't take her eyes off him as he raced around the basketball court—impressing the crowd with his ability, thrilling the girls with his flashing smile. He was devilishly good looking, and he knew it. Savannah knew it, too. And she had no business even noticing.

"Happy New Year," he said, "*Miss* Savannah."

His voice was disconcertingly deep, laced with the sarcasm that seemed to accompany every word he spoke to her these days. Savannah gave him a stony look.

"*Happy* New Year?" she repeated in a sarcastic tone of her own. "If you're trying to be festive, you're hardly succeeding."

Danny chuckled and rested a hip against the nearby railing. "If I were trying to be festive, I'd hardly be hanging around the Crossing, would I?"

"Good point. What *are* you doing here?"

He shrugged. "Taking in the night. What are *you* doing here?"

Thoughts about Clifford and New Year's and the future whirled through her mind. "The same," she said noncommitally. "Where's your mother?"

"Asleep. Where are your folks?"

"They haven't come home from the McKennas' yet."

"What about Clifford?"

"He's gone home. After all," she added swiftly, "it *is* one o'clock in the morning."

"Of course. And all nice boys should be home by one."

Savannah's hands left her throat to be planted squarely on her hips. "Are you going to start in on him again?"

Danny shifted away from the rail, gaining his full height so that he could look down on her. "Maybe."

Her chin came up. "Well then, if you'll excuse me . . ." She started to step away, but one of his arms moved to block her, and then the other. Savannah shrank back to the railing. She was fenced in, with only a foot of space hovering between her and the tall, dark figure of Danny Sawyer.

"What do you think you're doing?" she mumbled.

Danny didn't know why he was acting so crazy, but now that he was into it, he couldn't stop. "Asking you to stay."

"I didn't hear you *ask* anything."

"Sometimes people don't have to use words, Savannah. Or are you still such a baby you don't know even that?"

"I'm not a baby!"

"Oh, yeah? Prove it."

"I don't have to prove it. Not to you!"

Danny leaned slightly closer and saw her eyes widen. "I'm the only one here."

"Get out of my way!" she ordered haughtily.

Everything within him rebelled. For once he and Savannah were on equal footing. He stared down at her and didn't budge an inch.

"All right, then," Savannah muttered and tried to slip quickly under his arm.

But almost as soon as she moved, Danny's hands rose to stop her, closing about her upper arms in a hard grip that penetrated the fleecy robe. Savannah looked up in surprise.

"Get your hands off me!" she sputtered.

"Or what?" he countered.

Savannah's expression turned incredulous. "Or I'll scream."

"So?"

"So?! What's the matter with you, Danny? Are you drunk?"

"On New Year's Eve? Now what would make me want to get drunk on such a night?"

"Frankly, I don't care!" Savannah blazed. "I just don't like you inflicting your drunken condition on *me*. Now, please . . . go away!"

She tried to jerk away. Danny's grip tightened.

"Not until I get what I want," he said.

"And what in heaven's name do you want?"

"Not so much. A simple New Year's Eve kiss."

Savannah stared up at him. Starlight glistened on his hair as it shifted in the wind. Moonlight gilded the features of his face, and she saw again how handsome they were. A fearsome, unknown feeling rocked her stomach. She fought it the only way she knew.

"Afraid not," she managed in an airy tone. "I don't think Clifford would appreciate that, considering what he gave me tonight." She moved one of her constricted arms and flashed the ring under Danny's nose. The diamond sparkled, looking bigger than it actually was in the meager light.

"A ring," he said stupidly.

"A *pre-engagement* ring," Savannah supplied.

A pang of dread knifed through Danny, opening old wounds,

releasing the urge to strike out at her. "Pre-engagement, huh? Well, I guess that makes you something of a woman."

"*Clifford's* woman!"

"So you say."

The look in his eyes was hot. Ironically, a chill overtook Savannah, and she began to shake.

"Let me go," she tried once more.

Danny's heart was hammering and aching at the same time. "What are you afraid of, Savannah? That I could kiss in the new year better than Clifford Andrews?"

"I'm not afraid of anything! And certainly not of you!"

"Like I said before," he retorted, "prove it!"

The blue eyes before him had never seemed so large. Danny thought he detected a look of fear within them, but it did nothing to soften the drive to overpower her.

"Come on, Miss Savannah," he taunted. "I'll bet you don't even know how to kiss!"

Savannah peered up at him wordlessly, her breath puffing in quick clouds against the black night. She'd never been so insulted, so angry . . . so afraid. The emotions rushed through her one after the other, leaving her indecisive, immobile.

Danny moved a hand to the back of her head as she stood frozen. She felt his fingers in her hair and thought her heart would pound out of her body as she watched him bend closer. There was a whiff of champagne, and then his mouth was on hers—his lips, cool and firm, not at all like Clifford's. It was her last thought of Clifford. Savannah's eyes closed, and she submitted with the passivity of a lady.

For a moment Danny was stunned. But then his body took over, his arm encircling her, his face slanting across hers, his hand pressing insistently against the back of her head. Finally, her lips gave way and parted. His tongue moved inside.

Savannah squirmed in protest. But it lasted only seconds. Danny's mouth was commanding, his arms powerful, his tall masculinity exciting. She felt the softness of his sheepskin jacket against her cheek, the roughness of a manly beard on her face. But most of all she felt his tongue—filling, prodding, sleekly caressing the entirety of her mouth. A warm wave washed over her, melting her insides in its wake. Without conscious thought, she opened herself to him, began moving her mouth to his rhythm. One of her palms climbed up his back. *So this is what Libby meant . . .*

The thought came from nowhere, but suddenly a trio of faces leapt into her mind. Clifford, Mother, Mrs. Andrews—if they could see her now! Savannah's eyes popped open and took in the brief horrifying sight of Danny Sawyer's nose, his eyelids, his dark lashes. With a burst of strength, she pushed away.

Danny returned from some faraway place, reluctantly opening his eyes. Savannah stood there before him, her chest heaving, her eyes shining wide in the moonlight. Silence hung as they stared at each other.

"Well," he said, attempting a shaky laugh. "Guess I was wrong. You *do* know how to kiss."

"You're no gentleman!" Savannah hissed. "That's clear!"

Danny's smile faded. "Well, then. Since you weren't doing anything different from me, I guess that means you're no lady!"

Before she knew what she was doing, Savannah swung and gave him a resounding slap across the cheek. His head tipped with the blow. Slowly, he turned back to face her.

She couldn't bear his calm, accusing stare. *You allowed it to happen!* said the unsmiling eyes. *You liked it, and you know it!* Savannah pushed him out of her way and rushed off the veranda.

It was only seconds before Danny heard the slam of her door, followed by the distinct click of a lock.

"Just think of it, Jim!" Big Ed urged. "Kingsport needs more than a few fancy little spots like the Yachtsman and the Magnolia Club. Don't get me wrong—I mean, they're nice places to eat. But think about a real country club, something to put the resorts down the coast to shame—beautiful golf courses, a tennis center that would be second to none. Why, we could get a pro down here, and ten-to-one within a couple of years we could draw a World Championship Tennis tournament. Right here in Kingsport! Just think of what *that* would do for the city!"

It was one-thirty in the morning. The party was winding down. Big Ed had chosen his moment carefully, and now as he made the pitch, his eyes were shining. The look would be construed for excitement, but in truth, it was the thrill of laying the trap. Big Ed knew his quarry, and as he took in Jim King's look of interest, he knew he'd found the right bait.

"It's a worthy idea, I must admit," Jim said.

The man's naivety showed all over his face. Big Ed hid a feeling of contempt. This was almost too easy.

"Of course it is!" he boomed. "But it needs a man who knows tennis behind it. Why, when I found out you'd been a college champion, I *knew* you were the man to talk to. Of course, I must admit I'd like to back the club myself. Unfortunately, my funds are tied up for the next few years. And the Monroe parcel isn't likely to sit on the market for long. You know the way out-of-state investors are descending on us these days. It would be a shame to see that land gobbled up for a bunch of condominiums to put money in some Yankee's pocket! Particularly when it could be put to such a good use for Kingsport's own! Why, Henry Monroe would turn over in his grave."

Jim nodded solemnly. "That's true. In the last century, the Monroes were one of the biggest plantation families in the area, one of the few who managed to hold onto their assets after the War Between the States. Henry always did his best to funnel his profits back into Kingsport."

"That's right!" Ed agreed. "Of course, you knew him much better than I did."

"And you say a holding company has control of the land?"

"Yeah. A kind of historic committee I've been drafted into—me, the county commissioner, and Ben Cochrane from over at Waccamaw Bank. It was really Ben's idea to try and save the place before some outsider snaps it up. *You* know what happens when somebody dies without an heir. Well, apparently old Monroe was bedridden and senile. He didn't update his will, and the grandson he left everything to died a year ago in a car accident."

"Yes," Jim said. "I remember that. I also remember the Monroe place, though I haven't been there in years."

"There are a few fine points to the deal," Ed commented. "Considering the historic importance of the estate, the committee will have ultimate construction approval. I'm afraid we'll insist that any building or renovation be consistent with the authentic look of the antebellum home."

Jim gave him a look of indignation. "Why would anyone do it any other way? The Monroe house must be treated with respect."

"You see?" Ed blustered, slapping his thigh with enthusiasm. "I knew you were the man to talk to!"

Jim's head began to fill with the dream—the graceful white Monroe house, shaded walks winding through live oaks and

magnolias, sweeping golf courses, a dozen immaculately kept
tennis courts. He pushed aside the fact that he'd always sensed
something shady about McKenna. "Still," he said with a vestige
of hesitancy, "the price tag you mentioned is steep."

"I know it sounds high," Ed cajoled, "but I can supply the
materials and labor through Clancytown, and just think of the
return on the investment. Why, in a few years, whoever backs
this thing will be rolling in wealth! Not to mention having the
satisfaction of bringing something new and valuable to
Kingsport! Ben has offered to finance the whole thing through
the bank, but only if it's for someone he trusts—someone
Kingsport trusts."

Jim could already hear the tennis balls bouncing across the
clay. "I'll think about it," he said with a dreamy look.

"You do that, Jim. But I warn you—in a couple of years, as
soon as a few of my investments turn liquid, I want in!"

Ed extended his hand. Jim joined it.

"I knew it!" Ed exclaimed. "What a way to start the new
year. A toast!" he announced, raising his glass to his companion. "A toast to King's Club!"

Jim smiled. It had a nice ring. He touched his glass to that of
Big Ed McKenna and drank.

Libby hurried along the path. The gazebo was a garish structure with turrets, and Libby knew Mrs. McKenna's hair would
stand on end at the sight of it, even though it had been erected in
her memory. Still, the gazebo on the fringe of the woods had its
virtues—privacy, first and foremost. No one went there, and it
had become Libby's place, the spot she sought when she wanted
to escape her father, the McKennas, the world in general.

Ironically enough, she had seen Rory and a few of his friends
head in that direction. Her father was cleaning up after the party
guests. He thought she was already in bed. No one knew that
she was spying on Rory. Pulling the shawl tightly around her
shoulders, Libby scurried through the cold night and wished for
the first time that she was wearing something other than Savannah's emerald taffeta with the scoop neck. She crept off the path
near the gazebo and found a vantage point in nearby trees.

She couldn't make out what the guys were saying, though she
heard guttural comments and occasional bursts of laughter, and
could see that they were passing a flask. She stayed hidden in

the trees while everyone but Rory eventually drifted back toward the house, presumably to take their leave.

When Rory was alone, he lit up a cigarette. She watched, her
pulse racing. It was as if fate had brought him here, on the first
night of a brand-new year, to give her a golden opportunity.
Only when he seemed to be getting ready to leave did she work
up her nerve and saunter into the open.

"What are you doing here?" Rory demanded with a start.

"Just taking a walk." She struck what she hoped was a sexy
pose against the railing. "Got any of that liquor left?"

Rory looked down at the girl. As he noticed the full line of
the bosom she was flaunting, he remembered she wasn't just a
girl anymore. A spark of excitement flashed through him.

"Sorry. We drank it all. Why don't you come on up anyway?"

Libby climbed the stairs to the secluded platform. Rory's
white dinner jacket glowed in the moonlight, along with his
hair. She strolled a few paces, trying to appear cool and grown
up.

"You sure you were only taking a walk?" he asked.

"I'm sure."

"Out here to the gazebo? Nobody comes here!"

"I do . . . sometimes."

"Who knows you're here?"

"No one."

Rory smiled coldly. The alcohol had left him paradoxically
numb and alert. "I submit that you were not just taking a walk in
the middle of the night. I submit that you were following me."

Libby blinked. What could she say? How brazen should she
be? What approach could she use so that he might deign to kiss
her?

"You're right," she murmured breathlessly. "I . . . I just
wanted to wish you a happy New Year."

His smile broadened. "I'd like to wish you one as well. Come
here."

He's just a guy, Libby reminded herself as her shaking legs
moved her forward. *Just a guy.*

Rory regarded her critically. She was a bit short, but shapely;
common, but pretty. She passed inspection—for some things.

"I said, come here," he repeated.

Libby moved within a foot of him and gazed up at the handsome features, the eyes that were pale as ice. He was so perfect.
She saw him bend in her direction and expected his fingers to

cup her face, just as they had done with Hillary Cochrane. Instead, a rough hand yanked at her hair while an arm captured
her hips. His face came down hard, his teeth and tongue clashing with hers.

Libby's shawl fell unnoticed while her head reeled. At first
she tried to appease Rory. But when he forced her down on the
gazebo floor—one hand clenched in her hair, the other capturing her breast—she panicked. Her jaws slammed together, her
teeth closing on his tongue.

Rory drew away with a yelp, though his grip tightened. He
glared down at her, excitement and pain shining in his eyes as a
trickle of blood appeared at the corner of his mouth.

"So that's how you like it," he rasped, and hit her open-
palmed across the cheek.

When she screamed, his fist repeated the blow.

Libby slipped into a daze. She didn't hear the rending tear of
her bodice, didn't feel the bruising hands on her body, didn't
comprehend the fact that her skirt was thrown up, her underwear yanked out of the way. Finally, her defensive trance was
penetrated by a searing pain between her thighs. She wrenched,
and Rory's fingers went round her throat, threatening her wordlessly as he drove deep inside.

Libby's hands closed around his wrists. All she could do was
fight for breath and stare helplessly into the gleaming eyes
above her. Now she understood. The eyes were icy pale because
of the coldness behind them. The face was perfect as a statue
because there was no feeling to mar it. Girlhood fantasies froze
within her, shattering into oblivion as Rory shuddered to climax
. . . then settled heavily upon her. Gradually, his breathing
calmed, and he loosened his hold, though his hands remained at
her throat.

"Happy New Year," Rory said, then chuckled as the girl's
horrified expression seemed suddenly funny. "You came looking for it, and you found it," he added. "Don't try to act like you
didn't know what you were doing, like this was your first time
or something!"

"It . . . was my first time," Libby managed, her lips feeling
like two wooden planks.

Rory studied her dispassionately. "It won't be your last," he
announced. "This is only the beginning, my little servant girl.
You'll come when I call. You'll come when I snap my fingers. You'll come, and you'll keep your mouth shut!"

"No . . . please . . . I can't . . ."

"You *will*!" Rory decreed, his face hard and chiseled in the light of the winter moon. "Remember the way Mother looked? All still and staring at the foot of the stairs?"

Libby's breath stopped in her chest. It was her worst nightmare.

"I see that you do remember. Good. I want you to keep on remembering how fragile life is—how you can be hale and hearty one second, dead as a doornail the next."

Her face was white as a sheet, her eyes bulging with terror. Rory was satisfied . . . and exhilarated.

"Yes, you'll do," he muttered, his gaze falling to Libby's budding breasts. "You'll do quite nicely."

He withdrew, stood up, and fixed his clothing. Libby lay sprawled and unmoving as he smoothed his pale hair, walked casually down the steps, and disappeared.

The first few hours of 1976 had passed. Darkness lay across the lowlands like a cold blanket, while a nearly full moon shone from the starry sky. The early morning was crisp, still, quiet . . . seemingly peaceful. There was no one to hear as Libby sobbed against the freezing floor of the gazebo.

When no tears were left, she climbed to her feet, took a few slow steps, and tried to think of what she could do about the fact that she'd been beaten and raped by Rory McKenna. There was nothing . . . no one to turn to. Her father was the logical choice, but as Libby pictured his self-righteous, condemning expression, she laughed wildly into the deserted night.

"Harlot!" he would cry. "Just like your mother!" There would be no question that Libby had invited what happened. There would be no fault found with Rory. Abel Parker was blindly devoted to his employers; the word of a McKenna would override that of his daughter any day. She could almost hear, "Get down on your knees and pray!"

And then there was Rory. Fear swamped her anew as she recalled the cold eyes, the deadly threat, and knew she could put nothing past him. Holding the dress together the best she could, Libby stumbled back to the house and slipped into her room. As she approached the mirror, she almost screamed at what she saw. Her auburn curls were tangled, her skin streaked with dirt and blood, and her cheek swelled with a purple bruise.

Gradually the frightened look went out of her eyes and left them empty. The bruise could be explained as the result of a fall.

Her father would accept that. He was always saying she day-dreamed too much, that she paid no attention to what she was doing.

Libby undressed, bathed, and put on a flannel nightgown—all in the mechanical manner of a robot. When she returned to the center of her bedroom floor, she eyed the pile of clothing with a sense of distance. It seemed to have nothing to do with her. She picked up the shredded taffeta dress, noticed the red stain on the underlying crinoline. Virgin's blood. Without blinking an eye, Libby gathered the bundle to her breast and left the room.

The house was dark and quiet. No one else was up. She moved noiselessly past the foyer and into the game room where firelight beckoned. As she walked toward the hearth, she glanced at the trophies lining the walls. The prizes of the McKennas' . . . Rory, as well as his father. Laying the ruined clothes in the flames, she stepped back and watched the old Libby Parker go up in smoke.

Rory was right. She would come when he snapped his fingers, and she wouldn't say a word.

March 14, 1976

It was her birthday. Savannah looked in the mirror, searching for signs that she was a woman. All she saw was the same slim figure and the same hair pulled back in the same style she'd worn for years. With a disappointed sigh, she went down to breakfast.

Her parents were there. So was Danny, helping himself to coffee from the sideboard service as if he were an invited guest who belonged in the dining room of Kings Crossing. Savannah made the rounds—kissing her mother and father on the cheek, ignoring Danny, taking her place at the expansive table.

"Happy birthday, Kitten," her father said as she sat down. "It's beautiful outside. You've a wonderful day to celebrate."

"That's right," her mother confirmed regally. "It will be a perfect night for your Sweet Sixteen party."

Savannah smiled, thinking ahead to the posh celebration that had been planned at the Magnolia Club, the most exclusive dining and dancing spot in the city. Her parents had reserved the entire ballroom for the night of her birthday.

"Sweet sixteen and never been kissed," her father chuckled. "Isn't that the way it goes?"

"Oh, Jim!" her mother scolded as Savannah's gaze flew uncontrollably to Danny.

She remembered their deep New Year's Eve kiss as clearly as if it had happened yesterday. And as Danny smirked, she knew he was remembering it, too. Unnoticed by her parents, he raised his coffee cup in silent salute and left the room. Savannah desired nothing more than to throw her plate at the back of his head.

The irritable feeling stayed with her all morning. After school she decided to invite a few of the neighborhood girls over. The weather was perfect and the pool had just been filled. With Ophelia King's blessing, she called Hillary and Constance. When her mother left the room, she phoned the McKenna house and invited Libby. Now the four girls reclined on lounges about the pool, all in swimsuits except for Libby

"I tell you, it's positively devastating!" Hillary exclaimed. "If Rory doesn't stop kissing me like that, I swear I'll have to give in. And it won't be *my* fault, it will be *his!*"

Constance laughed one of her shocked, trilling laughs.

Libby's cheeks burned as she thought what a fool Hillary Cochrane was.

"Oh, Hillary, come on!" Savannah said. "If you let him, you let him! There's no excuse."

No excuse! Libby flashed an angry look in Savannah's direction. *What would you know about it? You've hardly even kissed a man, while I could give a lecture on positions that would curl your hair!* The anger quickly dissolved in a downpour of self-loathing. It wasn't Savannah's fault. It wasn't fair to hate her because she, herself, had sunk so low.

"That's right, Hillary," Constance chimed in. "If you let Rory have you, he'll never respect you."

"Maybe," Hillary returned. "But there are other things in the world, you know—like love . . . passion."

The girls tittered while Libby felt sick. She directed a mournful look at Hillary that somehow ended up on Savannah. The eyes that greeted her were clear and open, curious and concerned. Libby turned away. She had no right to look someone like Savannah in the eye. Libby felt dirty, tainted, nothing more than the whore her father had always accused her of being. She didn't belong out here on the patio with a bunch of rich virgins. She should go home and take a bath.

Savannah's attention remained on her auburn-haired friend. Today was the first time she'd seen Libby in weeks, and she was shocked by the dark circles under her eyes and the morose quiet of one who had always been so merry. It seemed to have started just after the turn of the year. Libby was a different person—keeping to herself, hardly talking. Yet when Savannah questioned her, she only turned away in tight-lipped silence.

Studying the dejected tilt of Libby's head, the air of sadness all mixed up with rage, Savannah wondered once again what could be so terribly wrong.

A short distance away, Danny wielded the clippers against the shoulder-high hedge, casting furtive glances toward the pool. His relationship with Savannah had only worsened since New Year's. There was a tangible enmity between them now. He could only guess at how she felt, but imagined that she despised him all the more each time he managed to deliver a sly barb. As for himself, the love and hate he felt for the girl continued to claw at his insides like two caged cats.

He *did* love her. There was no doubt, although the only one who seemed to know it was Ma.

His mind recreated the scene from last night. Ma was stepping behind the screen in her room as she changed out of her uniform and into a robe. They'd lived at the Crossing for nearly ten years, and the only times she was seen out of uniform was on Sundays. That was the way Mrs. King liked it.

"She's in your system like a sickness," Ma said as she slumped into a chair and looked at him with tired eyes.

"What are you talking about?" he said quickly.

"You know what. I tried to warn you about Miss Savannah long ago, but you never listened. And now you're in love with her."

"Ma!" he blurted, a look of protest transforming his face.

"Don't 'Ma' me. It's plain as day for anyone with half an eye."

Fierce denial welled up, but as Danny took in his mother's knowing expression, he saw there was no use. His puffed-up chest deflated as he released a heavy breath.

"You're only eighteen," Edna Sawyer went on, her voice comforting and wise, weak and weary. "It will pass. Just be sure you don't let your feelings spoil things, Danny. When you're on the basketball court, you must keep your mind on what you're doing—whether *she's* cheering for the other team or not."

He knew Ma was referring to the upcoming big game, the conference championship against Pine View Heights. Scouts from State and UNC and Wake Forest would be there, and Danny was hoping for the invitation to Chapel Hill that would mean he had a four-year scholarship locked up. The University of North Carolina had the finest journalism school in the state. It was where Mr. King had gone. It was where Danny intended to go.

He clipped a few more sprigs from the thick hedge. Ma was right. He had too much riding on tomorrow night's game to be thinking of anything but basketball. Still, his eyes lingered disobediently on Savannah. She was standing at the pool's edge, wearing a one-piece blue suit not quite as dark as her eyes. Her hair, falling straight to her waist, was still as pale as when she was seven years old. Her sixteen-year-old body was like a softly curving willow.

Mrs. King chose that moment to appear at the pool. Dressed in a flowing ensemble and sunhat, carrying a basket of newly cut spring flowers, she'd have made a perfect subject for a photograph in *Ladies' Home Journal*. The sight of her at the pool reminded Danny of that excruciating day several years back when she'd caught him watching her daughter. The memory was all it took to prod him swiftly along the hedge.

He was nearly to the end of the massive border, just opposite the courtyard, when the car horn began to blare. Danny stepped away from the hedge in time to see Mr. King's head pop up beyond the wrought-iron fence.

"All right, Kitten!" Mr. King called. "If you want your birthday present, you'd better come over here and see what I've brought!"

Unable to stem his curiosity, Danny headed to the front lawns as the chattering group of females fled the pool and hurried excitedly along the brick-lined path to the courtyard. Only Libby held back as the others spilled onto the drive.

It was a long, white, brand-new Cadillac convertible.

Savannah squealed and threw her arms around her father's neck. Mr. King hugged her and laughed with obvious enjoyment.

"Oh, Daddy, it's beautiful!" Savannah squealed as her friends exclaimed their admiration and Mrs. King looked on with a smile.

"You're a good girl, honey," Mr. King said. "You deserve it."

Savannah kissed him quickly on the cheek. "Can I take it for a drive?"

"That's what it's here for," her father announced.

"Come on, everybody!" Savannah ordered and jumped into the driver's seat as Hillary and Constance climbed into the back.

"You girls go ahead and have a good time," Mrs. King said. "But be careful!"

"We will," Savannah returned, and looked curiously in Libby's direction. "Libby? Aren't you coming?"

Libby glanced automatically at Mrs. King and beheld the expected arched brow. Turning back to Savannah, she managed a smile.

"Not this time," she answered. "I've got to get back. I'll see you later. Oh, and happy birthday!"

"Thanks!" Savannah called with a brilliant smile.

The radio volume went up a couple of notches, and then the Cadillac moved smoothly along the flower-decked driveway of Kings Crossing. Danny turned away. The image was so beautiful it hurt—Savannah driving away in that damned white convertible, her hair streaming in the wind.

That night he lay in bed and willed himself to sleep, trying futilely to rest up for the next night's game while he was tormented by her image. He'd always thought of her as a princess, and tonight she'd looked like one—all dressed up in a silvery white gown with a wide skirt, her pale hair coiled in artful curls atop her head. He'd never seen her with her hair up before; it showed off her long neck, made her look all grown up.

Concealed in a bulky chair in Mr. King's study, Danny had watched covertly as the party of five gathered in the foyer—Savannah, Mr. and Mrs. King, Clifford Andrews, and his mother. Ever since Mr. Andrews passed away, his widow had been leaning more heavily than ever on her son. Even Danny, who saw them only when they came to the Crossing, could detect the way the woman clutched at him.

Savannah, however, seemed oblivious to it. In the light of the chandelier, she'd shone from the top of her head to the polished tips of her fingers—a smiling portrait of grace in both form and movement, the epitome of the lady her mother had always decreed she would be. As she took the arm Andrews proferred and glided out of the house, Danny had felt so strong and sudden an ache it was as though someone buried a fist in his gut. Now, in the privacy of his bed, as he imagined her, the ache materialized once more . . . only lower.

Mr. King had invited him to the party—a gallant, dauntless gesture against the way things were. Everyone knew Danny had no place at the Magnolia Club, or Savannah's sixteenth birthday party, regardless of how long they'd lived in the same house.

"No thanks, Mr. King," he'd said. "I've gotta rest up for the game tomorrow night."

But so far he'd done anything but rest as he imagined Savannah whirling across the floor in the arms of Clifford Andrews. Then Danny brazenly removed Andrews from the picture and put himself there instead. His hardness became a painful thing. Danny leapt from under the covers and shrugged into jeans and a jacket. Slamming out of his room and onto the veranda, he circled aimlessly to the front of the house, failing to realize what he was doing until he sank into one of the wicker chairs outside Mr. and Mrs. King's front chamber.

The night was cool and peaceful, Danny's emotions hot and rowdy. He must be crazy to sit there like a night owl on a perch, watching for the celebrants to return from a ritzy club of which he had no part, waiting for a girl from a world of which he had no part.

"You're a damn fool!" Danny grumbled aloud, and yet knew he would stay.

"That really isn't necessary," Savannah said quickly.

It was after midnight. The party had been perfect, right up to the end when Clifford's mother announced she didn't feel well. Now a dozen or so stragglers were standing outside the Magnolia Club—Savannah and her parents, Clifford and Mrs. Andrews, Hillary Cochrane and her parents, Big Ed McKenna and Rory. Clayton hovered on the fringe of the group.

"I can ride with Clifford over to his house," Savannah went on. "Then he can take me home."

"Nonsense!" Big Ed boomed amiably. "There's no sense in y'all going clear across town, then driving back out to the Crossing—not when Rory's going just next door."

"Or *we* could drop you off, Kitten," her father said, apparently detecting her hesitancy. "Before we head over to Ben and Vera's."

Her parents and Big Ed McKenna were stopping over at the Cochranes' for a nightcap. Savannah picked up her father's look of concern and decided she was being silly. It was late and Hillary seemed to have no qualms about her escort driving Savannah home. Clifford had no objections. Still, as she waited for Clayton to climb into the back, then slid into the front seat of Rory's silver Corvette, Savannah experienced the same old pangs of apprehension that sprang up whenever Rory McKenna was nearby.

The feelings accelerated as they drove away from the club and Rory glanced over, his pale eyes sweeping boldly up her body to her face. She looked quickly ahead and kept her attention on the familiar landmarks of Kingsport and then The Cloisters. *Soon*, she thought. *I'll be home soon.* But her trepidation skyrocketed when Rory turned unexpectedly onto the dark drive of the McKenna house. He brought the car to a jolting stop in front of the house, climbed out, and pushed the driver's seat forward.

"Get out, Clayton," he ordered.

"Why?" Clayton voiced from behind Savannah, a small feeble sound against the forceful tone of his brother.

"Because I said so. Now get out. Time for all good little boys to call it a night."

Savannah sensed Clayton's reluctance, but he went anyway. Her heart was pounding by the time Rory pulled up at the Crossing, cut the engine, and extended an arm to the back of her seat.

"Thanks for bringing me," she said and swiftly reached for the door handle. But she'd no more than pushed the door open before he grabbed her other arm.

"Wait just a minute!"

It was the same tone he'd used on Clayton. Savannah's head snapped around. Raising a brow, she attempted to swallow the fright that loomed within her.

"For what?" she asked coolly.

"For this," Rory said and leaned toward her.

When she saw his intent, Savannah's eyes flew open wide, and all efforts to disguise her alarm vanished. She strained away, yanking at her captive arm. One of Rory's hands grabbed at her hair, dislodging a curl so that it fell across her face.

"Stop it, Rory!"

He only laughed. Fear swelled within Savannah, lodging in her throat at the thought that he wasn't going to stop—no matter what she said. She clawed at his hand, trying once again to free her arm. His fingers tightened savagely in her hair, jerking her head back so that she gasped. She caught a glimpse of his eyes, pale and shining, before being yanked out of her seat, feet flying off the floorboard, silver heels kicking in the air.

"Stop it, Rory!" This time, the words burst through her lips in a shriek.

Rory barely heard. He had no sense of anything but what he was after. Pinning Savannah across his lap, he took his hand from her hair, noting how an array of hairpins followed his fingers, freeing long blond tresses that spilled over his sleeve. Boldly, he ran an open palm across the silvery white dress covering Savannah's breasts. She screamed. Rory's sense of urgency spiraled. Once he kissed her, she'd give in. He bent down baring his teeth in a hard smile.

The driver's door flew open, and Savannah nearly fell out as Rory was snatched out of the car. Heaving for breath, she peered with a sense of shock out the open door.

Danny grabbed Rory by the stiff collar of his formal shirt. "Want to manhandle somebody?" he snarled. "Try *me* on for size!"

Rory's hands closed about his adversary's wrists. "Back off, Sawyer! You're forgetting who you're dealing with."

"Not hardly. I've dealt with you long enough to remember who you are, you son-of-a-bitch!"

Rory pulled once again at the fists, but was unable to budge them. He gave Danny Sawyer the scathing look he'd used on him since childhood.

"What are you going to do, Sawyer?" he taunted. "Hit me? You? Don't make me laugh. If you lay a finger on me, I'll see to it that you and that housekeeper mother of yours are tossed out of here so fast it will make your head spin."

Clutching Rory's shirt front with his left fist, Danny drew back his right. "It'll be damn well worth it!"

Savannah struggled out of the car. "No, Danny!" she cried and latched a restraining hand on his arm.

For the first time since the mess started, Danny looked away from Rory. When he saw Savannah's face and the look of fright that lingered there, his rage billowed like an angry flame.

"He's had this coming a long time, Savannah!"

"Maybe so," she said with a fixed, wide-eyed look. "But he's right. Daddy would understand, but Mother . . ." She shook her head. "Let him go, Danny. Just . . . let him go."

Danny looked back to the hated face before him. Slowly, reluctantly, he released his hold. As soon as Rory was free, he stepped briskly back, adjusting his collar and cuffs with jerky movements as he eyed the two of them—Savannah King and her faithful watchdog. Suddenly it came to him, and he snorted a chuckle of disbelief.

"You should know better, Sawyer," he remarked, then grinned with open derision. "But then you never *did* know your place, did you? You're nothing but a hired hand, Sawyer. A servant. You should know better than to get hung up on Miss Sweet Sixteen, here."

Danny took a threatening step toward Rory. Savannah stepped swiftly between the two of them.

"Get in the car, Rory," she commanded. "Get out of here before you stir up something we'll all regret."

Rory's eyes cut in her direction as he caught the inference. If he didn't go, Savannah would spill the story of his overture. Papa wouldn't like the idea of a scene at Kings Crossing. "Do what you want," Big Ed was fond of saying. "Just don't get caught at it." Rory flashed a look down Savannah's slender figure. If he'd gotten what he wanted, it might have been worth a lecture. But as it was, the whole thing had gone awry because . . . He turned back to Sawyer with a menacing expression.

"You think this is over?" Rory pronounced evenly. "It isn't. Not by a long shot."

"Damn straight," Danny returned.

Rory's pale eyes froze on Danny. Danny's hands curled once more into fists, and just when Savannah thought the thing was going to start all over again, Rory threw back his head and laughed—an eerie, joyless sound that smacked of the howl of a wolf. With that, the blond climbed into his flashy car, gunned the engine, and screeched away.

Savannah put shaking fingers to her forehead and walked into the courtyard. Danny shifted his stance and watched her go, his gaze racing from the shimmering dress to the disheveled hair tumbling down her back. He took long strides after her, catching up to her on the veranda.

"I can't believe he did that," Savannah murmured, more to herself than to him.

"Why not?" Danny returned sharply. "McKenna's always been that way. You knew it. Now that I think about it, it makes me wonder."

Savannah's gaze leapt to his. "What's that supposed to mean?"

"What were you doing with him?" Danny hurled. "You left here with Andrews."

"Clifford's mother got sick. And everyone said I should . . . well, it seemed the logical thing . . . Oh, never mind!"

Savannah swept in the front door, hurried through the foyer and up the stairs. Danny stomped after her, the sound of his footsteps loud in the quiet house. She was all the way to her room when he came up behind her and put a detaining hand on her shoulder.

"Are you all right?" he demanded gruffly.

Savannah halted in the midst of reaching for the doorknob. "I'm fine. Thank you for . . . intervening."

Danny shrugged at her back. "No problem." Her perfume reached him then, something like roses. His hand was still on her shoulder, and he was suddenly aware that two of his fingers were touching bare skin above the neck of the white dress. The offending hand shot away, his arm bringing it rigidly to his side. Savannah turned slowly to face him, and Danny was surprised to see a soft smile on her lips.

"You know what I just remembered out of the blue?" she said. "That time years ago when we became blood brothers. Friends for life . . . . remember?"

The memory caught him unawares, knocking the last few tempestuous minutes out of his mind. Danny stared down at her—the staining blush of her cheeks, the luminous eyes catching the light of the lamp down the hall. If he didn't know better, he'd swear that warm, sparkling look meant something.

"I remember," he muttered.

"So much has changed since then."

"Some things haven't."

Savannah saw the intense look in his eyes. Her breath caught in her throat as she continued to look up at Danny, knowing all the while that it was dangerous to lock eyes with him, that each passing instant charged the moment with more electricity. Yet she didn't look away, even when her heart began to thunder, even though the exhilarating sensation bore an edge of fright. She could feel the radiant closeness of him, as if he'd leaned closer though he hadn't moved a muscle. And then he did move. Taking a slow step forward, he raised a hand to cup her chin, bent toward her mouth . . .

"Please don't!" Savannah gasped and quickly jerked her face out of his fingers.

Danny took a deep painful breath and stuffed his hands in the pockets of his jacket.

"Am I as disgusting as McKenna, then?" he asked.

"It has nothing to do with Rory," Savannah answered, still staring into the shadows. "I'm sorry, Danny. I shouldn't have let that happen. I don't know what got into me."

"Maybe an honest impulse," he fired.

"I'm practically engaged to Clifford—"

"Ah, yes!" Danny broke in. "Clifford Andrews, the chosen one! Tell me, Savannah, where was Clifford just now when you needed him? Huh? Tell me *that*!"

"I told you, his mother—"

"His mother!"

The two words were all he said, but undertones of repugnance echoed across the hushed landing. Savannah studied the handsome face above her, hard-set now with a grimness that had become familiar the past year or so—an anger that encompassed her as well as Clifford, and Mrs. Andrews, and seemingly the whole of Kingsport. Her temples began to throb. She backed up against the door and found the knob behind her back.

"Good night," she said quietly.

And then she slipped inside and left Danny standing outside her door, his heart knocking with the familiar havoc only Savannah King could wreak.

Despite a near sleepless night, Danny was at his best the next evening. Somehow, when he stepped onto the basketball court, his personal life fled to the sidelines, and he became strictly a player of the game.

The smell of the gym was in his nostrils, the cheers of the crowd in his ears. Danny brought the ball down court, passed it deftly through his legs, around his back, and shot from twenty feet. The ball swished through the net. The crowd roared, and Eastway went up by four points.

He flashed a cocky grin at McKenna, who was glaring his

rage at having been outmaneuvered once again. Danny raised a triumphant fist in his direction, then took up his man as Pine View brought the ball back into play.

The guard threw the ball in. Danny swiped at it, tipped it, caused it to bounce high over the heads of the players.

Rory took the opportunity to try one of his old tripping moves.

His eye on the ball, Danny instinctively stepped around McKenna's outstretched leg, knocking it aside as he raced past in pursuit of the free ball.

Rory was caught off guard and fell.

As he sprawled to the floor, Danny stole the ball, dribbled back toward the basket and scored.

He could do nothing wrong. On this night, he owned the court, and by the time the seconds of the fourth period ticked away, the crowd was chanting his name.

The buzzer went off, and Eastway had won the championship—snatched it out of the jaws of the well-to-do Panthers. Almost immediately, it came across the speakers that Danny Sawyer had been named the game's most valuable player.

Adrenaline pumped through his veins, pounding in his ears as he trotted off the court and raised an acknowledging hand to the cheering throng.

Danny had entered the locker room with a dazzling smile. The scout from UNC had invited him to Chapel Hill. Now he felt as though he'd never smile again.

"What do you intend to do about it, kid?"

"Do?" Danny echoed. He gave Coach Glover a look of shock. "Nothing!"

Glover's face turned glum. "Thought you had more to you than that. You can't get a girl in trouble and just leave her stranded. That's not the kind of player or student they want at Chapel Hill! I knew you were something of a lady's man, but this . . ."

"I'm *not* the father of Roberta Sikes' baby!" Danny broke in.

"That's not what she told me, and Principal Standish. She said you might not admit it. That's why she came to us first."

Danny rubbed at a sudden pain in his forehead. "I can't believe this."

"Why would she lie? I mean, it's not like you're some super rich kid who can give her a life of luxury."

"Look! You've known me, coached me, for three years! Are you gonna believe Roberta Sikes or me?"

Coach Glover's face relaxed a little. "I'd like to believe you, kid. Just get this mess straightened out, all right?"

Danny walked out of the locker room feeling as if a two-ton weight had dropped on his head. It was too much—first, the triumph of being invited up to Chapel Hill, then this . . . this . . . blasphemy that could ruin everything. His thoughts were roiling as he walked blindly along. He didn't spot Roberta until he nearly bumped into her.

"Damn!" he sputtered as she moved out of the shadows.

"Danny, I gotta talk to you."

"Me? You want to talk to *me*?" His voice was snide, resentful. He couldn't help it. "Why in the world would you want to talk to me, Roberta? It seems you've already talked to everyone else!"

"Danny, please . . ."

"*Why*, Roberta? Why did you name me the father?"

"I had to," she said shakily.

"*Had* to? What do you mean? You know damn well we haven't been together in years!"

"I know, I know," Roberta said hurriedly. "But it was good between us, wasn't it, Danny? It could be good again."

He stared at her incredulously.

She misread his silence and reached for his arm. "It doesn't have to be so bad, you know. Just go along, okay? It would really help me out."

"Help you out?" Danny shouted. "Do you have any idea of the mess you've dragged me into?"

Most of the basketball crowd had already departed, but a few stragglers stared as Danny yanked his arm from Roberta's grasp and stomped angrily away. The onlookers glanced furtively at the obviously pregnant girl, then hurried on.

The parking lot was deserted but for the McKenna limousine, which was waiting for Rory as it did after every game. Mr. Parker and Libby were in the front, Big Ed and Clayton in the back, just like always. When Rory came out of the arena, Roberta ran up to him, sobbing at the top of her lungs.

Four sets of eyes zeroed in on the pair. It was startling to see Rory at a loss, but for a few fleeting seconds he clearly was—halting in midstride, raising his arms to fend off the girl. But then the Rory they all knew resurfaced. Shoving Roberta disdainfully away, he yelled something unintelligible. Whatever it was, it stopped her in her tracks.

And suddenly Libby knew. She wasn't Rory McKenna's only whore. She was just one of many. Her eyes stung as she watched the two of them out in the parking lot. Roberta Sikes stared at Rory. He stared back, probably with that cold distant look that had no humanity. She backed away. Rory walked nonchalantly to the limousine. And as he climbed in, Libby rubbed damp palms across her lap, as though she would scrub away some stubborn dirt that refused to be cleansed. She'd known she was low, but being lumped with the likes of Roberta Sikes showed her just what kind of trash she was.

The sleek car purred away from the gymnasium. The interior was dead silent, but the air buzzed with unspoken speculation. Rory? *He* was the father? It must be so. Why else would a Clancytown girl presume to waylay a McKenna?

Libby's eyes filled with scalding tears that knew better than to spill over. *Damn you, Rory!* she raged in silent, helpless misery. *Damn you to hell!*

"Well, that was certainly a disgraceful display," Big Ed ultimately announced in the silence of the car.

Rory gave him a calm look. "What exactly do you mean, Papa? Roberta or the game?"

"Both!"

Clayton savored the moment. He'd been on the butt end of Rory's cruelty all his life. It gave him an almost perverse pleasure to see his brother on the hot seat.

Rory shrugged. "I did the best I could in both instances. That damn Sawyer simply couldn't be stopped tonight."

"He s-sure made you l-look like shit," Clayton ventured.

"Shut up, you little pussy!" Rory exploded.

Clayton's dark eyes blazed with anger. He hated it when Rory called him that.

"No!" Big Ed boomed. "Clayton's right for once, and don't you be so damn careless about it, Rory! Tonight you let a servant make you look bad. A damn *servant* getting the better of a McKenna!"

"He'll get his," Rory returned shortly.

Big Ed merely grunted, and the tirade was over—far too soon to suit Clayton.

If Papa had been on *his* back, it would have lasted for at least an hour. He remembered the wrestling match Big Ed had at-

tended, one of nearly fifty Clayton had participated in during
the last few years. He'd been so preoccupied with the thought of
his father's presence that he'd fallen victim to a common hold
and had been pinned in a matter of minutes. When it was over,
his father had gotten loaded and carried on for well over an
hour—all about the McKenna name, the McKenna pride, the
tradition for hunting and sport which Clayton had never been
able to carry on. What made him think he could wrestle, for
God's sake? Clayton had virtually slunk out of the game room,
feeling the scornful eyes of every McKenna trophy that stared
down from the walls.

Clayton shifted in the plush seat, turning his thoughts away
from his own roasting and back to Rory's comparatively mild
one. Considering his poor performance on the court, and the
even poorer one with a tramp like Roberta Sikes, Rory deserved
far more of a tongue-lashing than he'd gotten. But at least it was
something. Clayton strained his eyes across the dark cab, imagined Rory squirming, and wished he could see lines of worry on
the perfect face. But he couldn't see anything at all until they
passed under a streetlamp, and then only the fleeting image of a
fixed stare turned coldly in their father's direction.

The hate and disgust Clayton felt for both of them welled up
in his throat until he thought he'd choke.

*The breezy, March night was alive, filled with the calls of
river frogs, the lapping of the water on the shore below, the distant honky-tonk of a neon-lit bar. The odors of Clancytown were
strong and raw—river mud, fish, the decaying wood of barna-
cled docks, an acrid smoke that hung in the air long after the
mills shut down.*

*It was good to be out after all the pent-up years—to hear the
sounds with her own ears, breathe in the night through her own
nostrils. Crouching in the shadows of the path behind the mill-
town shanty, she glanced once again at its black windows. The
hour was late, but the Sikes hut remained empty. Shifting carefully to a more comfortable position, she made hardly a sound.
Caution was a necessity. Roberta had three mean older brothers.*

*Such a tawdry piece of baggage! But then Rory had always
had a taste for the tawdry, along with the bizarre . . . and the sadistic. Even as a boy, the normal pleasures and fabric of life had
failed to touch him. And as he'd grown, he'd walked an ever*

darker path in search of excitement—finding it in the exhilaration of mastery over a stricken victim, the climax of inflicting pain. Only then did the ice-blue eyes sparkle with life. Like father, like son.

She still remembered the way Rory looked that fateful Fourth of July night. Something between fascination and thrill. No horror, no remorse, none of the things you might expect. Just a cold-blooded hunter caught up in the excitement of a kill.

There was a noise. Footsteps . . . one set of footsteps. Eyes gleaming, she twisted the scarf around a gloved hand and smiled into the darkness. Now it was his turn to be hunted.

Leo Crane glanced at the police photo, then snatched it up for a better look. Chills brushed over him. Roberta Sikes had been young and well along in pregnancy, but other than that . . . the pose, the scarf, everything was identical—right down to the mark on the left temple. It was like looking at Margaret all over again.

"This girl who was killed last night," he began. "She was strangled. Isn't that what the police report said?"

"That's right," Sergeant Colton returned. The late shift at the station was usually boring. And filing photos wasn't his idea of police work. He liked it when Leo dropped in to shoot the breeze.

"Was she beaten?" the doctor asked.

"No . . . not exactly. What are you getting at?"

"I was just wondering if she received a blow to the head."

The sergeant banged a palm on his cluttered desk. "How did you know? That wasn't in the report."

Leo smiled mysteriously, as though as a medical practitioner he had some sort of second sight.

His companion sighed. "Well, I guess it's no secret. Yeah, somebody hit her with something—just once, but it was probably enough to knock her out. It's possible she was unconscious when she was strangled."

"I see," Leo mused thoughtfully. He held the picture before his friend and pointed. "So this spot on her forehead is blood, then."

"It's blood, all right. Can't figure out how it got there, though."

"What do you mean?"

"The blow was to the back of the head. A little blood

there, but the medical examiner couldn't find any reason for it to be on her face."

Unless the killer placed it there on purpose, Leo thought. Just like he arranged everything else to be a replica of Margaret Clancy McKenna's death pose. Again, the chills. He gently returned the photo to the sergeant's desk.

"Thanks, Bill. I'll be seein' ya."

Leo pushed through the swinging doors and paused on the stoop to light his pipe. Nearly four years had passed since Margaret died in her "accident." He hadn't felt right about it then, and he sure as hell didn't now!

Tossing the match aside, he took a sweeping look across the lamplit commons. The spring night was cool and clear, and in his opinion there was no place more beautiful than Kingsport. But somewhere out there was a killer, and Leo had the uneasy feeling he would strike again.

Chapter Four

APRIL 20, 1976, would be long remembered at Eastway High. That was the day Kingsport police, at least a half dozen of them, stalked into Mr. Harding's chemistry class and arrested Danny Sawyer. The charge was murder. The news spread like wildfire, and by the end of the school day everyone knew Roberta Sikes had named Danny the father of her baby, that he'd been seen arguing with her the night she died, and that his truck had been spotted on the old river road that same night.

By dinnertime the next day, everyone in both Kingsport and Clancytown knew that Jim King had shown up at the police station with a high-class lawyer and gotten Danny Sawyer out on bail.

For Danny, the whole thing had the dazing effect of a nightmare. He was vaguely aware of presenting a sensible front to the outside world, but within he gaped like one caught up in a dream, horror-stricken and helpless as the fantastic events unfolded.

The police showed him pictures of Roberta, and he nearly lost his lunch. That anyone could even think him capable of such a thing was a shock, yet apparently the authorities did. Blood tests were taken, confirming that—indeed—according to blood type, Danny Sawyer could have fathered Roberta's unborn child.

Mr. Harper, the attorney Mr. King had retained, objected vehemently to the procedure, claiming that the issue of paternity had no relevance to the charge. But when the blood test news leaked out, public opinion stated quite clearly that it did. Danny was formally charged. He would stand trial. The story was all over the newspapers from one end of the state to the other.

Weeks passed. Danny watched them go with clouded vision. And then one morning, a glaring realization pierced the fog. While he wasn't watching, the prospective scholarship offer from Chapel Hill had fizzled into oblivion, as had those from smaller universities. Newly and painfully alert, Danny began contacting colleges he'd sloughed off long ago. No one replied to his letters. No one returned his calls. He'd been blackballed.

Mr. King told him not to worry, that after the trial things would change. Danny pinned his hopes on that theory as he made his way through each miserable, suspicion-shrouded day.

At school, he resisted the urge to defend himself against the curious looks. His buddies stood by him, but they didn't have the power to stem the horrified interest of the entire student body.

Around town, his footsteps were dogged by hushed conversations, which turned snidely accusing if anyone from Clancytown happened to be about. Most of Kingsport was furtively aghast at the sight of him, and virtually the whole of Clancytown spurned him openly. First, there were the Sikes brothers, who were spoiling for revenge. Then, too, most folks around the mill town remembered when Edna Sawyer took her boy and moved into Kings Crossing. They'd turned uppity after that, town gossips claimed. And through the years the boy had trifled with the affections of several other Clancytown girls. There was Susan McClain and, of course, Patty Sloan. With mounting yet futile anger, Danny found himself branded as some sort of lurid heartbreaker.

He had to bite his tongue to keep from lashing out at anyone . . . everyone. But Mr. Harper warned him to say nothing, do nothing. "Fade into the woodwork," the man said, an order that became harder and harder to abide as time dragged by.

The first week of June, Danny graduated from high school under the pall of the announcement that his trial would begin in a month's time, and that it would be held in a neighboring county due to "the intensity of public awareness in Brunswick."

That night, the Crossing was quiet. The Kings were at the Pine View Heights graduation ball, and Danny stood in the kitchen as his mother finished tidying up. Retrieving his diploma from the counter, he unrolled it and looked at the fancy lettering.

"I always thought I'd feel something when I graduated," he said.

Edna turned at the sink, wiping her hands on a towel. "It's quite an accomplishment. I wasn't able to finish school. Your father wasn't either. It's something to be proud of."

Danny tossed the document on the table. "I don't feel proud. I don't feel anything. What's going to happen now? No scholarship. No college. No career. Everything's over, and all because I slept with Roberta Sikes when I was fourteen!"

The words were out before he knew they were coming. Danny saw a mixed look of sadness and surprise rise to his mother's face.

"You might as well know it now," he muttered. "It will be coming out at the trial."

The surprise disappeared, though the sadness seemed to etch more deeply into her features.

"It didn't mean anything, Ma!" Danny blurted. "For God's sake, it was my first time. *She* seduced *me*! And then for some reason, years later she turns up pregnant and blames me! Ma, you know I didn't do it!" he concluded heatedly. "*Any* of it!"

"I know that, son." Glancing out the window at the dark sky, Edna sighed wearily. "God must have His reasons for letting this happen."

"For letting my life be wrecked?" Danny challenged fiercely, though his voice broke on the final word.

Edna came, raised her hands to his shoulders and looked up into her tall son's eyes. "You will be what you want to be, Danny. Nothing will stand in your way. Believe that, and nothing will."

Danny blinked. Sometimes his mother surprised him with her little pearls of wisdom. She patted his cheek, and when she turned and shuffled away, he had no idea it was the last time he'd see her walk anywhere.

Sometime around midnight Edna Sawyer suffered heart failure. She was dead before morning.

July dawned with record high temperatures. The sun broiled the air, a constant haze sealed in humidity, and the coast steamed. Tropical foliage thrived as everything else wilted. Most folks stayed indoors, and those who ventured out wore sunhats and ended up fanning themselves with anything handy. It was still and sticky, even on the beaches, where flies de-

scended in the lack of an ocean breeze to feast on a banquet of
unwary tourists, most of whom fled to the safety of screened-in
porches.

On those first, sweaty nights of July, Danny found himself
drawn out of the house and down to the old landing that had
often served as a haven. The slap of the water on the bank, the
creak of old timber, even the pungent smells of the riverfront
were a comfort—reminding him of happier days, or at least
more simple ones. The river whispered and flowed, rising
with the rains, shrinking with the droughts. But its winding
course never changed. To Danny, its very constancy was a
balm.

On the night of July third, he stretched out on the landing
and stared up at the sky. It was gray and sultry, the mere glim-
mer of a moon showing through a veil of luminous cloud. The
repetitive call of a river frog echoed clearly. There was no
breeze to stir the marsh grasses to muffle it, not even the song
of a katydid. Just that one lonesome frog. Danny closed his
eyes.

Four days. The trial began in four days. As soon as his guard
went down, the thought reared its head, and with it came the
other phrases that were prone to swirl through his muddled
brain these days. No family. No reputation. No future. All in a
matter of months. The chain of events seemed uncanny, un-
real. Danny could hardly relate it to himself; yet the approaching trial date was a chilling reminder that the phantasm was
real.

Danny broke out in a sweat and opened his eyes to the glowing, summer night sky. Concentrating willfully on the sky, he
theorized that tomorrow would be another blistering day. Yet it
wouldn't dampen the spirits of Kingsport, he knew, as the city
launched a typically fervent celebration of Independence Day.
The illustrious citizens of Kingsport were stewards of a legitimate Revolutionary heritage, and regardless of the heat, they'd
turn out in droves. There would be picnics, parades, and
speeches. In his current state of mind, Danny saw the whole
thing as pretty damn trivial.

Still, the next morning when Mrs. King complained that the
heat was going to "absolutely ruin the barbecue," Danny perked
up with a brainstorm. Keeping his plan a mysterious secret, he
had Mr. King call ahead to *The Watch*, authorizing Danny to
"borrow" anything he had a mind to take. Danny drove into

town in the old pickup, and when he returned, he was hauling three of the giant fans used in the mailroom. He set them up on the patio, succeeding in stirring up a breeze across a sizable circumference of back lawn. It wasn't as good as air conditioning, but at least it would keep the mosquitos off the Kings' well-bred guests.

Drawing a look of admiration from Mr. King and a short nod from Mrs. King, Danny started to walk away. Mr. King clapped a hand on his shoulder as he passed.

"You haven't attended the barbecue for a number of years now, Danny-Buck." He went on to insist that Danny attend the party that evening. At the moment Danny was about to refuse, Mrs. King's quick, disapproving look triggered him into rebellious acceptance. But later, as he pulled on jeans and a cool shirt, he rued the rash decision. Why the hell should he go? It would only be another arena where spectators could gawk at Danny Sawyer, where his upcoming trial was sure to be the main topic of conversation. In a town where once he'd been a star, he'd become a pariah.

That night he stood on the fringe of the crowd which, despite the heat, was sizable. This year, Mr. King had hired a ragtime band. Propping himself against the old oak by the patio, Danny secluded himself in shadow, content with listening to the music and nursing a beer. Occasionally, a mild breeze reached him from the nearest of the circulating fans. Suddenly, he caught the scent of roses. He stiffened but didn't turn.

"Hello, Savannah," he said casually.

She giggled and stepped around the tree. "How did you know it was me?"

Danny glanced in her direction. Her hair was pulled back from her perfect face, the lips parted in a bright smile. He was reminded of the first time he saw her, standing among the roses.

"If I told you, you wouldn't believe me," he muttered and took a pull off his beer.

Savannah took a step closer, idly swishing the skirt of the new dress of white eyelet. Her smile had drooped by the time Danny once again turned to look at her.

"Why are you over here all by yourself?" she asked.

He studied her from beneath furrowed brows. "I think that's pretty obvious, don't you?"

"No. I don't. You've never been the type to back down before."

Danny released a sharp laugh. "Give me a break, Savannah! I've never been on trial for murder before!"

Savannah chewed at the inside of her jaw. "It will be over soon," she said eventually and was awarded an angry look.

"What the hell do you want, Savannah?"

"I just wanted to talk to you. It's been a long time since . . ."

"Since your birthday?" Danny supplied. Since that night, she'd steered clear of him, and they both knew it. After all that had happened in the past few months, her warmest gesture had been a tearful hug when his mother died.

"Nearly four months have passed since then," he added. "What makes you to want to talk tonight?"

"Your trial starts in a few days. I—"

"I get it," Danny broke in with a biting tone. "You want the inside story."

Savannah took another step, searching through the shifting moonshadows to land a square look on his face. "I do *not* want the inside story, Danny. I only want to tell you that we'll be there at the trial, all the way through. You won't be alone."

The kindness of her statement left him paradoxically stinging. "I'm not afraid to be alone," he snorted, raising the beer.

"But isn't it nice that you won't be? Daddy says we'll drive you back and forth every day."

Danny hesitated in the midst of putting his mouth on the bottle, then proceeded to take a long swig. When he looked back at her, she hadn't altered her stance—only stood there in that damn white dress, looking up with that damn angelic expression. What would she do, he wondered, if he stepped over and took her in his arms? The impulse, more specifically the fact that he had to quell it, sharpened the set of his face.

"Where's Andrews?" he asked.

Savannah straightened a bit as she always did when Danny mentioned Clifford. "He's here," she replied.

Danny folded his arms across his chest. "Won't he be wondering where you are? After all, the two of you are pre-engaged, or whatever the hell you call it."

The sneer in his voice was excruciatingly familiar. Savannah pursed her lips.

"I don't know why you insist on making this ugly," she snapped. "I only came over to wish you well."

"How very gracious," Danny retorted sarcastically. "And from the princess of Kings Crossing herself."

"Oh!" Savannah sputtered, her eyes sparkling angrily. "You can be so hateful, Danny Sawyer!"

She turned her back on him in a whirl of blond hair and white eyelet. Danny's hand shot out and found her wrist before he knew what he was going to say. Savannah continued to face away from him, though she didn't tug her arm, didn't try to get away, simply . . . waited. He stared at her back as the waist-length hair settled into a still and shining mantle.

"I . . ." Danny tried and cleared his throat. "You can't know what this is like, Savannah."

She looked over her shoulder, limned by the light that spilled from the patio. "Daddy says Mr. Harper is the best attorney in the Carolinas and that there's nothing to worry about."

Her tone was so hopeful. Danny allowed himself a small smile as he glanced down at her hand, then released it.

"Right," he said simply.

He looked up, their eyes met, and Savannah hesitated—beset by the urge to step over and put her arms about his neck.

"So don't worry, okay?" she said instead.

"Sure."

Savannah stared at him another moment through the shadows, feeling that Danny needed more from her, that somehow he deserved more. She turned swiftly away before the notion could take root.

Danny watched as she broached the crowd and spoke smilingly to the mayor. Then Clifford Andrews put a hand on her arm and drew her to his side. Looking sharply away, Danny spun around the tree and retreated into the shield of darkness.

The morning after the barbecue, Savannah decided that enough was enough. Until this year, Libby Parker would have risked anything—including her father's punishment—to attend the Crossing barbecue. This year, when Savannah tried repeatedly to phone and invite her, Libby didn't even return her calls. Something was terribly wrong and had been for months.

It was barely nine o'clock when Savannah started through the pines toward the McKenna property. Overhead, the sky was pale blue, and already the sun was hot and melting through the limbs. By the time she arrived on the doorstep, she was perspiring, though she wore cool shorts and a sleeveless top. She stiffened when Rory answered the bell.

"I'd like to see Libby," she said. "Is she home?"

Rory, who was dressed in tennis duds, said nothing, but only indulged himself in a heated onceover she found insulting.

"Well?" Savannah snapped. "May I come in?"

He waved her in with a flourish. "By all means. I believe Libby is in her room at the back of the house. Servants quarters, you know."

Savannah flashed him a peeved look as she passed. "I know where it is, Rory."

Halfway along the hall, she came upon Clayton.

"Good m-morning," he stammered.

"Good morning, Clayton," she said cheerily. "How are you?"

"F-fine. What b-brings you here?"

"I came to visit Libby," Savannah replied. Clayton smiled shyly but said nothing more. "Well," she added, "see you later."

Proceeding along the hallway, Savannah was unaware that Clayton watched her progress with nothing short of adulation. When she reached Libby's room, she knocked but received no answer. Savannah tried the door, found it open, and stepped inside.

"Libby?" she called, scanning the room, then noticing the sound of running water in the adjoining bathroom.

Libby looked up with a start, her eyes colliding with her reflection in the mirror above the sink.

"Libby?" came the familiar voice once more, now from just on the other side of the partially open door.

Frantically, Libby began to splash water on her face.

"Are you all right?" Savannah asked.

Libby turned off the water and turned away to reach for a towel. "I'm okay," she said. "What are you doing here?"

"I was worried about you."

Libby patted her face a few times and turned. Savannah nearly gasped at the dark circles under her eyes, the pallor of her skin. Somehow Libby's face looked gaunt and puffy at the same time.

"You're sick!" Savannah said without thinking.

"It will pass," Libby replied and stepped around Savannah. Yes, it would pass, as it had for the past five mornings.

"Have you seen a doctor?"

"I don't need to. I know what's wrong." Libby let the statement hang as she walked into the bedroom. Part of her longed to talk to someone, but she recoiled at the notion of confiding in

Savannah. Turning in the center of the room, she looked across the distance, which seemed at that moment to swell to the breadth of an ocean. Savannah continued to stand at the bathroom door—so clean and fresh in her crisp little shorts . . . so naive . . . so virginal.

"Well, what is it?" Savannah asked. "The flu or something?"

It occurred to Libby that in a hundred years Savannah King would never guess the truth. She would never be able to imagine such tawdriness.

"Something like that," Libby said and, unable to tolerate her friend's innocent gaze, turned her back and crossed to the bed. "Thanks for coming, Savannah. But I'm trying to kick this . . . virus, and I really do need to rest. I'd like to lie down for a while. You don't mind if we cut the visit short, do you? I'll talk to you later, okay?"

Savannah eyed her doubtfully, but Libby proceeded to crawl under the covers and settle herself as if for a nap.

"You'll call me?"

"Sure." Libby smiled. "As soon as I get over this bug."

When Savannah was safely out the door, Libby flung an arm across her eyes. Tears welled up as she considered the difference in their lives—like two planets spinning in opposite directions, Savannah toward the clear heavens, herself to destruction. She wished she could climb inside Savannah's skin . . . live her life . . . *be* Savannah!

The hot tears receded as the silent tirade came to an end. Libby ran an arm under her runny nose and stared at the ceiling. It did no good to dwell on what she already knew. Some people were born to charmed lives, some were cursed. She'd found out which category she belonged in on New Year's morning.

Besides, there were other things to worry about—she glanced along the coverlet—like the bastard that was growing in her stomach . . . Rory's bastard . . . like Danny Sawyer's murder trial.

Libby closed her eyes against the awful truth. She almost hoped Danny would be proven guilty. Then at least she'd feel some relief that the killer was behind bars. Whether or not she'd turned into a total paranoid, Libby didn't know, but lately she'd been haunted by the idea that she and Roberta Sikes had quite a bit in common. And look what happened to Roberta.

* * *

It was the final day of the trial. The courtroom was packed, buzzing with hushed conversation and the swishing of hand fans. Savannah and her father sat pressed together in the third row. Behind them, she knew, was the entire McKenna household, all turned out for the finale—Big Ed, Rory, Clayton, Mr. Parker, and Libby . . . who, in Savannah's opinion, looked only slightly improved since their meeting a week and a half ago. Across the way, nearly half the benches were filled with on-lookers from Clancytown—the Sikes brothers and their rough-hewn entourage. "Mill trash," her mother would have declared with a sniff.

Savannah looked ahead. Soon the judge and jury would appear . . . and Danny. Today the attorneys would present their final arguments. Depending on how long the jury took to reach a decision, the verdict could come in as early as this afternoon. Perspiration broke out beneath her lightweight dress as she thought of it. Surely they would find him innocent!

To Savannah, the evidence had sounded ridiculously flimsy. But then, she was hardly impartial. Each day as she sat on the hard bench and watched Danny, sitting so straight and tall, her heart ached all the more. How he could sit there and hear his life torn apart, she didn't know. It was all she could do at certain times to refrain from standing up and shouting at the top of her lungs.

The prosecution had pointed out the time Sheriff Martin brought Danny home drunk. For heaven's sake, that didn't mean anything! All the boys in town got drunk! They reported the time when Danny was fourteen and had "relations" with Roberta Sikes. That little tidbit had stunned Savannah, while it left her mother completely scandalized. Ophelia King refused to accompany them after that, so it was Savannah and her father who drove Danny back and forth to the Columbus County courthouse.

It had gone on for eight long, hot, miserable days. The heat seemed to intensify every passing minute, every new thread of fabric being woven against Danny. Coach Glover testified that Roberta had named Danny the father of her unborn child . . . a couple who left the basketball game late reported they saw Danny arguing with her outside the coliseum . . . and Mr. Cosgrove "could swear" he saw Danny's truck on the river road that same fateful night. Good Lord! Mr. Cosgrove? Everybody knew he hadn't drawn a sober breath in twenty years! Yet that was the final piece of evidence that had given the prosecution justification to go to trial.

One afternoon, after Mr. Cosgrove testified, Savannah's father broke the silence that normally shrouded the car.

"I find it odd that Cosgrove would come forward."

Savannah was sitting in the front with her father. Danny was in the back. She sensed rather than saw his immediate attention.

"Cosgrove has never been one to volunteer," her father added with a glance in the rearview mirror. "If you catch my drift."

"You're saying he might have been . . . induced?" came Danny's voice.

"Stranger things have happened."

"Well, then, let's tell Mr. Harper," Savannah butted in with wide eyes.

"There's no proof, Savannah," her father said softly. She heard Danny slump back against the seat and looked out the window as she considered the notion. She'd never really thought about it before, but if Danny didn't kill Roberta Sikes, then who did? Maybe the same person who paid Mr. Cosgrove to testify?

Now, as she recalled those questions, Savannah glanced about the courtroom with probing eyes, wondering if the true murderer of Roberta Sikes might be sitting there right under their noses.

As the prosecutor began his speech, Savannah blocked him out with memories of good, hopeful moments from the trial. Dr. Leo Crane's psychological profile had painted Danny as an achiever, straightforward and ethical. But Mr. Harper had said that kind of thing didn't carry much weight. But then there was Danny's testimony! It had happened only yesterday, and Savannah felt a glowing pride in the way he'd conducted himself— admitting soberly that, yes, he'd been with Roberta Sikes when he was "a kid" but that he hadn't been around her in four years.

At that, one of the Sikes brothers piped up: "You calling my sister a liar?"

"Damn straight," Danny returned from the witness box at which point the courtroom erupted, and the judge ordered Mickey Sikes removed from the courtroom.

And yet Mickey was back today, along with Hal and Dick— the three Sikes brothers who had championed Roberta through this entire ordeal, and likely would champion her memory until somebody was brought before the bench to pay.

There was a brief recess following the prosecutor's summation. Savannah followed her father out of the courtroom and found to her distaste that the McKennas were waiting just outside in the corridor. Big Ed shook hands with her father and launched a business conversation about "the Monroe property" and "King's Club." Savannah paid scant attention, avoiding Rory's eyes as she felt rather than saw his leer. She passed a few comments with Clayton, who—although his stuttering complicated his presentation—was in full agreement that Danny couldn't possibly have committed the crime that had brought them all to the courthouse. Without realizing it, Savannah positively beamed.

The conversation with Clayton drifted to a halt, and she became aware of Rory's interested gaze. Before he could draw her into conversation, Savannah turned and spotted Libby a distance down the hall at the water cooler. With a brief "excuse me," she set off in that direction and left the McKenna boys looking after her.

Libby took another long, cool drink of water, feeling it cascade down her throat and into her parched insides. The heat in the courtroom had been oppressive, much like Rory's presence. He'd sat next to her on the bench, using the excuse of the crowd to press against her with a boldness he seemed to find amusing. She'd begun to think she was going to be sick when the judge announced a recess. Grabbing the opportunity, Libby had quickly excused herself and found a bit of privacy by the water cooler. Now she felt almost recovered, almost strong enough to produce the mien of calm that masked her quaking fear.

"How are you feeling?" Savannah asked.

Libby straightened and turned with a start. The sight of Savannah, all decked out in a pretty blue dress, made her feel instantly dowdy in her old gray outfit. But there was no help for it. She had to be careful about what she wore these days. The best she could figure, she was six or seven weeks pregnant. She could conceal her condition in the right clothes, but when she was naked, the changes in her body were obvious. Her breasts were heavier, her stomach rounder.

"I'm fine," she said.

Savannah disregarded the reply. Although Libby's makeup disguised her pallor, the darkness under her eyes hadn't changed.

"Have you thought anymore of seeing a doctor?"

Libby mustered a smile. "I'm fine, I tell you." Changing the subject, she added, "It doesn't sound good for Danny, does it?" Savannah's blue eyes leveled on her.

"What do you mean?"

"Well," Libby said and shrugged, "all the things the lawyer just talked about—Roberta pointing a finger at Danny, Mr. Cosgrove seeing him on the river road . . ."

"For heaven's sake!" Savannah replied on a scornful note. "You can't believe Danny was the father of that girl's baby! He hadn't been with her in years. *I* think somebody put Roberta up to accusing him. And as for Mr. Cosgrove, Daddy says it's possible somebody paid him to testify. But of course there's no proof."

"Why would anybody do that?"

"Why?" Savannah repeated with arched brows. "Why, to cover his own tracks, of course! Maybe the real father of Roberta's baby paid Cosgrove. Maybe the real killer!"

A shudder swept over Libby as she heard the two identities lumped as one. She thought of that night after the basketball game, the night Roberta was killed. Of course, no one who had been in the limousine that night would ever say a word about the revealing scene in the parking lot between Roberta Sikes and Rory McKenna—the scene that had left Libby certain that Rory was the infamous secret father of Roberta's baby. She remembered how he said Danny Sawyer would "get his," and she realized once again, but to a more shocking degree, that she could put nothing past Rory—maybe not even murder.

"Good afternoon, ladies."

Rory's voice came from just behind her, and Libby jumped as though the devil himself had just materialized.

Rory chuckled, then looked pointedly past her to Savannah. "And what are you two finding to talk about?"

"I've just been asking after Libby," Savannah returned in the clipped manner he always provoked. "She has been ill, you know."

"Oh?" Rory said, turning a mildly curious eye on Libby. "What's the matter with you?"

A tremor of terror rocked her. Libby clasped her hands over the inconsequential bulge under her skirt. "Nothing," she said. "Just a bug. Come on. Everybody's going back into the courtroom."

And as she walked along—Savannah on one side, Rory on

the other—Libby did her best to force a normal gait out of her shaking knees.

"Beyond the shadow of a doubt," Mr. Harper said, then paused dramatically to let the phrase sink into the jurors' ears. "Thank God for America," he went on. "Thank God for a judicial system which may well be regarded as the cornerstone of civilization. A civilized society, ladies and gentlemen, demands that guilt be proven . . . beyond the shadow of a doubt."

Danny tried to put a lid on his hopes, but his attorney was great! The more he talked, the more inclined Danny was to feel safe. Already Harper had discredited every shred of evidence as circumstantial. Now he was appealing to the jurors as fellow Americans with a mutual responsibility for justice. God, could the nightmare be coming to an end? Danny thought, and yet once again tried to caution himself against feeling secure. He had to be prepared for the worst.

Harper turned then and waved a palm in his direction. "Young Danny Sawyer, here, grew up in this community. He has been a good student, a sports hero, a responsible worker at *The River Watch*. His entire life is testimony that he could not have committed such a heinous crime. And the only marks against him? A confused girl placed blame on him for a difficult situation . . . Danny was angry when she unjustly accused him . . . Mr. Cosgrove *thinks* it was Danny's truck he saw on the river road early that morning."

Harper shook his head. "Ladies and gentlemen, circumstantial evidence is not proof. There is nothing to connect Danny Sawyer with the murder scene. Proof would be fingerprints . . . footprints . . . tire tracks . . . a witness who saw him commit the crime. It wouldn't even be proof if someone saw Danny near the scene! And yet no one did. No one saw Danny Sawyer in Clancytown that night because he was at the old riverfront landing at Kings Crossing—'thinking things out,' as he testified. And I, for one, find it understandable that he would need some time to think after the shock of Roberta Sikes' accusation."

Mr. Harper leaned forward, planting his palms on the jury box railing as he looked into the jurors' faces.

"Proof beyond the shadow of a doubt?" he queried. "I hardly think so, ladies and gentlemen. And if you agree with me, as you must, you will return a verdict of not guilty."

Mr. Harper took stately steps to the defendant's table, and everyone stood as the jurors filed out of the courtroom. Danny felt dizzy, as if he were floating at some giddy height and had lost the ability to touch solid ground.

The jury came back after only an hour and a half, and when the verdict of not guilty was announced, Savannah jumped to her feet, restraining herself from rushing to Danny only through a long and thoroughly ingrained sense of propriety. He looked so relieved, so happy, as he reached over to shake Mr. Harper's hand.

But then Savannah's gaze fell on the opposite side of the room. The prosecuting attorneys closed up their briefcases with grim faces. The Clancytown villagers filed silently from the courtroom. Savannah's smile drained as she saw their resentful expressions. And as she walked along the echoing courthouse corridor between her father and Danny, she heard grumblings that it would have been a different story if the trial had been held in Brunswick. She was certain Danny heard them, too.

Savannah glanced up at him. As she'd thought, his eyes were on her, glinting with a combination of defiance and hurt that she found almost unbearable. For a shining moment, she'd thought it was all over. But now, as she locked eyes with Danny, she knew it wasn't. The legal question of his innocence had been answered; the whispered one of the people hadn't.

"I'm getting the hell out of here," he muttered for her ears alone.

And Savannah knew he didn't mean just the courthouse. He meant Kingsport. She should have expected it, but she hadn't. A pang of remorse shot through her as she nodded in silent agreement.

Libby was on her way to light the lamps in the foyer when the bell rang. She started to answer it, saw Rory emerge from the game room, and ducked into the shadows of the hall.

"What the devil are you doing here?"

Rory's voice was angry. Libby edged a few steps along the hallway and craned for a look at the visitor. She heard mumbling, then Rory's sharp laugh.

"You must be joking," he said, still chuckling. "You want more?"

Again came the mumbling, and though Libby leaned daringly into the open corridor, she couldn't see anything of the mysterious caller. Rory blocked her view.

"I told you never to come here," came Rory's voice once more, now deadly serious. "It's a lucky thing I was around to answer the door. You have one strike against you. I wouldn't add to it if I were you." There was a brief, muffled exclamation and then:

"That's all, Cosgrove! If I ever see your face again, I'll knock it off for you!"

Rory slammed the door, but the thundering sound in Libby's ears was the echo of the name—*Cosgrove!* Savannah's theory burst into her mind: "Maybe the real father of Roberta's baby paid Cosgrove! Maybe the real killer!"

Rory turned, and Libby shrank back against the wall, her wide eyes turned and straining to watch as he swaggered through the foyer on his way back to the game room.

Then suddenly Rory paused, looked directly to where she stood in the shadows, and grinned. Chills broke out, flashing along her spine and limbs as if in warning—and yet Libby stood there, scarcely breathing as Rory's hard eyes bored into her. He wore a grin that reached no farther than his lips. Finally he looked away and continued into the game room. Libby remained frozen in the hall.

What that lethal grin meant, she couldn't be sure. That he knew she knew, and didn't give a damn? That her time was coming?

Libby lurched into movement and fled down the hall. All she could be sure of was that she must leave . . . tonight.

The Crossing was ominously quiet that night. Supper was supposed to have been a sort of celebration for Danny, but he either didn't realize that or didn't care. Whatever the reason, he was absent, preferring to use the time to pack his bags. He was leaving the next morning.

The heat, too, added to Savannah's stifled feeling. She reached up, lifted her hair off her neck, and in a swift move clasped it in a ponytail. She glanced back at the book she'd been reading with little interest.

Tick-tock. Tick-tock. The clock on the parlor wall kept time in the fashionable room. Savannah looked across the way to her father who was dressed in his smoking jacket, comfortably ensconced on the velveteen-covered loveseat. But he, too, had set aside his reading and was looking pensively into space. Only her mother seemed unaffected by the dismal shroud that had fallen over the house, as she talked busily on the phone in the next room, arranging some garden party or other.

Her father got up, stepped over to the front window, and looked outside. "That's curious," he murmured.

"What?" Savannah asked.

"What in the . . . Where's Danny?" he added urgently.

"Upstairs packing, I suppose."

"Listen to me, Savannah. I want you to go right now to the safe in my study . . ."

Suddenly alarmed, Savannah rose from her chair. "What is it, Daddy?"

"Listen to me, Kitten!" he said with a sharp look. "Go to the safe in my study. You know how to open it, don't you?"

Savannah nodded with wide eyes.

"Good girl. Take whatever money's there and give it to Danny."

"But why . . ."

"Tell him to hurry, Savannah. Tell him to grab a few things and go now, by the old field road."

"But . . ." Savannah stood rooted as she watched her father straighten the lapels of his jacket and start toward the foyer. "What are you going to do, Daddy?"

He gave her a sober look over his shoulder. "It's a mob, Savannah. There's no telling what they might do. I'll try and stall them the best I can. Now get going!"

"What's going on?" Ophelia walked into the parlor just as her daughter sprinted away.

"Call the police, Ophelia," Jim commanded.

"But . . ."

"Go!"

Ophelia King rarely bucked her husband, but this time the look on his face made her say, "I'm not budging one inch, Jim King, until you tell me what's happening."

"I think it might be a lynch mob, Ophelia," he said quietly. "I think they might have come for Danny."

"But it will take Sheriff Martin at least twenty minutes to get here!" she cried, promptly horrified.

"I'll just have to do the best I can until he gets here, then, won't I?" Jim returned. "Now go."

Ophelia fired a last belligerent look at her husband's back before she hurried to obey.

Savannah was shaking as she darted along the path to the pool house. It had taken her three tries to open the safe, and all the while she could hear the arrival of trucks, doors opening and slamming, and men's voices. And then when she ran up to Danny's room, he wasn't there! As she came again onto the landing, she heard her father's voice and darted into her parents' front chamber. Peeping between the curtains, she saw the array of vehicles crowding the drive—a group of men, milling about just outside the garden with torches, dogs, and guns.

"Come now, gentlemen," her father was saying. "I'll be happy to have you call at the Crossing most any time, but don't you think it's a bit late to be showing up on my front lawn?"

"We ain't got no quarrel with you, Mr. King," one of the men replied. "It's Sawyer we want."

At that, a rowdy cheer issued from the group, and the hounds began to bay. Savannah bolted out of her parents' room and down the stairs. She could only think that Danny had taken some things out to his truck. So now she ran, clutching the money in her hands, praying he was there behind the pool house. Rounding the corner in full stride, she nearly collided with him.

"What the—"

"Thank goodness!" Savannah puffed, fighting to catch her breath. "Take this," she said, thrusting the money at him. "It's from Daddy, almost fifteen hundred dollars. You . . . you have to go now, Danny . . . *right now!* A mob is here. Daddy says to take the old field road and circle round by the beach. It will take longer, but the drive is blocked."

Her chest was heaving, her eyes wide and frightened. Danny raised a calming hand.

"Slow down a minute, Savannah."

"Didn't you hear what I said?" she cried. "They have dogs and guns and . . . It's a *mob*, Danny!"

He stalked angrily away from the truck in the direction of the courtyard.

"Where are you going?" Savannah hissed as she hurried after him.

"I want to see."

"You want to see?" she repeated incredulously, but followed him anyway until the two of them could observe the goings-on at the front of the house through the cover of trees.

As she'd said, the drive was blocked by a half dozen trucks, and perhaps twenty men were gathered outside the courtyard. Some carried torches, others rifles. As Danny watched, a torch bearer stepped forward—one of the Sikes brothers.

He said something, but Danny was too far away to make out what it was. Then came an answering voice he recognized as Mr. King's. Danny's expression turned ferocious as he started forward. Savannah caught his arm.

"What do you think you're doing?"

"I'm not letting your father fight my battles for me."

"Are you *crazy*?" Savannah yanked on the captive arm. "Why do you think he's out there stalling them? He wants you to go!"

Danny considered her words, but then shook his head. "I was going to leave in the morning. I'm not going to run tonight."

"What are you going to do against a mob?" Savannah demanded in a fierce whisper. "What are you going to do when they take you down the river road and hang you from the first available tree? Now take the damn money, climb in your damn truck, and get the hell out of here!"

That got his attention. Savannah never swore. Danny's eyes took on a sudden new light.

"Do *you* want me to go?" he asked.

Savannah rolled her eyes, shifted her hold to his wrist, and slapped the money in his hand. "What do you think I've been saying?" As his fingers closed on the bills, she pushed his hand away in a rough manner that punctuated her irritation. "You don't seem to understand what's going on, Danny! There's a group of men over there, and they mean to string you up!"

She made quite a spectacle standing there in the faint light of a clouded moon, dappled by the shadows of the tree branches above. But beyond her Danny could see flickering lights, and he knew that the angry sounds that came from that direction were pointed directly at him. Savannah was right. They were out for his blood. Reluctantly, he stuffed the money in the pocket of his jeans and looked back at Savannah through the shrouding darkness. A sense of dread washed over him as he faced what was happening.

For the first time since she'd come upon him in such a panic, he looked at Savannah, really looked—knowing that he would remember she wore a pale dress, though he couldn't say what color . . . and that her face was flushed with alarm, though again, he couldn't see the blush in the limited light of the overcast July night. So this is how it would end, after all these years.

"Why should you care what happens to me?" he asked. She compressed her lips in a quick, impatient gesture. He'd seen her do it a hundred times.

"I care! Okay?" she chirped. "Now, would you please—"

The rest was lost as, without warning, Danny grabbed her and planted his mouth on hers. Savannah struggled to get free but could manage only to wrench her face away from his. Jamming her elbows against his rib cage, she forced the space of several inches between them and glared up at him. The question that popped into her head blurted out of her mouth.

"Why must you always want more than I can give?" she gasped and felt Danny's chest tighten beneath the lightweight shirt. His eyes burned down through the darkness. Savannah was aware of his height, his shape, his power.

"Because I do," he replied in a steady, low-pitched tone. "Because I've loved you since I was nine years old."

She stopped pushing at his chest, her gaze locking foolishly with that of the boy she'd been so close to long ago; the boy who'd grown into a mysterious, frightening man.

"I know," she breathed after a moment.

"You *know*?" Danny's brows shot up. "What kind of thing is that to say?"

Savannah glanced away. "I haven't always known," she murmured, still in the quiet tone demanded by the threateningly close presence of the raucous throng. They were entirely out of place—a blemish on the serene complexion of Kings Crossing.

"Most of the time I thought you hated me," she added. "It wasn't until recently I realized it must have been . . . something else."

Danny released her waist and in a quick move cupped her face in his palms and turned it back to him. Savannah met his gaze, and a peculiar thrill went through her. It was the dizzying sensation of being stunned, exhilarated, and frightened beyond drawing a steady breath, all at once—a sensation that only Danny had ever provoked.

"What about you?" he asked gruffly, his breath warm on her face. "Most of the time I thought you hated me. Was it something else?"

The air was hot and still. Sound carried. In the ensuing instant of silence, they both heard the upsurge of hostile voices from the front of the house.

"You must go," Savannah whispered urgently. "They're coming for you."

Danny shook her, once, firmly. "I'll know and know now. I'm about to leave, Savannah. You'll probably never see me again. What have you got to lose? Tell me the truth. All this stuff that's been going on all these years, this . . . clandestine attraction. Has it been one-sided?"

"It doesn't matter, Danny," she insisted, her hands closing about his wrists. "Don't you know that by now? I am who I am—"

"Has it?" he demanded with another shake.

Savannah's gaze darted between his eyes. In the meager light, their whites shone in disembodied slivers.

"No," she whispered.

Danny swallowed hard, overpowering the lump that sought to climb up his throat. "Then give me something to remember you by."

His deep voice rumbled like summer thunder, hanging in the sultry air during the brief moment Danny wrapped her unobjecting arms around his neck. Then his mouth was on hers once more. This time, Savannah kissed him back.

Danny's hands went through her hair, possessing the shining mass as he encircled her and pulled her tightly against him. He couldn't get close enough, even as his tongue claimed her mouth, and his hands her body—roaming over hips he'd only dreamed about. There was the urgency of a long pent-up drive suddenly freed. There was also the desperation of knowing it was his last chance, that in only a matter of minutes, he must turn and walk away. Danny reached for her hands and planted them on his hips, urging her to hold him as he was holding her.

For only an instant, Savannah's palms remained still where he had placed them. She felt the bottom of his belt with her thumb, the stitching of his jeans against her fingers, and beneath it the muscle of Danny's hips. But most of all, she felt his tongue, sleek and filling and masterful . . . *mesmerizing.* He slanted his face across hers, gaining a fierce new kiss, and Savannah's hands began to move over his back, registering the masculine form of him, absorbing the warmth of the skin beneath his cotton shirt.

In a vague dreamy sort of way, she felt his arm around her hips, lifting, settling her against him . . . or perhaps atop him, as his arm tightened and his hips began to move. He was strong and warm and . . . hard. A startling ache pulsed into being between her thighs, and as she realized what that shameful ache was calling for, Savannah's eyes flew wide. Jerking free of Danny, she stepped back, and before she even knew what she was about, had hauled off and smacked him fully across the cheek.

The cracking sound reached no farther than the nearest tree, yet to Savannah it seemed deafening. Danny turned back to face her, their eyes met, and she was swept back to New Year's morning. He'd kissed her then, she'd slapped him, and he'd impaled her with the same knowing look he was wearing now.

You liked it, his eyes accused. *You wanted it.*

No! Savannah's eyes shrieked back. *It's* your *fault! You make me do things, feel things, no lady should do or feel! You've always wanted more than I could give! Always!*

All this and more she would have said if she could have released a single word from her constricted throat.

A threatening chorus from the front of the house pierced the tense moment. Danny glanced beyond Savannah's shoulder. The torches were bobbing. The men were on the move.

He looked back at her, his cheek still stinging, his eyes watering at the sensation. Danny knew Savannah well enough to think she'd struck him out of fear, that she'd never felt the kind of passion that had just exploded between them. It had frightened her, and Danny knew then—if he'd never known before— that she had absolutely no understanding of how it could be between a man and a woman.

God, he longed to teach her, but even as the thought occurred, a grasp of reality rose to dry the moisture in his eyes. Whatever man would initiate Savannah to the act and beauty of loving, it would not be him. She'd been under his skin for so many years that he felt almost as if Savannah were part of him. But their being together had never been in the cards. Danny knew it, and at

the moment—with the daughter of Kings Crossing backlit by
the torchfire of a bloodthirsty mob—the breach between them
had never been more clear. The very idea of Danny Sawyer as-
piring after Savannah King seemed a profane joke. The thought
stiffened Danny's spine as well as his resolve.

"Good-bye, Princess," he said, and melted into the darkness.

Chapter Five

LIBBY WALKED along the shoulder of the road, keeping close to the stately oaks that lined Cloister Drive. It would have been easier going on the pavement, but she wasn't about to venture out in the open.

She'd waited until things were quiet in the McKenna house—her father listening to a gospel program in his room, Clayton reading in the gallery, Big Ed having slipped off in the direction of the new maid's room. Like father, like son.

The only one whose whereabouts were uncertain was the person Libby was seeking to escape. Rory had gone out after supper, and although she was relieved anytime he was away, she was unnerved that he could come driving around the next curve at any moment and spot her. The thought kept her moving at a rapid pace, her heart hammering, legs shaking. Cloister Drive had never seemed so long, but then she'd never tried walking to town before.

When she heard a vehicle approaching from behind her, Libby leapt instinctively behind an oak. As it came closer, she realized it was not a car, but a truck. It couldn't be anyone from the McKenna household. It was almost upon her when realization slammed into her. Sweeping up the pillowcase filled with her belongings, Libby ran for the street, waving her free arm. The truck came to a screeching, swerving halt, missing her by only a yard or two. Without hesitation, she hurried over to the passenger door.

"What the hell are you doing, Libby?" Danny shouted through the open window. "I nearly ran you down!"

"Can you give me a ride?" she asked, already in the process of climbing in.

Danny stared as she settled herself on the seat and deposited a bundle on the floorboard. "What the hell are you doing?" he asked again. She met his eyes with what appeared to be complete calm.

"What does it look like?" As Danny only continued to watch her, seemingly astonished, Libby added, "Could we get going?"

Recuperating from the shock of having nearly hit her, Danny suddenly remembered his own plight. "I'm not so sure you want to be riding with me just now," he said, his voice turning hard. "There's a lynch mob back at the Crossing, and they're out for my hide. When they realize I'm gone, there's no doubt they'll be coming after me."

"Well then, we should get going, don't you think?"

"You want to stay after what I just told you?"

"Danny," she said impatiently, "I'm not likely to get another ride, and I want to get out of here just as much as you do."

With a last questioning look, Danny put the truck in gear and moved ahead. Libby breathed a sigh of relief when they crossed the bridge and left The Cloisters behind.

"Where are you headed, anyway?" she asked.

Danny shrugged. "West."

"You're leaving for good?"

Once again in typical foul temper, Danny replied, "What the hell do you think?"

"West," Libby mused, unperturbed. "West is good."

Danny arched a testy brow. "I'm so glad you agree. Please do just invite yourself along, okay?"

"I need you to take me, Danny," she said firmly. "At least out of town."

"Why the hell are you running away, anyway?"

"You of all people should know how it feels to want out of Kingsport so bad you can taste it."

Danny glanced her way, but she'd turned to look out the window. "My reasons are well known," he said. "What are yours?"

"They're my own business is what they are."

Danny scowled and looked back to the road. They hardly spoke for the next hour, each finding it easy to sink into personal reflection on the events that had brought them to Highway 74 on a late July night. When they pulled into Lumberton, however, Libby pointed sharply to the bus station. At midnight, it was one of the few brightly lit buildings in the small city.

"You can let me off there," she said.

Danny turned dutifully into the parking lot, and Libby was

climbing out before the truck had reached a full stop. He quickly reached out and caught an arm.

"Where you going?" he asked when Libby turned with a surly look.

"South."

"That's a big place," Danny tried with a slight grin. "Got friends down there?"

"I intend to make some," she replied.

Taking a good look, Danny saw something in Libby he'd never noticed before. When had she become so grown up? She was only sixteen, like Savannah. He pictured Savannah running off on her own and hopping a late night bus, and his expression turned grim.

"Are you sure you want to do this, Libby? Granted, Kingsport can be pretty dull, but is it really so bad?"

"It's bad enough."

"Bad enough to make you do something stupid?" he demanded. "You shouldn't be taking off on your own—"

"Danny!"

She stopped him with a tone no sharper than the look in her eye. He closed his mouth, surprised once again at "little Libby."

"Years have passed since we kept up with each other, Danny. Things happen. I'm not a little girl anymore, and you're not the big protector who takes up for me and Clayton and Savannah." Libby didn't say "against Rory." She didn't have to.

A look of dawning came over Danny, followed by a murderous expression. "McKenna . . ." he began.

At just the sound of the name, Libby cringed. "Stop!" she broke in. "I don't want to hear his name! I don't want to see his face! I don't want to—"

She came to an abrupt halt, and Danny saw the change sweep over her. Out of a look of near hysteria emerged a mask of control.

"And now I don't have to," Libby finished quietly.

Whatever had happened to her, Libby had changed, and Danny realized quite suddenly that he had no influence on her whatsoever. The demons she was fleeing were as fearful as his own.

"Do you have any money?" he asked.

She closed the door of the truck. "Some," she said through the open window.

He hesitated, eyeing her youthful face, feeling that he should do something more to stop her, sensing that nothing he could say would make any difference.

"Take care of yourself," he said eventually.

"Yeah," Libby tossed with the nearest thing to a smile he'd seen all night. "You, too."

The last Danny saw of Libby Parker, she was disappearing into the neon-lit interior of the Lumberton bus station. Turning out of the deserted parking lot, he rejoined Highway 74 and continued west.

Sheriff Martin had managed to rout the Sikes brothers and their followers with relative ease, though Savannah's mother had been scandalized not only by "the sordid incident," but also by the fact that such "mill trash" had actually "tramped about the grounds of Kings Crossing!"

Nearly a week had passed, but talk about Danny Sawyer was still buzzing, and with new ugly undertones. The fact that Danny had been—more or less—run out of town had an effect that Savannah found both ridiculous and disgusting. More than once she'd heard someone say he'd "turned tail" and run, and somehow Kingsport was tending to equate running with guilt. Maybe those Clancytown folks had been barking up the right tree. After all, the authorities had no other suspects in the murder of Roberta Sikes. There was nothing to prove Danny did it, true; but there was also nothing to prove he didn't. And so the talk went on, and the name of Danny Sawyer lived in infamy.

On the other hand, the town hardly blinked an eye at the disappearance of Libby Parker, though it had been a blow to Savannah. She'd known something was wrong—she'd felt it. Why hadn't she insisted Libby open up to her? Now it was too late.

One morning, Savannah was strolling listlessly among the roses when her mother walked up the drive with the day's mail. She sallied over as her mother paused to sift through the collection.

"This one's for you, Savannah. For goodness sake!" Ophelia scoffed as she handed her daughter the missive. "Whom do you know who would use such hideously purple stationery?"

There was no return address, and it had been posted in some Georgia town Savannah had never heard of. Tearing open the envelope, she withdrew a sheet of paper the same offbeat color.

"It's from Libby!"

"Libby?" Ophelia pounced. "You mean that Parker girl?"

"Mother, please," Savannah mumbled as she raced through the letter. "She apologizes for not saying good-bye. She says she simply had to get out of Kingsport and will explain later—"

"I'll bet," Ophelia cut in sharply. "She had to get out so badly that she stole her poor father's nest egg to do it!"

"Mother!"

"Well, it's true! She took nearly five hundred dollars from the shoebox where her father kept his funds! I've always said she was a bad apple, and it's true." Ophelia sniffed. "What else does she have to say for herself?"

"Nothing really. Just that she'll send me her address when she's settled."

"You listen to me, Savannah King," Ophelia began in her most authoritative tone. "Libby Parker has never been good enough for you, and she's taken a definite turn for the worse. Dropping out of school, gallavanting about the country! It's obvious she's a complete undesirable, and I don't want you having anything further to do with her. Is that clear?"

Savannah replaced the note in the envelope and looked steadily into her mother's eyes. "She's my friend," she said, her voice neither loud nor hard, yet somehow unbending.

Ignoring the angry color that flooded her mother's face, Savannah turned and walked sedately out of the garden.

Days melted by. August carried on the hot, steamy tradition of July, and Savannah wished the summer would come to an end. Oh, there were the occasional parties, which she always attended with Clifford, the occasional dinners, mostly with Clifford. But by and large, the summer was boring and empty. Libby was gone . . . and Danny. Savannah had never thought about losing either of them. Now she saw that the gaps they left in her life were wide and gaping.

It was four weeks to the day since they'd both disappeared. Savannah was lingering at the breakfast table with her father, perusing the classifieds as he pored over the news sections of the morning edition.

"Mail's in," her mother said, and sacheted into the dining room looking lovely as ever in a lemon-yellow morning dress. "Bills and more bills," she muttered, her brow puckering as she sorted through the stack. "Ah, here's something personal, Jim," she said and dropped an envelope in her husband's lap. Savan-

nah went back to her reading as her mother opened a newly arrived magazine.

"My goodness," her father exclaimed after a moment.
"There's a hundred-dollar bill in here."

Savannah glanced up curiously.

"And a letter from Danny!"

"Danny?" Savannah piped, perhaps a bit too eagerly.

"Danny Sawyer," her mother said in an icy tone. "I'd hoped
we'd heard the last of *him*." She'd made no secret of her relief
that Danny Sawyer had left the Crossing and taken the stench of
scandal with him.

"Ophelia." Jim said the name scoldingly, absently, as his eyes
focused on the letter.

Her mother shrugged and went back to her magazine. Savannah eyed her father silently until she could hold her tongue no
longer.

"What does Danny have to say?" she asked casually.

Jim glanced again at the hundred-dollar bill and smiled.
"That he intends to pay back every penny I gave him that
night." He looked back at the letter, reporting as he read, "Let's
see . . . he's in Charlotte, and he's gotten a job at *The Charlotte
Observer*. Just running copy, but he intends to work his way up.
He's planning to start night school . . . Well, I'll be," Jim added
with a flush of pleasure. "He's going by the name of Buck Sawyer."

"Buck?" Savannah questioned.

"You know how I always called him 'Danny-Buck.' It seems
he liked it so well that . . . oh . . ."

Her father's expression dimmed dramatically. "What is it?"
Savannah asked.

"Well, he alludes to the fact that the change of his name has a
practical benefit, too—that even in Charlotte the name of
Danny Sawyer still draws a connection to Kingsport and that
whole messy matter." Jim read a bit more and set the letter
aside. "He concludes by saying he realizes now that he can
never come back here, at least not for a long time."

Her father got to his feet, strolled across the room, and looked
out the window. Savannah sensed his dejection. She, too, felt
the loss. She glanced toward her mother who was busily thumbing through the magazine.

"Anything for me?" she asked.

Ophelia looked up. "What, dear?"

"I asked if I got any mail."

Ophelia slipped her hand inside her skirt pocket, her fingers curling over the purple envelope.

"No, dear," she said. "Not today."

Libby peered out the one window afforded by the street-front room on the second floor. It was midday, and bright August sunlight poured over the street, spotlighting the dingy buildings across the way. Piedmont Avenue was definitely not one of the more fashionable streets in downtown Atlanta.

Still, she couldn't really complain. The apartment house to which the taxi driver had brought her was clean, if old and drab.

She was watching for the postman. He normally came just after lunch. Every day for the past four days, Libby had run eagerly down the stairs upon his arrival, hoping for a letter from Savannah. Today, she thought. Surely, it would come today.

The panic that had prompted her to write Savannah had been mounting day by day. Terrified of having an abortion, Libby knew nonetheless that she must. The problem was, she didn't know who to get to do it and hadn't enough money to pay a doctor anyway. Five hundred dollars had seemed like a lot when she left Kingsport, but between the bus trip, rent and food, the amount had dwindled to scarcely more than a hundred. Unknowledgeable as she was, Libby was certain it wasn't enough.

The only person she could conceive of calling on was Savannah. The Kings probably had a fortune just lying around the house. It would be easy for Savannah to lay her hands on a sizable sum of money that would probably never even be missed. But knowing her friend, Libby also knew Savannah would demand an explanation. Libby had kept the letter short and to the point. She could turn to no one else. She was pregnant. She needed an abortion . . . and she needed money.

She'd witheld the part about rape, as well as the name of Rory McKenna. Even now, just the thought of him struck terror in her heart. It was not farfetched to think that Savannah might confront him if she knew, and the idea of Rory's resulting anger turned Libby's knees to water.

Her spirits rose when she spotted the postman coming along the street, but fell when, once again, there was nothing for her. Libby had turned with a woebegone expression when Ginger came trotting up the steps to the stoop.

"Hi, there," the blonde greeted, her bright expression a perfect foil to how Libby felt.

"Hi," she returned glumly.

Along with a lot of other girls, Ginger—what her last name was, Libby had no idea—lived upstairs on the fourth floor. She was cute and friendly, though she wore far too much makeup and dressed in a garish way Kingsport would have considered scandalous. Today she was her usual, flashy self—her golden curls pulled up to display huge earrings, red midriff top clinging to her bosom, purple pants like a second skin. She was taller than Libby by a good six inches, and though Ginger appeared older, Libby knew she was only seventeen.

"How far along are you, anyway?" Ginger asked.

Libby looked up with a start, realizing that as she had studied Ginger, the blonde had been returning the gesture and was now staring quite openly at her rounded stomach. Heat rose to Libby's face and parched her throat. Unable to answer, she pushed through the apartment house door and started up the stairs. Apparently undiscouraged, however, Ginger tagged along.

"Well?" she prodded with that smiling voice of hers. "You can tell me, honey. I been there."

Libby stared at the threadbare carpet on the stairs. "As near as I can tell, close to three months."

"Whatcha gonna do about it?"

Libby glanced at her with a solemn expression, but again said nothing.

"Well, if you're planning to get rid of it," Ginger commented, "you better do something about it soon. See ya!" she added cheerily, and went bounding up the stairs with an energy Libby hadn't felt in weeks.

A few days later, after another fruitless trip to the mailbox, Libby ran into Ginger once more. Evidently her face was a mask of despair. The blond girl demanded to know what was wrong, and in an overwhelming upsurge of desperation, Libby found herself sobbing into Ginger's shoulder.

"I got a gentleman friend who might be able to help you out."

Libby looked up with a sniffle.

"He's a med student," Ginger added.

"I'm not sure I have enough money."

Ginger winked. "It never hurts to ask, now, does it?"

The next day, Ginger stopped by Libby's small, one-bedroom

apartment. "He'll come here," she reported. "And he'll do it for a hundred bucks."

The disclosure left Libby with contradictory feelings of relief and dread. Here was an avenue, at least—though the idea of an abortion still scared the life out of her. She would have preferred to go to a proper hospital, to a proper doctor. She knew that because of her age, she had to have some sort of medical excuse to be granted an abortion. She'd been counting on Savannah's loan to secure what she needed.

Libby chewed her lip and paced the room. Why hadn't Savannah gotten back to her? *Why?*

The next afternoon, when there was still no word, Libby gathered her courage, a few bucks in change, and went downstairs to the pay phone. She had to do something. Maybe Savannah had failed to get her pleading letter. Or maybe help was on the way. Maybe just the sound of Savannah's voice could soothe the ragged fright that had become Libby's constant companion. Her pulse was thrumming as the phone rang, rising with quick hope as someone picked up, stumbling with uncertainty as she heard Mrs. King's voice.

"Hello. Could I please speak to Savannah?"

"Who's calling?" Mrs. King asked, polite but firm.

"This is . . ." she hesitated. "This is a friend of hers. Could I speak to her please?"

There was a pause on the other end of the line, and Libby sensed what was coming even before Mrs. King spoke.

"Is that you, Libby Parker?"

Libby began to tremble. "Yes ma'am. Is Savannah home?"

"She's home," came the low, hissing reply. "But if you think I'll call her to the phone, you're sadly mistaken."

"I just wanted to know if she got my—"

"Letter?"

Libby jumped as though she'd been struck.

"Yes, she received your shameful letter," Mrs. King went on in a tone of revulsion. "Did you hear me? Shameful! How dare you presume to ask for money for such a sordid business? You should have thought about the consequences before you lay down in the gutter. Savannah was terribly upset . . ."

Belying the claim, Libby heard a sudden peal of laughter in the background . . . Savannah's laughter.

Libby virtually threw the receiver into its cradle, then stepped back and eyed it with a mortification that swelled to block out all other feeling. Savannah had told her mother? No, it couldn't be. But then, how else could Mrs. King have known?

Libby slumped against the wall, closed her eyes, and pictured Savannah. And suddenly she could see it—Savannah going to her mother with a shocked expression, the letter dangling from her manicured fingertips. Libby had known she was an innocent—a child, really, in so many ways in which Libby had been forced to grow up. Savannah would have been confused and horrified by her confessions, maybe even sickened.

A cold feeling settled in Libby's stomach, and when she opened her eyes, they were hard with the bitterness of having been betrayed. All her life she'd revered Savannah King. It was amazing how in one instant such idolatry could turn into a black resentment with all the power its pure counterpart had once possessed. The line between love and hate, someone had once said, was remarkably thin. Now Libby knew the truth of those words.

When the knock came on the door, Libby went to answer it on trembling legs. Soon, she told herself. Soon, it will all be over.

Except for the black bag he carried, the man who slipped quickly inside and closed the door didn't much resemble a doctor. Tall and painfully thin, he looked to be in his mid-twenties. Dark stubble showed on his cheeks as though he hadn't shaved in a couple of days, and although his suit appeared to be a nice one, it was definitely crumpled.

"Got the money?" he asked in a husky voice.

Libby reached into the pocket of her robe and withdrew the bills, noting the way he kept swiping at his nose and sniffling as though he had a bad cold. He thumbed through the money, then looked back at her with red-rimmed eyes.

"Take that off, and get on the bed."

For the life of her, Libby didn't think she could move. But then neither could she speak to call a halt to what was about to take place. He set down his bag, took off his jacket, and she saw stains of dried sweat on his white shirt.

"Well!" he then said in a harsh tone. "Let's get on with it!"

Surprisingly, her feet began to move toward the bed. Minutes later, she was positioned in the most degrading fashion she could ever have imagined. As she saw the man's face loom beyond her knees, she squeezed her eyes tightly shut, willing her mind to some other place. It retreated to Kings Crossing . . . the

old landing and the smell of the river, the marsh grass that made
a sighing noise when a breeze was up.

There was something cold and metallic between her legs . . .

And the way the beach looked at night, Libby thought desperately, with a full moon shining down and making a golden
path to the shore, and . . .

The image went suddenly red in a swift wash of color as her
insides were rent in two. Libby's eyes flew open, but still she
was blinded. Pain had a color, and it was scarlet.

The scream that tore from her throat rang with the anguish of
mortal agony, the terror of knowing that something was horri-
bly wrong.

The name Gracie conjured up the image of a petite belle with
flowing movements. In fact, Gracie Poteat was a voluminous
black woman who waddled more than walked. On hot days, she
wore a constant sheen of perspiration, no matter how high she
turned the damn air conditioner that was supposed to have
cooled her entire opulently furnished quarters.

"Piece of junk!" Gracie accused, slapping at the new unit
she'd had installed just last week.

Across the room, Dawn was curled on a loveseat reading a
magazine. She looked up with a grin.

"You ought to take it outa George's hide next time he comes
sniffing around after Lorna," she suggested.

"That's right!" Gracie huffed. "That man thinks he can come
round here and trade off his bill with some piece of junk like
this here? Hmph!"

With another whack for the ill-favored air conditioner, Gracie
proceeded to flutter the ever-present, hand-painted Chinese fan
that was virtually a trademark. She was still grumbling when
Ginger burst through the door.

"Oh, Gracie!" the girl cried with wide eyes. "You gotta come
quick! This girl I know on the second floor, I think she's *dying*!"

Dawn was at her heels as Gracie followed the nimble Ginger
as quickly as she could manage. When she walked into the
small, stifling room, Gracie beheld a sight that was, unfortunately, well known to her.

"Lord have mercy," she muttered, lowering her great girth to
the floor where the girl had apparently fallen, maybe trying to
get to the door and call for help. A trail of blood started at the
nearby bedside and was pooling around her thighs. Gracie

reached out and turned the girl's face toward her. It was pale as death, and cold to the touch.

"She's been butchered," Gracie announced. "And she'll damn well bleed to death if something isn't done in a hurry."

"Oh, my God," Ginger whimpered. "He said he was practically a doctor, that he'd done it a hundred times."

"There's time for regrets later," Gracie snapped. "For now, if you want to keep the girl in this world, you best find me a clean towel or sheet. Dawn, get on the phone and call Dr. Laurel."

Libby nearly died.

For ten days she had slipped in and out of consciousness. She vaguely recalled a gray-haired doctor, the words "staff infection" and "antibiotics," and Ginger's face.

The blonde had been in constant attendance since Libby finally regained consciousness three days ago. Ginger seemed to think it was all her fault, though Libby assured her that it wasn't—that in fact she had saved her.

"No, that was Gracie," Ginger had insisted.

And Libby had been told about Gracie Poteat, who had stemmed the flow of her life's blood and had the presence of mind to get Dr. Laurel there in a matter of minutes. She'd also paid the bills for daily house calls, as well as the necessary medicines. Libby had yet to set eyes on the mysterious woman who had apparently saved her life, though Ginger said Gracie had looked in on her quite often while she was delirious with fever.

Shifting up in the bed, Libby rested against the pillows and picked up the hand mirror Ginger had left the day before. The face in the reflection was still unfamiliar. All the roundness was gone. She actually had cheekbones, though the skin stretched over them was pale as ivory, and the dark circles above them made her eyes seem to loom too large.

She looked different. She *was* different. The looming eyes in the mirror were opaque, giving away nothing of what lay behind them. They seemed darker, too—perhaps, Libby thought, with the blackness of the wrath that enveloped her.

A date with the Grim Reaper did wonders for one's perspective. Libby saw everything with dazzling clarity and without the tremblings of one who had never faced death. Once she had been terrified of Rory, now his destruction was the bleak, single-minded purpose of her life. It would not happen soon,

Libby knew. But one day, somehow, she would see Rory McKenna destroyed.

A familiar knock sounded at the door, and Ginger walked in bearing a lunch tray.

"You're looking better today," she said brightly.

"I'm feeling better, too."

"Good. I'll have to tell Gracie. She's been asking how you're getting on."

Libby's brow puckered. "How am I going to pay her back, Ginger? I'm flat broke."

Ginger set the tray aside and shrugged. "Get a job. She'll wait. The important thing now is for you to get well."

"A job? I haven't finished high school. I don't know how to do anything, except maybe wait tables. The doctor's bills and all the medicine must run into hundreds of dollars." Libby looked away. "God, I've been on my own just a few weeks, and already I'm impossibly in the hole."

"Look at me," Ginger said, and when Libby complied, her friend proceeded to study her as if sizing her up for something.

"I'll bet you're a good-looking girl when you're healthy."

Libby's brows rose. "What brought that on?"

Ginger placed red-tipped hands on her hips. "I haven't finished high school either, and I bring in about four hundred a week."

"Four hundred?" Libby croaked.

"Look. Gracie takes a bigger cut than most, maybe, but she don't push you to do anything you don't want to, and she don't get her girls hooked on drugs, and . . ."

"Ginger. What are you talking about?"

The pert blonde gave her a searching look. "Don't you know?"

And suddenly Libby did. Gracie was a . . . a madam. Ginger worked for her, along with all the other girls who lived upstairs.

"Oh."

"Come on," Ginger said with infallible cheer. "You knew I was in the trade, didn't you?"

"I guess so."

"Well, what do you think?"

"About what?"

"You want to make some money?"

Libby considered the idea with the newborn detachment that marked her outlook toward everything. Should she be insulted?

Frightened? Horrified? She felt none of those things. In fact, the matter seemed to be of little importance.

A month later she stood in Gracie Poteat's lavish apartment, waiting as the immense woman looked her over. Libby had undergone the "Ginger treatment" and was dressed in a clinging black dress that reached only halfway down her thigh.

"You sure about this, honey?" Gracie asked.

Libby met the woman's questioning look with one of utter calm. "I'm sure."

Gracie nodded and broke into a smile. "All right, then. You've got good legs, a good figure, a pretty face. That hair of yours needs some attention. What's your name, again? Libby?" Gracie shook her head. "No, that'll have to go, too. How about something more exotic? Lily, maybe? Or Lilah?"

Libby Parker had entered Gracie Poteat's apartment. Lilah Parks emerged, and when she entertained her first client some weeks later, she derived a mild sense of amusement at how easy it was to wrap the balding man around her finger.

Chapter Six

MONOPOLIZING THE corner of Tryon and Stonewall streets, *The Charlotte Observer* building was tall and white. Buck hugged his jacket close as he darted through the crisp morning air, taking the granite steps two at a time until he broached the wide glass doors and passed into the hushed interior.

It was early. Most of the thousand or so employees wouldn't arrive until eight. As he stepped onto the escalator that would take him up to the fifth floor, Buck breathed in the smell of newsprint and felt the familiar thrill. Hallowed halls. It wasn't just *The Observer* that made him feel the unique sense of reverence. It would be the same with any good newspaper.

It had taken longer than he expected to work his way up—though, undeniably, his position had greatly improved. During three years of running copy, he'd grown friendly with a number of reporters, particularly Gil Jerome. And in the past year, Gil and he had become best buddies.

In some ways, they were an odd twosome. Gil was short, red-headed, and Buck's senior by ten years. But the two men had some basic interests in common—sports, for one thing. Gil was an avid basketball and tennis fan. But foremost, Buck supposed, was their common love of the newspaper. In the past months, Gil had critiqued his writing, encouraged his efforts, and upon his graduation from community college, arranged a job interview with the editor, Grant Spenser.

Spenser was a brilliant Harvard graduate with more than thirty years' experience in journalism. Buck still remembered how he felt that day some six months back—like a clod with a miserable two-year degree, and nothing but a few freelance stories in his portfolio. Spenser had shocked him by hiring him into Editorial, but Buck had been disappointed when he discovered his duties were basically behind the scenes. Oh, he wrote an occasional restaurant review or a calendar of events for the "Around Town" column. But by and large, he did legwork for the reporters whose names appeared in *The Observer* day after day.

Still, there were obvious benefits. Salary. A desk of his own. Primarily, the opportunity to sit in on Editorial meetings. It was there that he learned what was happening—locally, nationally, around the world. It was there that he felt the singing excitement that both whetted his appetite and confirmed what he had known for years. He was a newspaperman. He'd found it out the day Mr. King ran the story in *The River Watch*. Buck Sawyer had ink running in his veins, though he had yet to see his name in print.

That particular day in March, the afternoon turned unseasonably warm. After work, Buck and Gil got together for a few sets of tennis at Freedom Park. The front courts were usually reserved for the better players—an unspoken rule that a couple of girls on Court Six were apparently unaware of, or maybe they just didn't give a damn. Every ten minutes, one of their balls came sailing over the fence to bounce across Gil and Buck's court. It wasn't until the girls gave up their game and sauntered by that Buck thought perhaps the whole thing had been intentional. The blonde who gave him a blatant though wordless invitation with her onceover was definitely a number.

Buck had approached the net to retrieve a ball. In obvious acknowledgment, he came to a standstill and returned her perusal look for look.

"Oh, she likes you," Gil said in a soft voice.

Buck hadn't been aware of his friend's approach, and even after Gil spoke, he didn't break the look he'd established with the blonde. Finally she smiled and turned toward the parking lot. Buck watched her go—admiring the swing of her walk, the curve of her ass in the short tennis whites, the shapely legs . . .

"She's older than you by at least five years."

"So?"

"Fast as greased lightning, or so they say."

Buck turned at that and arched a brow. "Do they, now?"

"If she takes to you," Gil supplied with a grin. "Rita Nesbitt is picky, and she can afford to be. Old money, you know," he added in a singsong mimick of aristocracy. "Her father owns one of the biggest savings and loan outfits around, among other things."

Buck's expression turned to one of amusement. "Is that supposed to be something to hold against her? If you're trying to dampen my interest, you're not succeeding."

"She's a wild one, Buck. You know how some rich kids turn out? She plays the limits—fast cars, fast crowd, fast lane all the way. Word has it she parties with the Demons."

Finally, Gil thought, he'd struck a nerve.

"Demons?" Buck repeated. "The cycle gang?"

Most people who lived in Charlotte knew of the Demons, a Carolinas-based gang that maintained a house just outside the city limits, as well as a string of porn joints along Beaker Street. Just a few weeks back, Grant Spenser had mentioned them at one of the Editorial meetings. It seemed they were a pet peeve with him. "They flaunt the law and get away with it. But," Spenser had concluded with caustic resignation, "I may as well forget about them. There's no way to get to them without an inside connection. And there's no chance of that, so . . ."

With Spenser's comments fresh in his mind, Buck had paid special attention to the Demon whose path he'd crossed a few days later. Buck had been filling up the tank of his Harley at a gas station on the west side when the biker pulled up beside him on a noisy chopper. Cutting the engine, the guy climbed off and gave Buck an assessing look.

"Nice bike," he commented, his voice matching his rough looks. He was big and had long hair and a beard. Although it was a chilly February day, his massive arms were bare, the sleeves having been cut off the denim jacket that sported the word *Demons* on the back.

"Thanks," Buck returned, his eyes surveying the chopper. "Yours isn't bad either."

"You ride with an outfit?"

The question took Buck by surprise, and he glanced down at himself. He wore a leather jacket, jeans and boots—typical biker attire, he supposed, but he'd never considered the notion that he might look like one.

"Nah," he returned, giving his Harley a stroke. "This is just cheaper to run than a car. More fun, too."

That had been the extent of his conversation with the Demon, but now, as he remembered the biker's question, Buck's mind exploded with an idea. He looked sharply toward the parking lot as a flashy red Porsche screeched onto the street. Rita Nesbitt.

"Now where do you suppose a woman like that might hang out?" he mused.

"I don't know," Gil replied. "I saw her a few weeks ago at Whispers. Don't know if she's a regular, though."

Apparently she was. A few nights later at midnight, Danny had given up hope and was preparing to settle his tab when she breezed in—all alone and dressed to kill in metallic blue stretch pants and a matching low-cut sweater. A silvery white fur jacket was slung over her shoulder. Buck wasted no time. Before she even reached the bar, he was there.

"Can I buy you a drink?"

Rita looked up with an expression of irritation that turned to surprise and then sultry pleasure. "Sure," she replied, and sitting down, patted the stool next to her.

As the bartender stepped away to get their drinks, she turned and gave Buck a onceover he found entirely stimulating. At close range, he could see that her eyes were brown, her hair obviously bleached. Still, she was a looker, and the streetwise air about her made his blood run fast.

"Didn't I see you at Freedom Park yesterday?" she asked.

He nodded, his gaze dropping boldly to the ample bosom shown off by the sweater. "And I definitely saw you."

Rita's lashes fluttered down in seductive fashion as she returned his pointed look of interest, only lower.

"You look different tonight," she murmured.

In honor of her reputed taste for the Demons, Buck had worn jeans that fit like a second skin, a black T-shirt, and motorcycle boots. In a trendy place like Whispers, where most of the crowd was decked to the nines, he stood out as a fashion renegade.

"You don't like it?" he asked.

The lashes raised again—slowly, sensually. "I didn't say that. What's your name?"

"Sawyer. Buck Sawyer."

"Buck," she repeated, running the pink tip of a tongue over her lips as she considered the name. "And are you?"

"Am I what?"

"Wild as a buck?"

Buck settled his forearms on the bar and gave her a heated look that left no doubt of its meaning. "I haven't had any complaints."

When Whispers closed down at two, they went to her condo on the stately and wealthy south side of Charlotte. As Gil had said, she was obviously loaded. She was also, as he'd predicted, "fast as greased lightning." Before they were completely in the door, she was undressing him. Eagerly, Buck returned the favor, and Rita proceeded to knock his socks off.

Later, when she slept, he found himself wide awake in the feminine bed, staring up at the girlish ruffled canopy that seemed completely out of sync with the siren beside him. And then out of the blue the thought occurred. It was Savannah's birthday. Glancing at the clock on the bedside table, he saw that it was after four o'clock. March the fourteenth, 1980. Savannah would turn twenty today.

Buck turned his eyes once more to the canopy, though what he saw was the remembered image of a girl in a pale dress, her long blond hair limned by torchlight against a summer night. Nearly four years had passed since that last night at the Crossing. He rarely thought of Savannah anymore, but each time he did, her memory was accompanied by a shrill note of—what? He couldn't even put a name to it. It was more than longing . . . more, even, than love . . . something like the frustrated keen of an obsession denied.

Rita stirred then. Buck rolled over and proceeded to bring her awake with roaming kisses that presaged a second round.

"Now then," Spenser said, looking briefly up over the tops of bifocles before returning his study to the papers on his desk. "What was it you wanted to see me about?"

Buck was nervous but did his best to swallow the sensation by focusing on the plan that had gelled over the past week. He walked into the office with a sure and measured stride.

"I have an idea, Mr. Spenser," he said firmly.

"About what?"

"The Demons."

This time when the editor looked up, his attention was obviously piqued. "Sit down," he said, indicating one of the two leather chairs before his desk. "What about the Demons?"

"I was at one of their parties last night."

At that, Spenser snatched his glasses off the bridge of his nose. "Since when have you become privileged to the Demons?"

"Since I've been seeing Rita Nesbitt."

"Ah," Spenser mused, chewing absently at the end of a pencil as his gaze drilled into the young man sitting across from him. "And what's your idea?"

Buck drew a deep breath. "An exposé."

"Of the Demons?"

"That's right. A series."

"Reported by . . . ?"

"Reported by, written by, Buck Sawyer."

Spenser arched a brow. "You don't have the experience, Buck . . ."

"I'm talking about going undercover, Mr. Spenser. You yourself said that was the only way to get the goods on the Demons. You said it was impossible to get anyone on the inside. Well, I'm in . . . or I could be, given some time."

"Let me get this straight. You plan to infiltrate the Demons? Are you aware of the risk you'll be taking?"

Buck's jaw took on a hard set. "I'm willing to risk it. But on my terms. Put me in print, Mr. Spenser."

Spenser looked into the hazel eyes. There was great spirit in them, and determination. Plus, as he recalled, Buck Sawyer's writing wasn't half bad . . . with the proper editing, of course.

"We'll need reports along the way," he said with a cautious look that lasted only seconds as Buck's face lit up with a smile. Dissolving into helpless enthusiasm, Spenser offered a grin of his own. "And then, when you're ready," he added conspiratorially, "we'll send the Demons straight to hell."

May 20, 1980

At the windows of the study, a spring rain conducted rivulets along the panes. Outside, the world was gray and wet and unknowing. Inside the Cochrane mansion, Ben was facing the most odious decision of his life. It seemed fitting that it was raining.

"But do we have to destroy the man?" he pleaded, though he didn't brave the challenge of meeting his companion's eyes. "Why?" he added, the word like a breath on the wind.

"Yours is not to question why," came the reply.

Ben snapped around, instantly and thoroughly incensed. His gaze lit on the blasted Panama hat. He hated that damn hat almost as much as the man who wore it.

"What's the matter?" Big Ed asked lazily. "Did I misquote?"

"No. You did not misquote. Nevertheless, you did avoid the question."

With the flick of a finger, Big Ed tipped the Panama off his forehead. "You forget yourself, Ben," he drawled, the casual tone a direct contradiction to the look in his eyes. "The issue is not why, but when. I've done everything else that needed doing these past four years. All you have to do is play the final card. And the time is now."

"But—"

"Need I remind you, Ben, that we'll soon be related? In a matter of weeks, your girl and my boy . . ." Big Ed smiled and spread his palms. "Well, shall we say Hillary and Rory will join two of the finest families in Kingsport?"

"That has nothing to do with what we're discussing here." Ben straightened the lapels of his jacket and attempted to do the same with his spine. "We're discussing sabotage—no, more than that. We're discussing fraud . . . of the foulest kind."

Big Ed raised a brow. "Fraud?" he repeated in an inaudible tone. "That's your word, Ben. Not mine. I'm conducting business, plain and simple. There's always a winner; there's always a loser. In this case, the loser is Jim King."

"But he's one of the most respected men in . . . For God's sake, the city is *named* for his family!"

Big Ed's lips curled. "Precisely."

"So, this is to satisfy some whim of yours, some vendetta you've dreamed up!"

Ed's countenance lost its pleasant facade with mind-blowing speed. "I don't recall you being so reluctant when we first hatched this deal."

"Maybe I've had time to think—"

"Maybe you've had time to forget."

The words resounded in the quiet study where the only sound was the patter of rain.

"Don't forget what hangs in the bargain, Ben. You wouldn't want a certain naughty habit of yours to become public knowledge, now would you? Is that the right word? Habit?"

The word was *penchant*, though at that moment Ben hypothesized that Big Ed McKenna would have no knowledge of such a sophisticated word. Penchant was beyond Big Ed's vocabulary; it was not beyond Ben's. He'd been born into one of the finest families, schooled in the finest institutions, was president of one of the finest banks.

But he also had a penchant for young boys. He'd been discreet—he'd thought. But somehow Big Ed had found out. The image of the horrified faces of his wife and daughter chilled Ben to the bone. He couldn't bear it. It was either ruin himself or collaborate in the ruin of Jim King.

Ben looked up with watering eyes. "Who are you, Ed?" he asked in a hollow voice. "Where do you come from?"

Big Ed McKenna pulled the Panama low on his brow. "Does it matter?" he replied. "I'm here now."

May 24, 1980

"But Ben . . ." Jim's voice was as blank as his face. "You advised me to take out the final loan."

"Yes," Ben replied fervently. "And I still believe it was the only thing to do. You'd gotten in so deep, Jim, the only way you could have recovered was by getting the club up and running. You were close, so very close. Another month could have seen you through to the point that you could start getting a return. Who would have thought . . ."

Ben's voice trailed off.

"But why did you sell the loan out of state?"

"It's done all the time," Ben returned, trying his best to still the writhing in his gut. "It's called factoring. Second mortgages are often sold. If the note held by the first mortgagee comes due and isn't paid, the second holder has the legal right to buy out the first. Like I said, it's done all the time. I had no way of anticipating that this second company would call in the note. I'm sorry, Jim. Truly. You can't know how sorry I am."

Ben's voice broke on the last, but Jim King hadn't enough presence of mind to notice. In one fell blow, he'd been wiped out.

Actually it wasn't one fell blow, just the final one. The disaster had been building ever since he got involved with King's Club. Everything had taken longer and cost more than he'd planned. Jim had plowed stubbornly on, borrowing more and more as the project that once had been a dream turned into a nightmare. He'd sold the hardware store and gas station last spring, explaining to Ophelia that he was "consolidating." Now how could he tell her he'd lost not only *The Watch*, but also the Crossing?

The afternoon crawled by with painful sloth, each moment

like a bludgeon pounding the horrendous truth into Jim's brain. He drove aimlessly up the coast, the window of the black limousine open to a warm sea breeze that failed to soothe his roiling torment. Everything was lost—money, property . . . everything. The reign of the King family—founders of the city, guardians of a grand and glorious heritage—had come to an end. And it was all his doing. The only thing he had left to his name was the life insurance policy he'd remained steadfast in protecting. Thank God for that.

Shortly after dark, Jim turned the car back toward Kingsport. Stopping on the outskirts of town at Ira Lamont's liquor store, he picked up a pint of whiskey and was aware of Ira's curious look. Never before had Jim King darkened his shop doorway, and it was common knowledge he wasn't much of a drinking man. But of course Ira held his tongue. He never would have presumed to ask a King for an explanation of anything.

It was nearly eleven when Jim approached the tributary and pulled over to the shoulder of the road. Behind him, the coastal city was humming with the tourist traffic attracted by the warm May weather, but out here—where the picturesque bridge up ahead marked the beginnings of the south side—the night was shrouded with stately quiet. The only sounds were the songs of katydids and crickets, the only lights were the distant glow of the streetlamps along Cloister Drive.

Jim closed his eyes, his imagination taking him beyond The Cloisters and up the curving drive of the Crossing. He could almost see the glowing windows in the imposing white house, a solitary shadow pacing to and fro behind them. Cletus and the other servants would have long since departed. Ophelia was alone in the house. Savannah, of course, was in Raleigh, about to finish her sophomore year at Meredith College with the same sterling marks that had highlighted her entire scholastic career. The thought of Savannah was bittersweet, filled at once with overwhelming love and sadness. Jim opened his eyes, the proud smile that had crept to his lips disappearing to leave his mouth in a tight line. He had nothing left to bequeath her . . . nothing but the price of his skin.

Eyeing the bridge that spanned the tributary to The Cloisters, Jim drained the last of the whiskey, took hold of the steering wheel with nothing short of a death grip, and pressed the accelerator to the floor.

* * *

Savannah gazed idly out the classroom window. The college grounds were pretty in the springtime with their green lawns and bright azaleas. But Raleigh—despite its proximity to Chapel Hill and Clifford—was not Kingsport, and every year when the weather turned warm, Savannah found herself home-sick for the coast. *Just two more weeks*, she was thinking when a knock sounded at the classroom door. She was surprised—and then instantly worried—when the intruder turned out to be a messenger from Dean Whitman, who requested that Savannah King report immediately to her office.

"My dear," the woman said when Savannah entered.

She hurried to meet Savannah, her silver head bobbing, her wrinkled face drawn in an alarming expression of concern.

The next words she spoke were all Savannah heard before a loud buzzing exploded in her head, blotting out everything else Dean Whitman had to say, although Savannah could clearly see that the woman's mouth was moving.

Her father was dead.

Savannah's eyes rolled back as she fainted into oblivion for the first time in her life.

The alley on the west side of Charlotte smelled of garbage and was lit by flashing spillover from the neon signs on the street. The signs announced adult book stores, massage parlors, and an occasional bar. "Sleeze Street," Gil called it, and was openly reluctant about meeting there. Buck had insisted on it. He was in too tight now to be seen in the vicinity of *The Observer*, or anywhere in fashionable Charlotte for that matter, unless he had Rita on his arm. With Rita, he could crash that most lofty of upper crust havens, Myers Park Country Club—or even turn up at the Nesbitt mansion on Queens Road where Rita would relentlessly flaunt Buck Sawyer in the face of her cringing father.

"So, how's it going?" Gil asked.

"Good."

Buck handed over the envelope and ran absent fingers through his hair, brushing it back where it was prone to fall across his brows. He'd let it grow longer than convention permitted. Along with the tight jeans, boots, and leather bracelet, it helped him blend in with the Demons.

Over the course of two and a half months, he'd become generally accepted. His face had grown familiar, as had a sort of unspoken respect for the way he rode his bike. He was not a member of the Demons but nonetheless an expected presence among their number. As their wariness of him decreased, Buck had become privy to increasingly careless exchanges of "business." The main ones seemed to be prostitution and drugs, though he once had glimpsed a shipment of guns and had seen enough money flow through "Demon Den" to finance a small army.

He had enough material to blow the lid off the entire organization. And what was more, if put under oath, Rita would have to back him up.

"I want to ask you something, Gil," he said quietly. When his friend turned to face him, Buck added, "What happens when all this goes down?"

"Who the hell knows? Our job is to report the facts. Any action that's taken will be up to the authorities, but I'm willing to bet they'll pull a major raid at the very least."

"I mean, what's going to happen to Rita?"

"How deeply involved is she?"

"She's not really part of it, Gil. She just gets a kick out of playing at it."

Gil shrugged. "She plays at it hard enough for everyone in the city to connect her with the Demons."

Buck imagined the creamy thighs he'd left only hours ago, the tousled look of her hair in the morning.

"I've used her," he said, the words turning his mouth sour.

"Listen, Buck. I've thought about this. Rita Nesbitt has been pushing her luck for years. It's almost as if she wants something, or someone, to make her stop. Who knows? Maybe by cutting her off at this point, you're saving her from getting in completely over her head. There are some things her daddy's money can't buy, you know—like the chance to go on living if the Demons ever took a notion to turn against her."

Buck met his eyes, and gradually the haunted look went out of his own. "You're a good friend," he said and started to turn.

"There's something else," Gil called softly. Buck looked back, and Gil hesitated.

He'd been Buck Sawyer's confidant for a year now. He knew that Buck was, in reality, Danny Sawyer of Kingsport. He knew the specters that haunted Danny's past. He also knew a few of the good things—like the unimaginable lushness of a place called Kings Crossing . . . the beauty of a golden-haired girl named Savannah . . . the kindness of a man who was, Buck had said, the only true gentleman he'd ever known.

"It's bad news, Buck. A friend of yours died last night."

Gil felt rather than saw the immediate tension that straightened his friend's frame.

"Who?"

"Jim King."

The name fell on Buck's ear with the sweetness of a memory, the sharpness of startling grief. He opened his mouth, ultimately forcing out the question: "How?"

"Car accident."

In the dark recesses of the alley, the moisture that gathered in Buck's eyes was known only to himself. "Any other victims?"

Gil shook his head. "He was alone."

Buck nodded. Silence fell.

"Thanks, Gil," he said after a moment, and started back toward the neon lights of the strip.

The flowers he sent were to Savannah alone. The only deference he showed Ophelia King was the choice of roses.

June 8, 1980

Ginger, who was driving, was embroiled in a lively conversation with Dawn about some guy they both dated. Lilah sat alone in the back seat, gazing out the window as they sped along the northeasterly highway. Though well past eight o'clock, it was just getting dark, a soft twilight lying over the fields and trees of the Georgia countryside.

Of the dozen or so regulars known as "Gracie's girls," just the three of them had agreed to make the trip to Athens. Lilah knew there would be other hostesses from other sources. It was a combination bachelor and graduation party. The groom-to-be had just graduated from the University of Georgia and would be married the following week.

All this Lilah had been told, though she hardly bore it in mind. It was a stag party. In the past four years, she'd been to quite a few. They were all alike.

It was just past nine when Ginger turned the car into the parking lot of The Royal Coach, which was unquestionably the most posh hotel in Athens. Brocade wallpapers, gilded lamps and velvet-covered chairs adorned the ladies room where the three of them stopped to freshen up.

Lilah examined her appearance and proceeded to fluff her hair. The short curls danced with fiery highlights produced by a henna rinse. Her gaze slipped along the molding lines of the black strapless dress. She'd long ago decided black was her color—it contrasted so strikingly with the red hair and pale skin. She rarely wore any other color when she was working. With a final application of lipstick the exact shade of her hair, Lilah joined Dawn and Ginger and searched out "Royal Salon C."

She was pleasantly impressed as they stepped inside the banquet room. Chandeliers cast a soft glow over wainscoted walls, and liveried waiters tended bar. It was much more elegant than most facilities reserved for such occasions. Still, the room was filled with loud men and flashily dressed women, the sounds of music and laughter, the smells of booze and cigarette smoke—all reminding Lilah, once again, that although the party had a high-class tone, it was still just a flesh market, a bazaar where every attending man could shop for his own particular brand of whore.

The masking smile had just risen to her face when Lilah heard a guffaw that made her spin around. He was less than ten feet away and was devoid of the ever-present Panama, but other than that the man in the white planter's suit looked the same. Big Ed McKenna. Lilah's smile froze as she took an unconscious backward step, her gaze swiftly scanning the crowd. God, there was Clayton!

And then suddenly her eyes lit on the familiar form across the room. His back was to her, but there was no mistaking Rory. Lilah drew a sharp breath, unaware that she continued to hold it as though her lungs had forgotten how to work. She noted the ridiculous aluminum crown on his head, the wreath of flowers about his neck, and it occurred to her that he was the guest of honor . . . the graduate . . . the groom-to-be. He was dancing with a blonde whose long hair called to mind the memory of Savannah King. Lilah had seen her once or twice before—Amanda . . . Amelia . . . something like that.

Her mind went on with such gibberish until Rory turned, and she beheld his face.

The hatred that spiraled within her was like poison, nauseating Lilah so swiftly that she clapped a hand over her mouth and ran for the ladies room.

* * *

Ginger mosied through the crowd, sizing up the prospects; then she spotted a young attractive one standing all by himself against a wall. Licking her lips to give them sheen, she moved to join him.

"Hello, there," she opened smoothly, finding that she liked the looks of this one just fine. He was about her height, had nice brown hair and eyes, and looked to be no more than twenty if he was a day. At the moment a blush was creeping up his cheeks toward his scalp.

"I'm Ginger. Who are you?"

"Clayton McK-Kenna." He managed a smile. This one wasn't as scary as the other women in the room. She wore a lot of makeup, but she was pretty. Of course, he knew what she was, but as Clayton met the eyes that matched the green dress she was wearing, he found himself suddenly intrigued with the idea of being alone with her.

His newborn smile faded as he added, "Brother of the groom over there."

Ginger followed the direction of his gaze to the blond in the white dinner jacket. He was good looking, all right, but as she turned back to Clayton and saw the hard set of his face, she knew better than to pursue the subject of his brother.

"How about you?" she asked with a warm look. "You married?"

Clayton's brows shot up in surprise. "M-me? No, ma'am!"

"Ma'am?" Ginger smiled and tucked a hand inside his arm. "I like that. Where you from, sugar?"

With blossoming pleasure, Clayton found that he liked the feel of her touching him, leaning up against him. She smelled wonderful, and she talked in such easygoing fashion that he found himself responding in the same manner. His stammering diminished, a state that was completely unexpected considering the way his every nerve ending had come alert. He'd never been with a hooker before—never truly been with any woman, a fact with which his brother and father took endless delight in torturing him. As his blood heated with masculine urges, Clayton began to think that maybe tonight—with Ginger—he could put an end to all that.

It took the better part of an hour to work up the nerve to ask if they could go someplace private. But just as Clayton was preparing to voice the question, all hell broke loose in the center of the room, where Rory—apparently high as a kite and wild as a bull—had picked up his fair-haired partner and slung her over his shoulder. Now he stalked in the direction of the doorway, carving a bold path through an applauding crowd, his eyes gleaming as they lit on Clayton.

"What the hell do you think you're up to, brother?" he roared, coming to a halt. "Now, *I* know what to do with a package like this." Rory emphasized his claim by swatting the blonde on the bottom, then directing a scathing look over Clayton's female companion. "What the hell do you plan on doing with one?"

People had turned to watch. Clayton's chin went up, though he said nothing.

"Come on, boy!" Rory challenged in that bellowing tone. "Do you really think you can get it up?"

In response to his brother's taunt, Clayton felt his manhood shrivel to nothingness. Opening his mouth to retort, he discovered that his newfound flowing speech had deserted him as well.

Rory began to laugh, and Clayton thought he would explode if he couldn't escape the sound.

"Wait a minute, sugar!" Ginger cried as he snatched his arm out of her grasp and bolted toward the door.

But she was too late. Clayton moved just as his taller brother did. They collided, Clayton lost his footing and fell, and the blond man roared with new laughter. The girl hanging over his shoulder was laughing, too—as well as members of the surrounding crowd.

Ginger's attention swerved to Clayton who was red-faced with obvious mortification. She took a step in his direction, but if he saw her, he gave no sign as he scrambled to his feet and fled out the opposite door from where his swaggering brother disappeared.

She prepared herself in the practiced way of a soldier. Makeup. Dress. Wig. Gloves were the final touch. Picking up the scarf as she glided away from the dresser, she stepped into the deserted hall and turned in the direction of Rory's room.

In a way, it seemed eons since she'd been out on her own; in another, the time seemed to have passed in the blink of an eye.

The scenes could not have been more different. Then, there had·been the smell of mud and the distant sound of cheap music. Now there was the lingering aroma of expensive perfumes, the late-night hush of a deserted richly carpeted corridor. Still, trash was trash, whether it littered the Clancytown riverfront or the Royal Coach Hotel.

The girl was of no consequence—a piece of fluff already on the road to ruin, a justifiable casualty in a battle that began long ago. She was bait in a trap—probably the most noble role of her ill-begotten life.

One could only hope she would serve her intended purpose better than that little Sikes tramp, whose misconstrued demise had been completely ineffectual—pointing a finger at Danny Sawyer and failing to stir even a ripple on the placid surface of what should have been Rory's conscience.

This was different. Fifty people had seen him with the blonde. Fifty people could point their fingers.

She arrived without being seen and waited patiently, knowing it wasn't like Rory to invite a conquest to linger once he had his fill. Soon she would leave his room.

Soon . . . soon . . . the word came again and again in a secret, silent chant, whispering a death knell as she twined the scarf through expectant fingers.

It was nearly two in the morning when Lilah stumbled out the side entrance of the hotel and made weaving progress to the parking lot. She felt drunk—or drugged—as if she could hardly stand, much less put one spike heel in front of the other.

"Where have you been?" Ginger demanded, her irritation obvious as Lilah approached the car. "I've been looking for you for hours."

"I think I've come down with something," Lilah replied, putting a hand to her temple. "I've been sick all night."

Ginger's manner changed abruptly, and she slung a supporting arm about Lilah's shoulders. "Come on," she murmured. "Let's get you to the car. You didn't miss much anyway. After the groom disappeared with some blonde, the whole thing went downhill."

Two days later, the Athens paper carried a front-page story that *The Atlanta Constitution* mentioned briefly in a back section. The strangulation of a local Athens girl, Amelia Howard, might have deserved the front page in her hometown. But a known hooker turning up dead sixty miles away wasn't news in "Hot-lanta."

* * *

June 16, 1980

Buck propped himself on the pillow and peered through the flickering light of the candle on the bedside table.

"I want to ask you something, Rita."

"Sure," she murmured, trailing a painted nail from one of his nipples toward his navel.

Buck grabbed the hand and drew a look of surprise. "What would you say if I asked you to stop?" he said. "All the partying, the Demons, the whole thing."

Rita gave him an incredulous look. "Why, I'd say you'd lost your mind," she replied.

Buck leveled her with a solemn gaze but said nothing. Eventually, Rita smiled.

"Come on, my big, strong Buck. You knew what I was like from the first night. Why do you want me to change?"

"Because I do."

"But why?"

"Because you might get hurt if you don't."

That drew a look of alertness.

"What are you talking about?" she asked, pulling the sheet up over her breasts.

"I'm a reporter, Rita. I've been undercover these past few months, and everything about the Demons is about to hit the fan."

Her eyes went wide. "You're a what?"

"You heard me," Buck replied, his gaze intent and serious. "I never meant to use you, Rita. I guess I should have known it would turn out that way, but I was thinking about other things—the stories, the glory." He reached out and grasped a smooth shoulder. "But now I'm worried about you. The series is going to run next week. I want you to get out of town."

Rita glanced up at the canopy and emitted a short laugh as though the breath had left her. When she looked again at Buck, her eyes were searching, though to his relief they appeared to hold none of the rage he had feared might be there.

"You're worried about me," she said in a low, whispery voice. "At least that's something."

Out of the brief disconcerting earnestness emerged an impish expression that looked much more like the old Rita.

"I think I have a hankering to see Europe again," she then announced. "And the sooner the better."

Buck smiled and drew her into his arms. "I'll miss you, Rita."

She snuggled close and pressed a kiss to his neck that ended in a bite.

"Ow!" Buck winced, looking with surprise at her dimpling face.

"I'll miss you, too, asshole," she said.

The series made Buck Sawyer an instant star . . . and a target. Armed guards roamed *The Observer* building as the news reached Charlotte that the Demons were on the way, having gathered from clear across both Carolinas.

Buck was sent to lay low in a mountain retreat, and indeed they came—a long stream of angry, denim-jacketed cyclists. Traffic came to a standstill on Tryon Street, people crowded the windows of tall buildings to peer down at the spectacle, and police officers stood poised and ready for trouble. Yet the Demons ended up contenting themselves with a quiet parade through the city and past *The Observer* building—protesting the damning series in threatening silence but for the defining roar of their collective bikes.

When they departed, the entire day breathed a sigh of relief, and Buck returned to find he'd had a job offer from *The Washington Post*. Gil was openly envious.

"Here I am working my butt off for eight years, and you hit the jackpot with your first story!"

Buck grinned. "Yeah. I guess *The Post* is pretty much the jackpot, isn't it?"

"So?" Gil prodded.

"So what?"

"Are you going to take it?"

"What do you think?" Buck laughed, his expression dimming only when a sad thought crossed his mind. He sure as hell wished Mr. King could have known about this. He sure as hell did.

June 25, 1980

The chirping of birds drifted through the open French doors. Savannah stirred under the sheet, a smile curving her lips as her mind grasped for the interrupted dream and willed it to go on. She was dressed in white, and her father was twirling her across the ballroom floor of the Magnolia Club. He looked down with deep blue eyes only a shade darker than her own, and winked. She winked back. "Happy birthday, Kitten," he said. "Kitten . . ." the familiar voice echoed, now so faint and distant it evaporated in the face of the cheery twitter that wrenched her out of sleep.

She opened her eyes. Morning sunlight beamed through the eastern windows. For a moment, the smile lingered. But then reality closed in, wiping the smile away with a clammy hand that sent its chill through her body. She sat up and looked around the room, remembering. Today marked a month since she heard the news, exactly a month since her perfect world had spun off axis.

An ache started in her chest and made its throbbing way toward her throat. Savannah stemmed it in the odd way that had come to her in the past weeks, forcing it down, burying it in a dark, unreachable depth she'd never known she possessed. With measured movements, she climbed out of bed, dressed, and went downstairs.

The great house was quiet. It was still early, and her mother hadn't stirred—not that she would until near noon. Since the accident, and the shocking revelation of their circumstances, Ophelia King had retreated, by and large, to the haven of her rooms. Savannah had found it necessary to rise to the occasion and take control of things.

Most of the insurance money had gone to pay off the claim against the Crossing. There was nothing that could be done to save *The Watch* or any other of Jim King's holdings. Last week, Savannah had done what she knew she must and let Cletus and his family go. They'd left the Crossing with tearful good-byes. Savannah had remained dry-eyed, watching them drive away through the same peculiar fog that seemed to separate her from everything.

That afternoon Big Ed McKenna had come by to say he'd bought out the "sons-of-bitches" who had foreclosed on *The Watch* and intended to run the newspaper in honor of Jim King. Savannah supposed it was a gallant gesture, but her apathy must have shown.

"What the hell's the matter with you, girl?" the big man had demanded.

She didn't recall her reply, just as she didn't recall a great deal of what had been said to her in the past weeks. When she went out in public for one reason or another, she was vaguely aware of the whispers as she passed. She even detected a lack of the deference with which she'd always been greeted. But all those things failed to penetrate her numbness.

Walking into the deserted kitchen, Savannah found the dinner dishes just as she'd left them the night before—scabbed with congealed orange muck that someone had the audacity to market as a canned food. She'd never learned to cook, had never thought she'd need to cook. Now, as her nostrils flared and her stomach lurched, she wished she'd paid more attention to Loretta's frenzied, last-minute coaching.

She moved to the coffee pot. At least she knew how to do that, and after the smell of the brew filled the kitchen and a few hot sips went down her throat, she felt steady enough to attack the disgusting mess in the sink.

She was just about finished when her mother breezed in.

"Good morning, dear," came the voice from behind her. "Why, what on earth are you doing?"

"What does it look like?" Savannah replied, her gaze still directed at the murky water.

"You stop that this instant! If you persist in putting your hands in dish water, you'll absolutely ruin your skin! Where's Amaryllis? I'll have a word with that girl, and right now!"

Amaryllis?! With uncontrollable feelings of self-pity and exasperation, Savannah whirled.

"What are you—"

Her voice failed. Her mother was standing a mere few feet away, garbed in a silk dressing gown just as Savannah had seen her at midmorning for years, but . . .

"I can't imagine what must have gotten into you, Savannah. Too much time with the servant element, I suspect. Libby Parker . . . Danny Sawyer. I told your father what it would lead to, and I intend to take it up with him as soon as he gets home."

Where all else had failed, an explosive fear shattered the daze that had sheltered Savannah. Her wide eyes, sharp and clear for the first time in weeks, began to fill.

"Mother?" she croaked, the tears spilling over.

Ophelia stepped up and patted a wet cheek. "There, there. It's not as bad as all that. Come along now. We've both got to look our best for the auxiliary tea this afternoon."

Turning in a swirl of champagne silk, Ophelia exited the kitchen. Even after she disappeared, Savannah's blurred vision

continued to register the sight of her mother's hair—no longer
honey blond, but a shocking snow white.

Dr. Crane arrived in slightly more than a half hour, no small
feat considering how far he lived from the Crossing. Savannah
waited downstairs as he lingered in the master chamber. An
hour crawled by. She made a fresh pot of coffee, poured herself
a cup, then let it sit and grow cold on the kitchen counter. It was
past lunchtime when Dr. Crane finally joined her.

"Well?" she said anxiously.

"Well, physically your mother is perfectly healthy. I know
the sight of her hair gave you a start, but it connotes no physical
ailment. On the contrary, it seems to be only a symptom, a sort
of tangible testament to the occurrence of a mental—or maybe
even spiritual—battle."

"Please, Dr. Crane. Can you be more specific? I'm afraid I'm
not up to following a philosophical diatribe at the moment."

Leo withdrew his pipe and tobacco and proceeded to pack the
bowl as he chose his words. "She's escaping, Savannah, hiding
in the past. From what I can tell, your mother has disavowed everything that's happened since before your father died. Something within her is unable to accept it. If I had to pin a name to it,
I'd call it psychogenic amnesia. It could disappear tomorrow,
or . . ."

"Or?"

Leo sighed. "I'm sorry, Savannah. There's no way to tell if
the condition is temporary."

Savannah wrapped her arms about herself and turned away.
Leo lit his pipe and peered at her through the smoke.

"If it persists," he added, "she'll need a nurse."

"I thought you said she was healthy."

"Physically speaking, yes. But until she snaps out of this,
Ophelia should be watched constantly. You must understand
that for her, time has not proceeded beyond a few months ago.
In her eyes, your father and the servants are still here. She ex-
pects to be pampered and looked after just as before—"

"I can do that," Savannah said.

"You?"

She looked over her shoulder. "There's no one else."

"As I said, a nurse—"

"I'll be frank, Dr. Crane. I can't afford a nurse. When I turn
twenty-one, I can access my trust fund—"

"That's nearly a year away."

"That's right. And until then, I'm going to have my hands full simply meeting the lien on the Crossing."

Leo's expression turned dark. "I don't think you realize what you're getting yourself into, Savannah. There's a great deal to be kept up around the Crossing, and unless your mother improves, she won't be a bit of help—in fact, quite the opposite. It's too much for one person, particularly a young girl who ought to be living her own life."

Savannah turned to face him fully. "This *is* my life."

"It doesn't have to be."

She arched a brow. "No?"

"No." Leo took a slow draw off his pipe. "Your father wouldn't have wanted you to undertake such a struggle, Savannah."

She squared her shoulders against the pain that shot through her. "He'd have wanted me to do what's necessary, Dr. Crane. I'm the last of the Kings. There are no relatives to call on, no family to lean on. There's no one but me until Mother gets well."

"And if she doesn't?"

"I'll deal with it."

"There is an alternative, if worse comes to worse."

"And what is that?"

Leo looked beyond her shoulder, unable to meet her eyes as he said, "There are many investors who would fall at your feet to make an offer on the Crossing. Ed McKenna, for one."

Disbelief covered Savannah's face. "What are you saying?"

"I know you don't want to hear this, but you could sell the Crossing, let it go—"

"Never!"

The hiss of the word carried the incongruous ring of a cannon.

The shroud of shock had been ripped away. Now Savannah had nothing to shield her from a glaring reality of grief and fear.

A week passed. Her mother failed to improve; in fact, if any changed occurred, it was the settling of Ophelia King onto a plane of complete fantasy. Savannah waited on her hand-and-foot, preparing meals, excusing nonexistent servants, carrying on conversations that bore no relationship to their plight. When she wasn't needed by her mother, she threw herself into some chore or another: cleaning the house, pruning the rose gardens, even cutting the grass of the extensive Crossing lawns—an undertaking that left her with blistered palms and scratched legs.

Exhaustion became her ally, taking the edge off unspeakably slow-moving days, plunging her into deep sleep at night.

When the Fourth of July arrived, it was afternoon before Savannah recalled it was a special day. Withdrawing the flag from the closet, she hung it on the appointed column of the veranda, thinking that this was the first Independence Day of her life that there hadn't been the traditional barbecue at Kings Crossing.

In late afternoon, Clifford called. He'd been home from the university nearly a month, and Savannah had noted a dramatic drop in his attentiveness. But like most things outside the Crossing, the issue of Clifford's courtship seemed a distant concern.

He asked if he could stop by, and although she tried a graceful refusal, he insisted. Scarcely an hour later, the bell rang, and he stepped inside—impeccably dressed in deck pants, blazer, and ascot. Savannah drew a quick, mortified comparison to the wilted shorts and blouse she'd been wearing since morning. Still, it had been days since she'd seen anyone but her mother or Dr. Crane. Her lifelong sweetheart was a welcome sight.

"Come on in," she invited with a smile. He didn't return it.

"I'll be frank, Savannah," he announced, coming to a short halt in the foyer. "Mother is positively in a swoon."

"Oh? I'm sorry. I didn't know she'd fallen ill."

"She isn't ill!" Clifford barked. In a slightly mollified tone, he added, "It's you, Savannah. You're not yourself. It was bad enough when you dropped out of college a week before you were to graduate. But now we gather you've dropped out of everything. You're turning into a hermit!"

"I have a lot to do these days."

"Like what? Watching over your mother?"

"Among other things—"

"For God's sake!" Clifford exploded. "The talk is that your father killed himself and your mother's gone mad! I mean, really, Savannah!"

Finally the contempt in his voice pierced her consciousness. Suddenly Savannah heard what he was saying . . . what they all must be saying. Something within her crumbled; something hard and cold rose in its place.

"I see," she commented. "How awkward for you."

Completely missing her satire, Clifford breathed an obvious sigh of relief.

"It must have been so embarrassing," she went on, "coming back from Chapel Hill, seeing all the old crowd, everyone still associating you . . . with me."

He smiled, and for the first time Savannah found his attractive face completely disgusting.

"Thank heaven," he said. "I suppose I should have known you'd understand. After all, we cut our teeth on the same codes, the same rules. Reputation is everything, right? But you seem so different, Savannah. I wasn't sure what to expect. I was almost afraid there might be some kind of scene."

"A scene, Clifford? I really don't think you're worth the effort."

He could hardly miss the sarcasm of that. Clifford's face went rosy as he launched into some sputtering, blustering response.

Savannah barely heard. Without another word she pulled the small diamond off her finger and pressed it in his hand. And when she closed the door that night, it was on far more than the back of Clifford Andrews.

Part Two

❁

Those things that are the dearest to us have cost us most.

—Montaigne

Chapter Seven

January 12, 1990

LILAH STROLLED out of the bedroom, the ivory silk folds of her peignoir swirling luxuriously with her gait. Coming up behind Alfred, she pressed a kiss on the thatch of silvery white hair and took her seat across the breakfast table.

"Mornin', gorgeous," he said over the top of *The Atlanta Constitution*.

Lilah proceeded to pour herself a cup of coffee. The pot was of the finest bone china, a graceful piece in the expensive pattern Alfred gave her on the first anniversary of their meeting. Eight years had passed since then, but she still relished the feel of the smooth china in her hand, the cup against her lips.

"You're looking particularly delicious today."

Lilah took a sip, cradled the cup in her palms, and smiled across the table. "You always say that the morning after."

"It's always true," Alfred responded.

He went back to his newspaper as Lilah's gaze roamed the well-known, craggy features. Alfred Castle was more than thirty years her senior, but still attractive in his rugged way. The lines crisscrossing his face spoke more of the time he'd spent on a golf course than of age. Even so, his face had a definite gauntness that hadn't been there before the heart attack—his second, the one that nearly took his life.

The first one, Alfred said, had merely tapped him on the shoulder. The second "hauled off and knocked the shit" out of him. Lilah's fading smile settled in a grim line. There would be no recovering from a third. All the doctors said so.

Sitting there across from him—spring sunshine spilling across the elegant table Maria had set—Lilah found herself thinking back to the first time she set eyes on that weathered face with the bushy brows and twinkling eyes. A self-made businessman who had amassed a fortune in the stock market, Alfred was fifty-four when she met him at a party in downtown Atlanta. He'd made no bones about marching up to her, introducing himself, and virtually claiming her then and there. Lilah resembled a long-lost college love of his, and Alfred was a lonely man with a wife who'd been an invalid for many years.

After just one night in the arms of Lilah Parks, he declared himself bewitched. Later that week, he set her up in the condominium, and shortly thereafter, made her a present of it.

It had caused quite a flurry in Atlanta when the venerable Alfred Castle took a young mistress. But he'd taken the gossip in stride, firmly escorting Lilah into a lifestyle of exclusive clubs, expensive restaurants, and a steady stream of social invitations.

"Gracie's girls," and the nights of parties and dates and nameless men, were long behind. When Ginger married a salesman and moved west six years ago, Lilah's last connection to her former life had been broken. Nowadays, as for the past nine years, Lilah Parks was a lady of leisure—tended by a full-time maid, groomed by the most chic of salons, fawned over by the most outrageously expensive couturiers.

Lilah knew better than to think she was entirely approved of. Alfred Castle was a married man, and Atlanta—the old monied Atlanta of which he was part—looked disparagingly on the flagrant flaunting of good taste. As time went by, however, the old guard seemed to soften. After all, Alfred Castle's wife was a complete invalid attended by round-the-clock nurses, and rumor had it she'd long ago ceased knowing her husband or anyone else. Maybe the man deserved a bit of remuneration.

And so, through the years, Lilah had attained a sort of begrudged status. Everyone knew where she'd come from, but the lasting power of her relationship with Alfred seemed to make an impression. Whatever Lilah Parks had been once, she was now the mistress of a powerful man who adored her. She owned a luxury condominium on one of the most prestigious roads in Atlanta, wore only the finest clothes, was seen in only the best places. Lilah Parks was a woman to be envied . . . and it was all because of Alfred.

Her gaze caressed the top of the silvery white head across the table. The capacity to love, Lilah mused, had deserted her long ago. But if ever she could have harbored the fantasy emotion for any man, it would have been Alfred Castle.

"What are you thinking about?"

Lilah was suddenly aware of his eyes peering at her over the top of the newspaper.

"Oh, nothing." Bringing a brighter look to her face, she added, "Has *The Watch* come yet?"

The bushy brows lowered slightly. "Maria went down to fetch it." He had to pay special shipping charges to have the Carolina newspaper delivered in Atlanta. He didn't mind, of course, but Lilah's attachment to it was a frustrating mystery. She hardly looked at *The Constitution*, but each morning when *The River Watch* arrived, she descended on it with nothing short of voraciousness.

Today proved no different. When Maria arrived with the newspaper, Lilah proceeded to immerse herself.

"Why?" Alfred tried once more. "Why the hell are you so interested in a little paper published on the coast of nowhere?"

She looked up with an expression suggesting mild surprise. "I just like to keep up."

"With Kingsport, North Carolina? What's so special about it, Lilah? Is that where you come from?"

She took on the opaque look Alfred had come to recognize. It meant that the secret part of her had kicked in—the part that both intrigued and frightened him.

"I've told you before—I passed through there once, a very long time ago."

Her answer was delivered with cool finesse, but Alfred knew the signs. The creamy skin paled to alabaster, the eyes grew dark and fixed. It was the way she looked any time the subject of her past arose. Alfred had loved her since he first laid eyes on her nine years ago, and yet he knew nothing more of Lilah Parks than if she'd been born that night at the party.

One thing he did know. There was something within her, something that both burned her alive and froze her to a semblance of death. Despite his best efforts, Alfred had never been able to break through and find out what it was.

A few weeks later, Lilah was reading *The River Watch* with her morning coffee when she suddenly laughed—quite wildly—and darted away from the table and out of the room. Alfred picked up the issue and saw that it was open to the obituaries. Something told him that somewhere on that page lay a link to Lilah's mysterious past. He read the listings carefully, and all he could come up with was a man whose last name bore a similarity to Parks.

"Abel Parker," the item read, "employee of the Ed McKenna household for more than thirty years, died Saturday afternoon of injuries sustained in a freak accident while he attempted to repair his employer's vintage limousine. Reports say Mr. Parker was kneeling before the vehicle when it slipped into gear and plunged forward. Services will be held . . ."

Alfred tossed the paper aside and rose grumpily from the table. There was no reason to think Lilah was connected to the man. Hell, she'd given him no reason to think she was connected to anyone or anything at all, except for her odd preoccupation with a North Carolina newspaper.

In the plush confines of her boudoir, Lilah stared into the mirror—her eyes bright, her mind racing over all the times her self-righteous father had made her feel like a whore long before she became one, all the times he'd predicted a sordid future, the likes of which had become reality.

"Get down on your knees and pray, eh?" she murmured. "Didn't seem to do the trick for you . . . did it, Mr. Parker?"

She felt nothing, certainly no remorse, and was surprised when she saw a tear slide down her cheek.

It was only a month later that Lilah returned from shopping to the sight of an ambulance parked outside the condominium lobby. With a pounding sense of doom, she hurried upstairs to discover the worst. The third attack had struck. The doctor shook his head as he opened the door to the study. Alfred was lying on the couch.

"Now what did you have to go and do this for?" Lilah scolded with a brave attempt at levity. Inside, she felt an acute pain. Joining him on the couch, she lifted up his shoulders and slipped beneath him to cradle his head in her lap.

"This is it," he managed to say with a smile.

Lilah gazed down into the twinkling eyes and knew he was right. Reaching out, she smoothed the hair from his brow.

"You're the only decent man I've ever known," she said.

"Listen to me," Alfred returned rather urgently. "I don't have much time, and I'm worried about you."

"You're worried about *me*?"

"Something drives you, Lilah," he went on raspingly. "Something has consumed your heart until there's no room for anything else. Put it behind you, girl. Put it behind you, or your life won't be worth a plug nickel."

She felt the uncommon sting of tears in her eyes. "I can't, Alfred. Not until I make him pay."

He chuckled, the sound ending in a ragged cough. "So it finally comes out. Revenge, huh? Don't you know by now, girl? You can't win with revenge. With revenge, you're the one who pays. You're the one . . . who . . ."

Alfred's voice drifted off as his head lolled against her breast. Lilah bundled him close and rocked him comfortingly in the room he'd loved so well. But even as she held his lifeless body, she knew she'd never heed his final warning.

If the vengeance that burned within her demanded a price, so be it. One day she'd have Rory McKenna's head.

It was a short familiar drive into Alexandria. Carol parked by the stylish Old Town apartment house overlooking the Potomac and climbed swiftly to the second floor. Letting herself into Buck's flat, she stowed the groceries in the kitchen and shrugged out of her heavy coat.

The February morning was frigid, the chill of a freezing rain having sifted into the silent rooms. Washington winters could be picturesque, but they were also bitter. Carol shivered and moved into the den where she lit the fire Buck had laid on the hearth before he left. He'd been gone two weeks. It seemed longer.

The fire helped. She circulated through the room, opening blinds, turning on lamps, pausing by the bookshelves when her eye was caught by a picture in a silver frame. Picking it up, she went to the window for better light.

It had been taken a year ago in Nicaragua when Buck was assigned to investigate a guerrilla camp. He was wearing fatigues and looked so ruggedly handsome that Carol's pulse quickened. The assignment had proved dangerous, but then that was not uncommon for Buck Sawyer. Since coming to *The Post*, he'd exposed a drug smuggling ring in Florida, a pornography king in California, a gambling syndicate in Kentucky. In the past few years, his assignments had gone international—Nicaragua, Germany, and Japan where he'd nearly been killed before he could escape the reach of a powerful white slavery lord.

That had happened only six months ago, and when Carol found out about it, she'd almost fainted. Nearly killed? She'd talked herself blue in the face, but it hadn't done a bit of good. There was no getting Buck to slow down, to play it a little safer. Right now he was in Panama but was due back tonight.

Carol ran a caressing hand along the frame as she studied his smiling image. The name of Buck Sawyer, she supposed, was known around the world. Those who coveted his success labeled him a "sensation hound" who would take any risk for a headline. Friends knew that Buck simply lived on the edge. The fact that he could make a living by doing so was icing on the cake.

Carol hugged the picture to her breast and closed her eyes. God, but she loved him!

She thought back to the day they met, nearly a year ago. Ted Masters had brought him in. As a section chief in the FBI's records division, Ted was her boss. So when he came to her desk and said there was someone he'd like her to meet, Carol looked up from her computer with an obliging smile. She was unprepared for the jolt that went through her as she met the eyes of Buck Sawyer. Hazel, they were, clear and sparkling between lashes as dark as the brows above them. She must have been staring, for he suddenly broke into a smile, dazzling white against the sun-bronzed hue of his face.

Carol Kincaid was a pretty brunette with big brown eyes, petite, curvy, accustomed to drawing the eyes of men. She was not accustomed to being knocked off her feet by a single smile.

"Hello there," he said in a deep, spine-tingling voice . . . and she was lost. For her, it was love at first sight.

He asked her out to supper for Friday night. In the interim, Carol found out everything she could about him. He'd come to *The Post* from North Carolina, had been in Washington about ten years, and—most importantly—had been seen around town with a variety of women, most noticeably an attractive policewoman from the downtown precinct. It seemed Buck had connections there, as well as at the FBI.

Carol had been ecstatic when, after their first weekend together, Buck promptly narrowed his field of female companionship to her alone. But it took only months to realize that with Buck there was a definite limit. He saw no other women, but neither would he commit to anything more.

Once long ago she'd drawn up her courage and told him point-blank she was in love with him. The memory of his look of distress had restrained her from saying it again. Buck didn't love her, and it made him uncomfortable to think she might want more than he could give. Oh, he cared about her, all right—sometimes Carol thought he cared more for her than any woman he'd ever known. She told herself he was like the wind, that he had to be free to blow wherever circumstances might take him. She told herself to be content with what he could give.

Carol opened her eyes and ceased her daydreaming. Replacing the picture, she returned to the kitchen and set about preparing the hors d'oeuvres. She'd arranged a surprise welcome-home party for Buck, and she hoped he wasn't too worn out to enjoy it after tromping around some damn Panamanian jungle for two weeks.

As it turned out, he was obviously happy with the surprise and gave her a resounding kiss amidst the cheers of the guests. Carol's spirits were high as the night wore on. Buck was getting a little bit loaded, but then he deserved to let down. As he returned from the kitchen with fresh drinks, Carol was watching—she could never get enough of the sight of him—and so observed a brief exchange no one else would probably have noticed.

Buck was moving through the crowd in her direction when suddenly he stopped cold, the smile draining from his face. Setting down a drink on the nearest surface, he reached out and grabbed the arm of a woman with long blond hair. Carol was just close enough to hear the name.

"Savannah?" he demanded, his tone harsh and strangled.

When the woman turned, he released her arm, stepped back a pace and mumbled something Carol assumed to be an apology. By the time Buck arrived with the drinks, his smile was back in place. Through the remainder of the party, Carol did an admirable job of presenting a cheerful front—no small feat, considering she felt as though she'd been hit with a ton of bricks.

When the last of the guests departed, she followed Buck into the bedroom, watching for a moment as he paused before the dresser and stripped off his shirt.

"Who's Savannah?" she said.

The muscles across his back went tense as his gaze leapt to meet hers in the mirror. "What?"

Carol drew a sharp breath. "Come on, Buck. We've been together almost a year now—"

"Carol—"

She quickly held up a palm. "All right, all right. You've been

straight with me all along. You don't want to live together. You
don't want to commit. I have no claim on Buck Sawyer, right?"

He turned, his eyes bleary with more than drink. "You have a
claim," he rumbled.

Carol's lips began to tremble. "Well, then I have the right to
ask. All this time I thought the wall you put up between us had
to do with some—I don't know—some need to be free, to be
able to pick up and follow a story God-knows-where at a moment's notice. But that isn't it, is it?"

He looked genuinely perplexed. But she'd seen the look on
his face as he grabbed the blonde.

"Who's Savannah?" she asked once more. He actually
winced. "Dan?" she prodded, the use of his real name a cue as
to the seriousness of her question.

Grudgingly he sat down on the bed and began to talk.
Through the course of the next half hour, Carol found herself
both spellbound and stricken. Buck Sawyer was a communica-
tor by profession. His words were perhaps spare, but they
painted a portrait so real Carol felt as though she could visualize
each scene of his life—as a boy first arriving at the spectacular
Kings Crossing . . . a teenager, rebellious and helpless against
the staunch snobbishness of an Old South society . . . a young
man, for whom the world tumbled down when he was accused
of an unspeakable crime. And through it all was Savannah
King, the first girl he'd ever loved, the princess he couldn't
have.

He may not have spoken so openly if he hadn't been a little
drunk. Yet Carol had the feeling that somehow Buck was actually relieved to let the story out. As for herself, listening to it
was one of the hardest things she'd ever had to do.

Later that night, he made sweet love to her, so beautiful that
tears streamed down Carol's cheeks. For now she knew Buck
Sawyer would never be hers. Whatever time they had together
would be just that—a limited amount of time, a stop along the
way.

Some men were haunted, and he was one. She couldn't touch
someone who wasn't really there, couldn't capture a heart that
was being held outside her reach. He didn't even seem to realize
what was going on inside himself. Carol saw the truth quite
clearly. The man's heart was only the excruciating age of eighteen, and it lay somewhere on the North Carolina coast, in a
dirtwater town that bore the name King.

* * *

July 27, 1990

"Savannah!"

The imperious voice echoed across the hard wood of the landing. Savannah gave her hair a final brush and took a quick, assessing look at herself. The navy dress was old, of course—she had nothing new—but it looked more like business garb than anything else in her closet.

"Savannah!"

She couldn't prevent a slight grimace. Nonetheless, she stepped into pumps and made quick progress to her mother's rooms.

"What is it, Mother?"

"Ah, there you are," Ophelia said. She was seated at the small serving table by the French doors. Brilliant morning sunshine made its way through the curtains, lighting on her snowy hair. Except for that, it would have been easy to forget she was ill. She looked so lovely in a morning dress of pale rose.

"Dear, would you please tell Loretta that the eggs were a bit runny this morning, and send Amaryllis up for the tray? Oh, and tell Cletus I shall want the car brought round precisely at noon."

Savannah released a heavy breath as she crossed the room. "I'll take the tray, Mother," she said. "Amaryllis is busy."

"Thank you, dear. That's sweet of you."

Savannah paused at the doorway. "I'm going on a brief errand, but I should be back within a half hour. You'll be all right, won't you?"

Ophelia gave her a look of surprise. "Why, of course, dear. Whatever do you mean?"

Savannah merely smiled and withdrew, knowing it was safe enough to leave her for a short while. Ophelia King hardly left her rooms anymore, but for an occasional stroll among the roses.

Stashing the dirty dishes in the sink, Savannah turned and leaned against the counter, summoning her courage as her gaze traveled absently about the kitchen. The ghost of grandeur lingered in the sprawling room, but its trappings were undeniably shabby—the Wedgwood blue curtains faded, the ivory walls dingy, the once-fashionable linoleum with its pattern of wildflowers cracked and curling. Stepping away from the counter, she left the house by the side door and climbed into the old white Cadillac.

It was a quick trip from the Crossing to the McKennas'—too quick, Savannah thought as she drove along, oblivious to the lush coolness of the clear morning. In an hour it would grow unbearably hot once more, as it had been for the whole of July.

She'd rather have walked across burning coals than ask Big Ed McKenna for a job. But there was no help for it. The insurance money was long gone, her trust fund nearly depleted. She cringed as she approached the McKenna mansion. She hadn't darkened the doorway in ten years, and wouldn't now except that meeting Big Ed here seemed the lesser of two evils. She couldn't bear the idea of approaching him at *The Watch* where all those familiar eyes would watch her slink away in failure if he rejected her.

She was dismayed when the butler showed her into the game room and she saw that all three McKenna men were in attendance. They came to their feet as she entered.

"Good morning," she said. Clayton smiled with genuine fondness; the other two responded with what she interpreted as smugness.

"I believe we have an appointment, Mr. McKenna."

Big Ed tipped the Panama in acknowledgment. "Well now, why don't we all have a seat and talk things over?"

A pang of dread shot through Savannah. "All?"

The River Watch was a family operation in name only. Clayton was listed as business manager, but it was a bogus title. Even Rory, as publisher, was a figurehead. Big Ed pulled the strings and everybody knew it.

"I didn't realize that all of you . . ." she said, and to her shame, stumbled to an uncertain halt.

Clayton stepped forward. "It's all r-right, Savannah. If you want to t-talk p-privately with Papa, you have a r-right to."

Savannah smiled her thanks as he passed, then looked pointedly at Rory, who returned her stare with consummate arrogance.

"My brother has nothing to do with anything," he said. "If he wants to leave, fine. But if you're here to ask about a job at *The River Watch*, then I intend to stay."

"I made the appointment with your father," Savannah challenged.

"He's the publisher, after all," Big Ed drawled.

"You're the owner," she retorted.

"That's right." The big man smiled. "And now that we all know who we are and where we stand, why don't you tell us what's on your mind?"

She could press no further. Savannah knew it, and anger bubbled up within her as she forced herself to speak politely.

"I find that I'm going to be forced to seek employment. Considering the experience I've had at *The Watch*, naturally I hoped—"

"Experience?" Big Ed questioned. "I wasn't aware you'd had experience at *The Watch*."

"Not formal experience, perhaps, but I virtually grew up at *The Watch*. I trained with my father—"

"That was long ago, Savannah," Big Ed broke in gently.

The sickly sweet look on his face turned her stomach.

"Are you sure," he went on, "that you're actually up to taking on a job? Think of all the years you've been locked up in that house looking after your mother—very admirable, but has it left you prepared for the business world? Now, if you've gotten yourself in tight straights, I could arrange a loan—"

"I don't want a loan, Mr. McKenna," she said, her voice taut with pride. "I want a job."

"Grace Bowman is retiring," Rory offered casually.

Savannah's brows went up as she turned. "Grace Bowman?" she repeated on an incredulous note. "You mean, the Manners Lady?"

"Who better to take over as the authority on social graces than Miss Savannah King?"

Rory looked infuriatingly amused. Heat flooded Savannah's face.

"I was talking about reporting," she said levelly.

Big Ed rose from the overstuffed leather chair. "Well now, Savannah," he began in that same patronizing tone, "I think you know how fond I am of you and your mother. I'd do anything to help the two of you out, but in this case, I think Rory is right. Start small. There's no need to risk biting off more than you can chew."

Savannah's back went rigid. "I'm not biting off more than I can chew, Mr. McKenna."

He held up a silencing hand. "I'm afraid I'll have to consider our judgment best in this matter, Savannah. Now, if it turns out you can't get by, you come to me for a loan. I'd take the Cross-

ing as collateral any day, regardless of its condition. But for
now I'm leaving you in Rory's hands. Like I said, he's the publisher. He'll take good care of you."

With that, the big man lumbered out of the room. Trembling
with anger, Savannah watched him go and held her tongue. She
could do nothing else.

"He's right," Rory said, his voice low and silky. Savannah
turned and beheld the familiar disgusting leer.

"Just put yourself in my hands, Savannah. You won't be disappointed, I promise you."

Neither time nor marriage had changed Rory one bit. He
could still make her feel dirty just by looking at her.

Deliberately misreading his innuendo, she replied, "Does
that mean you'll consider me for a position other than Grace
Bowman's?"

"I'm afraid it's the only opening we have at the moment."

Savannah looked into Rory's jeering eyes and knew the truth.
Even if there were a better position, Rory wouldn't offer it. He
was enjoying manipulating her far too much. Well, she
wouldn't give him the satisfaction of groveling. She needed a
job, and whatever money he paid her would be more than she
was earning now. And working for *The Watch*—in whatever
capacity—would be better than trying to find some other job
doing . . . what? She couldn't even think of what else she could
do.

"What exactly are you offering?" she asked.

"You pick up when Grace Bowman leaves. A column a
week. Same benefits. Same salary."

"What *is* the salary?"

Rory actually smiled as he told her. Savannah's heart sank,
though she tried not to show it. She'd have to re-think everything. She'd been planning to work full-time and thus be able to
afford a companion for her mother. That was out. The paltry
sum Rory quoted would barely tide them over with expenses
cut to the bone, as they already were.

Rory came to his feet and gave her one of his leisurely
onceovers. "Of course, we did grow up together. I could promise to consider you if something better opens up."

Savannah produced a cold concealing smile. "How generous," she replied, wishing with the height and depth of her
being that she could reach out and knock Rory McKenna clear
into the next room.

"I would definitely be on the lookout for a more lucrative position if we could, shall we say, warm up that old friendship of ours."

"How would you warm up a friendship that never existed?" Savannah retorted.

Rory's eyelids lowered in slow, seductive fashion. "In ways you've never even imagined, *Miss* Savannah."

"And don't want to, I'm sure."

Rory gave her a sharp look from beneath lowered lids. "Friendly employees tend to rise through the ranks a lot faster than snooty little Southern belles. Perhaps when you get desperate, you'll change your tune."

"I'll never be that desperate," Savannah flashed, and turned on her heel.

Just outside the game room on the veranda, Hillary Cochrane McKenna listened to her husband's snide overtures. She'd heard them before. Almost from the first of their marriage, Rory had displayed a roving eye; in the ensuing years, it had turned into blatant lechery. The rare time he came near his wife was when he came to bed—usually long after she was presumably asleep. He had not exercised his husbandly rights in more than three years.

Hillary had found out early in the marriage that she couldn't have children, and for a long time she explained away Rory's behavior with that. But gradually she'd come to know otherwise. Children or not, Rory would have been the same.

Unsatisfied with simply ignoring her, he tormented her—making degrading remarks about her "inhibited sexuality" while flaunting his mistresses in her face. For a while, Hillary had been stunned into hurt, helpless confusion. Somewhere in the back of her mind, a hope had lingered—that the Rory she'd loved since girlhood would return, that this man was a passing stranger. It had taken years for it to sink in—this was the real Rory.

Two years ago, she'd dredged up the courage to ask him for a divorce. He'd laughed in her face.

"You're a good little hostess," he said mockingly. "I like things the way they are."

And then she understood. She was nothing more than a fixture, a social ornament that masked the debauchery of the true Rory McKenna. The thought sparked a brave anger that sent her to her father, but her pleadings had produced only a disappointing stoniness from Ben Cochrane.

"All marriages go through problematic times," he'd said.

"Have you been listening to me, Daddy? My husband despises me, he insults me, he runs around on me. He's seen to it that I have no money of my own. I want a divorce, and I need help!"

He only looked at her sternly.

Hillary's hopes plummeted. "If I can't get out of this, I'll just . . . die."

"Don't be absurd," her father snapped. "People don't die from unhappy marriages."

Her anger lashed out in a burst of dying strength. "Rory told me long ago that he and his father have you in their pocket. Is it true? Is that why you won't help me?"

"That's enough, Hillary!"

On her way out, her mother had hugged her with impotent sympathy. Ben Cochrane was the king of the castle. No one went against him.

Hillary returned to the McKenna house—whipped, beaten, resigned. Since then, she felt she'd lost the last thread of the happy life she once took for granted. She grew used to, and accepting of, Rory's ways. Yet now, as she listened to him try his wiles on Savannah, Hillary's eyes began to sting. Savannah King was part of the past happy life when Rory McKenna had courted Hillary Cochrane with a shower of attentions, making her the envy of most of the girls in Kingsport. Memories were all she had left, and now Rory was spoiling even those.

Hillary brushed away a tear just as the screen door swung open. Clayton walked over. She looked at him with glistening eyes.

"Wh-what is it, Hillary?" he asked.

"You know what it is," she returned through trembling lips.

Their gaze met and locked, a torrent of understanding passing between them. And suddenly Hillary was falling into her brother-in-law's arms.

Only moments later, the door again swung open.

"Well, well, isn't this cozy?" came Rory's sneering voice.

Hillary drew away to see that Rory stood only yards away. Savannah King had paused at the top of the veranda steps and was looking in her direction with an expression of concern.

"Don't the two of you make a pretty picture?" Rory went on.

"I don't know why I didn't think of it before. My wife and my brother. You're a perfect match!"

Clayton stepped forward. "D-don't say that. There's n-nothing going on between m-me and Hillary, and y-you know it!"

Rory snorted. "Do you actually think I would care if there was?" He turned a scathing look on Hillary. "Why don't you move in with him, honey? Maybe he'll be satisfied with your dull attempts at being a woman."

At that, Hillary flicked a mortified glance in Savannah's direction and fled the veranda. Clayton gave his brother an ineffectual look of anger and followed. Left alone with Rory, Savannah allowed the disgust she felt to show on her face. To her annoyance, he'd followed her out of the house. Now, after such a despicable display, he regarded her with calm nonchalance.

"You truly are the lowest form of animal," she said.

He smiled in that smug, superior way of his. "Don't knock it till you've tried it. I'll be waiting . . . *Miss* Savannah."

"Don't hold your breath!" she spat and whirled away, doing her best to ignore the mocking laugh that trailed her to the Cadillac.

Hillary did, in fact, move out of the marital bedroom that very afternoon and settled herself in one of the guest rooms along the hall. As weeks went by, she and Clayton grew close. They had lived in the same house for years, but somehow a special bond had formed that day on the veranda. For years, both of them had suffered pain and humiliation from the same hand. Now that the ice was broken, they became fast friends.

Many was the time they went for a walk about the grounds or simply sat in the gallery and read together. Rory took delight in taunting them about a "clandestine relationship"—together, Hillary and Clayton were able to shrug him off for the most part.

In the winter, Rory and his father went to South America on a hunting expedition. They were gone nearly two months and were absent for both Christmas and New Year's. It was the most peaceful time Hillary had known in years. Something within her seemed to heal. She felt stronger, more confident, and when Rory returned, she found herself meeting his taunts with uncommon rebellion.

One night soon after his return, Rory apparently grew bored

with drinking with his father and sought her out in the gallery. It was a chilly January night, and a cold rain pattered against the panes of the French doors.

"And what are you up to, my prim and proper little wife?"

Hillary rose from her chair by the fire. "I was just going to bed."

"Whose bed?" he accused and tossed down the last of his drink. "My darling brother's?"

Hillary raised her chin. "Why should you care if it is?"

Setting aside his glass, he came to stand before her, glaring down with a murderous look that froze Hillary's blood. It was then that she realized Rory had come looking for a fight. He hadn't needed much to set him off, and she'd provided it.

"You little bitch!" he hissed, and before Hillary knew what he was about, had slapped her fully across the cheek.

She backed away, her hand flying to her face, her eyes rounding with terror as he stalked her.

"Rory," she managed. "Stop!"

But it seemed to have no impact. He continued toward her, a wild look in his pale eyes.

"Stop it!" Hillary tried again. "You're frightening me!"

"Frightening you?" Rory threw back his head and laughed, though the look he turned on her had nothing to do with mirth. "My dear wife, frightening you is the least of what I plan to do."

He lunged for her, and Hillary twisted out of his grasp to scurry toward the nearest set of French doors. Casting a frightened look over her shoulder, she saw him prepare to follow. Swiftly, Hillary drew open the doors and ran for the safety of the dark, wet outdoors.

She was drenched and freezing when she returned the next dawn. Despite the best medical care, her racking cough turned into severe pneumonia. Within two weeks, Hillary Cochrane McKenna was dead.

January 24, 1991

When the news about Alfred Castle's will leaked out, it spread like wildfire. The multimillionaire had left his wife well cared for for the rest of her life, but the bulk of his fortune had gone to his long-time mistress, Lilah Parks.

Lilah had never considered what would happen when Alfred died. She'd known, of course, that he would provide for her, but she'd never imagined to what extent. The Castle empire was, for all practical purposes, hers. Alfred had always said she had a sharp mind with potential she had yet to fulfill; in death, he obviously intended to challenge her.

Lilah surprised herself with her instinctive grasp of the business world. The duties of being a major stockholder in no less than eight disparate companies proved surprisingly light. The investments ran themselves, a team of accountants ran the books, and Lilah Parks simply sat back and accrued the riches of an extremely wealthy woman.

Several months went by before it dawned on her. Now was the time to strike.

Procuring one of the most reputable and expensive private detectives in Atlanta, she sent him down to Kingsport and eagerly awaited the news that Rory had been caught in some despicable act. When, after six months, the detective reported that he could find nothing incriminating on the man, Lilah flew into a rage and fired him. The alternate she hired proved no better, however. Either the McKennas were lily white, or they had the money to whitewash their murky deeds. Lilah subscribed to the latter.

Nearly a year had passed since Alfred's death when she faced the truth. If she wanted dirt on Rory McKenna, she was going to have to dig it up herself. She was going to have to return to Kingsport and get inside his life. The question was how.

The day she read *The Watch* and found Hillary McKenna's death notice, Lilah faced the answer she'd fought against acknowledging. The only way she could get close enough to Rory to deal him damage was by using the weapon he himself had crafted. Moving into the bedroom, she began looking through her closets, rejecting one designer fashion after another as too ostentatious. Finally she withdrew an off-the-shoulder sweater dress of deep plum. Crossing the room to the dresser, she held it up and examined the effect.

"Welcome back, Libby," she murmured to the mirror.

It took a month to settle her affairs for a long absence. It was the end of February when she loaded a modest amount of luggage into the MG convertible she'd selected from Alfred's fleet and turned the car northeast. On the way to Kingsport, she polished up her plan. She had to have a credible story, and she had to be careful. Rory McKenna was shrewd as the devil.

The sun was warm, though the air remained crisp on the afternoon she crossed the Brunswick County line. Fifteen years had passed since she traveled the riverside highway lined with cypress and swamp. The night she'd fled Kingsport in Danny Sawyer's truck came rushing back to her, sharpening her resolve.

Libby slowed the car as she came within a few miles of Kingsport. After all these years, she wanted her meeting with Rory to appear to be by chance, and the most promising location she'd been able to think of was a little motel on the outskirts of town. It had a bar, it was out of the mainstream, and Rory kept the manager well paid to forget his face. It was a place he'd taken her several times all those years ago. She took heart when she went inside and discovered the same sleazy man who had always tended the place.

She hung around the bar for three nights running, dressed in a come-hither fashion, turning away a stream of men who took her for what she was. On the fourth night, she was dressed in the plum off-the-shoulder sweater dress when Rory walked in with a tall, lanky brunette. In spite of herself, Libby caught her breath at the sight of him. He'd hardly changed. Oh, he was a full-fledged man in his thirties now, but . . . he hadn't changed.

Libby ordered a whiskey, watching in the mirror as Rory helped the woman out of a long, black leather coat, then pulled his chair to hers so he could sling an arm around her. The brunette giggled as his hand reached down to fondle a breast. It was obvious that they were lovers. Tossing down the contents of the shot glass, Libby slid off the barstool and strolled over to their table.

"Hello, Rory," she said.

He looked up, his gaze racing over her figure before finding her face. "Do we know each other?"

Libby brought a smile to her lips and slipped into the act. "Intimately," she said.

Rory studied her face. Libby broadened her sparkling smile.

"Libby Parker?" he then said on a disbelieving note. "What the hell are you doing here?"

She rolled a bare shoulder. "I took a room a few days back. Just got into town."

"Damnation, girl," Rory muttered, his gaze drawn along the hourglass shape shown off by the clinging dress. "You've turned into a woman."

"You had something to do with that as I recall," she said, her leading remark drawing a glare from Rory's brunette companion.

"I'm Jane Wilson," she snapped. "You're an old friend of Rory's, I presume?"

"Friend is one way of putting it," Libby returned, hardly glancing at the woman as her eyes played games with Rory. "In fact, I was hoping to ask him for a little favor."

One of Rory's brows went up, but he said nothing.

"Favor?" Jane repeated sharply. "What kind of favor?"

"I'd like to talk to him in private if you don't mind."

Jane didn't like the way the redhead was looking at Rory, and she definitely didn't like the way he was looking at her. "Fat chance of that," she snorted. "You've got nerve, waltzing over here and thinking you can run me away from my own table."

"What's the matter, honey?" Libby asked smoothly. "Do I threaten you that much?"

Jane shot to her feet at that, her glare flashing from Rory to the redhead and back again. "I think I'll retire to the ladies room while you say good-bye to your friend!"

"Take your time," Libby returned.

As Jane huffed away, Rory folded his arms across his chest. "Why, Libby, I believe you've grown catty."

She rolled her weight to one leg, throwing her hips into voluptuous relief. "Among other things."

"Where have you been all this time?"

"Oh, just around," she answered, running a painted nail across the tabletop as she stepped closer.

Her provocative walk and air weren't lost on Rory. Little Libby Parker had turned pro.

"Why have you come back?" he asked casually. "As I remember, you were in a damn big hurry to get out of Kingsport some years back."

She shrugged. "Let's just say I found it advisable to pursue a change of address. You see, a certain—uh—businessman I used to work for became a little annoyed when I refused to work for him any longer."

"Cut the shit, Libby. You're a hooker, and you're trying to run out on your pimp." If his remark ruffled her at all, Rory didn't see it.

"A very high-classed hooker," she returned serenely. "And a very wealthy pimp. Carlos won't come after me himself. He'll send one of 'the boys,' and the first places he'll check are the motels. He'd never think of looking for me in The Cloisters."

The light of understanding dawned in Rory's eyes. "I see. You want a place to stay. But why should I take you in at the house? What's in it for me?"

Libby gritted her teeth and leaned down so his eyes were level with her impressive cleavage. "Your wildest dreams come true, big boy," she murmured.

It was amazing how easy it was to become the character she'd left behind ten years ago—smiling, luring, seducing, and all the while feeling nothing but a detached sense of contempt. Of course, with Rory it was different. With him, Libby had to mask a seething hatred that would prove her undoing if she couldn't control it.

"I'm not a little girl anymore, Rory," she went on, her gaze dropping to the juncture between his legs, then caressing its way up to his face. "I'm willing to bet that after one night with me, you won't even remember that brunette's name."

Rory's blood heated as he surveyed the ample curves before him. "I'll think about it," he said.

"Don't think too long. Unless I'm able to . . . improve my lodgings, I'll be moving on at the end of the week."

Rory's brows furled. "Are you actually trying to manipulate me?"

Libby reached out, took his hand, and filled it with one of her breasts. "Honey," she purred. "I'm trying to please you."

When two days passed and she heard nothing, Libby began to think she'd been mistaken about the hot look that came over Rory as he squeezed her breast. Her mind started exploring ploys to yield a second "chance" encounter, but then finally on Friday afternoon the phone rang. She was both relieved and repelled by the sound of his voice.

"I've cleared the decks," he said. "Get your tail over here."

Late afternoon sunlight dappled Cloister Drive, yet Libby felt a chill as she brought the MG to a stop before the ostentatious house—the home of her youth and her most vivid nightmares.

The plan had worked, though of course she had to pay the piper—first, with the looks of shock she received from the other men of the house, Big Ed's settling into a leer, Clayton's into something that looked like sadness. After all, Hillary was hardly cold in the grave, and here comes Libby Parker after all these years, like a bitch in heat ready to warm Rory's bed.

The image was a bitter pill, though it came nowhere near to matching the feeling of vileness that assaulted her that night. Rory mounted her like a wild animal. She came away from the ordeal with a bloodied lip, revived memories of his barbarous nature, and a steely commitment to endure whatever was necessary.

Saturday morning she rose late and took her time dressing. When she went downstairs, she heard male voices in the game room. Quickly passing, she found the dining room deserted, though the morning coffee service had yet to be cleared. Libby poured a cup, then noticed a copy of *The River Watch* on the sideboard. Settling at the great table with the newspaper, she took a sip of lukewarm coffee, turned to the local section, and nearly choked.

Early the previous morning, Jane Wilson had been found outside her beachfront cottage . . . *murdered*.

Libby was still in the dining room when the police arrived. Everyone in the household gravitated to the foyer as two officers stepped inside, and one of them proceeded to ask Rory about his association with the slain woman.

"Get on back to work, everybody," Big Ed ordered in a tone that sent the servants scurrying.

Libby retreated up the stairs, her mind seizing on the notion of Rory and Jane Wilson. Was that it, then? Cold-blooded murder? Was that the dirt she'd come to find on Rory McKenna?

She remembered the terror-stricken days when she'd linked him to Roberta Sikes. Now Jane Wilson. *Who's next?* she thought as she entered her bedroom, and had the creepy feeling that the stakes of her game had just gone higher.

Big Ed led the way into the sanctum of the game room, then turned with a beneficent smile. "Now then, officers. What's this all about?"

Lieutenant Steve Gilroy stepped forward and cleared his throat, fighting the inclination to be intimidated by the three men before him—Big Ed, Rory, and the other dark-haired son whose name Steve couldn't recall. He himself was new to Kingsport, and the McKennas were among the most powerful men in the city. He didn't relish stepping on their toes. At the same time, this was his first homicide. He had to do things right.

"You did know this woman, didn't you, Mr. McKenna?"

He held out a picture. Rory glanced down, and without missing a beat, replied, "Yes. I knew Jane Wilson. But I assume you were already aware of that or you wouldn't be here."

Big Ed and Clayton looked at the police photo of the dead woman, and in the rarest of occurrences, their eyes turned to each other, locked, and held—each of them thinking the same thing, each of them stunned by the inevitable conclusion that glared from the black-and-white picture. Neither said a word as Rory went on answering the detective's questions.

"Yes. I saw her Thursday night . . . I left about nine o'clock . . . No, I don't know if anyone saw me leave . . ."

Big Ed came abruptly alert. "Now wait just a minute!" he boomed.

In spite of himself, Gilroy jumped.

"You're not implying that my boy had anything to do with that woman getting killed."

"Just trying to get the facts. We have to interview everyone she saw that night. So far, it appears that Mr. McKenna, here, was the last person to see Jane Wilson alive."

"Damn, if that's so!" Big Ed retorted. "The *killer* was the last to see her alive!"

Gilroy reddened. "Well, of course—"

"And if you boys want to ask my boy any more of those fool questions, you'll just have to get yourself a court order. And knowing the commissioner as closely as I do, I'd be willing to bet he wouldn't be too happy about such a course of events."

Gilroy maintained as much dignity as he could. Closing his notepad, he stuffed it in his pocket and met the taller man's angry gaze. "Just trying to do my job, Mr. McKenna."

"Do it someplace else," came the reply.

"Come on, Sergeant," Gilroy said and, as he crossed the game room, indulged himself an obvious study of the trophies lining the walls. He turned at the doorway.

"Nice collection," he commented. "Who's the hunter?"

"They b-both are," Clayton volunteered.

"Shut your mouth," Big Ed growled, then, raising his voice to an authoritative level, added, "Good day, Lieutenant."

The three McKennas were silent as the officers withdrew.

"I always knew you were a k-killer," Clayton accused under his breath, but drew nothing more than an arched look from his brother.

Big Ed waited until he heard the starting of the car engine outside, then whirled on Clayton. "I thought I told you to shut your mouth. You're not to speak a word of this, boy—not a word! Do I make myself clear?"

His tone had risen steadily as he spoke. The word "clear" resounded in the paneled room. Clayton raised his chin in uncommon belligerence.

"Whether I s-speak of it or n-not, we all know what we s-saw."

"Get out of here!" Ed roared. "And close the doors behind you!"

With a final look of scorn for Rory, Clayton did as he was told. A soft click announced the closing of the game room doors. Ed peered into the ice-blue eyes that were a mirror of his own.

"All right, Rory. Let's have it."

"Have what?"

"You know damn well what! That picture . . . that woman . . . she looked exactly like your mother. So did the Sikes girl. So did that whore in Georgia."

Rory shrugged. "So?"

"So what the hell are you up to, boy?" came the thundering demand.

Clayton sagged against the doorjamb, drinking in the sound of his father's anger, grinning into the deserted hall.

April 1, 1991

Savannah parked in front of *The Watch* and darted inside. She was dressed in the faded jeans and T-shirt she'd donned quickly that morning and didn't venture up to Editorial. Leaving the weekly "Manners Lady" column with the lobby receptionist, she hurried back to the Cadillac.

As usual, she didn't enjoy being in town, though she stubbornly kept the convertible top down. Kingsport might gossip about her, might point her out as she drove by, but she'd be damned if she'd let them intimidate her into missing such a sunny afternoon.

On a final errand, she slowed the car on Providence Street and pulled up to Mr. Gibbons' store. Providence Sundries had everything anyone could possibly ever need, and she'd

switched around the light bulbs in the house until she now had
only six that burned.

She'd paid for the light bulbs and stepped out onto the shaded
storefront when someone called her name. Spinning, Savannah
looked along the porch, directly into the sunlight. Against it, she
beheld a female form but could see nothing more than a silhou-
ette. The woman approached.

"Hello, Savannah," she said. "My, but you've hardly
changed."

Shading her eyes, Savannah strained to see the face. When
she realized who she was looking at, she broke into a wide
smile.

"Libby?" she chortled. "Libby Parker?"

Libby regarded the tall blonde before her. "I've thought of
you over the years," she said. "But I never imagined you in
jeans."

Savannah glanced down herself then gave Libby a swift, assessing onceover. The impulse to step up and hug her long-lost
friend disappeared as Savannah saw how like a stranger she
was. Libby's hair was short and curly, and the most garish shade
of red. Her eyes appeared black as soot amidst heavy liner and
mascara. She was wearing a pink sweater with a matching skirt
that was indecently short, as well as a tall pair of heels that
brought her close to Savannah's own height.

"My word, Libby," she said. "You look so different."

Libby stiffened. "I'm not surprised."

"Where have you been? What have you been doing?"

Libby found her wide-eyed question immensely annoying.
"Does it matter?" she returned sharply.

Savannah blinked at that, momentarily taken aback, confused
at Libby's hostile manner. "When did you get back?" she asked.

"A month ago."

"Where are you staying?"

"The McKenna house."

"Whatever are you doing there?"

Libby's eyelids dropped guardedly. "The usual."

The implication went over Savannah's head.

"You've been back a month?" she said with an abrupt feeling
of hurt. "Why didn't you call me?"

Libby arched a brow. "Should I have? Gee, it seems to me I
tried calling you before, and it didn't do me a damn bit of
good."

Savannah peered at her. If she didn't know better, she'd swear Libby's hard expression spoke of hatred.

"What are you talking about, Libby?" she asked with a frown. "The last I heard from you, you were going to let me know when you got settled. That was fifteen years ago."

"The last you heard?" Libby blazed. "God, you've got a poor memory. As I remember it, I called you from Georgia, at the direst crossroads of my life, and you couldn't take the time to come to the phone! In fact, I heard you laughing in the background."

Savannah stared into the dark, flashing eyes, completely nonplussed. "I don't know what you're talking about."

"Don't you?!" Libby raged as the image turned crystal clear—herself, alone and scared, submitting her body to the knife of a butcher. "You always had an incredible knack for ignoring what was happening around you, Savannah. As if you lived in a bubble." Libby's face turned to granite. "I guess you still do."

"I don't understand! What call? What crossroads?"

Libby looked into the wide blue eyes and felt a momentary weakness. It passed almost as soon as it came.

"It doesn't matter, Savannah," she said coldly. "But if you've a mind to refresh your memory, why don't you ask your mother?"

Tilting her nose to the sky, Libby strode away, climbed into her car, and roared along Providence Street. After a moment of stunned immobility, Savannah did the same.

"Mother!" she cried as she bounded up the stairs. "Mother!" she bellowed again and burst into the master quarters.

Ophelia King looked up from her embroidery with surprise. "What on earth, Savannah?"

"Mother, I need to ask you something. You remember Libby Parker. Did she call here . . . from Georgia?"

Ophelia's lashes fluttered as she looked away. "Libby Parker," she repeated thoughtfully. When she returned her gaze to Savannah, the look in her eyes was sharp. "Libby Parker, that little hussy. I don't want you have anything to do with her, do you hear?"

Savannah's cheeks caught fire. "Did she call here, Mother?"

Ophelia tossed her head. "What if she did?"

"Mother!" Tears of frustration welled to Savannah's eyes. "What did she want? Was she in trouble?"

"How should I know?" Ophelia sniffed. "The girl is from the lower classes, Savannah. You should know by now that you have a position in society, a reputation to uphold. As your Grandmother Benton always said, a lady is known by the company she keeps—"

Savannah whirled out of the room and slammed the door. Almost instantaneously, she heard the humming from within that meant her mother was off on another daydream.

Savannah thought back to the years when she and Libby had been like sisters. *What had happened?* Something terrible . . . she'd known something was terribly wrong even before Libby disappeared.

So much time had passed, so much heart-breaking time. It had been so long since she'd had a friend, so long since she'd talked or laughed with anyone her own age. Now Libby was back, living just on the other side of the pines. But from the confusing sound of things, she might as well be on the other side of the world.

Savannah slumped against the wall in sudden, weary loneliness.

July 20, 1991

It was a warm summer night. Buck had the top off the jeep as he drove toward the downtown precinct house. Wind raced through his hair, the radio blared, and his spirits were high. He'd just returned from a successful trip to Colombia and was on his way to celebrate by hitting the bars with Bobby Woodall.

Carol wasn't wild about the way he intended to spend his Friday night—"getting drunk in Georgetown with that red-headed hellion!" Buck grinned as he remembered her outburst. Though reserved and strictly-by-the-numbers at the station, Bobby was in fact a kind of wildman when he was off duty. But he was Buck's oldest friend in Washington, and hardly a month went by that they didn't get together some time or another.

The two of them went back a long way—back to the early days at *The Post*, when one of Buck's first assignments had taken him undercover as a mugger. Police cooperation had been a must, and Bobby Woodall had been his phone man.

Bobby had proven invaluable. Born and raised in D.C., he knew everything about everyone in the District, and most everything about everyone else. Nothing major went on, either

criminally or politically, that he wasn't aware of, and it was ru-
mored that high-ranking officials made it regular policy to stay
in close touch with Bobby Woodall. He was a slick operator
with an incredible network, more like a businessman than a cop.
Buck had long thought of him as a broker—only instead of
stocks and bonds, his commodity was information.

Leaving the jeep in a reserved space out front, Buck went
into the station, pausing occasionally to shake hands with acquaintances on his way to Bobby's office. Tapping lightly at the
open door, he stepped inside and found Bobby studying a wall
map of the city.

"Hey, man," Bobby greeted, stepping over with a quick smile
and ready handshake. "How's it going? How was Colombia?"

"Hot." Buck grinned.

"Is it ever any other way?" Bobby continued to smile as he
stepped to his desk, which was covered with piles of reports,
files, and wire service photos. "I just want to put a couple of
these things away before we go. Prying eyes, you know."

Buck meandered toward the desk, eyeing its clutter. "How
the hell do you keep track of anything?"

"Hey, there's a divine order at work here!"

"If you say so." Shaking his head, Buck glanced at a group of
wire photos at the edge of the desk. His eyes started to move on,
then raced back to lock on the grainy photograph atop the pile.
Reaching down, he picked the thing up and stared in disbelief.

"Who's this?" he mumbled.

Bobby glanced over his shoulder, then moved to a file cabinet. "Local girl. Jane Wilson."

"When did it happen?"

"A few months back. It took a while for the photo to make it
up here. She moved away a couple of years ago. She was killed
on the North Carolina coast."

"Where—" Buck began in a croaking voice, then cleared his
throat and tried again. "*Where* on the North Carolina coast?"

"A rich little city near the South Carolina line. Kingsport."

A sudden throbbing hammered at his forehead. Closing his
eyes, Buck pressed his fingers to the juncture of his brows. God
in heaven! Letting the memory out of its dark cell, he remembered that day in the Kingsport station so long ago. Someone
had produced the police photo, and when he looked at it, he'd
nearly gotten sick. Forcing his eyes open, Buck stared again at
the picture in his hand. Fifteen years had passed since he'd seen

the likeness of that image—the bent-kneed pose, the scarf trailing from the neck. The inference was clear. Whoever killed Roberta Sikes had killed again.

"What is it?"

Buck looked up to find Bobby looking at him curiously. "This is important," Buck replied, slapping the photo in his palm. "*Very* important. I need a copy of this, Bobby."

"Hey, you know the rules—"

"I know, I know. I need you to bend the rules this time."

Bobby's gaze darted between the intent eyes. "It's really that important?"

"Yes. It really is."

"There's a copy machine in the corner over there," Bobby said eventually and headed toward the door. "I didn't see a thing," he added on his way out. "I didn't even know you were here."

July 27, 1991

Buck's editor was furious about granting a leave of absence, but he could hardly refuse when his only alternative was to accept a letter of resignation. Grudgingly, he even signed the letter of recommendation Buck drew up to send down to *The Watch*. Addressing it simply to Editor/Publisher, he kept the thing brief. He was on sabbatical from *The Post*. He'd become interested in a story on the North Carolina coast. Would *The River Watch* be interested in hiring a contributing reporter?

The reply must have burned its way through the mail. Within a week, Buck had received a contract and generous advance, as well as a glowing letter from Rory McKenna, Publisher.

Buck had to read the name twice to be sure his eyes weren't playing tricks. But, no . . . there it was at the bottom of the letter, and once again on the exorbitant check.

Buck hadn't kept up with *The Watch* since Mr. King's death, although he knew well enough that Big Ed McKenna had taken over all those years ago. What he hadn't expected was that Rory had become involved in the newspaper—and was now chaffing at the bit to hire on what he thought to be a hot-shot reporter.

It gave Buck perverse pleasure to sign the contract. Affixing his signature with a flourish, he detached a copy, held it up before him, and laughed aloud. He could only imagine the look on

Rory McKenna's face when he discovered that Buck and Danny Sawyer were one and the same.

The thought of leaving Carol was unpleasant; the thought of telling her his plans, even more so. She wasn't going to like it, and so Buck put off telling her until he'd made all the necessary arrangements. Finally, however, everything was set—including the subletting of his flat to a friend of Bobby's. He had no further excuse. He was leaving for Kingsport in two days.

Picking up dinner from their favorite French restaurant, he set a candlelit table and put champagne on ice. When Carol arrived, she smiled and looked so happy that he felt a pang of guilt.

"What's this all about?" she asked.

"I thought we both deserved it," he replied evasively.

When dinner was over, they stepped out on the balcony and looked out over the Potomac. In the distance, the Lincoln Memorial glowed white against the summer darkness.

Buck turned and ran a light palm along her bare arm. "I have something to tell you, Carol."

She looked over with a faint smile. "What?" she asked, the smile fading as she saw the look on his face.

"Something unbelievable has happened."

"What?" she repeated.

"I saw a police photo a couple of weeks ago. The woman was dead . . . murdered. She had a scarf around her neck."

Carol searched his eyes, failing to understand the sudden bleakness that clouded them. "I don't know what you're—"

"It happened in Kingsport, Carol. And the dead woman looked just like Roberta Sikes. Don't you see what this means? The killer is *there*, the same killer who went free all those years ago while I caught *his* hell! He's there, Carol. And I mean to find him."

A breeze skirted by, lifting her hair as her blood went cold. "You're going back."

"I have to."

"You're going back," she said again, this time in a mere whisper.

Buck reached out to put an arm around her. She pulled away.

"I can't turn my back on this, Carol. You shouldn't expect me to. I could no more resist tracking this thing down than I could resist breathing or eating or . . ."

"Or Savannah King?" she supplied.

He was clearly startled, just like the last time she'd spoken the name.

"What are you talking about?" he grumbled.

"It's true, isn't it? You were never able to resist her. You told me so yourself."

"Yes, when I was a boy!" His gaze flew over Carol's pretty, dark-eyed face. "That was years ago, a lifetime ago."

"She still has a hold on you, Buck."

"For God's sake, Carol! Don't be ridiculous. Even if what you claim were true, it wouldn't matter. By now, Miss Savannah is long married to Clifford Andrews and probably has a brood of little Andrews hanging on her skirts."

"No, she doesn't."

"What?"

"She doesn't have children. She never married. She still lives at your damnable Kings Crossing."

Buck's astonishment was obvious. "How the hell do you know?"

"It's all a matter of public record, Buck. For heaven's sake, I work in research. All I had to do was check, so . . . I did."

"When?"

"The day after you told me about her. More than a year ago."

By now, his face had taken on an added color she could detect even in the darkness.

"Let's get something straight, Carol. Whatever Savannah King's marital status, it has nothing to do with me. I'm going down there to clear my name. Period. There's no other reason I'd ever set foot in Kingsport again."

Carol's eyes were brilliant, shining, two steel shafts pinning him like a butterfly to a pad.

"Is that what you think, Buck?"

The question sounded deceptively simple. Behind it, he knew, was an unspoken accusation. A rebellious anger rose within him.

"I'm going, Carol," he said in a hard voice. "I can't do anything about your delusions as to why. I wish I could."

"And I wish I were the one with the delusions."

Buck peered at her a moment, then turned on his heel and went inside. Carol placed a hand on her churning stomach and pulled herself together. When she went in, she found him by the table. As she approached, he tossed down a gulp of champagne.

"I was intending to ask your help in this thing," he said without looking at her. "I suppose that's out of the question."

"What kind of help?"

"Run the MO through your computer. See if it spits out any other similar killings." As he voiced the last, Buck chanced a look in her direction.

"You know I'll help you," she said quietly. "I'll run the damn thing any way you want me to."

He stepped over, took hold of her upper arms and gazed down with warm eyes. "Then you *do* understand."

With a sinking feeling, Carol devoured the lines of the handsome face above her. "What I understand is that you're dead set on doing this. It wouldn't make any difference if I asked you not to, would it?"

He said nothing, though his features went tense all over again.

"I'll always treasure the time we've had together, Buck."

He gave her a little shake. "You talk as if I'm never coming back. A few months, Carol. If I'm lucky, maybe all I'll need is a few weeks. I'll call you as soon as I get settled. I promise."

Carol's gaze locked with his, and the familiar thrill pounded through her, although this time it was laced with dread. No man had ever affected her the way Buck Sawyer did. No man ever would.

"Whatever you say," she whispered. Lifting her mouth to his, Carol closed her eyes before he could see the tears within them.

Chapter Eight

It was after four o'clock on a sizzling-hot August afternoon. There was little traffic on Providence Street. Buck shifted down to second gear, keeping the jeep at a crawl as he took in the familiar sights with nostalgic thoroughness.

It was amazing how little Kingsport had changed. The historic buildings were just as stately, the lawns and gardens just as elegant. To the right, the palms stood like sentries along the boulevard. To the left, the median flowered with purple oleander, its sweet scent perfuming the seaside air.

Just ahead was Providence Sundries. Buck peered as he passed, confirming that the shaded storefront was still the downtown gathering place—with old-timers see-sawing back and forth in rockers at one end of the porch, while a group of teens lolled about a Coke machine at the other. Buck grinned as he recalled how many Cokes he himself had purloined from that machine. If it was the same one, there was a certain place on the side that you could bang, just once, and the machine would surrender a free drink. All the kids had known about it.

Casting a final glance in the rearview mirror, he looked ahead to the square at the heart of the city. The sun lit up the whitewashed buildings, and in their center the commons was a green island of grass and shade trees, distinguished every so often by a granite monument surrounded by flowers. It occurred to Buck, as he drove past, that he could name each and every one of those monuments.

Everything about Kingsport was so sensationally familiar. It was almost as if fifteen years had never passed. The eerie feeling intensified as he spotted the iron fence heralding *The Watch*.

The landmark dominated the corner of Providence and Clancy, the original face of the building overlooking the commons, the modern wing facing east. Nosing the jeep into a space at the side, Buck killed the motor and sat for a minute, just looking. It was as impressive as ever, regal in a way that only time could bestow. He'd been with two much larger newspapers in his career; now he realized that neither of them had ever quite measured up to his memories of *The Watch*. It was all mixed up with the hopes and dreams of his boyhood—part of him as no other paper could ever be.

His gaze passed the spear-tipped fence, touched on the statue of Josiah King, rose to the balcony on the fifth floor. He could almost see Mr. King standing there. In fact, he recalled a Fourth of July when he'd watched all three of them up there together, Mr. and Mrs. King, and . . . Savannah. Her image flashed to mind and lingered, as it had been prone to do ever since he drove into town. Irritated with the sudden dryness in his throat, Buck smoothed his hair with a careless hand and slid out of the jeep.

He was a day early, and it was late in the afternoon. There was really no reason to press seeing McKenna today—no reason except the tingling sense of expectancy that had propelled Buck along the highway like a rocket. Taking the steps two at a time, he pushed through the glass doors and strode into *The Watch*.

The ground floor interior was as he remembered—cool and hushed, except for the clicking sound of his footsteps as he crossed the tile floor. Stopping at the lobby desk, he identified himself and asked the receptionist to announce his arrival to Rory McKenna. The receptionist—a pretty, young brunette who reminded him of Carol—made the call, then looked up with a bright smile.

"Go right up, Mr. Sawyer," she said. "Mr. McKenna's office is on the fifth—"

"Thanks," he broke in. "I know where it is."

It was nearly five o'clock as he turned into the corridor leading to the office of the publisher. A good many of the employees in surrounding cubicles were packing up to go home, calling good night to friends, spilling into the hallway. The bustle failed to penetrate the sense of déjà vu that isolated Buck. The last time he'd walked this hall it was as a copy boy, and the man in the office ahead had been Jim King. Shaking off the solemn bent of his thoughts, he stepped up and knocked firmly on the door.

A hearty "come in!" resounded from within. Pushing through the door, Buck discovered not just Rory, but Big Ed as well. The latter sat in Mr. King's chair. Rory was on his way across the room, hand extended. Fair and tailored in a light summer suit, he looked as Buck might have imagined him . . . if he'd ever bothered.

It had seemed like a great joke back in D.C.—getting himself hired, at an extravagant cost, by the one man in his life who could be considered an arch rival. Now, however, the satisfaction of putting one over on Rory McKenna dimmed beside the hostility that flared to the surface. Buck met his handshake and looked him eye-to-eye.

"Hello, McKenna."

Rory's face froze in a half-formed smile. Yanking his hand away, he stepped back.

"*You!*" he expelled in a rush of breath. "*You're* Buck Sawyer?"

"That's right."

Searching beyond Rory's shoulder, Buck saw that Big Ed looked much the same in his white planter's suit and Panama hat. The years showed in his heavy jowls, and there was an unhealthy redness to his face. Other than that, the big man had changed little. Neither had the bitter regard in which Buck held him. The mere sight of him triggered memories of Clancytown and a long-dead father who'd been broken by Big Ed McKenna's mills.

"Afternoon, Mr. McKenna," Buck said with a crisp edge in his voice.

"What the hell are you trying to pull?" Rory demanded.

Buck looked aside. "Pull? Nothing. I just hit town. Thought I'd drop by and see what time you want me to report in the morning."

Rory adjusted his cuffs with cool disdain. "I don't want you to report at all, you bastard."

"I knew you were going to be glad to see me," Buck returned, "but please don't overwhelm me."

"Very clever. Unfortunately, your cleverness changes nothing."

Buck arched a brow. "I work here," he said. "As of tomorrow."

"You think so?"

"Yes. I do."

Rory chuckled. "You always were dense when it came to knowing your place. So you're Buck Sawyer these days. Fine. That name might carry some weight up in D.C., but you're in my town now."

It was Buck's turn to laugh. "Come on, McKenna. You sound like a gunslinger. What are you going to say next? The town ain't big enough for the both of us?"

His mockery hit its mark. McKenna's face turned to stone.

"If I'd had any inkling you were Danny Sawyer," he gritted from between clenched teeth, "I never would have hired you."

"Nevertheless, you did."

"Well, I'm *un*-hiring you!"

The words exploded from his mouth as Rory McKenna's icy mask shattered, his face turning a telltale red, his hands knotting into fists. Buck knew this side of him, remembered it from long ago. Keeping his tone, Buck countered with a look that was paradoxically menacing.

"I have a contract, McKenna, plain and simple. We've both signed it, and the check's been cashed. I don't think a judge would smile on your firing me for no other reason than . . . what? Past personal differences?"

Rory glared at him, speechless, in obvious hatred. Buck smiled in taunting contempt. Silent seconds ticked by, the tension mounting. And then a barreling laugh filled the room. Slowly, like a lumbering giant, Big Ed rose to his feet and joined them, his eyes on Buck.

"Danny Sawyer," he muttered, "come to challenge the lion in his own den, eh?"

"Challenge, *hell*!" Rory muttered, his eyes blazing. "I intend to have the company attorney here first thing in the morning."

"Hold on a minute," Big Ed cautioned. "The boy does have a point. You hired him, whatever his name is."

"Under false pretenses!"

Big Ed shot a sidelong glance at his son. "Don't be a fool, Rory. Buck Sawyer has all the credentials he needs to work for ten newspapers like this one. You paid for him. Use him. Who knows? Maybe he'll improve circulation even more than we thought. Give him a chance to prove what he's made of."

"I already know what he's made of," Rory sneered.

"Tsk, tsk," Buck parried with elaborate denunciation.

Once again, Big Ed laughed. "You two boys always did go at each other like a couple of pole cats! I see nothing's changed."

"Some things have changed," Buck responded levelly. "I'm not a boy anymore, Mr. McKenna, and some issues I take dead serious. Like a contract, for instance."

Big Ed's eyes narrowed beneath the brim of the Panama. "Welcome aboard, then," he said, "if you're sure that's what you want."

"Papa! I am not—"

"Shut up, Rory!"

Big Ed tossed the command with the barest of glances, his attention remaining on Buck. "You seem to think you've won something here, and maybe you have. But then again, the prize might turn out to be different from what you expect."

"I don't know what you're talking about," Buck stated.

Tipping back his Panama, Big Ed adopted a friendly expression Buck trusted about as much as he could fly.

"From what I understand, you've been a great many places since you left here and enjoyed a great many successes . . . as Buck Sawyer. But Washington, D.C., ain't Kingsport, boy. Folks around here and in Clancytown have long memories. The Sikes packed up and left some years back, but there are still lots of folks around here who remember Danny Sawyer—folks who might not be particularly welcoming if he showed up after all these years."

Buck stiffened. "I can handle anything anyone cares to dish out," he said in a low voice, his eyes flickering to Rory.

"We'll see," Big Ed pronounced with a smile. "We'll just see."

The man's remark rang in his ears as Buck stalked out of *The Watch*. Slamming into the jeep, he screeched out of the parking space and headed aimlessly toward the shore.

A lot of years had passed since he left Kingsport, years in which he'd grown into a successful, respected man. As he'd considered his prodigal return in faraway Washington, he'd felt strong and confident, even cocky. Now he saw his folly. For years he'd pretended the past didn't matter anymore. Big Ed had shown him how wrong he was in one fell stroke. His insinuation had struck like lightning—piercing the armor of Buck Sawyer with remarkable ease, setting fire to the smoldering anger and humiliation of the boy within.

Was Big Ed right? Did Kingsport still regard him as a murderer who deserved to be run out of town? And if so, just how hard was it going to be to shrug off the whispers, gossip, and stares that had made life hell so long ago?

Clenching his jaw, Buck pushed away the questions and looked ahead to the sea. It was nearly six o'clock. Behind him, the sun dipped toward the west, leaving the eastern horizon a deep blue meeting of sky and water. He turned onto Beach Drive, casting frequent glances at the ocean as he approached the strip of motels that catered to tourists. Here, a number of people clustered along the sidewalks, sunburned and all dressed up in summer finery on their way to a seafood dinner.

Beyond the motels was a district of stately seaside homes, and then the monumental shape of the old Ocean Forest Hotel. Built in an era of grandeur during the 1920's, the hotel was a huge Georgian structure of red brick, white columns, and tiled patios—long considered the most elegant hotel in Kingsport. On impulse, Buck turned in.

The interior was furnished with thick carpets, leafy plants, and polished antiques. Buck strolled across the lobby, caught sight of the Dogwood Room and decided to stop in for a drink. The bar of the Ocean Forest Hotel was elegant and dark, with more the air of a private club than a public bar. In fact, it had been private for fifty years or so when liquor by the drink remained illegal in North Carolina.

He took a seat on a leather stool and ordered a gin and tonic. The bartender was big and brawny and looked out of place in his formal white shirt and bow tie. Buck remembered him immediately. Hank Perkins. They'd played pick-up basketball together as kids.

When Hank returned with the drink, he took a long interested look.

"Do I know you?" he asked.

Buck grinned. "How are you, Hank?"

"Sawyer? Danny Sawyer?"

"How have you been?" Buck asked, reaching for his drink.

"Good. When the hell did you get back?"

"Just now."

Hank took out a cloth and began absently polishing the bar as his eyes remained on Buck. "How long has it been?" he asked.

"About fifteen years."

"What brings you back?"

Buck's pleasant expression tightened. "Unfinished business."

Hank nodded and moved away. "Good to see you."

"Yeah. Take it easy."

Buck drank slowly, impressions from the meeting at *The Watch* pummeling his brain: Rory's look of hatred . . . Big Ed's booming laugh . . . the air of self-indulged power that rose from both of them like a stench. It was going to be tougher than he'd imagined to fit himself to a role in which the McKennas were boss.

So engrossed was he in the recollections that he failed to notice the flurry of looks that turned his way as Hank made his way down the bar, or the woman who rose from one of the stools and moved in his direction.

"Hello, Danny."

Buck looked up through fogged eyes to behold a good-looking redhead. She seemed familiar, but damn if he could place her. Perching beside him, she proferred a languid, seductive smile.

"Cat got your tongue?" she teased.

"I'll be damned," he said slowly.

Swiveling on the stool, Buck took a good look. Libby Parker was wearing a sleeveless black dress that clung to her curves, and the way she was made up was unmistakably flashy. She looked like one of two things—a woman on the make or a hooker.

"I'll be damned," he said again. "The last time I saw you—"

"We were both on our way out of town," Libby supplied. "I never figured to see you back in Kingsport again."

"I could say the same thing about you. That night you seemed pretty definite about putting this place behind you."

"I was."

Buck regarded her assessingly. "When did you come back?"

"Just a few months ago."

"Why?"

She shrugged. "It was time. Why did you come back?"

He tossed down the last of his drink and gave her a hooded look. "I've taken a job at *The Watch*. I'm a reporter now. How about you? What are you doing these days?"

"Not much. Just getting along."

"Where are you living?"

Libby raised her chin. "The McKenna house."

"You're kidding," he said in such a derisive tone that she gave him a sharp look.

"No. I'm not kidding," Libby announced with a defiant gleam in her eye. "Seems we're both working for the family. I'm Rory's . . . private secretary."

It was not so much what she said as the way she said it. Danny's brows went up as he grasped her meaning. Libby was McKenna's mistress, and she was making no bones about it.

"Well now, that's a surprise," he said after a moment. "I got the impression some years back that you hated his guts."

"Very observant."

"Well then, why the hell—"

"Danny!" she broke in impatiently. "We don't always like everything we have to do, do we? I thought you and I learned that lesson long ago."

Buck shook his head, still unwilling to think of the girl he used to know as Rory McKenna's whore. "I guess you've got your reasons," he said.

"Just like you've got yours," she returned enigmatically. "Have you seen Savannah?"

Out of the blue like that, the name rushed through him like a current. "Not yet. How is she?"

Libby's expression turned inexplicably smug. "Things have changed, Danny. Or do you know already?"

"Know what?"

"Savannah is destitute. To hear Rory tell it, she's holding onto the Crossing by a mere thread."

"What?!"

Libby smiled. Somehow her expression looked more sly than anything else. "Guess you didn't know. When Mr. King died years ago, Savannah lost everything. On top of that, her mother went mad. It seems Miss Savannah has had an incredible streak of bad luck."

Buck held up a hand. "Wait a minute," he muttered a bit desperately. "What are you saying?"

Libby's smile disappeared. "I'm saying that Savannah King isn't the crown princess of the city anymore. I'm saying she's turned into a recluse, and from what I hear, the Crossing is nothing more than a run-down hermitage for an old maid and her crazy mother."

"Why the hell are you talking like that?" Buck bellowed, unaware of how his voice carried until he noticed people down the way looking curiously in their direction. "I thought you were her friend," he added more quietly.

Libby rose to her feet and retrieved her purse from the bar. "Not anymore, Danny. Like I said, things have changed."

With that, Libby Parker turned and sashayed out of the bar. When Buck settled his tab and hurried out moments later, he saw her speeding away from the hotel in an MG convertible.

Despite Libby's comments, Buck was unprepared for the scene that greeted him as he drove into the Crossing. Stopping the jeep halfway up the drive, he got out and walked toward the house, staring at the familiar trees that had gone unpruned, half of which had broken limbs hanging through their branches, the once immaculate front lawns that had been allowed to grow wild with weeds as tall as his knees.

When he entered the courtyard, he saw with relief that the rose gardens bore the stamp of care that once had marked the whole of the estate, but as he looked up at the house, his spirits dropped. Ivy climbed over the brick; the white paint of the columns and trim was weathered and cracked. At a third floor attic window, a shutter hung haphazardly from its frame.

Buck circled toward the pool house on the same path he'd taken a thousand times in the old pickup. He was further dismayed when he saw the pool. Obviously unused for years, it had been left to the elements. Vines had taken over, claiming the redwood deck until it was a muffled green shape. One of the corner lanterns had broken and fallen and was hanging upside down by a cord.

The sun went down as Buck continued his tour with mounting feelings of regret. The hedge he'd maintained so flawlessly was topped with shoots reaching higher than his head. The tennis court was littered with leaves and tree branches, the net loose at one end. The side yard that once met the pines in neat precision had melded with the forest, the undergrowth thick with brambles.

Stuffing his hands in his pockets, Buck meandered along the edge of the pines. Eventually the dusky gray light softened the ragged look of the grounds, and he became aware of other things—the briny smell of the nearby sea, the cloying accent of the river, and binding it all, the scent of summer grass cooling as evening set in. It was the smells and the upsurging chorus of katydids, that brought back the memories—long ago summer twilights when the grounds rang with cries of "Run Sheep Run" and "Ain't No Boogers Out Tonight."

He paused at the very back of the lawns and turned toward the house. In the soft light, it didn't look so bad. He started across the grassy expanse. By the time he neared the patio, night had just about fallen. Perhaps that was why he didn't notice the chicken coop until he was almost upon it. Perched between two elegant oaks at the back of the house, the wooden structure looked as ludicrous as the clucking of hens sounded against the traditional quiet of a summer night at the Crossing.

Chickens? Buck thought with wonder, but before he could do more than draw near the coop, a sharp crack split the air . . . followed by a searing pain in his left bicep. Grabbing his arm, Buck spun around.

There she was on the top step of the patio. The light was nearly gone, but there was no mistaking Savannah—the slender form, the long blond hair pulled up in a ponytail. She looked exactly as she did when she was sixteen, except that at the moment she was pointing a rifle at him. Damned if she hadn't shot him!

"For God's sake, Savannah!"—the first words he'd spoken to her in fifteen years.

Relaxing the firearm to a slightly less threatening position, she strained to see through the dusky shadows. "Who is it?"

"I'll show you damn well who it is!"

The voice was somehow familiar. Even so, as the unidentified man started toward her, Savannah raised the rifle to readiness.

"Hold it right there! This is only rock salt, but it can be awfully uncomfortable if you take it up close!"

Glancing down at his arm, Buck verified that the white cloth of his shirtsleeve was ripped and showing a bloodstain.

"You're telling me?" he boomed. "You winged me!"

"If I'd been aiming at anything more important, you might not be standing up just now!"

Thinking quickly back to when Mr. King taught them to shoot skeet, Buck knew she was telling the truth. Savannah had always been a crack shot.

"What are you doing at my coop?" she demanded. "I'm warning you. I've already alerted the police that I've had poachers out here. All it takes is a quick phone call!"

His arm continued to sting, but as Buck noted her defiant stance—the planted feet, the steady aim of the rifle—his shocked, angry expression settled gradually into a grin.

"So, you think I'm a poacher. Is that it?"

"Why else would you be hanging around my coop on a summer evening?"

He took a few steps but could see her no better in the dying light. "I'm not here to steal your chickens, Savannah."

The nagging familiarity of the voice swelled in her ears. Slowly, she lowered the rifle to her side.

"What are you here for, then?"

Buck walked toward her, still cradling the violated arm. "At the moment, I'd say a little first aid."

He stopped at the bottom of the patio steps, tall and broad-shouldered. Savannah peered down at his face but could make out nothing more than rather darkish hair falling across a strong brow. Then suddenly he smiled a crooked smile—the shape of it glowing white in the near darkness—and it hit her.

"Danny?" she whispered.

"Fifteen years I've been gone," he complained, "and when I come back, all you can think to do is shoot me?"

Savannah adopted a light, scolding tone as she dressed his arm, unaware that her pleasure at seeing him showed clearly in her sparkling eyes and heightened color.

"And just what were you doing out by my chicken coop?" she demanded.

She was standing above him as he sat in the kitchen chair. Buck glanced up, his eyes performing a quick hungry scan of her face.

"Just looking around," he replied as he thought how incredibly little she'd changed. The hair was the same as when she was a girl—long, shining, sunbleached to the palest ash blond. The skin glowed a sunny, rosy gold he recalled from long-ago summers. The cut-off shorts and oversized shirt she was wearing were incongruous with the girl he remembered, but other than that . . .

"When did you get back?" Savannah asked.

"A few hours ago."

"There now," she muttered, fastening a bandage on the offended arm. "Hardly a scratch, but it should teach you not to turn up unannounced at my chicken coop."

She stepped back and gave him a teasing smile. Buck's gaze lifted from her mouth to her unforgettable eyes. They, too, remained the same—the deepest, most shocking blue he'd ever seen. A charge ran through him, and still she regarded him with that innocent, ignorant smile. God, it was still the same. She undid him with the simplest of gestures and never even knew it. Turning to his arm, he went about rolling down his shirtsleeve.

"Where on earth have you come from, anyway?" she asked.

"Washington."

"Oh, yes. I should have known. Buck Sawyer has made quite a name for himself at *The Post*."

He looked up in surprise. "You knew that was me?"

"I knew. You wrote to my father about it years ago, when you first started at *The Charlotte Observer*." The image of her father crossed her mind, draining the absent smile that had played about her lips. "He'd have been very proud of you," she added. "He loved you like a son."

A lump rose to Buck's throat. "What happened? I never really knew what happened."

"A car crash." Gathering up the first aid materials, Savannah turned away. "It happened just after he found out he'd lost everything. All the money, *The Watch*, even the Crossing."

She walked across the room to the sink. Buck watched her go, noting the stiff way she held herself. An ache rose within him, something born of the urge to protect her and the knowledge that such an urge was far too late. He took another look about the vast kitchen. Merciless overhead fluorescence showed the furnishings to be the same as when he left, except that everything had grown faded and dingy. Just like the whole of the Crossing.

He got up and went to join Savannah. Resting a hip against the counter, he studied her profile as she went about washing up the few things she'd dirtied while tending his arm. It struck him that he'd never seen her perform such a chore.

"How could such a thing happen, Savannah? Your father was rich as Midas." She didn't look up.

"King's Club," she said. "We never knew, Mother and I, what was going on. Later they told us that for years Daddy had been pouring everything into the development of the country club. Then one day there was nothing left."

Turning off the faucet, Savannah reached for the dish towel.

"You said the Crossing was lost," Buck commented, "but obviously you're here."

She dried her hands, discarded the towel, and looked up. Now, Buck thought, he could see a difference. There was a stern set to her face, a haunted look he never would have associated with the girl of his past.

"It took most of the insurance money to pay off the claim on the Crossing," she said flatly. "The bank carried us for about a year until I turned twenty-one and could get into my trust fund. Now that's gone, too. I took a part-time job last year, but it isn't enough. The truth is, I'm months behind on the mortgage, and it's purely through the generosity of Ben Cochrane that Mother and I haven't been turned out."

Buck swallowed hard. The story didn't disturb him as much as the cold, lifeless way in which she told it.

"How *is* your mother?" he asked.

"Years ago, just after Daddy died, she became ill. Dr. Crane said she simply couldn't accept what had happened."

"I don't understand."

"She doesn't live in the real world, Danny. She hasn't for a long time. For Mother, time stopped. For her, Daddy's still alive, the fortune has never been lost, and the King family is still the toast of Kingsport."

Buck tried to picture the staunch Mrs. King as out of her mind and found he just couldn't do it. She'd always been so sure of herself, so maddeningly superior.

"Where is she?" he asked.

Savannah's gaze drifted to the window and the darkness beyond. "Upstairs. She hardly leaves her rooms anymore."

"And you take care of her?"

She nodded.

"For all these years?" he added in a deep voice. When she nodded once again, the dismal picture of what her life must have been like flashed through Buck's mind.

"You mean you've been stuck out here since your father died? All alone? Taking care of your mother?"

Savannah turned and gave him a steady look. "There was no one else to do it."

"A nurse—"

"I couldn't afford a nurse, Danny."

"What about Clifford Andrews? The two of you were practically engaged. He could have helped."

A very small, very cold smile touched her lips. "Clifford Andrews. Now there's a name I haven't called to mind in a long time. No," she went on, the smile disappearing. "I mean, it really was a social disgrace, you know. Who could expect an Andrews to abide such gossip about his fiancée, or worse yet, his wife?"

"What kind of gossip?" Buck demanded.

"What kind?" Savannah snapped, the old resentment returning. "Oh, the usual kind, I guess. You see, Daddy had just lost a fortune. People said he crashed the car deliberately, and that the only reason the insurance company paid off was because the owner is a family friend. And then, of course, when Mother went off the deep end, there was a new blaze of controversy. Why, even to this day, we're the talk of the town. They're convinced Mother is crazy, and they're not too sure about me. 'Those crazy King ladies,' they say. 'Those crazy Kings—' "

"Stop it, Savannah!"

Shoving away from the counter, Buck rose to his full intimidating height, glowering as though she'd done him a personal injury.

"It's true."

"I don't give a damn if it's true! I don't want to hear it!"

His tone pierced the murky bitterness that had overtaken Savannah. It had been years since she'd talked of such things to anyone. She was surprised at the way everything had rolled out of her mouth, particularly since she hadn't seen Danny in half a lifetime. But then, he *was* Danny, and despite the years that had passed, there was an undeniable bond between them.

Sharpening her gaze, Savannah studied him. There was a new maturity about his face, but the angry flush was the same, as were the flashing hazel eyes. And suddenly there emerged that same, heart-stopping sensation she hadn't felt since she was all of sixteen. Savannah took a quick backward step, a wave of fright washing over her. Her guard had slipped since Danny Sawyer showed up on her doorstep. Now it returned in full force. She took another step back, the wary distance that had become second nature settling over her like a familiar cloak.

"What are you doing here, Danny?" she asked.

"Following a story."

"How long are you staying?"

Buck sensed her withdrawal. Her face was tense, her questions carrying the edge of an interrogation.

"I don't know yet," he replied. "Could be months, maybe longer."

"It must be quite a story for *The Post* to let you go for that long."

"I've taken a leave of absence from *The Post*. Actually, the McKennas have hired me on and at a pretty little price."

He tried a small grin but saw it was the wrong thing to do as Savannah's expression flitted from surprise to outrage.

"The McKennas?" she fired.

"Yes. I'm reporting for *The Watch*."

"That's great. That's just *great*!" Twisting away, Savannah slapped frustratedly at the counter.

"What the hell's the matter with you, Savannah?"

She spun around and let her temper fly. "Oh, nothing! Nothing at all! I've only been working for the McKennas for over a year now. For peanuts! All the time they kept me stuck in that miserable little Manners Lady job, they kept assuring me there was nothing else available. And now you show up, and all of a sudden they're offering the moon!"

Buck shrugged, his brows knitting. "I'm sorry. I didn't know."

"Savannah!"

The voice rang down the stairs, and Savannah whirled toward the kitchen doorway.

"I'm here, Mother!" she called. "What is it?"

"Tell that girl, Amaryllis, I want to see her in my chambers at once. It's after eight o'clock, the house is dark as pitch, and the lamps haven't even been lit!"

"I'll see to it!" Savannah waited at the doorway for a moment until she was sure Ophelia King had returned to her haven. Then she walked back into the kitchen, keeping a safe distance between herself and Danny.

"It's good to see you, Danny," she said solemnly, "but as you see, I have things to do."

Buck took the hint, but he did not want to go. "Listen, Savannah. I could help you out around here."

"What?"

"I took a look around the place—the pool, the grounds, the house. Everything needs work."

Savannah's back straightened as she suddenly saw the Crossing through his eyes. "Thank you very much, but we get along. I don't have time for things like grounds and pools, but then I gave up worrying about appearances long ago."

"I could help you out another way."

"And what is that?"

"Rent."

"Rent?"

"I need a place to live, Savannah, and the Crossing is plenty big enough to house me. I may as well pay you as someone else."

"I don't want your charity," she snapped. "I've been getting by all these years—"

"You just told me how well you're getting by."

"Well, I certainly didn't tell you in order to elicit some sort of . . . proposition."

The term carried a sexy undertone Buck couldn't resist noting, not when he was standing there looking at Savannah. His gaze raced down the length of her. The oversized shirt hid her figure, but the shorts revealed long, shapely legs. His eyes burned their way back to her face. No, he did not want to go.

His lingering look didn't go past Savannah. There it went again—that nagging tingle, sizzling up her spine.

"The idea is preposterous," she remarked.

"Why?"

"Mother and I are alone here. It wouldn't be proper for a single man to move in." Her brows went up at a sudden thought. "You are single, aren't you?"

"I'm single," he said with a grin.

"Well then."

"Well then, what?"

"It just simply isn't done," she sniffed, as if that settled that.

He shook his head, though the grin broadened. "Still the same, ever-proper Miss Savannah. I thought you said you'd given up worrying about appearances."

She gave him a sharp look.

"Think of it," Buck said, undaunted. "What better way to get back a little from the McKennas than by taking their money from me?" Her attention seemed to perk up at that, and Buck whipped his wallet out of his back pocket. "Room and board. Four hundred a month. What do you say?"

"Four hundred?" Savannah repeated in surprise.

"All right then, five." Fishing five one-hundred-dollar bills out of his wallet, he held out his hand. "Here. Take this. Tomorrow, after I have a chance to set up an account at the bank, I'll draw you a check for another five."

Stepping swiftly forward, Buck pressed the bills into her

hand. Savannah looked at the money, then back up to his face, clearly astonished.

"A thousand dollars?" she squeaked.

Buck replaced his wallet. "That's the customary way. One month's rent for deposit, the first month in advance."

Slowly she began to shake her head. "I can't take—"

"It's late, Savannah," he broke in, sensing that he'd won the battle as her gaze drifted back to the money. "I don't relish the idea of trying to find another place to stay tonight."

With that he turned and headed for the kitchen door.

"Where are you going?" she called through her daze.

"To get my things. I left my jeep in the drive."

"Danny—"

"I go by Buck, now," he told her, pausing at the doorway.

Thankfully, some of Savannah's sense returned, along with the urge to recover some sort of control. Her chin went up as she stuffed the bills in the pocket of her shorts.

"I don't think I could get used to that," she remarked contrarily. "You'll always be Danny to me."

He flashed her another of his crooked smiles.

"I can handle that," he said and stalked into the summer night, thinking that Savannah was more right than she knew. Ever since he set foot in Kingsport, he'd had the feeling that he'd come home to being Danny once more.

When he returned to the house, he found her making up the bed in his old room. Nostalgia welled up within him, but it was quickly overpowered by other instincts as his gaze lit on the trim backside bent over his bed. The house was quiet, the room dimly lit by a single lamp. An air of intimacy bloomed, and Danny was certain Savannah felt it just as he did. He leaned against the doorjamb, enjoying the spectacle as she stretched and extended a long, bare leg behind her. It was obvious she was hurrying, yanking at the sheets, seemingly anxious to be out of the bedroom now that he was in it. Some things about her had changed, some had not. She was still skittish as a colt in springtime.

"There," she said, tugging the bedspread taut with a final flourish. "You may find that the linens smell of cedar, but they're clean."

He said nothing.

"I hope you don't expect maid service after this," she added. "I'm afraid I have too much to do."

"That's okay. I'll manage."

Savannah turned from the bed, locating him at the doorway from the corner of her eye, but loath to look him in the face. She'd felt his eyes on her while she worked. Now her heart was racing, and she could feel the heat in her cheeks. Drawing a quick breath, she turned and walked in his direction, still avoiding his eyes.

"Well then, good night," she said, and would have made the break out of the room. But at the last moment, he raised an arm across the doorway, blocking her exit. She had no choice but to look up.

"Savannah."

He said the name caressingly, and a heightened sense of alarm swarmed over her.

"It's been a long time," he added. "Do you think we could talk for a while?"

"No. I can't. I have to see to Mother."

"Can't it wait a half hour? A quarter of an hour?"

She glanced away. He was too attractive. Too masculine. His mere presence seemed to . . .

"No, Danny. I'm sorry. She has a certain routine. It's best that I stick to it."

She started to step under his arm. He detained her by placing large hands on her upper arms and turning her to face him. Her gaze flew to his like a startled bird.

"Please don't!" she said, shrinking back. "I don't like to be touched!"

His dark brows lowered. "Since when?"

"Since always."

Sparkling eyes searched hers, delving deep.

"Always?" he repeated, his deep voice probing along with his eyes.

Savannah pushed at his hands. His hold remained firm.

"Let me go, Danny!" she blurted. "If you're going to stay in my home, then please do me the courtesy of respecting my wishes. I said I don't want to be touched!"

By the time she finished, her voice had risen to a near shriek. In a theatrical gesture, Danny spread his fingers wide, yanked his hands away, and stepped aside.

Without another word, Savannah fled the room.

The next day was Tuesday. She was disconcerted to come downstairs and find the coffee already brewed and Danny sitting in the breakfast nook and reading the morning paper—as if he'd been there for a lifetime, as if he'd never left.

"Good morning," he greeted pleasantly.

Savannah offered him toast and eggs—which he refused—and went about her normal morning task of preparing her mother's breakfast tray. As she started out of the kitchen with it, he rose to his feet and delivered his coffee cup to the sink.

"Guess I'd better be on my way," he said as he passed. "Don't want to be late my first day." Straightening the knot of his tie, he asked, "How do I look?"

He was wearing tailored gray slacks, a white shirt, and a stylish, striped tie of red, black, and gray. Savannah had never seen a more handsome man in her life.

"Fine," she replied.

He headed for the door, and she stood there, foolishly rooted to the spot, the silver tray in her hands.

"By the way," he added. "What time is supper around here?"

"Seven."

"I'll look forward to it," he responded, his voice deep and unsettling despite the breadth of the room between them. "Have a good day, Savannah."

"You, too," she managed.

With a final parting grin, he was gone.

Savannah climbed the stairs with a sense of wonder. They'd exchanged only the merest of comments, and yet the difference between this morning and all the silent mornings she'd known for years was as blatant as night and day. Was this how most women felt each morning? Sending their men off into the world with wishes for a good day?

Irritably, she dismissed the notion. Danny Sawyer was not "her man," and she wouldn't know what to do with him if he were. Nonetheless, the thought of him stayed with her throughout the day, and as the afternoon drew to a close, she caught herself listening for his arrival.

She was in the kitchen when his jeep pulled up at the back of the house. It was half past six. The pork chops were sticking to the pan. The mashed potatoes were full of lumps. Suddenly he walked in.

"Hello there," he greeted. "Something smells good. Do I have time to wash up?"

"Sure," Savannah tossed over her shoulder. She had no idea

why she felt so ridiculous, standing there before the stove as she had every evening for as long as she could remember.

Scraping the damnable chops out of the pan, she prepared her mother's tray and took it up. When she returned, she found Danny sniffing about the stove.

"Sit down," she scolded with a faint smile. "It won't take a minute to put it on a plate."

They settled in the breakfast nook, and he dove into the food with obvious relish. Savannah picked at her portion.

"This is good," he said after a moment, and she was inordinately pleased. "When did you learn how to cook?"

"Loretta left me her recipes."

He looked up. "Loretta," he repeated with a fond smile. "Many's the day I've dreamed about her homemade biscuits. How is she? And Cletus and Amaryllis?"

"Cletus died years ago," Savannah answered. "Loretta and Amaryllis moved away shortly after that."

"Sorry to hear it," he said.

Savannah met his eyes and found herself caught up in them. They'd always been one of Danny's best features—a deep green flecked with brown and gold, fringed with lashes much darker than his sunstreaked hair. At the moment, those eyes held a touching look of sadness. She looked swiftly down at her plate.

"How did you find things at *The Watch*?" she asked.

"As you know, there have been a lot of changes."

"No, I don't know."

"What do you mean? Last night you said you write a column."

"I usually mail it in," Savannah explained, her voice tightening. "I have no desire to frequent *The Watch* or to see Rory lolling about my father's office as if he belongs there."

Danny slowly chewed a piece of meat as he studied her. "I see."

Savannah looked up and brought a livelier expression to her face. "You said there have been changes," she said. "Like what?"

"New machinery and the like. An inserter that takes up the whole mailroom. A new press. Actually, come to think of it, aside from new gadgets, the guts of *The Watch* are pretty much the same. A lot of the same people are still there . . ."

Danny kept her entertained through the rest of the meal with

anecdotes about the old-timers they both remembered: Abe
Reynolds, who had proposed to his wife, the food columnist, by
taking out an ad in the classifieds . . . Miriam Hinshaw, who
continued her long-unrequited love affair with sportswriter
Larry Sage . . . Jack Doggett, who had grown only more snide
with age and had developed a habit of brown-nosing Rory
McKenna. Danny's expression sobered at that point. Pushing
aside his empty plate, he leaned forward, planting his forearms
on the table as he gazed across at Savannah.

"Rory McKenna," he repeated with a note of distaste. "You
know, when he hired Buck Sawyer, he had no idea he was getting me. He was mad as hell when I showed up and would have
broken the contract if I'd allowed it. I guess the most interesting
highlight of my day was when he called me into his office to
give me my first assignment—an insignificant city council
meeting tomorrow afternoon. He took obvious pleasure in it,
and his meaning was clear. He may have to honor my contract,
but he doesn't have to put me on any decent stories."

Danny shook his head, a glint coming into his eyes. "As soon
as I looked at McKenna, all the feelings I had as a kid came
rushing back. Part of me is gloating at the way I took him in.
Part of me still can't stand to be around him."

"I can relate to that," Savannah replied earnestly. "I can't
stand to be around him, either."

Their eyes locked, an old feeling of camaraderie springing up
between them. Danny reached tentative fingers across the tabletop where her hand rested.

"What in the world do you think you're doing, young man?"
rang the imperious voice.

In spite of himself, Danny jumped as he twisted to face
Ophelia King. Standing there in the center of the kitchen, she
made a striking picture as the overhead light glinted off her elegant, silk-blue robe . . . and a shocking crown of white hair!
Danny got swiftly to his feet, staring, unable to keep his eyes
from it.

Savannah slipped out of her seat. "Mother," she said gently.
"You remember Danny, don't you? Danny Sawyer?"

Ophelia shot her daughter an impatient look. "Remember
him? For heaven's sake, Savannah, do you think I'm daft?" Her
eyes swerved back to Danny. "Listen to me, young man. That
little episode this past weekend was a disgrace. Sheriff Martin
bringing you home in the middle of the night, in *that* condition!

It won't happen again without serious repercussions. Do you understand?"

Danny's mind reeled. The incident she was describing had happened when he was fourteen years old.

"Yes ma'am," he managed to say. "I'm sorry. It won't happen again."

"Mother—" Savannah tried with a weary look.

"Also," Ophelia went on to Danny, "I want you to know I'm aware of certain liberties you've been taking in regard to my daughter. Watch yourself, Danny. I've already spoken to your mother about this, and I shan't hesitate to do so again!"

With that, Ophelia King whirled out of the room. Danny listened as she ascended the stairs. Shock, more than anything else, prodded him into a low chuckle.

"Don't you dare laugh at her!" Savannah flashed.

Helplessly, Danny broke into open laughter, though he targeted Savannah with an apologetic look all the while. Gathering the dinner plates in a quick, efficient huff, she moved to the sink. He picked up his glass and followed.

"I'm not laughing at her, Savannah," he insisted as he joined her. "I'm laughing at the situation. It is kind of funny, don't you think? Here I've been away fifteen years, and—if I say so, myself—have made a few strides. But sometimes you get slapped in the face with something unchanging. Your mother, Savannah. Ill or not, one thing's for sure—she's consistent!"

Savannah surrendered a smile. Glancing up, she admitted, "I guess you're right about that."

His smile broadened. Hers disappeared as her stomach did a peculiar flip.

"Tell me something," Danny murmured. "What have you been doing all these years?"

"Doing?"

"If Clifford's been out of the picture, who's been in?"

Savannah turned back to the sink and reached for the dish soap.

"No one," she answered. "Not in the way you mean."

"No one?"

"Look, Danny," she said in an exasperated tone. "There are limits, you know. Some things I prefer to keep private. How would you like it if I started asking you about your love life?"

"What would you like to know?" he drawled.

Savannah chanced a sidelong glance and shouldn't have. The

look he wore was just the kind that had set her quivering long ago, only now it carried the matured impact of a full-grown man.

"I don't want to know anything," she said briskly. "That's the point. Sometimes you have a way of . . ."

"Of what?" he asked, searching her eyes.

"Of—I don't know—of going too far." Looking back at the sink, Savannah began scrubbing a plate with a vengeance. "There are parameters to this relationship, Danny. I'll respect yours, and I expect you to respect mine."

"And what exactly are your parameters?"

"Those of a . . . business associate. We'll be polite to each other, cooperative—"

"I see. But nothing more."

Setting the plate aside, Savannah grabbed up a soapy glass. "Exactly."

"No familiarity."

"No more so than you'd show any other landlady. That's the only way this leasing arrangement can possibly work."

Danny's eyes raced over her, and as he noted the tense set of her body, he knew better than to press.

"All right, then, landlady," he said, producing his wallet. "Here's the check I promised you. I'll put it over here on the counter and bid you good night."

Savannah looked up with both surprise and relief as he strolled out of the room. Finishing up in the kitchen some time later, she climbed the stairs, her eyes turning uncontrollably to the strip of light under the door across the landing. The thought of Danny stayed with her, creeping in as she bathed, and then later when she crawled into bed with a book. It was well past eleven when she got up and wandered restlessly to the French doors.

Danny leaned against the column, gazing out across the moonlit grounds, breathing in the strong familiar scents of summer flowers and honeysuckle. Dressed in the flattering light of the moon, the Crossing seemed just as it was when he left. He thought of his mother, Mr. King, and childhood memories he hadn't called to mind in years.

He glanced along the veranda where a light shone from Savannah's room. And then, shockingly, she stepped out. Time screeched to a halt and flew backward. All of a sudden, he was smack in the middle of a night a lifetime ago, a night when he'd watched Savannah step onto the portico, her long hair catching the light of the moon. Fifteen years had passed, yet the tightening in his chest was the same—as was the wide-eyed look on her face as he emerged from the shadows.

"Nice night," he offered.

Savannah clutched her robe front. "You startled me. I guess I forgot I'm not the only one on this side of the house anymore."

Danny glanced out across the grounds. "Being here sure brings back a lot of memories."

"Good memories?"

"Some of them. In fact, when you stepped out on the veranda, I was reminded of a certain New Year's Eve. Remember?"

Savannah's face grew warm. He'd kissed her that night, almost in this very spot.

"I remember," she replied, moving warily away. "I remember a lot of things." Gaining a safe distance, she peered at him through the darkness. "I'm surprised you've come back, Danny. Once, as I recall, you wrote Daddy that you planned never to return to Kingsport. What changed your mind?"

Danny studied her a moment. "This is not for common knowledge, Savannah. Have you ever heard of a woman named Jane Wilson?"

"Wilson," Savannah repeated. "The name is familiar. Wait a minute. Wasn't she the one who was killed a few months ago?"

"That's right. The same man who killed her killed Roberta Sikes."

"What?" Savannah whispered. She hadn't heard that name in years; the sound of it triggered images of a courtroom and a lynch mob.

"I saw the picture of Jane Wilson in D.C.," Danny went on. "There's no doubt about it. Whoever killed her killed Roberta all those years ago. And he's here, in Kingsport."

Savannah shuddered at the morbid speculation. "How can you be sure?"

"I'm sure," he answered firmly. "I've gained some experience over the years, you know. This is the story I left *The Post* to track down."

Savannah studied him through the muted light of the summer night. "You intend to track down this killer," she said, slowly pulling together her thoughts. "And in doing so, clear your own name. That's why you came back."

A breeze rustled by, lifting her shining tresses in a glimmering wave. Moonlight sparkled in her eyes. *God!* Danny thought.

"I had to come back," he said gruffly. Moving in her direction, he caught the scent of roses. "Now I'm glad I have for more reasons than one."

"Oh, really?" Savannah returned with pointed lightness.

"I think you know what I mean. You're more beautiful than ever, Savannah."

Her chin snapped up. "Please don't say things like that."

"Why not? Most women enjoy hearing a compliment."

"I'm not like most women, Danny."

He cocked his head to one side. "What makes you so different?"

"A lot of things."

"Like what?"

"Like all the things I told you about last night."

Danny considered her for a long, thoughtful moment. "You told me about things that must have been hard to take. You didn't tell me about anything that should make you different from any other beautiful woman."

"I asked you not to say that."

"And I asked you why not."

"Because it makes me nervous, okay?"

"A simple compliment makes you nervous?"

"The thought of what it implies does," she stated bluntly.

Danny crossed his arms across his chest, amused—but saddened, too—by this show of the old, stalwart Savannah.

"And what does it imply?" he pressed.

"That you're regarding me in a certain light, through which I don't wish to be regarded."

"Whether you wish it or not, Savannah, I don't intend to ignore the fact that you're beautiful or apologize for the fact that I find you completely desirable."

Heat flashed to her face and prickled her scalp. "Then it appears we have a serious problem with this housing arrangement."

"Calm down, Savannah—"

"No! Listen to me, Danny. I'll not be made to feel uncomfortable in my own house. I well remember how you were as a boy—"

"And how was I?"

She raised a defiant brow. "Smooth enough so that I'm certain you've been entirely successful with a great many women."

Danny laughed. "A few," he admitted, his smile settling as he focused once more on the haunting face before him. "That doesn't mean I didn't think of you, Savannah. There were times I wondered how you were, what you were doing. Did you ever think of me?" he added. "Even once?"

His question tugged at the old Savannah she kept locked away—the Savannah whose life had been a golden thing of which Danny Sawyer was an indelible part.

"Of course I've thought of you," she responded.

"And what have you thought?"

The husky tone of his voice pulled her focus back to the moment and to the prowling look in his eyes.

"Don't look at me that way, Danny," she warned. "This is exactly the kind of thing I want you to stop."

"Well, then, I guess you're right."

She raised a questioning brow.

"We *are* going to have a problem because I can't do a damn thing about the way I look at you. It was this way before, and I'm finding it hasn't changed. You heat my blood, Savannah. The fact that it shows is something over which I have no control."

As he spoke, her eyes had grown huge and luminous. Danny smiled reassuringly.

"Don't look so scared, for God's sake. I'm not going to hurt you." Reaching out, he swept a lock of pale hair over her shoulder, his fingertips grazing lightly across the shoulder of her robe. She jerked away as though he'd struck her.

"Stop it!" she hissed. "I told you I don't—"

"I know," Danny broke in, his smile disappearing. "You don't like to be touched."

It was at that moment that he grasped the severity of what had changed within Savannah. She'd always been reserved, but somewhere along the way, she'd completely withdrawn. She was so locked up inside herself it was almost frightening. The realization made Danny instantly, unspeakably angry. Suddenly he sensed how much time and effort it would take to break through to her. Suddenly he knew he would invest it.

"We'll play it your way," he said, stuffing his hands in his pockets and turning away. "Good night, Savannah."

In the next few days, Savannah came to believe that Danny
intended to stand by his word. Each morning he greeted her
pleasantly before leaving for *The Watch*. Each evening he
thanked her for the meal and even helped her clean up before retiring to his room. He was friendly and companionable, but he
kept a respectful distance both physically and verbally.

The thousand dollars he'd given her made scarcely a dent in
her debt, but Savannah took great pleasure in drafting the check
to the bank. If not a solution, it was at least a step in the right direction. She told herself that gratitude lay behind the gradual
but unmistakable softening of her guard against Danny.

By the time the end of the week rolled around, however, she
had to admit that gratitude wasn't all there was to it. She'd have
been crazy not to enjoy the change Danny created in the household. The comings and goings of a man injected instant life into
the place. Now, instead of silence, there were the sounds of radio music, a running shower, Danny whistling as he trotted
down the stairs. Now, instead of the dull routine of tending her
mother and the house, there was morning coffee and the evening meal to look forward to.

Danny surprised her on Saturday morning by announcing he
intended to spend the day working at the pool.

"Who knows?" he joked on his way out the kitchen door.
"Maybe when a thousand or so vines are cut away, we'll discover it still holds water."

At midday, Savannah started for the pool with a sandwich
and a tall glass of iced tea. As she drew near, she saw him at
work. Having pulled off his shirt, he'd donned work gloves and
was hacking away at a thick cluster of honeysuckle. Already
he'd succeeded in freeing the entire facing redwood wall. Some
slats were broken, but all in all it looked far better than she'd
imagined it could look, considering how long it had been buried
beneath a choking shroud.

"This is great!" she announced brightly.

Danny paused, buried the large knife he'd been using in a
nearby stump, and walked over. Wiping his arm across his forehead, he reached eagerly for the drink. Savannah would have
had to be blind not to notice the way the sun played off his muscles as he raised the glass to his mouth. His expansive chest was
dusted with dark hair; his skin a rich caramel color that at the
moment boasted a sheen of sweat that made him positively glis-

ten. Catching herself, Savannah looked up and saw he was watching her over the rim of the glass.

"You've really made progress out here," she said quickly.

"Yeah," he answered with a raking look. "Maybe one night soon we can go for a swim."

It was an innocent enough remark, but the image it conjured up made Savannah's heart race a little. Swimming with Danny? Alone? At night? She made a hasty retreat back to the house.

When she ventured out once more to the pool, it was to call him in for supper. By then, he was more than halfway through with the vines and had climbed on the deck to inspect the planks.

"Save it for me, will you?" he called. "Now that I've started this, I'd like to keep at it."

For some odd reason, a feeling of pride came over her as she walked back to the house. Danny worked into the night, apparently taking advantage of the summer glow that lit the sky until well past nine. Savannah glanced at the clock when she heard him come in. Nearly ten. A moment later, the sound of running water filled the old pipes. She closed her eyes, relishing the sound of his movements and feeling wicked for it.

The next morning when she came down, she discovered a note that he was back at the pool. Humming lightly under her breath, Savannah went about her morning chores. She'd just put together a lunch of cold chicken, bread, and fruit when Danny bounded in through the kitchen door.

"Hey, Savannah!" he called, his deep voice sounding boyishly excited. "Come on out here. I want to show you something."

"Well, I've just finished making lunch—"

"Bring it out," he suggested with a grin. "We'll have a picnic at poolside."

The big excitement was that he'd repaired the pump so that crystal clear water now spiraled into the long-empty basin.

"Of course, the interior needs to be scrubbed," he said, pointing toward the dirt-streaked walls of the pool. "But it seems that all the basics are sound enough. In a couple of weeks, I'll wager I can have it up and running."

The warmth Savannah felt spilled into her smile. "It's wonderful, Danny. It's been a long time since I've seen anything at the Crossing come back to life. Thank you."

"You're welcome," he returned, his lighthearted expression

settling, beginning to turn into something else. Savannah turned away and busied herself with spreading the blanket and setting out their lunch.

"Come on," she invited, sitting down so that her calves hung over the edge of the pool. "Let's eat."

After a moment, he came to join her, sitting down as she had done, dangling his legs over the side. Savannah handed him a drumstick and bit into her own. Nearby, the sound of running water was a cheery accent to the songs of birds, the buzz of honey bees. The high summer sun poured down on their bare limbs, taking them back to other summers spent round the pool. Before long, they dropped into a medley of stories from the past.

"Remember that time the mayor had too much to drink at one of the Fourth of July parties?" Danny said. "He fell in the pool right there, right in the middle of all those water lilies your mother had imported for the occasion!"

Savannah laughed. "Oh yes, I remember! How about that time Constance Webb wore a two-piece bathing suit for the first time? When she jumped in, she lost her top!"

"No!" Danny exclaimed. "I didn't know that! Constance Webb? Oh, well," he added with a teasing grin. "If I remember Constance correctly, I don't think I could have missed much."

"Danny!" Savannah scolded, though she laughed along with him.

Gradually, the sounds of their laughter melted away, and there was only the gurgling of the water and the flirting twitter of birds. Savannah glanced aside. Danny's attention was on her, seemingly targeted on her bare legs. Suddenly he raised his eyes, meeting hers squarely. An alarm went off inside her, though she didn't move as he reached out to cup her chin.

"Come here," he commanded, tugging her face gently toward him.

For a split second, Savannah went along with him. Then, as if on cue, she twisted out of his fingers to stare safely away.

"I've been so happy the past few days, Danny," she said in a low voice. "Please don't spoil it."

Capturing her chin once more, he pulled her back in a way that brooked no nonsense. "I'm not going to spoil it, Savannah. I don't think one kiss is too much to ask for all this work, do you?" Keeping a tight rein on his inclinations, Danny forced a light smile. "Hell," he added, "even at sixteen, you allowed a little kiss now and then."

He bent toward her. Savannah's heart slammed up to her throat, and then his mouth was on hers, gentle but firm as it parted her lips. Her eyelids fell, and he began kissing her as she remembered, his tongue filling her mouth. She felt his hand slip through her hair to the back of her head, leading her, positioning her so their faces melded . . . shifted . . .

A long instant later, Savannah realized with a jolt just how thoroughly she was kissing him back. A deep-seated instinct sprang to life and she pushed at his chest, tearing her mouth away.

"Please stop!" she murmured breathlessly. His hand was still in her hair. When he insisted on turning her to face him, she focused on his Adam's apple.

Danny's fingers caressed the back of her head. "Why stop?" he asked softly. "I thought that was kind of nice."

"You said we'd play it my way," Savannah reminded him.

She raised her eyes. A look of fright was within them. From only inches away, Danny studied her, his faint smile fading.

"I guess I did, didn't I?"

Releasing her, he got to his feet and walked across the deck where he sank to a crouch and resumed his examination of the pump. As far as Savannah could tell, he didn't look up when she left.

When he came in that afternoon, he announced—rather briskly—that he would be going out for supper. Savannah heard him come in some time around midnight, and the next morning when she went down to the kitchen, he'd already gone.

Chapter Nine

ON MONDAY MORNING, Danny arrived early at *The Watch*. Sunlight streamed through the tall windows, throwing bars of gold across the sprawling editorial area of the fifth floor. No one else had arrived. The place was uncharacteristically quiet as he wound around empty desks on his way to the cubicle McKenna had assigned him—a cramped little corner affair located as far as possible from the publisher's offices.

Settling down at the desk, Danny took out his notebook and reviewed the scribbles comprising his file on the phantom he'd labeled "The Strangler." As he read, the feelings that had driven him from Washington returned—urgent sensations that he alone was aware of the link between Jane Wilson and Roberta Sikes, that he alone was responsible for tracking the fiend. As Danny saw it, he was pitted in a one-on-one match with a killer who had won the first round years ago. This story was personal, *real* personal.

The killer was out there. Danny could sense it. Like a shadow moving just outside his range of vision, the Strangler had taken on a vague but definite presence. He was somewhere in Kingsport or Clancytown. The culprit could be a native who'd lived here in 1976 and still did. The scarf should hold a clue since it appeared to be The Strangler's stamp. Only a unique kind of madman would strangle a woman, then arrange her like a fashion plate with the murder weapon trailing from her throat. What would provoke such a maniac? What was it about Roberta and Jane that had set him off?

Establishing the link between the two women was the obvious first step to take. And as Danny perused his notes, a feeling of self-reproach gathered within him. He had done no work on this exposé since arriving in Kingsport. The truth was, he'd al-

lowed himself to be sidetracked. In addition to the trivial assignments McKenna had been firing his way nonstop, there was
Savannah. When Danny wasn't absorbed in work, he was thinking about her, imagining what she was doing, itching to get back
to the Crossing.

He stared at the blank wall beyond his desk as Savannah's
image materialized. He'd stayed purposely out of her way since
yesterday's kiss at the pool. He'd thought it would be easier,
playing it her way. But when she pushed him away like that,
something inside him wrenched—something that called to
mind those long-ago brooding days when she demanded he
keep a respectful distance.

Time had passed. They were both full grown. Still, Savannah
insisted on playing the untouchable princess.

He had enough experience to know when a woman was responding, and she *had* been—at least for a moment, before that
pious ghost from the past rose up to slam him back in his place.
The bottom line was that nothing had changed. He was only
good enough to give Miss Savannah a passing thrill.

Danny had driven along the coast until nearly midnight with
such poisonous thoughts circling his brain. A few hours sleep
helped cool him down, and although he'd left the Crossing that
morning without seeing Savannah, he went to work with a more
level-headed perspective. He'd known she was a challenge
from day one. If he was going to give up at the first setback, he
ought to just throw in the towel. That he was not ready to do.

His gaze drifted back to the notebook, the names of Roberta
Sikes and Jane Wilson glaring from the page.

Yes, indeed, Savannah had sidetracked him—had climbed inside him all over again with uncanny ease. If he didn't watch
himself, he could get so caught up in her that he'd forget what
brought him back to Kingsport altogether.

Straightening in his chair, Danny set aside the notebook and
turned on his terminal. Editorial began to fill up, and the news-
room launched into its usual bustling hum. He scrolled through
a story, supposedly proofing copy, though his eyes strayed frequently to the phone. There was something else he'd neglected
to do. He'd been gone more than a week and hadn't called
Carol. Now, as he considered it, he cringed at the thought of
telling her he'd moved in at the Crossing.

Eventually he leaned over and dialed her work number with
brisk determination.

"Carol Kincaid."

The familiar voice came over the line, and Danny smiled as he pictured her. "Hello there, Carol Kincaid."

"Buck . . ."

"Yes?"

"I—well—it's good to hear from you."

"Sorry I haven't gotten in touch sooner," he said casually. "This jerk of a publisher has kept me hopping."

"I understand. Any luck with your mystery man?"

"Not yet," he hedged.

"Nothing here yet, either. I've sent profiles to bureaus across the southeast, but it will take time for everyone to report back."

"Thanks, Carol. I really appreciate what you're doing."

"Don't mention it."

"How are you?"

On the other end of the line, Carol rubbed at her throbbing temple. "Fine," she said lightly.

The conversation lagged.

"I want to give you my phone number," Danny said after a moment. "Got a pen?"

Carol dutifully copied down both work and home numbers. "So, where is home?" she asked.

He flinched. "I'm back at the Crossing."

Silence.

"It turned out to be the logical place," he added.

"How is Savannah?"

Danny noted the brittle tone, imagined the tense set of Carol's pretty features. "Not good," he replied rapidly. "Savannah's broke and has been for quite a while. That's the main reason I'm renting a room at the Crossing."

"And what is the other reason?"

"Come on, Carol," he chided. "Let's not—"

"Be honest with me!" she said. "If you can't give me anything else, at least give me that. You know what I'm asking. How do you feel now that you've seen Savannah?"

Danny's eyes rolled to the ceiling as he released a heavy breath. "All right," he said in a low tone. "I'd be lying if I said I didn't feel . . . something."

Carol buried her forehead in her palm. "I was right, then."

He bit briefly at his lip. "Maybe so," he admitted after a moment. "Listen, Carol, I'm sorry—"

"Don't say it," she broke in. "Let's just leave it at that. I'll be in touch when I know something. Good-bye, Dan."

The phone clicked in his ear, and Danny got the distinct impression she'd been about to burst into tears. He replaced the receiver with a frown, swiveled in his chair, and became suddenly aware that someone was standing behind him. His gaze lifted to meet that of Jack Doggett.

"Hear anything interesting?" Danny challenged.

If possible, the man's face pinched into even more disapproving lines. As Managing Editor, he liked to think he was above everyone else in Editorial. He didn't appreciate flippancy, and as a result, Danny delighted in dishing it out.

"I don't know what you mean," Doggett snapped. "I just arrived. Mr. McKenna wanted me to give you this assignment."

Danny's vision dropped to the paper Doggett held out, and for an instant he entertained a ridiculous hope. As chairman of a committee reviewing erosion along North Carolina shores, State Senator Bob Gaines was making a tour of the coastline. He was arriving Thursday and staying through the weekend— the first legitimate news Kingsport had offered since Danny returned.

Snatching the paper from Doggett's hand, Danny gave it a quick scan and looked up with an arched brow. "Shrimp boats?"

"That's right."

"May I ask," Danny added with grueling calm, "who's covering the senator's visit?"

Doggett puffed out his chest. "I am. And although it might be difficult for a big-time reporter like you to believe, I have everything well in hand. There are quite a few scheduled events— press conference, public speech on the commons, even a full-fledged ball Saturday night at King's Club."

"Great." Danny tried to manage an indifferent smile, but the attempt faltered as he glanced again at his own assignment. "Shrimp boats," he repeated derisively.

"It's a big industry that supports a lot of folks around here."

"Give me a break."

"Some might say you've been given a break already."

Danny's gaze leapt from the paper to Jack Doggett—a dark, sharp-eyed little man who brought to mind the thought of a weasel for more reasons than one.

"I know I'm going to regret asking this," Danny returned, "but exactly what kind of a break are you talking about?"

Doggett crossed his arms across his chest and looked down his nose. "Everyone here knows Mr. McKenna didn't want to honor your contract. Everyone knows you bulldozed your way in. Why you should want to return here—a man with your past—is beyond me."

Danny's eyes narrowed to slits. "Then it's a lucky thing it's none of your business, isn't it?"

Doggett tossed his head and moved away. Danny watched him make quick progress toward the publisher's office and imagined him reporting back to McKenna with gossipy relish.

One of these days, Danny thought, he was going to catch Jack Doggett at the right time and place and punch his lights out.

Savannah dashed through the house, performing her usual chores with noisy disregard, often muttering under her breath. Finally her mother demanded what on earth was the matter with her.

"Nothing," Savannah snapped. "It's just hot, that's all. I think I'll go outside for a breath of air."

She went out the back, letting the screen door bang behind her, and moved toward the location that had drawn her thoughts since yesterday afternoon. Climbing the stairs to the deck, she looked along the pool's edge to the spot where she'd spread the picnic blanket. The heat of the sun was intoxicating, sensual, as it had been the day before. She could almost see Danny and herself there, almost feel his mouth . . .

Savannah fled the site, but the image stayed with her, the memory of Danny's kiss triggering a mixture of wonder and fear. For a shattering moment, she'd surrendered . . . until the long-entrenched inhibition that formed her very core jerked her back to her senses. The fearful thing was that part of her had wanted more. Now, as she considered the inevitability of what "more" would lead to, the hair at the back of her neck bristled like a bunch of quills.

Stomping into the house, Savannah threw herself into the task of polishing the furniture. Still, as she moved the cloth in vigorous circles across the dining table, her thoughts lingered on Danny. He was angry, she knew. Her temper flared in matching anger. She'd told him how things stood. He was just so stubborn, so cocky; he never could take no for an answer.

Speeding up her efforts, she gave the dining table a final slap and moved into the parlor. Okay, so she liked having him here:

talking with him, laughing with him. She even liked looking at him—he was, after all, an incredibly handsome man, especially when he flashed one of his rakish smiles. What she couldn't bear was that Danny seemed intent on making her pay for enjoying his presence.

"Come on," he had said. "I don't think one little kiss is too much to ask for all this work, do you?"

One little kiss? To him, maybe that's all it was. To her, it had been something else—a gauntlet thrown in the face of her peaceful self-containment. It wasn't fair. Just when she was feeling carefree and happy with Danny, he turned into that intimidating male bent on pushing her to a precipice, beyond whose edge was the fathomless, terrifying unknown.

He'd come back on a crusade to clear his name. Once that was done, he'd be gone. What right did he have to drop in after fifteen years and upend her world?

By the time Savannah had made her way through the whole of the downstairs, however, her mood had shifted, the belligerence sinking beneath a growing weight of melancholia. In all fairness, she couldn't fault Danny. Men and women went around kissing, or whatever, all the time. She was the abnormal one for whom such interaction had become a foreign, impossible thing.

Thinking back, Savannah tried to pinpoint exactly when she'd turned down the path on which she now found herself. In the beginning, it hadn't seemed to be a road of no return. In the early days, a proper young lady was expected to say no, to slap a boy's hands away if he became too bold. But somewhere along the line, the rules had changed. Sometime—while she was pent up in the Crossing with no one for company but a mother who lived in a world of her own—the time for discovery had passed.

The girls she'd grown up with were married and had children. The boys were fathers, except perhaps for wild bucks like Danny—whom, she imagined, had played the field for years with any number of willing females. She alone remained locked in a shell which, by its very unsuitability, was impregnable.

Since she was nineteen years old, Savannah had been kissed by only one other man, a good-looking young drifter who'd helped Mr. Kiker patch the roof a few winters back. The guy—Tom something-or-other—had come into the kitchen for a cup of coffee, grabbed her, and had swept her up in his arms before

she knew what was happening. Savannah had sent both men
packing without delay. As a result, the roof continued to leak.

For years she'd lived her life a certain way—immersing herself in the role of provider, and struggling to meet financial ob-
ligations. There had been no time—no wish—for the female
part of her to grow into a woman. Now it was too late. The
Southern belle's code of propriety that kept her pure as a young
girl had stiffened into the staunchness of an old maid. Savannah
King was a thirty-one-year-old virgin who'd locked herself
away far too long to remember how to open up—if, indeed,
she'd ever known.

Pausing by the mirror in the hall, she took a long look at herself. Lifting her chin, she scanned the long neck, searched for
infirmity, and found none. The skin was toned with the tensile
muscularity that marked the whole of her lean body. If nothing
else, the rigorous years of outdoor chores and housework had
kept her in shape.

She still considered her brows a little too dark to suit the rest
of her coloring, and she'd never liked the way her nose turned
up on the end. Still, she recalled girlhood days when she'd been
considered a beauty and supposed she hadn't changed very
much. Danny had said she was more beautiful than ever.

Savannah watched the reflected cheeks begin to blush. It had
been easy to disregard the void of experience that evolved with
her solitary existence—easy, that is, until Danny had returned.
There was no doubt he had a tremendous effect on her. It had always been so, even long ago. She remembered the years with
Clifford, the dull, lifeless kisses she hadn't known were dull and
lifeless until Danny kissed her, stealing her breath, melting her
with his tongue until she lost her senses.

It had happened then, and it had happened yesterday. Despite
her limited experience, Savannah knew enough to realize something extraordinary happened when Danny touched her. There
was an undeniable chemistry, the kind of thing most women
dreamed of. He didn't have to kiss her to start her insides quaking; he merely had to give her one of those heated looks that
seemed to undress her, seemed to demand . . .

A shiver flashed from her scalp to her toes, stirring taboo
parts of her body into willful alertness. Savannah's surprised
gaze dropped to her shirtfront; through the light fabric, she
could see the thrusting outlines of nipples that had turned hard
as pebbles. She stared, and despite her mortification, experi-

enced a flash of fascination, a spark of curiosity, even a flicker of arousal. All were swiftly extinguished as the inescapable facts closed over her like a cold rain.

Savannah's gaze rose to meet the eyes in the mirror, her flushed face taking on a determined set. There were simply some ways a person couldn't go against herself—some corners that, once turned, led only to destruction. She was reminded of the passage from *Hamlet*: "This above all, to thine own self be true."

She was what she was, and that was that. The cards had been dealt long before Danny showed up on her doorstep, and she would be holding the same hand when he left. She wished that while he was here they could be friends. But if not, she could exist without friendship. After all, she'd done it for a dozen years.

Feeling more like her old rigidly controlled self, Savannah marched to the kitchen and went about the business of preparing lunch.

Shrimp boats. No further direction, just a fluff piece for the Saturday "Living" page.

Danny spent most of the day hanging around the docks. It was a clear day and the boats were out, so he contented himself with talking to a few old salts who'd been left behind. He picked up a few stories. If worse came to worse, he could string them together for a nostalgia piece.

It was late afternoon when he passed the Donnelly place—a small shrimping operation that had been in the family for generations. Danny paused as he saw a silver-haired man stride away from a newly docked boat and head up the ramp in his direction. He'd never known the Donnellys personally, but thought he recognized the short muscular man as one of the family.

"How was the haul?" Danny asked with a friendly smile.

The man paused, returning Danny's smile with a wary look. "All right, considering we only took out half the fleet. Who are you?"

Danny extended a hand. "Name's Sawyer." A brawny mit met his hand, tentatively at first.

"Sawyer," the man repeated, withdrawing his hand and burying it in a pocket. "*Danny* Sawyer?"

Danny stiffened defensively. "I see word travels fast."

"It's a small town. Nothin' much of interest happens. When somethin' does, folks are liable to take note and remember."

"So I've been told. Actually, I guess I knew that all along, even before I decided to come back."

The shorter man's gaze sharpened. "You got your reasons, I reckon. What are you doin' hanging around my place?"

"My job. I'm with *The Watch* now."

"What's *The Watch* want down here at the docks?"

"The usual. A story."

"About what?"

"Shrimpers."

A thoughtful look came over the man's weathered face. Danny detected something, but he wasn't sure what. "Know any good shrimper tales?" he prodded.

"Depends on what kind of tale you're interested in."

"What kind do you have, Mr. . . . ?"

"Donnelly. Nate Donnelly. Is it true what they say? About you reporter fellas protecting your sources?"

Danny's pulse quickened as it always did when he sensed something about to break. "It's true," he replied.

Nate squinted up at the sky. "Hot day," he said. "How'd ya like to buy me a beer?"

In the private shadows of a waterfront bar, Danny learned that Nate's twenty-year-old son, Luke, had been lured into using one of the shrimpers to haul "unidentified" cargo. Once they got him on the payroll, the "druggers"—as Nate called them—had threatened Luke into complying with their demands. Since the beginning of the summer, he'd been ordered to make a half dozen late-night hauls—meeting an offshore speedboat and returning to have the clandestine shipment unloaded by a trio of sleazy characters. Nate had known nothing about it until his son confessed in desperation. He was in over his head, and Nate had been afraid to call in the police for fear his boy would bear the consequences.

"But you," Nate concluded with a sharp look. "You could be doing a story down here at the docks and maybe catch wind of something that makes you want to take a closer look."

"Absolutely," Danny responded in a quiet tone. "Got any idea when these guys are going to make their next move?"

"Friday night."

"*This* Friday night?"

Nate gave a short nod.

"You're sure," Danny pressed.

"As sure as I can be. Luke says once he's been contacted, they've never missed."

"The police will have to be notified," Danny cautioned. "Coast Guard, too."

Nate's face took on the look of a thundercloud. "The only reason I've told you this is that I want my boy out of it without getting hurt. If I can't be sure of that, you can forget the whole thing."

Danny's blood was racing along with his thoughts. Finishing off his beer, he set the bottle aside and leaned forward.

"I think there's a way," he said, "although the timing will be tight. Just tell Luke to go along like always."

Nate gave him a doubtful look.

"I can handle it, Mr. Donnelly," Danny said earnestly. "Do you trust me?"

Eventually the man surrendered a grin. "Yeah. I guess I do."

It was after five o'clock when Danny walked into the police station. The place seemed small and deserted compared to the round-the-clock bustle Danny had become used to in D.C. No one stopped him as he walked through the lobby and along the corridor—simultaneously remembering and trying to forget the last time he'd been inside these walls.

Spotting a solitary man bent over a desk in one of the offices, Danny paused, read the name on the door, and stepped inside.

"Lieutenant Gilroy?"

He looked up. He was young, maybe thirty.

"Yes," he said. "Can I help you?"

"My name's Sawyer. I'm with *The Watch*. I have a story you might be interested in. Mind if I close the door?"

Without revealing names or dates, Danny gave the lieutenant a sketch of his plan. As they talked, Danny knew he had the right man. Gilroy was new in town, new to the department. He had a good head on his shoulders, and he was hungry. Yes, the thing could be orchestrated with the Coast Guard. Yes, his own men could be trusted to handle things at the docks.

"There's just one thing," Danny cautioned toward the end. "The shrimper is my informant. He's not to be singled out in front of the smugglers, but neither is he to be prosecuted."

"Well . . ." Gilroy shrugged.

"Well, nothing," Danny returned firmly. "That's the only way this bust is going down."

Gilroy studied the man across the desk. His expression was solemn, unyielding.

"Okay, Sawyer," he said, extending a hand. "We have a deal."

It was past six when Danny drove into the Crossing, stopping the jeep out front as he spotted Savannah in the rose garden. He was in high spirits, as he always was when a story was breaking.

Loosening his tie as he walked, he eyed her through the fence. She was kneeling at the base of one of the rosebushes, wearing white shorts and a T-shirt, her slender limbs gleaming a rosy gold in the light of the setting sun. Joining her in the courtyard, he stopped only a foot away. She must have known he was there, though she didn't look up.

"Miss me?" he quipped.

"Oh, yes. Terribly."

A corner of Danny's mouth turned up. She was a spectacle without seeming aware of it. The long blond ponytail was a shining streak to her waist, the smooth suntan interrupted by the brief white of her clothes. A familiar hunger knotted within him.

"What's for supper?" he asked.

"I wasn't sure you intended to show up. There's just salad. I was going to have a grilled cheese sandwich with it."

"Delicious," he commented.

But when Savannah looked up, she gathered he wasn't talking about supper. His gaze was moving along her legs. She gazed up the tall length of him, unable to prevent a thought of how attractive he was in business slacks and shirt. His sleeves were rolled to the elbow, his collar loose . . .

"Your legs make me hot," he said.

Her gaze leapt to his, and if she'd been able, Savannah would have climbed inside the rosebush to hide the limbs in question. As it was, she climbed hurriedly to her feet and began yanking at the fingertips of her garden gloves.

"I think you do it on purpose," Danny added.

"Do what?" she snapped.

"Parade around here with your behind barely covered."

Smacking the freed glove in her palm, Savannah attacked the other one with short, jerky movements. "I do *not* parade, Danny Sawyer! And my behind is perfectly covered, thank you!"

He dipped his head to one side. "Perfectly is right." He grinned at her red-faced speechlessness.

"Admit it, Savannah," he added. "You want me to notice your legs. You *want* me, period."

Sunlight radiated off his chestnut hair and limned his face. He was despicably good-looking, and he'd always known it. All this passed through Savannah's mind while she searched for a retort.

"Don't flatter yourself!" was all she could come up with.

But later, after she'd stalked into the house to the sound of his low laughter, she had an inspiration. Taking off the brief shorts and top, she dressed carefully in the rust-streaked work pants she reserved for grimy jobs. Adding a billowing, denim shirt of her father's, she buttoned it up beneath her chin and went down to the kitchen with a smug smile on her face.

Danny glanced over from the breakfast nook as she came in, then did a double take, noting the outrageous clothes she was wearing as well as her smug expression. The August evening was sultry. Typically, Savannah would have been wearing brief, cool garb that exposed a tantalizing amount of her flesh. Tonight she looked like a ditch-digger dressed for a hard day. Looking stubbornly back at his newspaper, Danny refrained from saying anything as she puttered around the stove.

Eventually she served salad and the hot sandwiches, and sat down opposite him. Danny set aside his paper.

"Thank you," he said.

"Room and board," she returned. "That's the arrangement."

Her tone was cool, in contrast with the beads of perspiration clinging to her upper lip. Danny hid a smile.

"Nice outfit," he remarked casually. "Is it for my benefit?"

"Why, Danny," she said as she lifted a forkful of salad along with her brows, "whatever do you mean?"

He took a bite of the grilled cheese, chewing slowly as he considered her. She was taking great enjoyment in her little ploy.

"Why don't you go upstairs and change? You've made your point."

She gave him a sweet smile and went on with her salad.

"It's not doing you any good to sit there sweating in those ridiculous clothes," he said eventually. "I can easily imagine what's underneath."

Her face, already flushed from the heat of the stove, turned a

shade brighter as she caught his look of amusement. With one
remark he'd turned the tables on her. Now she felt all the more
conspicuous in her voluminous costume. Snatching open the
collar button of the shirt, she rose to her feet.

"You're right," she huffed. "I *am* uncomfortably hot. I think
I'll retire and clean up these dishes later."

Danny leaned back in his chair and looked up, unperturbed.
"Will it be worth my time to wait around for the kitchen detail?"

"What?"

"Are you coming back down in shorts?"

Suddenly, his conceited, amused onceover was more than she
could bear. "Oh!" she blurted. "You are the most vulgar man it
has ever been my misfortune to meet!"

Turning on her heel, she was halfway across the room when
he stopped her with another remark.

"It isn't vulgar to admire someone, Savannah."

She sent him a scathing look as she turned. "You don't admire, Danny, you leer! I told you from the beginning that I don't
intend to put up with that kind of thing."

The careless grin faded from his face. He got to his feet at a
slow, unthreatening pace. Still, Savannah felt a pang of uncertainty as he glared across the few yards between them.

"And I told you I didn't intend to hide what I think or feel."

The uncertainty swelled. "I'm asking you, Danny," she said.
"Please stop these . . . innuendos."

He shook his head.

"This is just a game to you," she said in a tight voice. "It is
not a game to me. Why do you insist on making me so terribly
uncomfortable?"

"Maybe you need to be uncomfortable."

Savannah's chin went up. "I don't think that's your decision
to make."

"If I care about you, it is."

His deep voice rumbled in the quiet room. Savannah's knees
felt weak.

"If you care about me," she managed, "you might consider
doing as I ask."

"I did consider it. I said we'd play it your way, remember?
But I didn't mean forever. It might be different if I didn't know
how we are together."

"And how are we?"

He started toward her. "Shall I remind you?"

She stepped quickly back. "Stop it, Danny."

He came to a halt, the familiar ache pounding through him. Half of him wanted to grab and kiss her; the other half wanted to slap her.

"You might choose to sublimate the fact that you're a woman," he said quietly, "but don't expect me to behave as something less than a man."

Savannah searched his eyes—beautiful and determined. The unwelcome tingle overcame her. This time when she turned she fled the kitchen at a near run, slowing only when she reached the sanctuary of her bedroom. Irritated with herself and burning up in the stifling clothes, she stripped and spent the better part of the next half hour in a cool shower.

The next few days passed in fleeting moments of taut civility. Savannah kept to herself, and Danny had need to be away from the Crossing. Between maintaining appearances at *The Watch* and clandestine meetings with Nate Donnelly and Lieutenant Gilroy, he found his days and nights consumed.

On Friday afternoon, he handed in a collection of shrimping yore from days gone by. A short while later, Jack Doggett paraded by with the story in hand. Normally his patronizing nod of approval would have provoked a taunting riposte. This time Danny swallowed the urge, taking satisfaction from the fact that the preening peacock had no idea the story was a ruse.

It was the best plan he'd been able to devise. Neither Doggett nor McKenna would approve the daring story he was hoping to substitute for the copy he'd just submitted. If either of them had the slightest inkling of what he was up to, Danny was certain he'd be yanked off the assignment so fast his head would spin. His only chance was to slip it past them.

The timing would be crucial. Luke Donnelly was embarking at eleven and was due back some time after midnight. Things had to go right, both offshore and at the docks, for Danny to make it back to *The Watch* in time to sweet-talk the young pressman who launched the morning edition at two a.m.

That evening, after a solitary supper during which Savannah was conspicuously "required" by her mother, Danny changed into dark clothes and gathered notebook, pen, and recorder. When he stepped outside his room, he saw the light under Savannah's door. A grim set came to his mouth. They'd hardly spoken in days. Walking swiftly over, he rapped at the door.

"Savannah?" he called.

She'd been in the midst of changing. Spinning around, Savannah clutched her nightgown to her bare bosom and peered at the door as if the man on the other side could see straight through it.

"What is it?" she answered shrilly.

"I'll be out late tonight. Just thought I should let you know."

Savannah blinked as the conclusion struck her. *A woman!* The word rang in her head like a jarring bell, and as it chimed, the image of Danny smiling one of his crooked seductive smiles flashed to mind. Of course! A woman! That was what took him away the past few evenings! A shower of heat washed over her, and Savannah knew it for what it was—pure, burning jealousy. What did she expect? That he would take on the lifestyle of a monk just because she lived like a nun?

Danny tapped again with a single knuckle. "Savannah? Did you hear—"

"Have a good time!" she cut in with uncontrollable sharpness.

"It has nothing to do with . . ." Grimacing, Danny came to a halt. "What the hell," he muttered to himself. Vaulting down the steps, he stalked out of the house, yanked the convertible top off the jeep, and sped away from the Crossing.

By the time he reached the appointed copse of palms and joined up with Gilroy and his men, Danny had put all else from his mind. His heart was pounding, nerves jangling, as they watched Luke Donnelly board a shrimper and move away from the docks minus his running lights. Time crept by. An occasional breeze stirred the clear August night, failing to lift the air of tension that blanketed the group hiding in the palms.

As it turned out, the plan moved along like clockwork. While Gilroy and his team stayed out of sight at the docks, the Coast Guard seized a speedboat and arrested two men. A half hour later, the shrimper chugged up to the Donnelly docks. As Luke killed the engine and left the boat, a white unmarked van pulled into the deserted parking area. Luke was well away, and the van half-unloaded of its illegal cargo, when Gilroy made his move—netting a respectable haul of marijuana and cocaine, as well as four drug-runners, without finding it necessary to fire a shot.

The docks came alive with flashing lights, milling officers, and the crackling sound of police radios. Danny stood apart with Gilroy and watched as the perpetrators were cuffed and read their rights.

"Ten to one we find out these guys are part of a ring I heard about that stems out of Miami," the lieutenant said.

Danny looked sharply at him. He'd been talking into his recorder. He left it running as he asked, "Is it too early to put that in print?"

Gilroy's brows went up, his face taking on a look of amusement. "Just say it's a possibility that's being looked into. God, you're greedy. Isn't it enough you've masterminded a significant bust here?"

"Oh, yeah," Danny said, grinning. "It's enough."

"Will it be on the front page tomorrow?"

Danny glanced at his watch. One o'clock. "Actually, I'll be pulling off a miracle to get it in at all. I gotta get going."

"Good work," Gilroy offered.

"Same to you."

"It helps if somebody walks in with everything wrapped up in a neat little package. You can contact me with a 'story' any time."

The thought of Jane Wilson flashed through Danny's mind. "Now that you mention it, there *is* something I'd like to talk over."

"What?"

"Some other time," Danny said.

"Just let me know," Gilroy replied and, with a passing salute, walked off toward the crowd.

Racing back to *The Watch*, Danny banged the story into his computer terminal, waited impatiently as the type went through, and proofed the copy on the way downstairs to the pressroom. After a cajoling speech and the exchange of a fifty-dollar bill, the new story was plugged onto the "Living" page. Danny backed away, covering his ears as the giant press went into motion . . . and grinned like the Cheshire cat all the way back to the Crossing.

Morning sunlight shafted across the banquet-sized table, illuminating Rory and Big Ed to Nordic brilliance, while it cast Clayton into the shadows. Libby set aside the newspaper and took a sip of coffee as she studied Rory from beneath lowered lids. He was poring over *The Charlotte Observer*, which he read every morning in preference to *The Watch*.

"Interesting story on the 'Living' page," she remarked.

"If you like shrimping lore," Rory smirked without looking up.

"I thought you said it would be a cold day in hell when you'd put Danny Sawyer on an important story."

"It will be."

"I'd call busting a drug ring a fairly important story."

He looked up at that. "What are you talking about?"

Libby picked up the section and passed it across the table. Rory looked at the page, then grabbed it up, his expression changing from shock to fury.

"That son-of-a-bitch," he snarled.

Big Ed looked up. "What are you muttering about?"

Rory's eyes flashed to his father. "That son-of-a-bitch!" he repeated in a near yell.

"Not so loud," Big Ed growled.

Studying the man, Libby noted his bloodshot eyes. He was obviously hungover, as he was most mornings.

Rory leapt to his feet and smacked the newspaper down in front of his father. "This is not the story I approved! This is not what was supposed to go to press! Somehow or other that bastard pulled off a substitution!"

Cringing against Rory's loudness, Big Ed began to read the "Living" page. Glancing to her left, Libby caught the look of unmistakable satisfaction on Clayton's face. Raising her coffee cup to her lips, she hid the beginnings of a smile. After a moment, Big Ed emitted a rumble of low laughter.

"What's so funny?" Rory demanded.

Big Ed looked up. "You wanted an ace reporter, and you got one."

"You're missing the point, Papa! Sawyer went behind my back!"

"Obviously. Otherwise the piece never would have made it into the paper, and he knew it."

Rory's eyes narrowed. "I'd like to know why you're so complacent about this. As I recall, you're the man who never let anybody get away with anything . . . *ever!*"

The smile drained as Big Ed rose to his feet and looked his son eye-to-eye. "It seems that he's already gotten away with it. You know, every now and then you have to surrender a little respect to a worthy adversary. Every hunter knows that."

"Surrender?" Rory repeated sharply. "That's a word I never

would have heard from you a few years back." He shook his head in derision. "The truth is, you've lost the killer instinct. You've gotten old, Papa. Old and soft."

Big Ed grabbed Rory by the shirt collar and pulled him so close that they were nose to nose. "Not so old that I can't keep a buck like you in line. You'd do well to remember that, *son*."

An instant of awkward silence ensued, with Rory glaring rebelliously into his father's eyes but holding his tongue. After a dramatic moment, Big Ed released him and left the room without a backward glance.

Clayton left his chair as well. He took a few steps, then turned to his brother with a grin.

"M-makes me think of a certain b-basketball game some years b-back," he said. "Sawyer m-made you look like shit then, too."

"Get the hell out of my sight!" Rory boomed, and as Clayton walked out, turned a blazing look on Libby.

Raising her shoulders, she regarded him with wide, innocent eyes. "I didn't say anything," she offered, and held back a beaming smile until he'd stormed safely away from the table.

Having found it impossible to sleep, Danny had been up since dawn and then decided to take advantage of the cool morning to resume his work at the pool. By the time nine o'clock rolled around, he'd succeeded in freeing the back wall of its strangling vines and had worked up a powerful thirst. After burying the jungle knife in a nearby stump, he picked up the T-shirt he'd removed earlier, hung it around his neck, and walked up to the house.

The phone rang just as he stepped into the kitchen. Glancing about the room, he saw that it looked just as he'd left it hours ago. Savannah apparently hadn't come down yet. He reached for the phone and had barely said hello when Rory McKenna lit into him. Phrases like "flagrant insubordination" and "grounds for dismissal" blared in Danny's ear. He held the receiver away, eyeing it with disgust before he responded.

"Shut up a minute, McKenna," he broke in. "If you want to talk to me about something, then *talk*. But I'm not going to stand here and listen to a harangue."

"I said I just finished reading your little surprise story on the "Living" page. That was not approved, and you know it!"

Danny's face hardened. "No shit. But it makes your paper

look pretty good, doesn't it, McKenna? I don't know of any publisher who would complain about such an exclusive. If he did, he'd look like a damn fool."

Without answering, McKenna slammed down the receiver. Danny responded in kind and turned to find that Savannah had come into the room. She was standing just a few yards away, regarding him with an odd, almost glowing, expression.

"So this is what you've been up to the past few days," she said.

She held up a copy of *The Watch*. It was open to his story. Danny nodded.

"However did you figure it out?"

"I had a tip."

"The anonymous shrimper?"

"That's right."

Savannah shook her head, her eyes shining. "You're gifted, Danny. Truly, you are. Daddy used to say so, and it's true."

Caught off guard, Danny stared for a moment. No praise had ever touched him quite so deeply.

"Thanks," he mumbled. "To both of you."

Savannah smiled, her gaze drifting innocently over him, her smile faltering as she took note of the masculine spectacle before her. Faded gym shorts hung low on Danny's hips. His muscular legs and chest were bare, his face rosy with sun, his hair damp with sweat. Turning away, she moved to the stove, set aside the newspaper, and reached for the coffee pot.

"So that's how you've been spending your nights?" she asked in the most casual tone she could manage. "Following a story?"

"Yeah. Like I said . . ." A look of dawning broke across Danny's features. He took a few slow steps in Savannah's direction, his gaze sweeping her body. She was wearing shorts and a sleeveless top. Her legs and arms were enticingly bare.

"Why?" he asked. "Did you think it might be something else?"

She sidestepped to the sink where she turned on the faucet and began rinsing the pot.

"A woman, maybe?" Danny prodded, stepping closer.

Savannah stared at the running water. "You'd have every right—if you wanted to see a woman, I mean."

"But you wouldn't like it, would you?"

The words came from just behind her head, stirring the wisps of hair at her ear. In a swift motion that showed her irritation, Savannah turned off the faucet and stepped away, pot in hand.

"Excuse me," she said, glancing briefly up as she moved around him on her way along the counter.

Danny followed, a small hope flickering within him as he watched her reach for a dish towel and begin swiping at the pot.

"You've been jealous," he said.

"For heaven's sake, Danny—"

"Admit it."

Her hands stopped moving. Hesitating an instant, Savannah turned her back to the counter and faced him.

"What I'll admit is that I've missed you these past few days, Danny. I don't want to be angry with you any longer. I don't want you to be angry with me. I want us to be friends."

"We are, Savannah. I think you know that."

"We don't seem to act like it most of the time."

"Maybe that's because we're more than just friends."

Her gaze darted between his eyes. "We don't seem to act like that either."

Danny's surprise showed in the quick rise of his brows. "I can fix *that*," he said and leaned toward her.

"No," she blurted, planting a quick palm on his chest. "I'm sorry. I didn't mean that as an invitation."

He looked down at her hand. Suddenly conscious of the warm bare skin beneath her fingers, Savannah snatched her hand away and would have slipped aside, but Danny placed quick hands on each side of her, effectively trapping her against the corner. His knees brushed against her bare legs. Savannah's heart skipped.

"Why you fight such a good feeling is beyond me," he said.

The eyes that met his were sapphire blue and wide as an ocean, filled with that shimmering look he remembered from the pool. Danny straightened and backed away a step.

"Don't look like that," he commanded.

"Like what?"

"Like a little girl about to be molested."

"In some ways," Savannah said after a moment, "I guess I *am* a little girl."

"Not that I can see," Danny commented with a raking look.

His irritation was growing by the second. It occurred to him the feeling had less to do with Savannah than with the emasculating sense of restraint that had suddenly come over him. She was less than a foot away, and he had the feeling that if he took her in his arms, she'd give in. Why, then, was he backing off?

"Appearances can be deceiving," Savannah commented. "You're a full-grown man, but sometimes I see the boy I knew long ago."

The unwelcome answer dawned on Danny. He didn't want a look of fright, but of desire. She'd defeated him with those wide blue eyes—unmanned him, by God! His brows furled in a dark line.

"Didn't realize you'd noticed," he snapped.

Savannah regarded him questioningly, aware of his mounting anger, nonplussed as to the cause. "Noticed what?"

"That I'm a full-grown man. Seems more like you're dead set on turning me into some sexless mannequin like yourself."

Standing so close and glaring down at her, he was instantly aware when tears filled her eyes. She looked swiftly aside and started to move. Danny's arms lurched into motion, his hand closing on her shoulder. She looked from his fingers to his face. Her eyes were swimming, but at least she didn't cry out the dreaded warning about not wanting to be touched.

"I'm sorry," Danny muttered. "I shouldn't have said that."

She stared at him mutely, and he found himself pulling her into his arms. For the first time in his life that he'd held Savannah, it had nothing to do with the flesh, but all with the spirit. Apparently sensing the difference, Savannah allowed the embrace. They said nothing, but simply stood there, her arms hanging by her sides, his wrapped around her. After a moment, Danny became aware of a growing damp spot against his neck, just where her closed eyes were resting. Looking up at the ceiling, he positioned his chin on the top of her head, feeling sorry that he'd hurt her.

"Please, Danny," she mumbled against his throat. "Just be my friend."

The thick tone of her voice tugged at him. Danny ran a caressing palm along the trail of hair reaching down her back, his hand coming to a halt as he brought himself up short. She was doing it again. Stepping abruptly back, he looked down with hard eyes, no longer softened by the wetness that spiked her lashes.

"I'm not some boy you can twist around your finger, Savannah. You said yourself I'm a full-grown man, so stop trying to rob me of that very manhood."

She blinked, momentarily stunned by his remarks. "No one's trying to rob you of anything. I just asked you to be—"

"I'll be what I am!" Danny broke in ferally. "Nothing more. Nothing less."

Savannah's chin went up, the lingering sheen in her eyes adding a poignant impact to her defiant gaze.

"And so will I," she said.

Danny peered at her a long, punishing moment before stalking out. Savannah jumped as the screen door banged noisily behind him.

It was nearly lunchtime when Danny heard his name. Looking up, he saw Savannah standing a safe distance away in the side yard, shielding her eyes against the sun as she peered in his direction.

"What is it?" he called.

"The phone!" she yelled back.

He stood and brushed a forearm across his brow, then reached for his discarded shirt and rubbed it across his moist chest. That was all it took. Savannah bounded away like a scared jackrabbit.

His skin was scorched and his throat parched, but a few hours' purgative labor in the hot sun had improved Danny's mood. Now, as he watched her scurry toward the house, he grinned. Slinging the shirt around his neck, he followed, casting an inquisitive look at Savannah as he stepped into the kitchen. She was facing away from him, seemingly so absorbed in grating carrots into a bowl that she couldn't spare so much as a look. Danny reached for the phone.

"Hello?" he said on a questioning note.

Minutes later, he hung up and looked in Savannah's direction.

"What are you doing tonight?"

She gave him a mere glance. "What I do every night, I suppose."

"No."

"No?"

"That was State Senator Gaines. You're going to a senatorial ball." That got her attention. She looked up from her bowl.

"He liked my story," Danny went on. "We're invited to a ball in his honor. All the big shots in town will be there. Eight o'clock at King's Club."

"King's Club!" Savannah looked back at the salad bowl. "I'm not going to King's Club," she said.

"Why not?"

"It was my father's dream, and his last hope. The McKennas took it over, just like they took over *The Watch*. I've never set foot inside the place and don't intend to. Anyway, I've told you before—I don't go into public anymore."

"Do you think I'm any less scandalous than you?" Danny asked. "Everyone around here remembers Danny Sawyer. Everyone whispers when I walk by. There comes a point, you know, when it's time to face off. That time is now, Savannah. Let's go to this thing, look everyone dead in the eye, and imply they can go straight to hell."

She chuckled ruefully. "I'm not like you, Danny. I'd prefer just to stay here and let things be."

"Hide, you mean. Let them exile you to this piece of land as they have for years."

Savannah met the glint in his eye with one of her own. "I have not *let* them do anything, Danny. It was my choice."

"Right."

His sarcasm spurred her temper. "What good will it do for me to show up at a gathering where the big shots—as you call them—want nothing more than to peer down their roses and whisper to each other when I pass?"

Danny regarded her sternly. "You used to have more spunk."

A single brow shot up. "I can't just go gallavanting about at night," Savannah returned haughtily. "Someone has to stay with Mother."

"Are you telling me you've never left her alone? Not a single night in twelve years?"

"Occasionally I've had to."

"Who stayed with her then?"

Savannah glanced down at her hands. "Dr. Crane."

"Call him," Danny commanded.

"But—"

"Call him!"

Savannah spun around. "I told you I'm not going, Danny."

"Well, *I* am, and I don't intend to go stag." Folding his arms across his chest, he gave her a stony look. "This is an honor for me, you know—to be contacted by the senator, personally invited to meet him. You asked me to be your friend, Savannah. Why don't you try being one yourself?"

His remark hit home. Savannah caught her bottom lip between her teeth, her mind racing. "But this is Saturday. Dr. Crane probably has plans for the evening."

"You'll never know unless you ask," Danny returned relentlessly.

He stood over her as she made the call, arching a brow as she hung up the phone. "Well?"

"He'll be here at seven-thirty." Savannah's eyes lifted. "Danny, I'm really not so sure . . ."

"I am," he returned firmly. "Come on, Savannah. Let's walk into that club, heads high, and have the best time of anybody there. Let's rub their faces in it together. What do you say?"

She gave him a last doubtful look. "Together, then."

Danny's tense expression gave way to a grin. "Damn straight," he confirmed. Heading for the door, he retrieved his wallet and keys from the highboy where he'd left them early that morning.

"Where are you going?" Savannah asked.

"Into town. I've got to pick up a tux."

"Tux?!"

"Yeah," he threw over his shoulder. "It's black tie."

"Black tie?" Savannah echoed as he went out the door. A senatorial *ball*? Of *course*, it was black tie! For a moment she stood transfixed, her mind's eye thumbing hurriedly through her outdated wardrobe.

"Good heavens!" she muttered, and hurried for the stairs.

Chapter Ten

LIBBY CRAWLED to the edge of the bed, swung her legs over, and pushed up to a sitting position. The light that made its way through the shades was muffled, but she could tell the sun was low. Soon it would be time for supper.

Well, she wouldn't have to make supper tonight, though she was expected to be dressed to the teeth for the damn ball due to start in a few short hours. Looking down at herself, Libby found it hard to believe she could ever be presentable again. Even in the dim light, the marks showed—three sets of teeth, two raking scratches, assorted bruises and abrasions . . . all on the torso between breast and thigh, all inflicted in locations that could be easily covered.

Even in his madness, Rory was cunning.

She dreamed briefly of begging off for the evening, but knew she couldn't. Rory enjoyed showing her off, like a new car or piece of clothing. He'd demand an explanation, and there was none she could give. To maintain the lurid cover that permitted her inside Rory's life, it was necessary not just to submit to his barbarism, but to pretend to like it.

Libby pushed to her feet, took a step, and cringed. The spot between her legs was another matter. He'd bitten her there, too, and as she glanced down, she saw a trickle of blood staining the inside of her right thigh. Fury blossomed within her, carrying her forward when the pain of moving made her long to stop in the center of the room and cry her eyes out.

She moved into the bathroom and turned on the shower, leaving the light off, recoiling at the idea of seeing in the mirror what she knew was there. She climbed gingerly into the tub, and the water hit—stinging and urgent, purity clashing with foulness. She thought of Alfred, and for a desperate moment was actually glad he was dead; at least he would never know the shameful indignities she was suffering, the perverse depths to which Rory was dragging her.

He was getting worse, pushing further. Libby wasn't sure how much longer she could endure it. And yet she knew she would, until she caught him or until she died. Maybe that was what happened to Jane Wilson—maybe Rory had simply gotten carried away in one of his fiendish fantasies and killed her.

The water was scalding, but Libby turned it hotter still, cleansing her body while her mind dwelled in the dingy alleys that had become her reality: brutality, revenge, and murder.

By the time she finished, the small, closeted room was stifling with steam. Wrapping a towel loosely around herself, she opened the door and was stopped in her tracks by what she thought she saw. Just before the steam billowed out of the bathroom, she could have sworn she saw . . . *Mrs. McKenna?*

For a heart-stopping moment, Libby peered blindly into the cloud of steam. And then the mist cleared, jolting her with the revelation of the image that had managed to terrify her, in a fleeting second, with the unfamiliar blankness of its stare.

Not a ghost, not a phantom, just her own reflection in the facing mirror.

"I still don't approve of your going out with that Sawyer boy," Ophelia snapped. "But a fat lot of good it would do me to object. Your father is just as soft for the boy as you are!"

"I am not—" Savannah broke off, flinching as her mother jammed a pearl-headed pin into her upswept hair. "Ow!" she complained. "Are you finished, I hope?"

Ophelia stepped away from the vanity and eyed her critically. "Stand up, Savannah," she said with an impatient flick of her hand. "I can't see how you look while you're squatting there like a toad on a log."

Savannah rose and turned. Ophelia beamed a smile of approval.

"Lovely," she pronounced, the smile fading as she considered her daughter's shockingly mature appearance. "In fact, you look quite grown up," she added, perplexed.

Savannah moved to the full-length mirror. Her mother was right. She did look grown up, thank heaven. Earlier, as she'd plunged through her closet, every cellophane-shrouded dress had seemed hopelessly girlish and out of fashion. It was at the very back of the wardrobe that she'd discovered the ivory gown with its yoke and overskirt of ruffled lace. A few strokes of the scissors had denuded the frock of its lace and yielded a sleeve-less, satin gown with a tight-fitting waist and flowing skirt. By its very simplicity it was sophisticated and, Savannah decided as she gazed in the mirror, quite flattering.

Her mother, a wizard at hairdressing, had arranged the "horse's mane" in a sleek twist with curls secured at the crown by her own treasured collection of pearl-headed hairpins. Pearls were repeated at ear and throat, Grandmother Benton's choker having proven the ideal length for the modestly scooped neck of the gown. The final touch was Savannah's own full-length kid gloves—retrieved from the cedar chest packed with treasures from days gone by.

Savannah breathed a sigh of relief. She might not reflect the latest fashion, but the classic look she'd achieved never really went out of style. Now if she could just manage to still the but-terflies in her stomach.

"Savannah . . ."

She turned to find her mother studying her with a worried look.

"Where's that pretty, tea-length gown I bought you early in the summer? Perhaps it would be more appropriate for a young lady—"

"Mother," Savannah interrupted gently. "The dress is fine." Retrieving an evening bag covered with seed pearls from the di-van, she paused at the door and cast a look over her shoulder.

"Thanks for doing my hair."

Ophelia tipped her head to one side, her own platinum locks catching the light and shining like a halo.

"You really do look quite lovely," she remarked, the compli-ment shadowed by an expression of complete puzzlement.

Savannah smiled. "Thank you, Mother. Good night."

Leo poured hefty portions of brandy into two glasses. "I'd heard you were back out here at the Crossing. How long you planning to stay?"

"I'm not sure yet. A few months maybe."

"What brings you back?"

Danny hesitated. He'd always liked Dr. Crane, but . . . "Just needed a break from the fast lane," he replied.

Replacing the decanter in the otherwise empty liquor cabinet,

Leo turned. "Ophelia's private stock," he confided, and with a conspiratorial grin, offered a snifter. "Cheers."

Leo took a healthy gulp, eyeing his companion as he followed suit. The last time he'd seen Danny was when he testified at his trial; since then Danny Sawyer of Kingsport had become Buck Sawyer of *The Washington Post*. The man had made great strides, and it showed. Dressed tonight in black-tie formality, Danny looked every inch the accomplished gentleman—a man who would be just as comfortable in the parlor of the White House as the one here at Kings Crossing.

"A great deal of time has passed," Leo observed. "It's hard to believe you're the same barefoot boy I used to see running wild about the Crossing."

Danny smiled. Apart from the graying of his hair, the gangly doctor had altered little.

"You, on the other hand, haven't changed a bit," he said.

"Oh, but I feel the years in my bones," Leo returned amicably. Setting the drink aside, he fished for the pipe and tobacco in his breast pocket. "Ophelia and Savannah have been alone far too long," he added on a more serious note. "I'm glad you're back."

Danny chucked wryly. "That makes you a member of a very exclusive group: yourself and me."

Absently packing his pipe bowl, Leo kept a sharp eye on the younger man. "Savannah, too, I imagine. As I recall, the two of you were always exceptionally fond of each other."

Danny nearly choked on his brandy. *"Fond?"* he wheezed through a veil of laughter. "Sorry, Doctor. I don't mean to laugh, but it's just that through all the years Savannah and I have known each other, we've been . . . well, not fond."

Leo lit the pipe and peered through a cloud of smoke. "What would you call it? I remember the way she and Jim stood by you through your trial. I'd say that connotes a certain fondness."

Danny's smile dimmed. Leo went on, unperturbed.

"And now this. Savannah hasn't been out for an evening in . . . well, more years than I care to count. How the deuce did you convince her to go to this ball? And to King's Club, no less?"

Danny glanced down into the amber depths of his glass. "To be honest, I guess I bullied her into it."

"Well, then, bully for you," the doctor returned.

Danny looked up with surprise.

"Savannah's a bright young woman," Leo added, "but her stubbornness overrides her good sense in some things."

"I'll agree with that."

"You say that on a note of humor. But what I'm talking about is dead serious. In case you haven't figured it out, Savannah is not the girl you used to know. She'd just turned twenty when her life changed. In a matter of weeks, a debutante who'd never had a care in the world became the sole caretaker of both Kings Crossing and a mother who ceased to function on any plane of reality. I tried to talk Savannah out of it, but she was stubborn as a mule."

A corner of Danny's mouth dipped. "She always was."

"I suppose it isn't an altogether unhappy trait; she's needed a good dose of mule-headedness to make it through all these years."

Danny took a drink. Leo puffed on his pipe, his eyes narrowing.

"I'm glad you're taking Savannah out," he resumed. "And I'm glad you're here. But along with the stubbornness that brought Savannah to this point, there developed a certain vulnerability. While you were out there in the world making a name for yourself and sowing—I'm sure—your share of wild oats, Savannah was stuck in this house, virtually alone. She's not one of your fast-lane D.C. ladies, Danny, and I'll thank you to remember it."

Danny's brows went up. "Are you telling me to keep my hands off?"

"In a manner of speaking."

Danny's expression of amused surprise slipped gradually away. "Maybe it's best for her if I don't."

"Not if you intend to light out of here in a few months, leaving Savannah high and dry with her world turned upside down."

"I think this is getting a little personal, don't you, Doctor?"

"Where Savannah is concerned, I feel personal. Jim was a good friend. I won't stand by and see his daughter hurt."

"I have every respect for Mr. King, and I would never willfully hurt Savannah!" Lowering his voice, Danny regarded the doctor steadily. "But I'll tell you just like I told her. I don't intend to hide what I feel or want. Savannah's a grown woman. It's high time she started acting like one."

"And that's the way it is."

"That's the way it is."

Leo considered him thoughtfully. The jaw was set, the eyes determined. Danny Sawyer had always adored Savannah King; despite any other changes in the man, that trait apparently remained.

"You care for her a great deal, don't you?"

Danny frowned as his face flooded with heat. "Like I said, this is getting a little personal."

Leo smiled. "Sorry. Occupational hazard. At any rate, it appears we're not at odds after all—not as long as we agree Savannah should be handled with kid gloves."

Danny met the doctor's insightful eyes. After a moment he mustered a grin.

"Has anybody ever gotten anywhere using kid gloves on a mule?"

Leo chuckled and raised his glass in salute. Danny started to take a drink, heard something, glanced at the doorway and . . . froze.

"Good evening, gentlemen." Savannah glided into the parlor, her smooth gait belying the agitated state of her nerves. Extending a hand to the doctor, she gave him a gracious smile. "I do appreciate your coming, Dr. Crane. And on such short notice, too."

Leo smiled. "Happy to do it, Savannah. You know I enjoy visiting Ophelia, even if she does cheat shamefully at gin."

Savannah laughed airily. The doctor released her hand, stepped back, and looked her over.

"And *you*, my dear. It was worth the drive out here just to see you all decked out. You're lovelier than ever, Savannah."

"Thank you," she murmured, and for the first time looked fully at Danny. A charge ran through her. He was beautiful—his face bronze from the sun, his tall form spectacular in formal attire. One hand was in the pocket of black trousers, carelessly tucking a white dinner jacket behind a hip; the other, poised in the midst of raising a brandy snifter to his mouth. And he was . . . staring.

"Danny? Is something wrong?"

He cleared his throat and seemed suddenly capable of motion. "On the contrary." Tossing down the last of his drink, he set the glass aside and offered an arm. "Ready to go?"

Fireflies flickered against the twilight as they drove toward town in Danny's jeep—a military-looking vehicle painted in a pattern of camouflage. It was a beautiful summer night, but Savannah was unable to derive any pleasure from it, nor from the unexpected outing that was the first break from the routine of the Crossing she'd had in years. As she stared out the window in seeming composure, her heart pounded with trepidation. How could she have allowed herself to be roped into such a situation?

Glancing aside, she saw the answer—Danny, with his hot looks and cajoling ways. *Be a friend,* he'd challenged. And now she found herself manipulated into spending an evening with people she hadn't seen in a dozen years, people she'd vowed to spurn. Savannah's gaze fell to the casually clasped hands in her lap. Within the gloves, her palms had gone moist; within her skin, her nerves twitched like electrified wires.

She fired an angry look at Danny. He wasn't helping a bit! He hadn't said a word since they left the house.

"For someone who was so determined to go to this thing, you're awfully quiet!" she snapped.

He turned, his gaze touching her face, sweeping down her body and back up again. "I guess that's understandable," he rumbled. "Considering you take my breath away."

He looked back at the road. As Savannah grasped his meaning, a blush of surprise leapt to her cheeks.

"Really, Danny," she muttered. Her tone was chiding; nonetheless, a feeling of pleasure rippled through her.

"It's true," he replied, still looking ahead. "When you walk into that place, you'll turn heads. Believe me."

Her fragile sense of pleasure evaporated. *That* place. King's Club. Savannah turned once again to the window, noting the familiar landmarks of the skyline as they bypassed the city, remembering her father and the way they often stood on the balcony of *The Watch* and simply drank in the beauty of Kingsport.

He'd loved it, just as his forefathers before him had. The Kings had built the city, safeguarded it through generations much like a royal family and its dominion. The newspaper . . . the church . . . businesses that had gained their beginnings in loans from the King coffers. There was hardly a long-standing family in all of Kingsport that hadn't been touched one way or another by the Kings. And yet, there was not one Savannah could think of that had not turned its back—particularly among those bluebloods who'd once fluttered around Jim King like flies drawn to honey.

The old wrath boiled up within her, straightening her spine, lifting her chin, and glistening in her hardened eyes.

Clayton had accompanied Rory to the bar in one corner of the ballroom, where they'd come across Ben Cochrane. The older man had stood there with a reddening face as Rory proceeded to degrade him with a series of tongue-in-cheek slurs. Finally, Clayton had turned away in disgust, wondering why Ben Cochrane tolerated such behavior, and realizing that he himself had reacted in the same impotent way for as long as he could remember.

Now Clayton moved along the fringe of the elegant crowd, nodding occasionally as someone greeted him, hurrying on in mute rejection of any tentative invitation to stop and chat, knowing such invitations came only because he was Big Ed McKenna's son—"the odd one with the speech problem." Looking ahead, he saw that Libby remained alone at their table, not that Clayton would have expected her to join in the festivities, much less that anyone would stop by to say hello.

Libby Parker was a fallen woman. The fact that she was mistress to one of the most powerful men in Kingsport didn't alter the fact that she was a whore. Polite society would have recoiled at the mere idea of being seated at the same table with her. But that hadn't stopped Rory from bringing her. He enjoyed flaunting her in the face of convention.

As he drew near, Clayton wondered how Libby felt about that, how she felt about anything. He hadn't talked much with her since she returned a few months back, shocking him with the obvious change the years had wrought. It was hard to believe she was the same girl he'd grown up with. Occasionally he saw a twinkling smile that called to mind the expression she'd worn most often all those years ago, but by and large her eyes emitted a strange darkness that overpowered any passing look of contentment.

For some reason, Clayton felt a kinship with the darkness in those eyes.

As he drew near, he studied her. Dressed in a chic black gown with a high neck and long sleeves, she didn't look much like a whore tonight, except for the outrageous hair that glittered beneath the chandelier like a red flame.

"W-would you like something to d-drink?" he asked as he arrived.

She looked up, her face carefully composed.

"How about a little arsenic?"

Clayton surrendered a small grin. "Is it that b-bad?"

"Pretty bad."

The orchestra started up then, and the strains of a classical melody filled the ballroom, overriding the noise of the crowd.

"At least the music's n-nice," he commented.

"I guess so. Where's the rest of the illustrious McKenna clan?"

He inclined his head toward the bar. "Rory's over there. Papa's s-still at his p-place at the entrance."

Libby looked across the room toward the distinguished members of the receiving line: Senator Gaines and his wife, the mayor of Kingsport and his dowdy mate, a county commissioner . . . Her gaze lit on Big Ed just as he gulped down a drink and reached behind himself to release the glass almost before a black waiter could step up to catch it on a silver tray.

"Your father was half loaded before we left the house," Libby muttered. "Somebody ought to tell him to slow down."

Clayton followed her gaze. "Yeah," he returned. "S-somebody ought to t-tell him a lot of th-things."

"Why *don't* you, then?"

Why not, indeed? Clayton thought. The familiar taste of self-loathing rose to his mouth. Letting Libby's question go unanswered, he glanced over the crowd and noticed that Rory had left the bar and was moving toward their table, a prestigious one adjacent to the head table reserved for Senator Gaines.

"Here c-comes Rory n-now," he said.

"Hooray," Libby returned sarcastically.

Clayton looked down at her pretty but undeniably hard face. "If you f-feel that way, why have you m-moved in?"

Her eyes took on that unfathomable black look. "It's a long story."

"I've got t-time."

Her red lips parted in the semblance of a smile. "You wouldn't understand, Clayton."

"T-try me. I'd l-like to understand what l-led you t-to . . ."

His voice trailed off as Libby's smile vanished.

"What's next?" she asked in a low, cutting tone. "What's a nice girl like me doing in a place like this?"

Clayton's face flooded with heat. "I'm s-sorry. I didn't mean t-to—"

"No," Libby broke in quietly. "I'm the one who's sorry. You didn't deserve that. Guess I've been spending too much time with your brother."

"*Too much* time, darling?"

Clayton turned as his brother stepped up behind Libby's chair and placed a hand on her shoulder.

"Careful," Rory added as Libby looked up. "Someone might think you didn't treasure every moment we spend together."

"But of course *you* know that I do," she purred smoothly.

Clayton studied Libby's artful smile for a moment. The way she leaned into Rory's touch, anyone would presume she welcomed it. He looked away with a sinking feeling, his glance skirting through the elaborately dressed people, idly turning to the open doors across the dance floor. That was when he saw her.

"Savannah!" he whispered, awed by the sight of her and shocked by her public appearance.

She was all in white, poised at the doorway like an angel that had just touched down on earth. Clayton caught his breath, not noticing the way his companions' eyes swerved in the direction of his gaze.

Clayton had always had a soft spot for Savannah. It had started when they were children, continued through the awkward teen-age years, and maintained into adulthood even though he rarely saw her anymore. Despite the fact that the Crossing backed up on McKenna property, Clayton had not set eyes on her in months. Years had passed since she'd last deigned to grace one of these unholy gatherings with her presence. He'd always admired that about her, the way she'd turned her back on the whispering crowds.

But she had appeared tonight, and the years melted away. Heads turned—just as they always had when she entered a room—and although the orchestra continued to play, there was an obvious skipped beat in the attention of the crowd.

"She's with Sawyer," Rory hissed.

Libby rose to her feet, craning for a better look as the couple proceeded toward the receiving line.

"That's no surprise," she remarked. "Danny's out at the Crossing again, and he's always had an obsession for Savannah."

"That's right," Rory said thoughtfully. "He *has*, hasn't he?"

And when Clayton glanced up at his brother's face, the evil smile he found chilled his blood.

The ballroom glittered beneath a trio of crystal chandeliers, their lights dancing across a polished floor, reflecting off mirrors, sparkling on a pale brocade that covered the walls up to a chair railing and was repeated in draperies framing the French doors across the way. At one end of the sweeping room, an orchestra played a courtly allemande, and lining the dance floor, a series of tables covered with white linen were lit by candles.

Savannah might have thought it lovely, but for two things—the way the crowd of a hundred or so turned, their looks of interest holding beyond the point of politeness, and the fact that this was, after all, the King's Club ballroom. The antipathy she felt for the place had swelled as she crossed its threshold. Now she was hard-pressed to maintain a guise of pleasantness as Danny led her toward the receiving line. They were still a couple of yards away when the silver-haired senator stepped up to greet them, his hand extended to Danny.

"Buck Sawyer!" he resounded. "I recognize you from your picture in *The Post*. Happy you could make it!"

"Hello, Senator." Danny smiled, joining the man's pumping handshake. "It's nice to meet you."

"The pleasure is mine. Once again, allow me to say how gratified I was to see that piece in *The River Watch* this morning." His eyes turned to Savannah. "And who is this lovely lady?"

Danny introduced her. The senator presented his wife, and the receiving line enclosed them—all but Big Ed McKenna—the community leaders falling all over themselves to follow the senator's lead, fawning over Danny, welcoming Savannah as though she were a long-lost daughter. *Hypocrites!* she thought.

"It's so good to see you, Savannah," the mayor's wife chortled. "And how is dear Ophelia?"

Dear Ophelia? Clarissa Hinshaw had been one of the first of Ophelia King's bosom buddies to desert her when the scandal hit.

"Fine," Savannah replied stiffly.

"Be sure to give her my best, won't you?"

Savannah forced her lips to smile.

The senator leaned back to smile at Big Ed McKenna who stood some few feet away.

"You're a sly dog, Ed. However did you manage to lure someone like Buck Sawyer away from *The Washington Post*?"

"Just lucky, I guess," the big man answered.

"My compliments on that piece in *The River Watch* today," the senator went on, oblivious to the way Big Ed's eyes narrowed on Danny. "I assume you were in on the whole thing from the beginning, but what a surprise it must have been to land such a school of fish in one net!"

"That's an understatement, Senator. It was more than a surprise. In fact, my son Rory and I were discussing it just this morning."

"Yes," Danny put in obliquely. "Your son was kind enough to call and convey his opinions."

"Allow me to add my sentiments to those of my son," Big Ed returned.

"I'd expect nothing less," Danny parried.

"Well, I see more guests are arriving," the senator said, clapping a friendly hand on Danny's shoulder. "Why don't you and the lovely Miss King join the party? I've made arrangements for you at my table."

Danny and Savannah excused themselves and would have left the receiving line behind, but for the loud *harumph!* that made them pause near Big Ed McKenna.

"I think you misread me, boy," he said to Danny.

"Oh?"

"I admire nerve. There's no greater quality in my book, as long as it's backed by a certain amount of know-how. And you, my boy, have know-how."

"I'm not your *boy*, Mr. McKenna—"

"Slow down, son! I'm about to thank you. The wire services picked up your story. By tomorrow morning it'll be clear across the country. That kind of thing does wonders for circulation, which does wonders for advertising, which does wonders for my wallet. You're putting money in my pocket, Mr. Buck Sawyer, whether you ever intended to or not!"

Big Ed broke into rumbling laughter. Danny put a hand to the small of Savannah's back and turned away.

"No matter what Rory says, boy, you've got a place at *The Watch* as long as you want it!"

The remark was followed by another laugh. Savannah glanced up, saw Danny's stony expression, and felt a similar one form on her own face. She looked ahead, refusing to ac-

knowledge the interested looks as they moved around the circumference of the dance floor.

Across the way, backing up to a row of mirrors, was the table
to which Senator Gaines had gestured. The other tables sat four.
This one was twice that size, trimmed with gold bunting and
presided over by a magnificent centerpiece of peach gladiolas.
Relishing the moment she could sit down and escape the feeling
of being on parade, Savannah focused on the gladiolas—
glancing aside only as she and Danny drew near. Her eyes fell
on the three people standing just ahead in their path. Rory, Clayton, and Libby.

She would have continued past them with a regal nod, but at
the last moment, Danny commandeered her elbow. Savannah
glanced up, noting with surprise that in the few moments it had
taken them to walk around the room, Danny's hardset expression had completely transformed. Now he was absolutely aglow
with pleasantness! She certainly felt no such sentiment as he
drew her aside.

"Hello, everybody," Danny said brightly. Reaching over, he
extended a hand. "Haven't seen you since I got back, Clayton.
How have you been?"

As Clayton smiled, Savannah's gaze darted among the trio.
Rory and Clayton were sporting identical tuxedos, but looking
as different as two men could; one tall and fair, the other slight
and dark. Between them, Libby was all in black.

"I've been f-fine," Clayton said, shaking Danny's hand. "It's
good to s-see you. I liked that s-story in *The Watch* today."

His remark drew a grin from Danny, a stony look from his
brother.

"Hello, Libby," Savannah said.

Libby targeted her former friend with dark eyes. Savannah
looked just as she always had, beautiful and pure.

"Hello, Savannah," she replied coolly.

Savannah recalled the day they ran into each other outside
Providence Sundries. The air of hostility about Libby hadn't diminished. If anything, it was more intense. Savannah stiffened.

"I want you to know I spoke to my mother," she said.

Libby rolled a hip, achieving a stance that was both provocative and snide. "Oh? About what?"

"I never knew about that phone call, Libby!"

Catching the sharpness of Savannah's voice, Danny looked at
her curiously. "What's going on?"

Savannah's eyes remained on Libby. "I never knew," she repeated.

"This is not the time or place to discuss it," Libby replied shortly.

"You're looking particularly lovely tonight, Savannah," Rory interjected, drawing all four pairs of eyes his way.

Assuming a self-satisfied smile, Rory reached to adjust a diamond-studded cuff link and zeroed in on Danny. "Enough to make a man's mouth water, eh, Sawyer?"

"Eat your heart out," Danny returned.

Rory's smile faded, and the two of them eyed each other.

Like a couple of lions squaring off, Clayton thought. *Just like always.* Before he knew it was coming, he let out a laugh. Everyone turned in his direction.

"It's j-just th-that . . ." he stuttered. "I was th-thinking of long ago when the f-five of us . . . Well, a lot of y-years have p-passed, b-but nothing's ch-changed."

"You're wrong about that," Libby said, her eyes leveled on Savannah. "Everything has."

"That's right!" Savannah bristled. "There once was a time when one friend might have given the other the benefit of the doubt!"

Libby's mouth opened, but Danny swiftly intervened.

"I think it's time we moved on, don't you?" he said. Putting a firm arm around Savannah's waist, he directed a parting look around the group.

"Hell of a reunion," he added and steered Savannah away. Within the circle of his arm, she was stiff as a board.

"What the hell's wrong between you and Libby?" he muttered under his breath.

"Watch your language, Danny," Savannah snapped.

They moved toward the senator's table. Several people were seated there, and when Savannah's gaze lit on the dark-haired man between two women, she faltered in midstep. It had been twelve years since she faced Clifford. In the interim, he'd married a hosiery heiress and fathered two little girls whom, Savannah had heard, were overseen by the staunch chaperon of their paternal grandmother, Belle Andrews.

That austere lady was on Clifford's right—older, plumper, but instantly recognizable. The woman on the left was an attractive brunette. Clifford's wife.

"What is it now?" Danny asked as Savannah came to a full halt.

"Clifford. Of all people—"

"We're going to have the best time of anyone here, remember?"

Danny propelled her forward. Clifford came to his feet as they arrived.

"Good evening," he said in the familiar nasal voice. "The senator informed us you would be joining our table. I think both of you know my mother."

Belle Andrews inclined her head. Like a dowager queen greeting peasants, Savannah thought.

"But I don't think either of you has met my wife," Clifford went on. "Doris, allow me to present Miss Savannah King and her escort, Mr. Sawyer."

"Charmed," the brunette offered, looking and sounding so like Clifford that Savannah was struck with the notion he'd married the female image of himself.

Savannah sank into the chair Danny pulled out, appreciative of the fact that he left two empty seats between themselves and the Andrews. Just as they sat down, a liveried waiter stepped up and offered a round of champagne. Savannah selected a glass, set it down before her and looked up to find three pairs of dark eyes hovering on her and Danny. She glanced aside and found him presenting a rather forced smile.

"So!" he began, looking around the peering group. "How 'bout them Tar Heels?"

Clifford's mouth drew down at the corners, but otherwise he ignored the flip remark.

"When did you return to Kingsport, Mr. Sawyer?" he asked crisply.

"A couple of weeks ago."

"I understand your home is in Washington now. Will you be staying long in our fair city?"

Danny gave Savannah a quick sidelong glance. "That depends."

"Wherever have you managed to find a place to stay at the height of the tourist season?" Doris questioned nosily.

Danny grinned and stretched an arm around the back of Savannah's chair. "Actually, Savannah has been gracious enough to let me stay at the Crossing."

Mrs. Andrews' brows shot up before twisting in a disapproving line. Doris and Clifford exchanged a swift look, then turned in unison to offer countenances which, in their strict politeness, were intolerably condemning. Savannah felt as though her face had caught fire. The orchestra launched into a forties melody, and she turned to Danny with bright eyes.

"Do you think we could dance?" she asked.

Clearly surprised, he nonetheless unfolded his tall form from the chair and offered a hand. Only two other couples were on the dance floor. Danny led her to a spot in the center, as far away as possible from the gawking onlookers lining the edge, yet spotlit—Savannah thought—by the giant chandelier directly overhead. Stepping into his open arms, she raised a hand to his shoulder and looked up.

"Are we having fun yet?" she asked.

Danny threw back his head and laughed. "Ah, Savannah," he said, "what would I do without you?"

Without further word, he twirled her in a series of circles that took her breath away and brought an uncontrollable smile to her lips.

"You're making me dizzy," she complained after a moment.

Danny halted the whirlwind twirl and gazed down with a merry expression. "You truly are a master," he said.

"Of what?"

"Of satire." He glanced down at the shifting toes of her slippers. "Of dancing."

He looked at her face, his smile settling. "Of me, I suppose," he added.

Savannah looked over his shoulder, absently watching the swirling backdrop of the ballroom as her pulse began to thrum with more than outraged nerves.

"Don't tease," she said.

"I'm not."

"I'm edgy enough as it is, Danny. Don't complicate things."

His first impulse was to lash back with something like: "You're the one who's making things complicated!" But his recent conversation with Dr. Crane came to mind. Tonight, if tonight only, he'd handle her with kid gloves.

"She hates me, you know," Savannah said.

The comment shattered his train of thought. Danny looked down with surprise.

"Who hates you?"

"Libby."

He tipped his head. "Libby's changed. I don't think she likes much of anything anymore . . . or anyone."

"What happened to her, Danny? She thinks I betrayed her in some way, and I don't even know what she's talking about."

"Who knows? Libby chose her direction long ago. To tell you the truth, I had a feeling about the way she was going the night I drove her out of town all those years ago."

Savannah's eyes widened. "Did you?"

"Yep."

"You mean the same night the Sikes brothers—"

"Yep," he confirmed. "She was clearing out of Kingsport—wanted out bad. I never thought she'd come back here, much less to McKenna's bed."

Savannah blinked. "His *bed*?"

Danny returned her shocked look with one of amusement. "Of course, his bed. What else do you think she's doing there?"

"She's Rory's *mistress*?"

"That's a genteel way of putting it, yes."

"I can't believe it," Savannah murmured.

Danny felt a pang of annoyance. "Why not? Some people do have sex, you know."

Savannah caught the irritation in his voice, but could think of no reply—certainly nothing that would smooth over the subject that was a source of such awkwardness between them.

Danny raised his chin and looked over the top of her head. Although he drew her a little closer, it was only to benefit their swaying steps.

"In all the time we've known each other, this is the first time we've danced together."

"Is it?" she asked.

"Yes."

"I suppose that's odd."

"Not really, considering the distance that always existed between us."

Savannah leaned back and dared to face him. "What distance?"

"What distance? Come on," Danny said with a tight chuckle. "You were the princess; I wasn't fit to be your lackey."

She gazed up with eyes full of amazement. "Is that what you thought?"

"That's what I knew. When we were children, it wasn't that way. But then, childhood is a fleeting thing."

Removing her eyes from the probing intensity of his gaze, Savannah looked safely at his black bow tie. "Everything is fleeting, Danny. Nothing lasts. Nothing can be counted on."

"That's a pretty dismal outlook."

"But a realistic one," she countered just as Danny drew back. Someone was tapping him on the shoulder . . . Rory!

"May I cut in?" he asked in the haughty tone Savannah had always despised.

Expecting Danny to refuse, she was both surprised and alarmed when he smoothly transferred her gloved hand into Rory's. She barely had time to fire a fuming look at Danny's disappearing back when Rory pulled her into his arms.

"As I mentioned before, you're looking particularly beautiful this evening," he complimented.

She said nothing.

"What brings you out on this occasion, after you've passed up so many others?"

"Danny wanted to come."

"Ah . . . and whatever Danny wants, Danny gets?"

Savannah looked up with a sharp denial in mind, then abruptly changed her tack. "That's right," she replied.

Rory seemed a bit startled, but not as much as she'd have liked.

"Lucky man," he muttered, and swept her around in a way that rivaled the circles Danny had instituted at the beginning of the dance.

Head reeling, Savannah bit her lip to keep from complaining. There was something within her that rebelled against showing Rory McKenna any weakness whatsoever.

Looking pointedly away from his smirking face, she wished only that the music would end; a feeling that grew stronger when she caught sight of Danny leading Libby Parker onto the dance floor.

She was definitely sexy. But as Danny took Libby in his arms, he had none of that in mind.

"What do you have against Savannah?" he asked.

Libby looked up. She was wearing spike heels; still, he towered over her.

"You asked me to dance when no other man in the room would have dared," she replied, "but don't think that gives you any special license."

"Why can't you tell me?" Danny pursued. "Is it some deep, dark secret?"

"It won't be if I tell you."

"She doesn't understand—"

"Give it a rest, Danny. Miss Savannah can go one night without you fighting her battles for her, can't she?"

Danny looked into Libby's eyes, expecting the lively sparkle he remembered from the old days, but finding they were devoid of anything except the hard glint of a stranger.

When the music ended, Savannah virtually leapt out of Rory's embrace. Applause rippled through the dance crowd, and Rory joined in, grinning. She turned her back on him and walked off the floor unescorted, refusing to look as Danny walked by their table with Libby on his arm. A moment later, he took his seat next to her.

"Why did you let Rory cut in?" she hissed beneath a covering smile.

"What did you want me to do?" he returned in similar fashion. "Challenge him to a duel?"

Cutting a quick look at Clifford and his attendant females, Savannah had the small pleasure of shaming them into looking away.

"And you just had to dance with Libby?" she resumed.

Danny cracked a grin. "Jealous?"

One of her brows arched painfully high.

"Relax," he added. "I tried to find out what she's all fired up about where you're concerned."

Savannah's expression switched to one of instant interest.

"Sorry," Danny supplied. "She ain't talking."

The senator and his wife arrived then. Conversation bubbled up to greet them, and Savannah knew the relief of feeling like part of the crowd, rather than its focal point. From then on, the evening improved. Hors d'oeuvres were served; champagne was replenished. The chatter of the ballroom crowd swelled to a pitch above the music.

At the head table, talk flowed at a lively pace. The senator was a charming conversationalist, though a noticable majority of his dialogue was directed to Danny. He'd been reading Buck Sawyer's work for a number of years and made no bones about enjoying the opportunity to talk with him face to face. Savannah found that she could sit back and say little.

Buck Sawyer, celebrity. She'd been impressed by his story in *The Watch*. She should have realized how bright he was, but she hadn't—not really. It had been too easy to perceive him as the Danny she'd always known to anticipate the heights at which his mind worked. Politics. International events. The state of the world. He discussed them all with casual aplomb, and the senator was positively enthralled. Occasionally Clifford introduced a line of conversation the table would take up for a moment or two. In each case, Senator Gaines responded politely, but ultimately his attention returned to Danny, as—it seemed—did that of the entire table.

Eventually, the Andrews party excused themselves to mingle with the crowd, leaving Danny and Savannah alone with Senator and Mrs. Gaines. Perhaps an hour had passed when Savannah realized that—along with the senator and his wife—she, too, was hanging on Danny's every word.

Not only that, but the strangest feeling of pride was coursing through her, and not just pride in Danny. She was proud to be the woman at his side. It was something she'd never felt before—something different from the heart-pounding reactions he often wrenched from her. This was warm and glowing and . . .

The music faded to a distant hum, the conversation to a low-pitched whine. She watched fixedly as Danny reached for his glass of champagne. It was a simple gesture; yet as he raised the glass toward his mouth, she found herself enamored with the long fingers wrapped around the stem, the suntanned brown of his hand against the white sleeve, the flash of a grin before his lips met the rim. Her thoughts barreled toward a fearful conclusion. Before they could reach their destination, she shot to her feet.

Conversation halted as the group turned expectantly in her direction. Savannah peered down at Senator Gaines, noting his curious expression as she groped for something to say.

"Savannah?" Danny voiced questioningly.

Her gaze darted to his cursedly handsome face, and the strange sensations started anew . . .

"Excuse me," she managed to say.

Then she was escaping through the crowd, heading for the ballroom doors through which they'd entered, sweeping into the relative seclusion of the foyer. Turning down an adjacent corridor, she came across the ladies lounge, slipped into the elegant chamber, and found it thankfully deserted.

Savannah moved toward the extravagant gilded mirror above the vanity. Her gaze was on her own reflection, but she was seeing the chiseled lines of Danny's profile, the way his sunstreaked hair lay across his collar where he'd allowed it to grow long in back.

Stripping off the long gloves, she moved into the washroom. She was still there some minutes later when she heard the door to the lounge open, and then the sound of voices. Selecting a monogrammed towel from the counter, Savannah dried her hands and pulled on her gloves once more, absently listening to the women just outside the washroom, then coming instantly alert as she caught the gist of their conversation.

"At least you must agree they make a handsome couple, Belle."

"Hmph!" Belle Andrews snorted. "Handsome is as handsome does. Danny Sawyer is from *Clancytown*, Millicent. Not to mention that sordid scandal that drove him from town all those years ago. And *Savannah* . . . well, I'm perfectly horrified. You should see the way they look at each other. It's obvious they're lovers. With no one else at the Crossing but a mindless invalid, heaven knows what goes on behind closed doors.!"

Savannah pulled open the swinging door to the washroom with a dramatic whoosh and stepped into the lounge. She barely noticed the way Millicent Brewer's hand flew to her mouth. Her attention was all for Belle Andrews.

"Mrs. Andrews," she pronounced with all the disdain she could summon, "I'm sure you must realize such speculation smears my name."

Another woman might have been thrown into embarrassed confusion, but not Belle Andrews. Her jowls settled in disapproving folds at the neck of her pearl gray gown.

"What could you possibly expect, Savannah? I didn't plan to confront you, but since you're here, I may as well bring out in the open what everyone is whispering. First, the McKennas take in that harlot, Libby Parker. And now you and that . . . *accused murderer*. Whatever could have possessed you to do such a thing?"

"Danny is a boarder," Savannah replied evenly. "He pays

rent like any boarder at any establishment. Frankly, I need the money."

Mrs. Andrews' nose went up. "There are some things a lady doesn't do for money."

Outrage made Savannah long to fly at the older woman. Propriety, so deeply embedded it overruled such riotous impulses, made her stand there like a marble statue.

"Perhaps you wouldn't be so discriminating if you found yourself without it someday," she said.

"I hardly foresee that happening," Mrs. Andrews commented haughtily. "Prudence and wisdom safeguard a fortune, you know. But of one thing I'm certain. If such a thing came to pass, I would continue to conduct myself as a lady—a course which you have obviously forsaken!"

"Since when did back-alley gossip become the mark of a great lady?" Savannah retaliated crisply.

"Well!" Belle Andrews exclaimed.

Puffing herself up with indignation, the woman reached a swift, new dimension of plumpness; in contrast, her companion seemed to shrink within her powder blue gown. Savannah looked from one to the other, her eyes glittering with unmistakable anger though her face remained flawlessly composed.

"Good evening . . . *ladies*," she added, and swishing past the two of them, made her exit with painstaking stateliness.

As she stepped outside, however, the facade crumbled and the trembling began. Up the way to the right, a number of people had spilled out of the ballroom entrance and into the adjoining foyer. Spinning left, Savannah hurried down the corridor and came across a side exit that opened onto the terrace. With great relief, she rushed outside, taking a great gulp of night air as she moved into the darkness.

Up ahead, the French doors of the ballroom threw rectangles of golden light across the slate floor of the terrace bordering the rear of the building. A few people were gathered at one set of open doors. Moving in the opposite direction, Savannah came to rest at a white railing with a trail of clematis weaving through the posts. Reaching out to touch a snowy blossom, she stared across the starlit grounds.

Nearby a mimosa stretched its branches toward the terrace, its sweet scent rivaling that of the gardenias in the garden immediately below. Beyond the garden, a hedge-trimmed path stretched away from the house, and far in the distance was the dark, symmetrical shape of a tennis court. The sight reminded Savannah instantly of her father, and joining the vibrant hatred that had her fairly shaking, came the familiar ache of loss.

All this would have been his if not for . . . what? An error in judgment? A twist of fate? Savannah raged against them all—and even destiny, itself—as she stood alone in the moonlight. Some time later she became aware of the music drifting out of the ballroom and then the sound of approaching footsteps. She turned just as Danny arrived.

"What the hell are you doing out here?" he demanded.

"I needed some air."

"You left the table forty minutes ago. You might have told me if you planned on disappearing."

"I didn't plan on disappearing until I ran into Mrs. Andrews in the ladies room."

The angry knit of Danny's brows unfurled. "And what did she have to say?"

"She actually accused me of—" Savannah broke off and looked swiftly into the darkness. "Never mind. You were right about them all those years ago—Clifford and his mother, I mean. Rich, spoiled, self-righteous, small-town snobs. Damn them!" she concluded fiercely. "Damn them all to hell!"

Taken by surprise, Danny laughed.

Savannah gave him a sharp look. "What's so funny?"

"Did you say 'damn them all to hell'?"

"You heard me."

"Sorry. I don't think I've ever heard a single oath cross your lips. Hearing two in one breath kind of shocked me."

Savannah turned away. Danny's smile disappeared as he studied her profile—the unsmiling mouth, the stubborn set of the chin.

"I really am sorry," he added. "I didn't realize how upset you are."

"*Upset?* I don't think upset covers it. I'd give anything to be able to walk up to Belle Andrews and laugh in her face."

"You could do that now."

Savannah turned her back to the rail and looked up at him. "You don't understand," she said heatedly. "Money is the only thing that matters to them. Belle Andrews, Clarissa Hinshaw, all of them! Oh, they may talk about breeding and heritage, but it all comes down to money. If you have it, they'll overlook almost anything. If you lose it, they turn on you like a pack of wolves!"

"What is it you want, then?" Danny asked. "Money?"

"No," Savannah replied succinctly. "Revenge . . . for every slur against my father, every insult to my mother, every degrading remark about the King family. I want to be on top again and look down my nose at every one of them! I want—"

"Hey, now, slow down a minute," Danny broke in.

"I'd sell my soul to have it all back," she added insistently.

"Careful," Danny cautioned with the hint of a smile. "You never know when the devil might be listening."

"I mean it, Danny."

His gaze swept over her, his smile vanishing again. Standing there so defiantly—her hair, her eyes, her dress, everything glowing in the moonlight—she appeared to be unearthly. The thought had crossed his mind before, but this time it was different. This time he saw something in addition to the ethereal beauty, something completely unreachable, something that seemed to separate Savannah King from everyone, including himself.

"I can see that you do," he replied. "I didn't realize until now just how deeply you've been hurt."

Savannah raised her chin valiantly, though the irrepressible trembling was making its way to her lips.

"Could we go now?" she asked.

"What the hell did that old cow say to you in the ladies room?"

"It doesn't matter. Do you think we could make our excuses to the senator and just . . . go?"

Her lips were shaking now. Danny saw her fight for control and felt the pain of it. "I think we could arrange that." Watching her a moment longer, he stepped forward and opened his arms. "Come here a minute."

Savannah eyed him with glaring defensiveness.

"It's all right," Danny encouraged, "No strings. Just a shoulder to lean on, if you want it."

"Thank you, but I'm all right."

His arms fell, his palms slapping the legs of his trousers.

"Could we just go?" Savannah reiterated.

"Of course."

She sensed rather than saw Danny's disappointment, for she refused to meet his eyes as they walked back to the ballroom.

* * *

Clayton searched the crowd and then confirmed that Libby continued to sit alone, ignored, at their table. He stalked out of the ballroom, through the foyer, and found Rory outside on the front veranda.

"Libby's all alone in th-there," he announced.

Rory glanced carelessly at his brother. "Go sit with her, then."

"She's your c-companion. *Your* responsibility!"

Rory looked back into the night. "There are finer fish to fry, little brother."

Clayton followed his brother's gaze and found it targeted on a couple disappearing toward the parking lot. The light of the September night sky illuminated the man's white jacket and the woman's shimmering gown. Clayton looked swiftly up at his brother, and for the second time that evening was chilled by the intent way he was watching Savannah.

"What are you th-thinking?" he asked.

Rory glanced aside, but Clayton would never know what he might have answered; for at that moment a series of screams reached their ears. Rushing back inside, they saw that chaos had erupted in the ballroom. And when they managed to cut through the gasping crowd near the bar, they found their father lying still as death on the floor.

The ride back to the Crossing was quiet. Pulling up in front of the house, Danny went around and helped Savannah out of the jeep. She withdrew her hand as soon as she found her footing. He would have expected nothing else. They walked into the courtyard.

It was nearly midnight. The moon was high, softly lighting the garden and the white columns of the house beyond. The air was filled with the songs of katydids and the scent of roses. In another few moments, they would be inside and the night would be over.

"Hold on a minute," Danny said.

Savannah watched from the walkway as he stepped over to a nearby rosebush, then returned to offer her a long-stemmed bud.

"For the belle of the ball."

"Hardly the belle of the ball," she murmured. "But thank

you." Raising the newly opened blossom, she sniffed of its fragrance.

"Thank *you.*"

Savannah looked up questioningly.

"For going with me tonight. Was it absolutely gruesome?"

A light laugh escaped her. "Not all of it." She surveyed his tall form. God, he was handsome standing there in the moonlight! "*You* were very nice, for instance. Charming, in fact."

"You're kidding. Charming?"

"Why, yes. I thought Mrs. Gaines was going to swoon at any minute, not to mention the senator himself."

Danny chuckled. Savannah smiled up at him. Danny stepped closer and raised a hand; his fingertips trailed gently along the side of her face.

"You know, Savannah, if this little assignation were a typical date, this is about the time a kiss would be in order." His hand fell away. "But I just don't think I'm up to being pushed away. Not tonight."

Looking up, Savannah had the sudden urge to offer her mouth. The impulse must have shown. Danny looked into her eyes, and in contradiction to his words, bent to kiss her.

It was a sweet kiss—lips parted, tongues mingled, but gently . . . tenderly. Danny's arms stole around her waist; Savannah's hands crept to his shoulders. Danny savored every second of the unexpected warmth. Too soon, she was drawing away. He opened his eyes, scanning her upturned face.

"Well, that was nice," he murmured. "Shocking, but nice."

"Good night," Savannah rasped, and backed out of his arms.

"Wait a second." Stepping forward, Danny replaced his arms around her waist and drew her to him. "There's no reason to rush inside. Not right now." He bent once more, seeking her mouth.

"Danny, don't."

"Come on—"

"No!"

Her tone pierced his entranced state. Savannah reached behind her back to dislodge his hands, and Danny saw that everything had returned to normal. The closeness had been nothing more than a dream—fleeting, elusive, gone upon awakening.

"You can't tell me you didn't like what just happened," he said, his tone as wooden as he felt inside. "For once in your life, stop saying no long enough to decide if you really want to."

Savannah looked away, shifting her gaze to the safety of the rose still clutched within her gloved fingers.

"I never should have allowed that to happen," she said.

In sudden, ungovernable aggravation, Danny snatched the flower from her hand and tossed it aside.

"Why the hell not, Savannah?"

She raised defiant eyes. "Because it can't lead anywhere."

"Tell me one more time!" Danny boomed in her face. "Why the hell not?"

"Just *because!*" she yelled back.

Turning on her heel, Savannah hurried up the steps and into the house, forgetting for the moment that Leo Crane was there, stopping short when she nearly collided with him in the foyer.

"Dr. Crane!" she exclaimed breathlessly.

"Savannah? Is something wrong?"

"No . . . nothing," she replied. Lifting a hand to her temple, she added, "I have a bit of a headache." And it was true. Her head was pounding, along with her heart.

"How's Mother?" she asked.

"Fine. She's been asleep the past hour or so."

Danny came in then. Savannah looked over, their eyes met, and Leo noted the explosive look that passed between them. Savannah turned curtly away as Danny started in their direction.

"Thank you again for coming, Dr. Crane," she said. "If you don't mind, I'll let you see yourself out. Excuse me."

With that, she made for the stairs, her gown rustling with every step. Danny joined Leo, and the two men watched as she ascended swiftly to the second floor and passed out of view. Leo glanced aside.

"How are the kid gloves holding up?" he asked flippantly.

Danny flashed him a look of irritation. "Frankly, Doctor, they're about to come apart at the seams."

With that, he vaulted up the stairs and disappeared in the opposite direction from Savannah. Seconds later came the sound of a door slamming overhead. Shaking his head, Leo walked across the silent foyer and turned out the light.

"Love," he muttered, and locked the doors to Kings Crossing behind him.

Chapter Eleven

THE GALA honoring Senator Gaines ended in an uproar. Among the guests were several physicians. They bent over Big Ed's unmoving body, exchanging grim looks as a cacophony of sirens converged on the entrance of Kings Club. The ambulance was the first to arrive, followed closely by police cars and a fire truck. Medics jostled into the ballroom with an array of equipment; the guests parted to make way, turning to each other with horrified whispers as the stricken man was loaded on a stretcher and carted away.

The following morning, word spread from the hospital. Big Ed McKenna had suffered a near-fatal stroke that had left him paralyzed. His pale eyes appeared alert, but aside from the random blinking of his eyelids, there was no movement. Days went by with no change in his condition. Specialists were flown in. Partial recovery was possible, they agreed, but severe damage had been incurred. The patient might, with time and therapy, recover the ability to speak. Beyond that, they refused to speculate.

By Thursday, board members of a half dozen corporations were clamoring for some sort of action. Big Ed was without doubt the most powerful man in Kingsport and probably all of Brunswick County. His holdings constituted an empire; his absence affected thousands. That afternoon, five days after the debilitating stroke, Big Ed was declared incompetent.

It came as no surprise that Rory was appointed his legal guardian. By the end of the business day, he was also acting chief of the McKenna empire.

On Friday morning, Savannah was in the midst of washing up the breakfast dishes when the doorbell rang. It was the florist

from town, delivering an arrangement of white lilies. When she
read the card, she was moved to fury. Dumping the flowers in
the trash, she hurried to the phone and called *The Watch*. Rory
hadn't arrived. She dialed the McKenna house.

"What do you mean, I'm fired?" she demanded.

"I'm sorry, Savannah. But as you may have heard, I've succeeded my father in all his business roles, including chairman of
the board at *The Watch*. I'm afraid some streamlining is in order. Of course, if you'd care to discuss the matter with me in
private, say, over a candlelit dinner . . ."

Before the image of Rory's smirking face could fully materi-
alize, Savannah slammed down the phone.

It was past noon on Friday when Rory swaggered into *The
Watch*—looking, Danny thought, like the proverbial cat who'd
swallowed the canary. It occurred to him that now, without his
father's staying hand, Rory might very well do what he'd
threatened when Danny first returned: call in the company attorneys and have him dismissed. The McKennas virtually ran
Kingsport; even if Danny sued, he knew it could be years before
the issue was settled.

Finishing his latest trite assignment in short order, Danny left
the building early and headed to the police station. He'd called
Gilroy a couple of times the past week but hadn't been able to
catch him. Today he found him in his office. Tapping briefly on
the open door, Danny stepped inside.

"You busy?" he asked.

Gilroy looked up, then rose to his feet with a smile. "Not really," he replied. "Come on in."

As Danny approached, the lieutenant leaned across the desk
to offer a handshake. "Have a seat," he added. "What's on your
mind?"

"Remember last week when I said there was something I'd
like to talk to you about?"

Gilroy nodded.

"Know anything about a woman named Jane Wilson?"

Gilroy's brows went up. "What's your interest in her?"

"Unsolved homicides are intrinsically interesting, don't you
think? Do you know anything?"

"I ought to," Gilroy replied. "I'm in charge of the damn
case."

"What can you tell me about her?"

"Damn little that's of any use, I'm afraid." Gilroy reached inside a desk drawer and produced a file. "Let's see. She was single, twenty-eight, good-looking. Care to see the police photo?"

"I've seen it."

"Okay." Settling back in his chair, the lieutenant went on. "Jane Wilson lived alone in a small cottage up the beach. She'd been in Kingsport a few years. Didn't have many acquaintances, other than a fairly constant stream of men. Seems Miss Wilson lived off the kindness of gentleman friends, if you catch my drift. Her most constant companion during the month or so before her death was Rory McKenna."

"McKenna!"

"Yeah. Does that mean something to you?"

Covering his surprise, Danny shrugged and shook his head.

"They had a hot thing going, but McKenna says he broke it off, coincidentally enough, on the night she died. From what I could determine, he was the last person to see her alive, although there wasn't a shred of evidence to connect him with the crime. We couldn't find anything at all at the scene. Hey," Gilroy added with a bright look, "it's a slow afternoon. Want to drive out and take a look?"

They took Danny's jeep and headed for the coast. The cottage Jane Wilson had rented was on a lonely stretch of beach north of the city limits. Like Roberta, she'd been murdered late at night just outside her home. Like Roberta, she'd offered no clue as to the identity of her assailant. No skin under fingernails, no hair or blood or even a thread of fabric that couldn't be matched to her own body and clothing. In all probability, a blow to the head had rendered her unconscious, and the murderer had gone about his foul business without the hindrance of a struggle. He'd left no tracks, either by foot or tire.

Danny and the lieutenant scanned the area outside the vacant cottage. It was the first Friday of September; the air was hot and sticky, the sky overcast and glaring. Danny squinted as he peered up the highway from which The Strangler must have approached.

"Guess he parked up here on the road," Danny theorized. "There's no traffic out here, even now at the beginning of Labor Day weekend, when the rest of the beach is bustling. Late at night, off season, there would be little danger of anyone spotting a car."

"He picked his time and place, all right," Gilroy commented. "He's no dummy. Damn clever, in fact."

"And sick," Danny added soberly. Turning once more to stare up the highway, he fantasized about The Strangler's presence in this very spot, wished he could turn back time and catch a glimpse . . .

"There's more to it than just an interest in homicide, isn't there?"

Danny looked over his shoulder and found Gilroy studying him with a pensive look. Ignoring the question, he said, "It seems to make sense that the killer was one of her 'gentleman friends.'"

"I questioned them all—all that I could find, anyway. Most of them were tourists, vacationers just passing through. Only a few were locals, and none of them had been seen with her for months except, as I said, Rory McKenna."

On the drive back to Kingsport, the name chimed in Danny's brain, resounding with the echo of rightness. Rory McKenna. Could it be that, after all these years, Danny would find that The Strangler was one and the same with the man who'd been his archenemy since childhood? There was a certain poetic ring about it that sent chills up Danny's spine.

He was preoccupied as he dropped Gilroy in front of the police station and thanked him for his time. Backing onto the street, he noticed at the last minute that Dr. Crane had walked down the steps and was joining Gilroy. The doctor waved. Danny raised an obliging hand, shifted into gear, and drove on.

"What did he want?" Leo asked straightforwardly.

Gilroy glanced aside with a faint look of amusement at the doctor's nosiness. "Background on that homicide some months back—Jane Wilson."

A conclusion popped into Leo's head, and he knew he was right. Stepping to the curb, he raised a hand to shield his eyes and peered after the jeep.

Danny Sawyer had explained away his return with a blithe comment about needing a break from Washington. But that wasn't it—that wasn't it at all. The accused murderer of Roberta Sikes had come back to catch a killer.

It had been gray and muggy all day, the clouds hanging low and threatening rain that failed to fall. Up in the gabled attic of the Crossing, the air was musty as well as stifling.

Savannah heaved once more at the window. Finally the thing gave way with a loud creak that brought it halfway up. There it stuck and refused to give another inch, leaving just enough leeway for her to crawl through on her belly and out onto the roof.

It had been several years since she'd been up here—not since she'd chased off Mr. Kiker and that drifter, Tom. Now she saw the sad shape of the roof she hadn't allowed them to finish repairing. There were a half dozen spots where tiles were missing altogether, sources of the leaks that often made their way through the attic and into the second-story rooms. She simply must have the roof repaired, although she couldn't imagine where the money would come from, especially now that she'd been fired from *The Watch*.

Her expression brightened. Maybe Danny could—

Savannah stopped herself before the thought went any further. She could not depend on Danny. He'd been markedly distant since the night of the ball, leaving early, coming home late. In the objective light of his absence, she'd examined herself with scathing eyes, realizing with a mix of fear and self-reproach just how deeply she'd allowed him inside her life. Whether she wanted to admit it or not, she had slipped into depending on Danny for a great many things. The idea of his leaving filled her with dread.

Rebelling against the sense of loneliness that had overtaken her the past week, she'd kept herself busy with chores about the Crossing. Today it was the shutter hanging from a broken hinge outside the third-floor attic window.

The roof was steep, the tiles offering little foothold. Savannah inched her way around the gable, and bracing herself against its side, took hold of the shutter and looked up at the rusted hinge. It would take a good push to dislodge it. Shifting her hands to the bottom, she grasped the weathered wood, and a splinter pierced her palm. She yanked her hand away.

"Damn!" she muttered, Danny's influence spilling from her mouth as his face loomed in her mind's eye. "Damn straight," she could hear him saying around the white slash of a grin. The image lingered as rain began to fall—a few heavy drops heralding the swift beginning of a steady downpour.

"*Now* it rains!" Savannah remarked irritably.

Taking hold of the shutter, she pushed with all her strength. The thing broke instantly free, toppling away from the wall, clattering to the roof beside her. Savannah clambered for it, slipped on the newly wet tiles, and made a mad grab for the windowframe. The window slammed down with a bang just seconds before she heard the crash of the shutter on the steps below.

The rain was falling in sheets now. Carefully positioning her tennis shoes on the slippery tile, Savannah pulled herself up to the window, holding onto the frame for dear life with her left hand as she used her right to try and raise the treacherous window. It didn't budge. Her position was so precarious that she couldn't risk putting all her force behind a struggle she'd barely been able to accomplish from inside.

"Mother!" she yelled, but knew her voice carried no farther than a few yards in the squelching rain.

Crawling carefully back to the meager shelter of the gable, Savannah drew up her knees, settled in the safest position she could devise, and proceeded to call herself every derogatory name she could bring to mind.

Danny stopped by *The Watch* and learned that Carol had called. Glancing at the clock, he saw that it was nearly five, so he quickly dialed her number.

"Carol Kincaid."

"Carol? It's me. What's up?"

"My, my. Aren't we brisk?"

"Sorry," he apologized sheepishly. "I've spent the afternoon with a police officer down here, and I've had my mind squarely on The Strangler. I was hoping you had something to report."

"Something, yes, but I'm not sure what. I got a reply from a bureau in Georgia. Seems the MO your boy uses fits a crime that occurred down there a number of years ago."

"Georgia?"

"That's right. If it turns out to be the same guy, looks like his hunting ground is a bit more expansive than you thought. I don't know any details yet. They're forwarding a transcript, but I won't have it until next week."

"Georgia," Danny repeated glumly, the theory he'd had about Rory McKenna seeming to fly apart.

"You sound disappointed. Why?"

"I was beginning to think maybe I was onto something, but . . . oh, well. The truth is what I'm after, whatever it is. Thanks for letting me know. You'll call when you get more information?"

"You know I will. Still no idea of how long you'll be down there?"

"Not yet."

There was a brief silence.

"I miss you, Dan."

For the first time since he'd caught up with Gilroy, Danny's thoughts settled on something other than The Strangler. Picturing Carol's pretty, dark-eyed face, he found that he could hardly visualize her features. He'd barely thought of her in weeks, and the realization made him feel instantly guilty.

"I miss you, too," he said.

"Really?"

"Really." It wasn't a lie, for then and there he found that he did in fact miss her . . . Washington . . . the whole scheme of a life that now seemed a world away, an eon ago.

"How are things in D.C.?" he asked.

"The same. *The Post* seems a little dull without Buck Sawyer, though. I saw the story the wires picked up from *The River Watch*. Nice work."

"Thanks."

"How are things in Kingsport?"

"Okay, I guess."

"And with Savannah?"

Danny flinched. "Very . . . uncertain."

"You're in love with her, aren't you?"

"I—" Danny rubbed his forehead. "It's awkward talking to you about this, Carol."

"That's no excuse to leave me hanging. It isn't fair to string me along when there's no hope."

Releasing a defeated sigh, Danny glanced behind him to make sure no one was near. "I don't know, Carol," he said quietly. "Whatever I feel for her, I wish I didn't."

"Why?"

"Because it makes me miserable."

"I can relate to that," came the tight reply. "Good-bye, Dan."

Danny walked out of *The Watch* into a steady rain. It suited his increasingly dour mood as he drove to the Crossing. He thought of times he'd shared with Carol—the uncomplicated fun, the great sex. Stacking that up against the past few frustrating weeks, he decided he must be a total idiot.

There had been good moments with Savannah since he came back, but by and large he had experienced a series of disappointments. The night of the senatorial ball, he'd done his damnedest to approach her with tenderness. She'd only ended up flying off the handle as always, and they'd hardly crossed paths the past week.

By the time Danny turned up the drive, he was livid, not just with Savannah, but also with himself. Stomping into the house, he decided to put an end to the cold war and meet her head-on.

"Savannah!" he bellowed.

Silence. No sound but the pattering of rain. He went upstairs and called again. Nothing. Walking brashly into her bedroom, he found it empty. Without hesitation he stalked across the landing to the master chamber and rapped on the door.

"Mrs. King?"

"What is it?" came the imperious voice.

"Is Savannah with you?"

"She and her father went into town," came the crazed reply. "You'd do better, Danny Sawyer, to forget my daughter's whereabouts and keep your mind on your chores!"

Danny rolled his eyes and went downstairs, eventually going to the front doors and stepping out on the veranda. That was when he noticed the smashed shutter on the steps below. Oblivious to the rain, he trotted down and looked up at the attic window. What he saw made him scrub his eyes with his fists and peer again up the towering height of the house.

"Savannah?!" he yelled.

"I'm stuck!"

The words barely reached him, though he was certain she must have shouted at the top of her lungs. Seconds later, Danny was racing up the flights of stairs, his heart pounding as he re-created the image of her precarious perch on the tiled roof. The door to the attic was open. He galloped across the dusty floor and grabbed at the window. It resisted, and he formed a quick idea of what must have happened. She'd crawled out, and it had slammed shut behind her. Changing his grip, he gave a mighty push. The thing groaned and flew up, though the opening it surrendered was less than a foot high. Sticking his head out, Danny saw her an arm's length away, soaked and clinging to the gable for dear life.

"Of all the stupid, idiotic, ridiculous . . ."

The angry words pelted Savannah along with the rain. "For heaven's sake, don't scold me!" she yelled. "*Help me!* The tiles are slick as glass!"

Stretching half his body out the narrow opening, Danny took firm hold of her wrists and pulled. Feet scrambling, Savannah wriggled to the window, made her entrance headfirst, and landed in a belly flop on Danny's outstretched body. The window fell with a bang just as her tennis shoes cleared the sill.

Danny glared up from his position beneath her. "What in blue blazes were you doing out there in the rain?!"

Savannah was dripping from head to toe. Blinking rapidly against the streams running into her eyes, she did her best to return his glare. "Did you ever stop to think it might not have been raining when I went out there? Let me up!"

Instead, Danny rolled with her, swiftly pinning her body full-length beneath his own. Bracing his forearms on each side of her head, he stared angrily down at her.

"What would you have done if I hadn't come along?"

"I'd have thought of something!" she fired, her voice becoming more shrill as his weight forced her breath.

"Anybody knows better than to go out on a rooftop without somebody around in case of trouble! Don't ever do anything like that again!"

"I don't plan to!" Twisting her head from side to side, Savannah pushed at his shoulders.

Danny's hands secured her head and stilled her movements. "If you'd fallen, you would have been killed!"

The words rang out in a hoarse cry. Looking helplessly up from her imprisoned position, Savannah met his eyes, her brain gathering a sharp reply, faltering in the midst of it, then losing altogether the thread of what she was going to say.

Time stumbled and seemed to slow like the gears of a machine grinding to a halt. In the sequestered attic, there was the patter of rain, the plunk of heavy drops leaking into a nearby pot, and—in Savannah's mind—a crackling sizzle as awareness struck.

She saw a raindrop slide from Danny's hair to his furled brow, smelled his aftershave, heard his breathing. Charged to acuteness, her tactile sense registered the weight of his body, the warm covering of his trousers along her rain-soaked legs, the contrasting wetness of the shirt beneath her hands, where her fingers were spread defensively against his chest.

Injecting strength into those fingers, she silently pushed. Danny rebuffed with a steady descent against the pressure. Savannah's elbows bent beneath his strength, her eyes searching his, watching them shift to her mouth. Undermining the effort of her hands, her lips parted to meet his.

The warm wetness of her mouth closed about Danny's tongue, shocking his system. He settled into the kiss, face slanting, tongue driving. Savannah met it, returned the kiss, and he was swept over some brink beyond which there was only mindless passion. He moved a knee to the pair beneath him, pushing until they parted, and slipped his hips into a position of unprecedented intimacy.

Danny lay still between her legs, hard and throbbing, a shred of willpower urging him to wait for her reaction, even as his mouth sought to seduce her. When Savannah went on with their smoldering kiss, it was all the signal he needed. His pelvis began to move in rhythm with his tongue.

Some time later, he became aware that Savannah's legs had moved. Having planted her feet on the floor, she was straining against him. Her movements only heightened the mindblowing friction between their bodies. She made noises in his mouth. Danny ignored them. She tore her lips away, and his moved to her neck.

"Danny!" she panted.

The sound was dim and far away.

"Stop it!"

Danny went still, though his manhood continued to press urgently against her. He propped himself up on shaking arms and looked down.

"You let me up this instant!" Savannah hissed, punctuating the command with a violent shove against his chest.

Danny's entire body stiffened as he resisted, stubbornly lowering himself so that his nose was an inch from hers.

"And if I don't?" he muttered breathlessly.

She twisted away from his nearness. "I was crazy to let you back into the Crossing! Get off me!"

The tone of her voice wrenched Danny to his feet. He watched tensely as she scrambled up, ready to catch her if she tried to run. He wasn't through yet.

"Don't worry, Miss Savannah," he said as she straightened. "Everything's still intact."

Savannah's gaze leapt to his.

"Just as sweet and pure as the day you were born," Danny added, unable to keep the snide tone out of his voice.

Savannah's back went rigid. "You have no right to be sarcastic with me."

"Oh, yes, I do."

Danny took a stiff step toward her. Savannah held her ground.

"Do you think you're the only person here with any feelings?" he demanded. "God, you're selfish."

"I'd hardly call it selfish to—"

"Yes! Damn selfish! You're not the only one you're cutting off anymore, Savannah. You're cutting me off, too."

"I told you from the beginning not to expect anything from me," she replied. Her breath was slow in coming; her chest began to heave. "You're just so . . . so conceited you can't believe there's a woman alive who doesn't appreciate your manhandling!"

"You appreciate it, all right." The control Danny forced over himself came less from a gentleman's code than the overwhelming feelings he had for the woman before him.

"I'm no fool, Savannah," he went on quietly. "Do you think I haven't been around enough to know when a woman is responding? What are you so afraid of? That if you get carried away, I'll make love to you? You're right. If you do, I will."

"Don't say that, Danny!"

"I *will* say it. I'm going to make love to you, Savannah. And don't worry, I'll make it good. Even though it will be your first time."

She stared, her heart hammering, unable to produce a sensible thought, much less a retort.

"It doesn't take a genius to figure you're a virgin," Danny continued. "That's it, isn't it? That's what holds you back."

Savannah pushed a swallow past her constricting throat.

"All the more reason the first time should be with me," he added and leaned toward her.

She leapt back like a frightened doe. "Promise me!" she cried. "Promise me you'll stop doing this!"

"No," he answered.

"Well, then, I want you out of my house!"

"No."

"What?!"

"I said I'm not leaving."

Savannah's flushed face took on a look of incredulity. "You

haven't changed a bit! You always wanted more than I could give! Stop tormenting me, Danny Sawyer!"

"Not a chance," he murmured. His gaze fell to where the long wet ponytail had swung over her shoulder to lodge between her heaving breasts, then rose to re-engage her eyes with earnest steadiness.

"Mark my words, Savannah," he went on in a low tone. "It won't be today and probably not tomorrow. But one day soon, I'll hold you down by that long hair of yours and kiss you until you're moaning to give yourself to me. Do you hear me? *Moaning*."

If he'd shouted the words, Savannah thought they would have carried less impact. As it was, the quiet threat reverberated not only through the attic, but through her body as well. She spun and ran out of the room.

Moaning, *eh*?

Savannah bolted into her bedroom and locked the door, her eyes searching, though it had not yet fully dawned on her what she was about to do.

She was halfway through the dastardly deed when her glazed eyes conveyed the reflection in the mirror to her consciousness. A look of horror formed on her face. But by then it was too late.

When seven-thirty rolled around and there was no Savannah, Danny paced the deserted kitchen, peering first at the desolate stove, then up at the ceiling. It might be like her to ignore him, or even her own suppertime hunger. But it was completely atypical for Savannah to slight her mother's needs.

Grabbing up the newspaper, he planted himself in the breakfast nook and pretended to read, his gaze darting every few minutes to the old clock hanging above the pots and pans on the west wall. At eight o'clock, he got up and headed for the stairs.

Savannah was seated before the vanity. She'd taken a shower, washed her hair, and curled it with a hot iron she found in the depths of a long-neglected drawer. The iron had succeeded only in shrinking what was left, curling it into a pale halo about her head. She'd been brushing out the curl, off and on, for the past hour. Now her face was framed with blending waves, but there was nothing she could do to stretch the length. When a knock sounded at her door, she jumped as though she'd been shot.

"Savannah?" came Danny's voice.

Her gaze froze on the mirror. She'd dressed in fresh shorts and blouse but had been unable to make herself leave the companionship of the shocking reflection.

"Savannah? Open up!"

The call was accompanied by a renewed round of knocking. An insistent hand tried the knob.

Danny was preparing to knock once more when he heard the click of the lock. "Listen, Savannah," he began as the door opened. "There's no need to—"

He swallowed his words when he saw her. He stared for a moment, his brain registering the sight over and over again.

"Let me see," he mumbled senselessly.

But Savannah knew what he meant. Dutifully, she turned the back of her head for him to see, then quickly pivoted to stare him directly in the eye.

"Where is it?"

Her eyes shifted, targeting a spot across the floor. Danny walked over and picked up a handful of the golden hair. With a sense of shock, he rubbed its silky texture through his fingers. Images flew through his mind—Savannah as a child, a girl, a budding woman. In each he saw her hair, long and shining. His words came back to him: "I'll hold you down by that long hair of yours and kiss you . . ."

In an explosion of anger, Danny dropped the shorn lock and whirled on her. Spanning the distance between them in two long strides, he reached for the hair that was now the length of his own and jerked her face up to his.

"There's still enough to grab and hold," he said through his teeth. "What do you intend to do next? Shave yourself bald?"

Savannah stared mutely up at him, unable to move or to control the tears that suddenly filled her eyes. Danny saw them, and abruptly releasing her, began to back away, his eyes still locked on her.

"God!" he exploded, grabbing his head as though it were a source of sudden, intolerable pain. "You make me crazy!"

Having delivered the declaration, he stalked out. By the time Savannah walked dazedly to the doorway, he was slamming out of his room, flashing her a look of fury as he stuffed his wallet in his pocket on the way to the stairs. Without a word, he started down. She moved to the head of the staircase on weighted legs.

"Where are you going?" she called inanely.

He turned at the bottom of the stairs.

"Do you really give a damn?"

His voice thundered up from the foyer, resounding against the quiet of the house.

"I . . ." Savannah paused. "Of course, I—"

"Forget it!" Danny boomed. "I'm long past expecting you to admit you give a damn about me or anything else, except maybe the long-lost fortune of the illustrious Kings!"

"What's going on out there?" her mother's voice intruded from behind the door across the landing.

Savannah turned an impatient look toward the master chamber, and in the space of that instant, Danny strode into the foyer. She hurried down several steps.

"Danny!"

He halted, though his back remained stiffly turned.

"Please . . ."

"Please what?" He cast a harsh look over his shoulder.

"Please wait," Savannah managed, taking another step down.

Danny's hands flexed at his sides. "I don't think that would be wise. We need some time apart, Savannah. Before we really hurt each other. Maybe you're right. Maybe I should move out."

His words stopped her. Savannah's hand tightened spasmodically on the rail as she noted from a great silent distance the way Danny's gaze lifted.

"Your hair . . ." His words were barely audible, as disbelieving as the shock that surfaced on his face. And then he walked out.

Savannah peered into the empty foyer, listening futilely as his footsteps receded. When she heard the bang of the kitchen door, she turned and retraced her steps up the stairs. She'd opened the door to her room when that of the master chamber flew open.

"I've never heard such carrying on!" Ophelia King announced from across the landing. "What in the world is going on between you and that Sawyer boy?"

"Nothing, Mother," Savannah replied. Closing her bedroom door, she leaned against it and stared unseeingly across the room.

It was still drizzling as Danny leaped into the jeep. He was nearly out of the courtyard when another vehicle swerved in front of him, lights blaring, horn honking. Danny slammed on the brakes and skidded to a stop.

"What the hell—!" he yelled, thrusting his head through the window. "Oh, it's you, Dr. Crane. What the devil are you doing? We almost had a head-on!"

Leo grinned. "Sorry. Didn't want you to get away. I drove out here to have a word with you. Where are you off to?"

"Hell if I know. Away from here."

"Feel like a drink?" Leo asked.

Danny's feverish eyes met the doctor's calm ones. After an instant of consideration, he killed the engine and climbed out.

"That's exactly what I feel like," he said and, leaving the jeep outside the courtyard gate, circled round to the passenger's side of the doctor's old Ford.

They went to the Ocean Forest Hotel and settled at the bar. It was crowded, and as always the Dogwood Room was dark. Neither of them noticed the man at the far table who straightened in his seat as they walked in, watched attentively as they ordered drinks, then rose and made a discreet exit.

Danny tossed down a whiskey and motioned Hank for another.

"What's the matter?" Leo asked. "If you don't mind my saying so, you seem mad as a bull."

Danny gave him a sullen look. "A rather constant state since I came back to Kingsport."

Leo reached inside his jacket for his pipe. "Funny you should bring that up. That's exactly what I wanted to discuss with you—your return to Kingsport."

Eyeing the doctor, Danny reached for the second whiskey.

"Last weekend when I asked why you came back, you said you wanted a break. That isn't the whole truth, is it?"

"What do you mean?"

Leo lit the pipe, took a few puffs, and tossed the match in a nearby ashtray.

"I talked with Steve Gilroy today. He said you were asking about a homicide that took place here early in the year."

Damn! Danny thought. He should have told Gilroy to keep his mouth shut. He did away with the shot before saying, "So?"

"So, I figure you made the same connection I did—between Jane Wilson and Roberta Sikes."

Resting his forearms on the polished bar, Danny gave the doctor a long, steady look.

"Their police photos are virtually identical," Leo added.

The grisly details rose in Danny's mind. "I know," he said gruffly.

"Same MO: blow to the head, strangulation, a scarf tied—"

"I know!" Danny interrupted and motioned for another drink.

"Maybe there's something you *don't* know."

"Like what?"

"Like both of those murders were duplicates of another death," Leo supplied quietly.

Something both thrilling and terrifying charged through Danny. Turning on the barstool, he faced the doctor fully.

"Go on," he said.

Leo took a puff off the pipe. "You were only a boy when she died, but Margaret McKenna always wore a scarf."

"McKenna!"

The name burst from Danny's lips. Leo raised a cautioning hand.

"McKenna?" Danny repeated in a near whisper. "What are you saying? That she was murdered?"

"No. She fell down the stairs and died of a broken neck."

"But you said—"

"I said both victims, Roberta and Jane, appeared to be replicas of an earlier death."

Danny looked away, considering the doctor's words as his fingers toyed with the shot glass. "This is the second time today I've heard the name McKenna in connection with this thing. Gilroy said Rory McKenna was Jane Wilson's lover and possibly the last person to see her alive. But there's nothing to link him with Roberta."

"No one ever learned the identity of the father of her child," Leo commented.

Danny's gaze rose with startled swiftness.

"It wasn't you," Leo resumed, cocking a brow. "Was it?"

"No, even though she said it was."

"What if she was shielding the true father?" Leo theorized. "What if he was rich and powerful, downright overwhelming to a Clancytown girl? What if he could intimidate her into naming someone else as the father?"

"Rory McKenna."

"I've often wondered," Leo said.

"You're sure about this?" Danny said with a searching look.

"I can't be sure about the father of Roberta's unborn child,"

Leo said. "I *can* be sure that both she and Jane Wilson were killed by the same person, and that somehow or other the killer is connected to Margaret McKenna."

"And you say Roberta and Jane were . . . replicas?"

Leo nodded. "I went to the McKenna house that night, as soon as I heard the news. Margaret was still lying there, her right arm outflung, her legs bent at crazy angles. There was a streak of blood on her forehead and a scarf around her throat."

"Jesus!" Danny raised his arm and motioned swiftly to Hank.

"Ed refused to let me see the boys that night," Leo went on. "They were young, vulnerable. A thing like that could be pretty traumatic, and when trauma is involved, you can never predict how someone will react."

"So, the killer is *repeating* Margaret McKenna's death?"

"Or avenging it."

As Hank stepped up and poured another round, Danny suddenly remembered his conversation with Carol.

"Wait a minute," he said when he and the doctor were once again alone. "There might be something that doesn't fit. I spoke with a contact of mine today. It seems there was a similar murder down in Georgia."

Leo peered at him through a ring of smoke. "When?"

"Some years ago. That's all I know at the moment."

Leo put aside his pipe. "Some years ago? As it happens, Rory McKenna went to college in Georgia *some years ago*."

Danny's eyes widened. "You're kidding."

"No," Leo returned solemnly. "I never kid about murder."

It was after nine when Libby started for the stairs, a long luxurious bath in mind. It had been a peaceful evening; Rory hadn't been home since he left at midday.

Glancing into the game room as she passed, she saw Clayton sitting alone in the dim light of a single lamp. She'd always thought of the game room as Rory and Big Ed's domain, never as Clayton's. He seemed as misplaced in it as he was among the McKenna males. She detoured into the room.

"What are you doing in here?" she asked.

"N-nothing."

Libby lit a cigarette, warding off a light shiver. "I've never liked this room. I wouldn't have thought you do, either."

"I d-don't."

"Then why are you here?"

Clayton raised a brandy snifter and took a healthy draught. "Where's my b-brother?"

"Who knows? Probably out celebrating. I get the feeling he's been itching to take your father's place for quite a while."

"Who b-better? They're two of a k-kind."

"You seem depressed, Clayton. Is it because of your father?"

He snorted in a way that reminded her of Rory, but offered no reply. Libby stepped to the fireplace and tossed the cigarette on the hearth. "I get the picture," she said. "None of my business, right? Good night, Clayton." She walked away.

"Libby!"

She turned and looked across the room. Clayton rose from the leather chair that was his father's favorite.

"I want to w-warn you."

"Warn me?" Libby said and backtracked a few steps. "About what?"

"Rory."

"I don't think there's anything about Rory—"

"You d-don't know everything," Clayton broke in on a shrill note. "You should l-leave this house. And this t-town."

She gave him a slight puzzled smile. "Why? You're not making any sense, Clayton."

"I'm making p-perfect sense. Something t-terrible could happen. It has before. You don't know how b-brutal Rory can be when he loses interest."

Libby arched a brow. "Loses interest?"

Clayton nodded. "He's got his eye on s-someone else."

"Who?"

"Savannah."

"Savannah?" Libby laughed. "Little Miss Perfect?"

But her laughter died as she thought about it. Maybe Clayton was right. Recently, there had been a waning in Rory's attention. When she first arrived, he'd wanted it every night. Now, nearly a week had passed. She couldn't be unhappy about his absence, but she was worried that all her careful plotting would be for naught if Rory turned to another woman. But Savannah?

Libby looked at Clayton with hard eyes. "He'd gobble her up for breakfast. Besides, Savannah wouldn't give Rory the time of day. She's always detested him."

Clayton tossed down the remainder of the brandy. "Maybe that's why he's after her," he said without a single stutter.

* * *

Having turned out the lights in the parlor, Savannah was on her way back upstairs when she heard the sound of an approaching car.

"Danny," she whispered and paused on the stairs, waiting, listening as the engine was killed and footsteps approached the front door. A hand tried the lock, and then the footsteps retreated. Still not moving, Savannah turned and peered blindly through the darkness, sensing the direction from which the next sound would come. Moments later she heard the kitchen door open. Glancing down the front of herself, she confirmed that she was hardly dressed to confront a man. The old sleeveless nightgown reached to her ankles, but was as light as gauze after years of washing.

She hesitated, thinking of the way he'd left, the way he'd threatened to leave the Crossing. The urge to reconcile overpowered her sense of propriety, and she made her bare feet move down the stairs.

"Danny?" she mumbled, moving into the kitchen and turning on the overhead light. What she saw stopped her in her tracks.

"The back door was open," Rory said with a smirk. "I happened to see Sawyer out on the town and thought you might be lonesome."

"I'm not. Please go."

He walked rebelliously into the room. His hair was windblown, his eyes red. He'd been drinking.

"The least you could do is offer me a drink," he said.

"It appears you've had quite enough of that already."

"What's the matter, Miss Savannah? Still mad because I canned you? I told you on the phone how easy it would be to mend our . . . friendship."

"Don't be obtuse, Rory. There's nothing to mend. I can't imagine what prompted you to show up here tonight."

"No?" he questioned with a lazy up-and-down look. "Are you sure about that?"

Suddenly remembering the meagerness of her gown, Savannah folded her arms over her breasts. "I don't care to expend any energy trying to figure it out."

"You've cut your hair," he observed. "I like it."

"I'm so pleased. Now, would you go?"

In contrast to her request, Rory ambled closer. "I like it a lot. It makes you look older . . . like a woman."

Alarm pounded through Savannah. She thought of her sixteenth birthday, the way he'd attacked her in his car. Turning her back, she walked stiffly to the sink where she eyed the dishes in the drying rack, her gaze coming to rest on a butcher knife.

"Still," came Rory's voice from behind her, "there's something undeniably girlish about you. A real man could fix that."

"There's nothing about me that I want fixed," she retorted.

"Anything Sawyer can do, I can do better. You don't know what you're missing."

He was so close that his breath stirred her hair. To Savannah's horror, he placed a hand on her shoulder. Still, she refused to believe what seemed to be happening.

"I'm sure you're right," she said steadily. "But I'd prefer to miss it all the same."

"I'd prefer you didn't."

In a surprise move, Rory twirled her around and jammed her up against the counter.

"Come on, Savannah. You can't deny there's chemistry between us."

"Of course I can deny it! With every shred of my being!"

She saw him grin, and then his face swooped toward her. Savannah dodged as much as she could manage, considering the way she'd allowed herself to become trapped. Rory's mouth landed on the side of her neck. There was a flash of pain as his teeth captured tender skin, accompanied by a hard sucking that drew her flesh into the wet cavern of his mouth. Yanking her head violently backward, Savannah tore herself loose, wondering if her neck was bleeding. The thought was fleeting as she heard Rory's insolent laugh. She shoved him with every bit of her strength. He stumbled back a pace.

"You must have lost your mind!" she accused.

He chuckled and placed a hand on his chest. "Maybe my heart."

"Get out of here, Rory!"

"I don't think so."

"Get out!" she shrieked.

"Go ahead. Scream. In fact, I'd like it. There's no one to hear but your crazy mother. Do you think she could stop me?"

"Perhaps I could," came the ringing words.

Both Savannah and Rory spun around. Ophelia King stood in the kitchen doorway, wearing a frilly feminine peignoir that contrasted sharply with the rifle she was pointing in their direc-

tion. It was only loaded with rock salt, Savannah thought frantically, but Rory didn't know that.

"Mrs. King," he said, a slow smile rising to his face. "I didn't
think you were up."

"Obviously," Ophelia returned. "I can't tell you how disappointed I am in you, Rory. Boys will be boys, I know, but some
things are inexcusable . . . I wouldn't!" she cautioned quickly as
he took a step toward her. "I don't intend to tolerate this nonsense, even from a McKenna. My husband isn't home, but I as-
sure you he's instructed me well in the use of this rifle."

"Your husband—"

"Shut up, Rory!" Darting away from the counter, Savannah
joined her mother and took the rifle. "Get out," she reiterated,
leveling the barrel point-blank at Rory's chest.

He laughed. "You should see the pair of you—"

"Don't be impertinent, young man!" Ophelia commanded.
"Your mother was one of my dearest friends, but don't delude
yourself. I intend to have a word with your father first thing tomorrow!"

Rory guffawed at that. Savannah glanced aside.

"Go on to bed, Mother. Thanks for coming down, but
everything's all right. Rory was just leaving."

Savannah added the last with a hard look in Rory's direction
as her mother exited, muttering under her breath about the demise of Southern chivalry. Strained seconds passed.

"The chase is on," Rory muttered.

He grinned, the expression evil and threatening. Savannah's
alarm skyrocketed anew, but then, thank goodness, he backed
away. She made herself breathe with forced regularity as he
walked across the room, pausing at the door to impale her with
steel-blue eyes.

"I'll have you before I'm through," he said. "I've tracked the
best, and I've learned the old saying is true. There's more than
one way to skin a cat."

Savannah mustered a show of strength. "Even as a child, I
could always outwit you, Rory. That hasn't changed."

"Don't bet on it, sweetheart."

And then he was gone, leaving the kitchen door wide open.
Minutes passed, and Savannah stood rooted to the spot, rifle in
hand, unable to make her feet move in the direction in which
he'd disappeared, but knowing she wasn't safe until she'd
locked the door. She began inching her way along the counter,

drawing fortitude from the idea of how Rory would laugh if he could see her slow, fearful progress. That saw her through. Reaching the door, she slammed it, threw the bolt in place, and raced upstairs.

The next morning she woke with a start and found that she was drenched with perspiration. Kicking off the covers, she glanced at the clock and saw that it was past eight. She must have fallen asleep some time near daybreak, for she knew she hadn't closed her eyes as long as darkness remained.

She'd heard Danny come in around midnight. The thought of Danny was curtailed by the memory of Rory, his hands on her body, his mouth on her neck. Moving into the bathroom, Savannah looked in the mirror and was newly shocked by the short locks curling round her forehead and cheeks. Craning to one side, she examined her neck and gasped. The mark was a mix of purple and red, its shape that of an open mouth.

The revulsion she felt for Rory McKenna swelled until she thought she was going to be sick. After pulling on cut-off jeans and a T-shirt, she tied a red bandana about her neck, successfully hiding the blot that was in a sense, she thought, Rory's brand.

Stepping onto the landing, she saw that Danny's door was closed. Still sleeping. At least he'd come back. Hours ago, as the minutes ticked toward midnight, she'd tortured herself with the notion that he wasn't coming back at all. The relief she'd felt when he did hadn't sustained her very long. For all she knew, when he came downstairs this morning, he might very well have his bags in tow.

She descended the stairs lethargically, feeling weak and groggy, hoping a cup of coffee would help. She was nearly through the foyer when she saw the slip of paper lying on the floor near the door.

"Stay away from Rory," it said. Four simple words; yet as she read them, Savannah was chilled to the bone.

Danny rolled over and opened a lazy eye in the direction of the clock. Ten . . . *ten!* He bolted up, remembering it was Saturday too late to prevent the resultant pounding in his head. Sliding to the side of the bed, he pushed slowly to his feet. His tongue felt as though it were the size of Nebraska. God, he should never drink whiskey.

After a shower and shave, he felt better. Walking into the

bedroom with a towel wrapped around his hips, Danny considered what he was going to do with the free day. It was Labor Day weekend. Another man might go to the beach, meet a pretty lady, line up a night out. He grimaced as he stripped off the towel and pulled on gym shorts and a T-shirt. He'd spend the damn day working out at the pool—unless Savannah had decided to run him off the Crossing posthaste.

He had no idea what to expect from her. Would she be openly angry? Silently withdrawn? He considered the possibilities as he went downstairs and poured himself a cup of coffee in the deserted kitchen. Glancing out the window, he spotted her at the chicken coop. His stomach lurched at the mere sight of her, just like always. It didn't matter that she'd chopped off her hair. In fact, now that he saw it shining in the sun, he kind of liked it. Folding up a bag of feed, she tucked it under her arm and started toward the house. Danny returned to the coffee pot and poured a fresh cup.

She walked briskly in, hesitating the slightest bit as she saw him standing there, then continued across the room.

"Morning," she said.

So, he thought, *at least she's speaking.*

"Good morning," he returned. Leaning back against the counter, he waited while she stored the chicken feed in the pantry. When she turned and started toward the sink, he noted the bandana. It reminded him instantly of the women who'd been on his mind since yesterday—Roberta Sikes . . . Jane Wilson . . . Margaret McKenna. All dead. Suddenly the bright cloth about Savannah's neck seemed to mark her as a victim.

"Would you mind taking that off?" he asked.

She looked up from washing her hands. "What?"

"That scarf."

Turning off the faucet, Savannah reached for the towel. "Why?"

"I'd just like you to, that's all."

"Danny, really. A simple bandana—"

"Do it!" he commanded.

Turning to face him, she saw the determined look in his eyes. Reaching up, she untied the simple knot and pulled the cloth away.

"That's better." Danny started to take a sip of coffee, then looked swiftly back. "What the hell is that thing on your neck?

It looks like . . ." He met her eyes with a startled look. "I didn't do that yesterday, did I?"

It wasn't you! Savannah longed to cry. *It was Rory! Rory!!* But for some reason, she covered for the bastard. For some reason, she found herself in the midst of a stupid lie.

"No. I . . . I did it myself when I was out on the roof."

Danny assumed a faint look of relief. "Nasty bruise."

"Yes. I must be more careful."

He sought her eyes, and then she knew why she'd lied. If she'd revealed the truth, Danny would have stormed over to the McKenna house at that very moment. And she was afraid for him. There was evil in Rory, and ever since that morning when she read the anonymous note, she'd felt that she was somehow caught up in it.

"I thought I'd go out to the pool," Danny said. "Another day or two of work, and I ought to be able to fill it up."

Savannah looked up, a fearful hope shaking its way through her. "You're not leaving, then?"

Danny's gaze darted between her eyes. "Do you want me to?"

"Danny, I . . . I need to talk to you." She drew a deep breath, letting it fill her cheeks while her mind raced over her feelings.

"Well?" Danny prodded.

She expelled the breath. "I have something to tell you."

Danny set his coffee cup aside, his pulse suddenly racing. "Yes," he said. "What is it?"

"I . . . I was fired yesterday morning. And although the column didn't mean much money, it was the only regular income I had, until you showed up, that is. Yesterday afternoon, up in the attic, I spoke hastily. The fact is I need you to stay at the Crossing, Danny, at least until I can find some sort of job."

It was blurted in a rush, and it was the coward's way out. But at least she'd asked him not to go. Savannah studied him but couldn't read his face. It was as though he'd pulled on a mask.

"That's right," he said eventually. "The month is nearly up. Rent is due."

Something about his tone grated. Savannah's chin went up.

"I don't intend to beg, Danny. If you're not happy here—"

"Shut up, Savannah."

Her brows went up, and then her mouth snapped shut. Pushing away from the counter, Danny gave her a long onceover.

"You'll have your check," he added and headed for the door.

Pausing as he stepped outside, he stuck his head back in the door and looked at her.

"Last night I said I should move out, and I probably should. Something's going to break here, Savannah. I hope you were prepared for that when you asked me to stay."

To say she understood would have implied she condoned a situation she could not accept. To say she had no idea what he meant would have been ridiculous. They both knew what he was talking about. Savannah regarded him silently.

"You have until tomorrow to change your mind," Danny concluded, and closed the door.

Chapter Twelve

DANNY SPENT all day Saturday working at the pool. The rainy skies from the night before had cleared, baring a grueling sun. By the end of the day, his skin was scorched. When he returned to the house and stripped for a shower, he saw the clear outline of his shorts on his skin. The rest was a hot, reddish brown burn.

Still, there was something nostalgic about the feel of pulling fresh clothes over a sunburn. It made him think of summers long ago when, after a day at the beach, he joined up with the guys and went out on the town. The girls they hawked on those nights had sported bright sunburns, too.

He trotted down the steps whistling an old tune and got a cold beer from his stock in the refrigerator. It was past six, but Savannah was nowhere around. He hadn't seen her since morning. Recalling the warning he'd issued, he figured it was entirely possible she would approach him that evening and say it was best, after all, if he left the Crossing.

Danny strolled through the house and went out on the veranda, sipping his beer as he surveyed the grounds beyond the rose garden. Late sun filtered through the trees, shining on the tall untended grass. There was only a shadow of the lawns' former grandeur in the untamed growth. It had been so beautiful once.

It could be again, Danny thought, with someone to look after it.

The notion that had been dancing in the corners of his mind came forward. He wanted to be that someone. He didn't want to leave the Crossing or Savannah . . . ever.

The admission settled over him, monumental in its ramifications. Leave *The Post* for good? Relegate himself to anonymity in the hometown he'd long despised?

Yes, Danny decided. That's what he did want—but only if he had Savannah, and only if his name was cleared. He drank the rest of his beer thinking about the Strangler and picturing Rory McKenna's face in the place that had always been a blank.

Walking back inside, he crumpled the beer can, tossed it in the kitchen trash, and moved to the phone. Carol wasn't home. Her answering machine picked up.

"Hi, Carol. It's me," he said. "It's Saturday, about six-thirty. I found out something last night, and I'd like you to confirm it for me as soon as you get the transcript from Georgia. Please look it over and call me immediately if you come across the name Rory McKenna. It could very well be the connection we're looking for. That's McKenna, first name, Rory—"

The machine beeped in his ear. Danny jerked the receiver away and hung it up. He hated talking to those blasted machines, but Carol was obviously unavailable. It was Saturday night; she was probably out with some new guy. The thought stirred a certain sadness, but it passed. Mentally, Danny had cut his ties to both Washington and Carol.

He was completely sure of it when Savannah walked in a short while later, and the familiar charge ran through him. She was wearing sandals, a faded blue skirt that reached below her knees, and a plain white top that resembled a T-shirt. The short blond hair, apparently still damp from a shower, hugged the shape of her head.

"Hi," he said.

"Hello." The greeting was tossed over her shoulder as she moved to the refrigerator and began removing the makings for salad.

Danny's gaze roamed over her slender form. "I have an idea. Why don't we order out tonight?"

She looked up. "Order out?"

"You know, from a restaurant. Hamburgers, hot dogs . . ." He grinned. "Nothing but the best."

She moved to the counter, vegetables in hand. "Very nutritious."

"Seafood, then. I'll bet that little place down the causeway still has the best around. My treat, on one condition. After supper, you go for a jeep ride with me."

Savannah turned and backed up to the counter. "Why are you doing this?" she asked.

He shrugged. "It's Saturday night. Is that a good enough reason?"

She arched a brow.

"Okay," he added. "I'm trying to break the ice. Things are a little tense between the two of us right now."

"I'd hardly call that unusual."

"Maybe," he replied solemnly. "But at least I'm making an effort to get past it. What have you got against doing something a little different for a change? You might actually enjoy it."

And so he picked up the seafood. Ophelia made one of her rare appearances in the dining room. The three of them proceeded to devour platters of shrimp, oysters and scallops, french fries, cole slaw and hushpuppies. When dinner was over, Ophelia patted her mouth with a napkin, a dainty gesture that contrasted with the obvious relish with which she'd cleaned her plate.

"That was really quite tasty," she announced and rose to her feet. "Please convey my compliments to the chef."

As she walked out, Savannah glanced at Danny, and they exchanged a smile. She sank back in her chair.

"I'm stuffed," she said. "And the best part is, there's nothing to clean up. Thank you, Danny."

"The best thing to do after a meal like that is get moving," he remarked. "Come on. Let's go for a ride. There's a place I've been hankering to visit."

They went out to the jeep, and Danny removed the top.

"Strap yourself in good," he instructed as Savannah climbed in.

"Where did you get this thing anyway?" she asked. "It looks like an Army jeep."

"Very observant. The best they ever made. Nothing goes over rough terrain like this baby. Hold on now," he added, and with a flashing grin, floored the gas pedal. The jeep screeched off across the back lawns, bumping along at a mad pace. Savannah shrieked with laughter.

"You're crazy!" she yelled.

The rush of the wind was wild; its smell, that of eternal summer, its force, seeming to blow the years away. No longer was Savannah thirty-one, but a teenager, surrendering herself to an exhilaration she'd not known even then. But the feeling was bittersweet; for even as she smiled into the wind, it whispered of time gone by and an age never to be recovered.

Danny slowed the jeep when they reached the cypress near the river, picking his way along the well-remembered path. When they reached the landing, he killed the engine and sat back. It was a starry night. The murmuring river shone like silver.

"I should have known you were coming here," Savannah said.

He glanced aside with a smile. "How many times do you figure we sneaked out here to the forbidden landing?"

"Lots more than we got caught."

"Yeah. I guess our record was pretty good."

Danny looked back toward the river. The calls of bullfrogs accented the night, along with the remembered smell of the riverbank and the sound of a light breeze rustling through the cypress.

"The last time I was here, I was eighteen," he said. "A lot of things have changed, but not this place."

"No. Oh, the landing may have rotted away in another space or two, but years mean nothing to the river. It was here centuries ago. It will be here when we're all dead and gone."

"That's an uplifting thought."

"If only everything were as unchanging as the river," Savannah murmured thoughtfully.

Danny considered her solemn profile, then suddenly broke into his deepest, most resounding bass. "Old man river, that old man river . . ."

Looking at him with a start, Savannah cracked a smile and slapped playfully at his arm.

"Stop making fun of me," she chided as his singing dissolved into laughter.

"You take everything so seriously," Danny said. "Lighten up."

The brief smile faded. "Sorry. There are some things I just don't take lightly."

"You know," Danny said after a moment, "I saw something in you the night of the senator's ball. For lack of a better word, I'd have to call it obsession."

"Obsession? For what?"

"The past. That's all that really matters to you, isn't it? The loss of the King fortune?"

"Not just the fortune. Everything that goes with it, position, respect, honor—"

"Honor doesn't come from money. If you believe that, you're no different than Belle Andrews."

Savannah's chin snapped up. "You're right," she admitted stiffly, "but that doesn't change the way I feel. Somewhere in the back of my mind there's this dream that someday, somehow, everything will go back to the way it was. That dream is what kept me going the past twelve years. It's what I live for."

"That's a ridiculous thing to say, Savannah."

"Why? There are lesser things to live for."

"And greater ones."

"Like what?"

"Like happiness, accomplishment, friends, family, chil- dren—"

"Children!" she interrupted with a short laugh.

"What's the matter? Don't you want children?"

Suddenly, as she peered at Danny's starlit face, Savannah pictured a little boy with chestnut hair, hazel eyes, and rosy cheeks.

"I haven't given it much thought," she replied and glanced away.

"You could turn out some pretty ones."

Savannah tried a chuckle. It sounded as forced as it felt.

"Come on, Danny. We both know what my life is. I hardly think I'm going to end up with a brood of children."

"Why not?" he asked. "You're thirty-one years old, Savan- nah. Stop talking as if your life is over."

"Some things are over."

"Some haven't even begun."

He stretched an arm across the back of her seat. Savannah's pulse began to thrum. He looked at her fixedly, then raised a hand to run it over her hair.

"You know, now that I'm used to this, I kind of like it," he said. "Although it was rather a drastic measure."

"I was feeling rather drastic at the time."

Danny's hand dropped to the seat. "I'd like to talk about the attic."

"I wouldn't."

He hesitated, studying her in the starlight. "You're going to have to face it sometime, Savannah. Things might have moved a little fast—"

"A *little*?!"

"For a while you were right there with me, all the way."

"That's it!" she flared. "All the way! That's how you've always been, Danny—pushing and pushing! Just once I'd like to kiss you on *my* terms!"

His brows shot up. "You would? Be my guest."

She turned in a huff and stared out at the river. "It's getting late, Danny. Let's go back."

"All you need is a good teacher," he said.

Her eyes flashed in his direction. "And what of your own obsession?" she demanded. "Have you made any progress with your mystery killer?"

"Some."

"Well! And as soon as the truth is known, where will my 'good teacher' be then? Gone with the wind!"

"I don't have to be."

Hope and fear, sharp as razors, sliced their way through Savannah. In the soft light, Danny's tempting face was dark against the open throat of a white polo shirt. She looked away as fear won out.

"You know how I feel, Savannah. Are you saying you're not the least bit attracted in return?"

"I'm saying I'd like to go back!"

Danny started up the jeep and drove obediently back to the house, unsure of whether he'd furthered his cause or made things worse. He suspected the latter when Savannah bade him a curt good night and stamped into the house.

The next morning, he finished cleaning the pool and turned on the water. As the sweltering day crept by and the basin slowly filled, he repaired the broken lantern and checked every inch of electrical wiring. When dusk fell, he threw the switch. What he saw took him back fifteen years. If nothing else came of his return to the Crossing, at least he'd managed this one resurrection. He walked back to the house and found Savannah washing dishes in the kitchen.

"I saved supper for you," she said.

"Thanks."

"It's just cold chicken and salad. On such a hot night—"

"It *is* hot," Danny broke in. "Just right for a swim."

She looked at him fully for the first time since he walked in. "The pool's ready?"

He nodded.

"That's wonderful," she said with a smile.

"Come swimming with me."

The smile dimmed. "I have a lot to do, Danny. Mother's sheets need changing, and I didn't get around to it today."

"That can wait."

"But she can't go to bed until—"

"Put on your suit, Savannah."

"Really, Danny. I need to—"

"I'm not going to jump you, if that's what you think."

She looked up uncertainly.

"Just celebrate with me, Savannah. The pool looks great. I don't want to christen it alone."

She acquiesced and ascended the stairs, thinking all the while that she was letting herself in for something. She found a tank suit she'd worn only a few times, navy blue with a white racing stripe down the side. Against her better judgment, Savannah stripped off her clothes, pulled it on, and stepped to the mirror. It had been ten years since she wore the clinging suit, but it fit as well as ever. As she eyed the scantily covered body in the mirror, apprehension beset her anew. Turning abruptly away, she donned a short terrycloth robe and went down to the kitchen to join Danny.

He'd taken off his shirt and hung a towel round his neck, but he still wore the brief gym shorts. His eyes swept the length of her.

"Come on," he said and flourished a welcoming hand toward the open door.

As their bare feet trod the path side by side, Savannah was reminded of years gone by, childhood summers when those very feet had run along the path together in carefree abandon. And then as they rounded the copse of trees she saw it, the pool just as it had been before, all lit up and beautiful and . . . Her eyes began to sting; she kept them carefully trained on the pool.

"It's beautiful," she murmured.

Danny looked down, his eyes tracing her profile. "Yeah," he said. "Come on. Let's see if it feels as good as it looks."

They did laps together, then paused to rest at the shallow end. Danny stretched his arms out behind him on the deck. Savannah bobbed a few yards away, her slender lines haloed by the backlight of the underwater lamp.

"So, what do you think about the pool?" he asked.

"Good as ever." She smiled merrily. The water and exertion had blotted out her nervousness. It had been years since she'd gone swimming, and at the moment, in the midst of the humid summer night, the water felt wonderful. Dipping below the surface, she came up with her hair neatly slicked back.

Danny continued to loll at the edge, watching her. She trailed her fingers across the water's surface. His gaze flickered to the point where the water swirled about her breasts. When he looked up, he caught her studying him in much the same way.

"Come here a minute," he said in a low tone.

"I don't think so."

"Come on. I won't grab you. I won't even move my hands." Danny patted the deck with his palms. "They'll stay right here, I promise."

Savannah moved cautiously in his direction, leaving two feet of space between them when she stopped.

"I want you to do something for me," he said.

"What?"

"Kiss me."

"Danny!" she objected in a singsong voice.

"What I said before stands. My hands will stay right here. It will be your show . . . your move. Just like you said. Your terms."

Savannah stared, not moving a muscle. Around them, the crickets sang and the water lapped.

"You know, Savannah," he said eventually. "Things aren't usually as insurmountable as they seem. You just have to go about them one step at a time. A kiss is a good first step."

What he suggested was impossible . . . wasn't it? Apparently not, for as she stepped up to him, it became apparent to Savannah that she was about to take him up on his offer. Raising her palms to each side of his face, she went up on tiptoe and kissed him. His lips were warm beneath her cool ones, receiving her touch willingly but passively.

She pulled back, looking into his eyes as her arms rose and her wrists locked about his neck. Her toes left the pool floor, her body floating up against him as her mouth found his. This time, his lips parted beneath her open ones. Her tongue slipped in tentatively at first, then in slow, searching strokes.

Danny's fingers clawed at the deck. When she moved away, it took him a few seconds to open his eyes. By that time, she'd backstroked away to the side of the pool.

"Jesus Christ!" he muttered hoarsely.

Savannah smiled at his breathlessness, feeling a sense of

power she'd never experienced before, the power—she supposed—of a woman.

"Can I move my hands now?" he asked. She nodded, and Danny dropped below the water's surface, coming up sputtering and spraying as he shook his head from side to side. Rubbing his palms over his wet hair, he started toward her.

"See there?" he said, producing an outrageously sexy grin. "That wasn't so bad, was it?"

"Pretty good, actually," Savannah quipped.

They were shoulder-deep in water. Danny rested a hand on the deck beside her head.

"Anyone who can kiss like that won't have trouble with anything else," he said. "Making love isn't much different. Just better."

Savannah caught her lip between her teeth. "There's something I have to tell you, Danny. Last night you asked . . . well, the truth is, I *am* attracted to you."

"What news," he returned, his light smile covering a mixture of shock and elation.

"You're incorrigible," she scolded, her answering smile slipping as he moved a hand to her shoulder.

"But that's not the whole picture," she added hurriedly. "Maybe if you understand, you'll stop thinking things can be different. This isn't easy to put into words, but . . . Even if I wanted to . . . Well, I've said no for so long that . . ." She drew a sharp breath. "There's just something inside me that . . . shuts down."

It was the hardest, most awkward admission she'd ever made. Savannah searched his face, looking for understanding, finding instead that his expression turned stone cold.

"That's bullshit."

"Danny!"

"No, it *is*! I mean it!"

Her gaze darted to his eyes as she was flooded with anger. "I should have known better than to confide in you!"

Diving swiftly away from him, Savannah swam to the ladder at the deep end and climbed out. Danny raised himself up on his forearms, his body dangling over the side. She stomped angrily along the deck in his direction and reached for her robe.

"Nothing inside you shuts down, Savannah," he said as she stooped nearby. "Trust me. Everything's in perfect working order. You've just got things built up in your mind—"

"Thank you, Danny!" she cut in. Rising to ramrod straightness, she flashed him a vehement look. "I think I've had quite enough of your psychoanalyzing for one evening!"

Planting the robe around her shoulders, she high-stepped away.

"About the check!" Danny called. "You know, the rent money?"

Savannah halted and looked over her shoulder.

"It's on the counter next to the kitchen sink."

"Thank you," she muttered stiffly.

Danny cocked his head to one side. "You *do* remember what I said? Something's gonna break, Savannah. Be prepared."

She spun around. "You are infuriating!"

He raised an index finger along with his brows. "Ah, but you're attracted all the same."

Savannah couldn't make her feet move fast enough as she fled the pool, the summer night, and most of all Danny Sawyer's unbearable cockiness.

September was hurricane season. The talk at *The Watch* the next few days was about Zelda. Born as a tropical storm off the coast of West Africa, she achieved hurricane status when she bashed Guadeloupe with winds exceeding ninety miles per hour. In the three days since, her strength had grown as she moved across the sea. Now she was designated a Category 4 hurricane, with winds at a hundred and thirty-five miles per hour, and a northwesterly course that targeted the Carolinas.

Danny was gathered near the TV with a bunch of other reporters, watching the latest weather bulletin, when Jack Doggett sauntered up to say Danny was wanted in the publisher's office.

"Sit down, Sawyer," Rory commanded when he walked in.

Danny lumbered to the desk and sprawled in one of the chairs. *This is it*, he thought. The axe was about to fall.

"Hurricane Zelda is expected to strike somewhere between Charleston and Myrtle Beach tomorrow evening."

"I'm aware of that."

"I want you to drive down the coast and cover it."

Danny blinked. "What?"

"You've been bitching about your assignments. Well, here's one that could be the biggest news story of the year. Be there tomorrow morning. Stay through the night. Take a portable, and send your reports from the scene."

Danny stared, surprise written on his face.

Rory looked briskly down at the papers on his desk. "That's all, Sawyer. Take the rest of the day off and pack your bags."

Danny got up and walked away, suspicion overriding his initial surprise. Opening the door, he turned.

"I don't get it, McKenna. I thought that now, with your father out of the picture, you'd pull every trick in the book to fire my ass out of here."

Rory looked up with a glib smile. "The thought crossed my mind," he said. "But frankly, the image of you battling it out with a hurricane is far more appealing."

When Danny had gone, Rory sat back in his chair, his smile broadening until it erupted in resounding laughter.

Ben Cochrane picked up his private line, his expression souring as Rory McKenna bade him a good afternoon.

"I understand you're moving your father out of the hospital," Ben said. "Does that mean there's been some improvement?"

"No. Just that the same things can be done for him at home."

"I suppose you've hired nurses—"

"I didn't call to discuss my father," Rory cut in.

A sense of doom swept over Ben. "What do you want?" he demanded, his tone unmistakably sharp.

Rory smiled as he absently twirled a pencil through his fingers. "Come now, Ben. I'd say a little more courtesy is in order. As you know, I've been appointed Papa's legal guardian, and part of my duties include a thorough evaluation of the estate of my ward. It's come to my attention that we own more of Waccamaw Bank than you do. That sort of makes me your boss, doesn't it?"

In a way, Rory was right. Over the years, Big Ed McKenna had infiltrated Waccamaw Bank—gradually, discreetly, cunningly—just as he'd done with many businesses in the city. Ben's mouth set in a grim line.

"What do you want?" he said again.

"I need a favor, Ben. I've been admiring a certain property for some time, and I've just come up with a way to get hold of it."

"How?"

"Foreclosure. The bank owns the mortgage, and from what I gather, it's long overdue."

"What property is it?"

"Kings Crossing."

Ben snatched his glasses off the bridge of his nose. "You mean put Savannah and Ophelia *out*?"

"That's usually what foreclosure means."

First Jim King, now his heirs. "I won't do it!" Ben snapped.

Rory chuckled. "Of course you'll do it. You would have done it for Papa, and you'll do it for me. Papa and I have always been extremely close, Ben. Everything he knew, I know. Do you understand what I'm saying, Ben?"

Ben covered his eyes with his hand; it failed to cover the ugly self-image that formed behind his eyelids.

"It would be a shame for such a reputable, respected man as yourself to be held up to public ridicule," Rory commented. "Whatever would Mrs. Cochrane—"

"Don't!" Ben rasped. Opening his eyes, he looked at the picture on his desk. His wife and dead daughter smiled from the frame. How in God's name had his life become such a mess? But even as the question formed, Ben knew the answer had nothing to do with God. He'd opened the door to hell with his own debauchery, and the devil had sent him the McKennas.

"Well, then," Rory went on pleasantly. "I assume your silence means agreement. Two o'clock tomorrow. I'd like Savannah notified precisely at two. Oh, and Ben . . . drive out there yourself with the news, hmmm? I think it would be a nice touch."

The September afternoon was muggy, the air wet and still. The only sign that Hurricane Zelda was somewhere offshore was the cloud cover that sealed the humidity to the earth like a blanket.

Savannah exited her mother's room, balancing the laundry basket on her hip with a single hand while she wiped perspiration from her lip with the other. She was wearing the briefest shorts she owned and a stretch-band top that was a mere strip around her breasts; even so, her body glistened with a sheen of sweat.

Moving to her own quarters, she went into the bathroom and gathered up towels. As she turned to leave, she caught sight of herself in the mirror over the sink. She paused for a moment, and—bam!—there he was again, smiling through the reflection of her crimson cheeks. Ever since the night at the pool, Danny had been so heavily on her mind, she was scarcely able to think of anything else. Picking up the laundry basket, she walked briskly out of her room, her feet slowing as her gaze darted across the landing. She eyed the closed door. He wouldn't be back for hours yet. Setting the basket aside, she went into Danny's bedroom and closed the door behind her.

She hadn't been inside the room since the night of his arrival. Now she saw how entirely Danny had made it his own. His clothing from yesterday was tossed across the rocker, his possessions littered the dresser top, and his aftershave scented the air. How empty the room would seem if he left.

Meandering to the rocker, Savannah ran her fingers over the light blue fabric of his discarded shirt. A moment later she was pulling it on, hugging it close. Shocked with herself for doing such a thing, she turned toward the bed and shocked herself further by climbing onto his rumpled sheets.

She sat there for a moment in the middle of his bed, knowing all it would take was a word, and she could be here with Danny, in this very spot . . . making love. Weeks ago, she couldn't even have allowed such an idea to form. But lately the notion had been stealing into her thoughts, teasing her, seducing her.

Closing her eyes, Savannah lay back against his pillow and allowed her thoughts to slip down a road they had never before dared to traverse.

Danny tossed a last look at the sky and went inside. The old house was quiet. He was back early. Figuring Savannah was out on the grounds somewhere, he scaled the stairs, intent on changing into cooler clothes before he sought her out and told her of the surprising assignment that would take him away the next morning.

Loosening his tie as he moved along the hall, he threw open the door and walked in unsuspectingly, his gaze nonchalantly passing the bed, then veering back. He came to a dead halt, his breath stopping as he confirmed what he was actually seeing— Savannah lying in his bed, wrapped in one of his shirts.

For a long instant they stared at each other. His eyes darted to the shapely legs bared by brief shorts, to the shirt that had been donned over a midriff top, back up to the eyes which by now loomed like two blue disks. Danny's breathing resumed, deep and heavy, his blood turning to liquid fire in his veins. Slowly he reached behind himself and pushed the door closed.

Within a paralyzed outer shell, Savannah strained like a madwoman, her eyes growing ever wider as she watched his long fingers reach up to his shirt collar, pull the tie from around his neck, and drop it to the floor. The fingers returned to move methodically from one button to the next—disengaging, freeing, until a dark strip of tan skin showed between the open fronts of the shirt. And all the while Danny's smoldering gaze held her like a branding iron that had pinned her to his bed.

He shrugged out of the shirt. The air was heavy, so thick with tension the very room seemed to buzz. Savannah saw his chest rise and fall . . . rise and fall . . . and thought her heart would crash through her ribs any second.

After a few more impossible moments, he tossed the shirt aside and took a step in her direction. Suddenly she lurched into movement, her legs catapulting her from the bed and leaving the box springs creaking. Her feet hit the floor moving backward, away from his steady approach.

Danny took a step. She matched it. And on they went in a slow chase across the room. Predator and quarry, she thought wildly—a rabbit caught in the den of a lion. On he came, tall and bronze, his intent so blatant he fairly radiated with it. Savannah could say nothing. Her throat had closed up, and all she seemed able to do was back away automatically, her blood knocking in her ears, flaming in her face. She bumped into the wall, flattening herself against it as he stepped up to tower over her.

She threw a panicked look to her left, prepared to dart away. "Don't!" Danny ordered, swiftly capturing her shoulders. "Don't fight, Savannah," he added, his tone low and imploring. "For once in your life, don't fight."

He leaned down, and she squirmed with the frightened outrage of one who knows only how to refuse, placing feeble palms against his chest, digging nails into his bare skin. His thumbs merely tightened on her collar bones.

"Let me, Savannah," Danny urged. Joining the whole of his body in the plea, he moved against her, his hardness pressing into her stomach. She gave him a swift, startled glance.

"Just let go," he whispered.

"I . . . can't."

"You can."

He bent toward her. Savannah cringed away. Releasing a heavy sigh, Danny lifted a hand and smoothed the hair from her forehead.

"Just let me kiss you," he murmured. "You can do that, I know."

"Not when I know what else is going to follow."

He took her gently by the chin. "Look at me, Savannah." When she did, he added, "There's nothing to be afraid of. It's the most natural thing in the world."

"That's easy for you to say. You've done it hundreds of times, probably thousands!"

A grin pulled at his lips, then disappeared before it formed.

"Never with you, my love," he replied, looking into her eyes, thinking—hoping—he saw some of the fright go out of them.

With painful slowness Danny lowered his face and settled his lips on hers in a chaste kiss. She complied for a mere instant, then yanked her head aside. He stayed with her, his fingers closing firmly on her jaw, turning her back to his searching mouth. When she gasped, he slipped his tongue inside.

She began to squirm anew, her fingers raking at his sides. Danny went on kissing her with the wildness of a desperate man—knowing he had no intention of stopping until he broke her down and made love to her, knowing she might never forgive him.

He'd needed her so long—during childhood years before he knew what it was to want a woman, hot-blooded years when he first turned into a man and fell asleep night after night aching for her. That was nothing compared to the searing longing that had flared to the surface since he returned to the Crossing. Her teeth clashed with his. Tearing his mouth away, Danny peered stormily down at her.

"Haven't you made a fool out of me long enough?" he demanded, his voice harsh with emotion. "Give it a chance, dammit!"

The desperation in his tone broke through, and although Savannah's heart continued to pound like a jackhammer, she went still, her only movement the raising of her eyes. Danny's were glittering with golden sparks only inches above, and with a sheen she couldn't define. Something unknown washed through her, something that held her like a statue as his arms stole around her.

Her hands closed around his biceps tentatively, and that's

when she felt it—a repetitive tremor running through his muscular arms. He was shaking! The fact zoomed to her brain, momentarily overpowering the unsureness that had her quaking. When he bent haltingly toward her, Savannah lifted her lips. And then he was kissing her once more in the way that only he ever had, caressing her with his tongue, with a sort of primeval rhythm that drew her mouth into its beat.

Kissing Danny had always been an erotic taboo, but this time the difference was that she allowed it to go on, to unfold without the slam-down barrier that normally corraled her responses like a diligent sheepdog. Minutes passed, and then it happened—not gradually, but like wildfire. The sensation was overwhelming, the reasons to protest gone like a puff of smoke. Suddenly her only reality was Danny: the taste of his mouth, the feel of his body. A luxurious languor flooded her veins.

Danny knew the instant she surrendered. With one last roaming stroke of his tongue, he pressed her lips in parting, looked down, and reveled in the trancelike expression on her face.

Savannah couldn't open her eyes, couldn't make a move. Somewhere within the foreign being that had overtaken her, she knew she wasn't going to stem the tide. For the first time in her life, she wasn't going to stop. The name that was circling her brain slipped unconsciously from her lips.

"Danny," she whispered.

He kissed her again, the feel of her willing embrace almost more than he could bear. God, it was Savannah in his arms! God, she was a virgin! Danny lifted his mouth and drew a shuddering breath, his lips resting somewhere near her eyelids.

Savannah's eyelids opened halfway, her gaze falling on the line of his chin, and below to his heaving chest. His arms moved, and she was no longer imprisoned, except by an invisible force that bade her to stay there and not move a muscle. His breath came in puffs against her forehead as his hands moved—gently, like a bird's wings fluttering against her shoulders—lifting the fabric of his own shirt, maneuvering it along her leaden arms, allowing it to drop to the floor. Her eyelids fell as his fingers grazed the bare skin of her midriff on their way to the waistband of her shorts. The zipper slid down, and her shorts followed the way of his shirt. And then there was little left.

Savannah stood there—eyes closed, near naked, the air stopped in her lungs as if she had no further call to breathe. There was a moment of absence of contact, and then she was

swept off the floor, one strong arm around her back, the other
collecting her legs. He lowered her to the bed, and covered her
with his long body.

He was still wearing trousers. A warm hand crawled between
their bellies, and seconds later Danny was as unencumbered as
she. He repositioned himself on top of her, and Savannah knew
the full pressure of his maleness through the meager barrier of
underwear. His lips reclaimed hers, his tongue diving toward
her throat—his hand no longer tentative as it moved along the
hollow of her waist to reach up and fill itself with her breast.

His fingers moved beneath the stretchy top, kneading the
softness of the mound, a thumb brushing back and forth across
her erect nipple. Savannah's arms encircled his back, her fingers stroking the taut skin above his waist. Danny moaned into
her mouth, then slipped his lips along her chin, along the column of her throat, leaving a cool trail with his tongue. His hand
pried away her top, and his mouth took over on her breast. Savannah tensed as he clamped his mouth around the nipple, sending shimmering waves outward from the spot to ripple through
her body.

A voice that sounded vaguely like her mother's screamed in a
corner of her mind; it was silenced by an internal roar as
Danny's hands moved to her hips. He rose to his knees,
smoothly drawing her panties along her legs and off her feet.
Then he settled once more between her thighs. Savannah's head
rolled on the pillow as his hardness pressed between the folds,
tracing a path to the opening that had never before been
touched. He stopped there, poised, the pressure of his manhood
eliciting urges she'd never known she'd possessed.

Danny reached a palm to her cheek and kissed her, gradually
lowering his torso to hers, maintaining the same erogenous
pressure, teasing her body with his presence, denying her—and
himself—the thrust their flesh cried out for. As though of their
own volition, Savannah's hips rose, and she enveloped him.
Danny's breath caught. She felt it in her mouth as his hands
reached for her knees and pulled them up.

He was large and hard within her, his breadth forcing her
body to accept him. He withdrew, rubbed up and down along
her, then slipped inside once more. Savannah arched, taking on
more of him, feeling the first shaft of pain. Her hips fell. He fell
with them. His tongue filled her mouth as he plunged in with
slow deliberation.

The enchantment was instantly gone. *No!* Savannah thought. *No more!* Yet there was more. Gradually, grindingly, Danny filled her, kissing her all the while with feverish abandon.

Savannah felt as though the dry walls of her inner body had caught fire. She lost track of time. Minutes—or hours—later, it was over. As soon as he removed the monumental log from inside her, she rolled off the bed.

"Wait!" Danny protested, flinging an arm after her.

"Don't tell me to wait!" she hurled, and proceeded to grab up her clothes with frantic speed.

Danny sat up, staring at her, scrambling across the bed as he prepared to follow.

"Don't!" Savannah warned, lifting her bundle to shield as much of her body as possible. Ignoring the pain that continued to burn between her legs, she found that she couldn't dismiss the look on his face that darted somewhere between confusion and abject misery.

"I need some time to myself," she managed to say and walked stiffly out of his bedroom.

That night, of all nights, Mrs. King accompanied Savannah into the kitchen, hovering about her daughter, chatting, even pitching in with supper preparations.

Sitting alone at the breakfast nook, Danny conjectured that Savannah had engineered the whole thing, just so she wouldn't have to be alone with him. He took a swig of his beer and decided he'd never felt more awkward. Savannah wouldn't even look at him, and her mother's imperious voice was getting on his nerves. Eventually he got up and went outside.

The sky was solid gray, imbuing the muggy September night with a faint glow. The calm before the storm. Danny took a gulp of cold beer and strolled down the patio steps, thinking of Hurricane Zelda and his trip the next morning. He should leave at daybreak, but after what happened this afternoon, he didn't want to go. Even though he'd held back as much as humanly possible, he knew he'd hurt Savannah. The abrupt way she left his bed showed it, as did the blood on his sheet.

She said she needed time. What could he do but give it? Still, Danny knew he couldn't drive away from the Crossing the next morning, not until he had at least spoken to her. When he returned to the house some twenty minutes later, he found his supper set out on the table and the kitchen empty. Leaving the plate untouched, he got another beer and went upstairs to pack.

The radio played beach music as the night sweltered on. Stripping down to gym shorts, Danny set his duffel bag by the door and went down for another beer. When he returned, he paused at the head of the stairs, then walked firmly across the landing and knocked on Savannah's door. No answer.

"Savannah?" he called.

"I'm tired, Danny," came her voice from behind the barrier.

Danny put his palm against the door. "I want to talk to you."

"Not tonight."

"It *has* to be tonight!"

Silent seconds ticked by.

"Savannah?" he said. But there was no further reply, and when he tried the knob, he found it locked.

When midnight rolled around, Danny was leaning against the veranda rail outside his room, gazing across the way to the light that spilled from Savannah's. Setting aside the empty beer bottle, he walked the distance and stepped up to the French doors. Without hesitation, he tried the door, found it unlocked, and stepped unabashedly into the room.

Her bathroom door was closed. He could hear water running. Acting purely on instinct, he crossed the room and entered the private sanctum. She must have heard the door open. She looked around the edge of the shower curtain, then yanked it to her body.

"Danny!" she trilled. "What are you doing?"

"I need to talk to you." His eyes registered her beautiful face, gleaming shoulders, the outline of her body in the shower curtain, which was now plastered against her.

"Hell, I need more than that," he added. Looking her straight in the eye, he peeled off his shorts.

"Oh, my God," Savannah mumbled, cringing back as he stepped into the tub. He tipped his head and let the shower drench his hair. A curtain of water ran off his shoulders, down his chest . . .

"Oh, my God!" Savannah repeated as her gaze fixed uncontrollably on his erectness.

"This feels great," he rumbled. "I didn't know you liked cold showers."

"It's a hot night," she replied without thinking. It was a perfectly normal response in a perfectly abnormal set of circumstances. Tearing her eyes away from his engorged manhood, Savannah looked up at his face.

"It isn't anything you haven't seen before," Danny said and smiled.

"What do you think you're doing?" Savannah asked. "You can't just come barging in here like this!"

He moved toward her. She made her gaze lift to stay with his eyes, though at any second it threatened to succumb to the lure of the spectacle below—the outrageous maleness that was pointing at her like a spear.

"You know the old saying. When you fall off a horse . . ." Danny reached up and caressed her cheek, his smile waning. "It won't hurt this time," he said. "This time, it's all for you."

Savannah stared up at him, her hands frozen on the shower curtain. "I can't . . . You can't expect me to—"

"Shut up," Danny interrupted, his palm trailing down her neck, along the wet smoothness of her shoulder.

His hands moved to hers. With a quick jerk, he yanked them free of the curtain, which swirled to its appointed position outside the tub, leaving nothing between them. Taking another step, he raised her clenched fists to his mouth and proceeded to kiss each rigid knuckle.

Savannah's instinct was to cover herself with her hands, but her hands were at Danny's mouth, her fingers uncurling, responding . . . She began to ache shamefully between her thighs.

"Danny, please stop."

Her tone verged on a sob. Danny glanced up from her hands and saw the fear in her eyes.

"It all begins with a simple kiss, remember?"

He bent to her mouth, which was open and ready, despite her objections. His tongue moved inside, his arm moved around her, and he kissed her thoroughly. When he pulled her naked body against his own, it was as pliant and obliging as though Savannah King made love every day.

Desire exploded within him. Danny fought it off. Pulling away long enough to turn off the shower, he picked her up and headed for her bed.

"Danny, I—"

He stopped her words with a wet kiss, and Savannah had no further use for speaking after that. He crawled with her on the bed. His mouth moved to her neck, her breasts, her stomach . . .

Savannah forced her eyes open and saw the frilly canopy

above her. Thinking of how she'd slept in this bed since she was a little girl, she peered down the front of her body and saw her fingers twining in Danny's hair. His head was somewhere near her hips. And then his hand moved between her legs, and she lost the capacity for thought.

Her thighs parted, and Danny's mouth followed his fingers. When she arched against him, he lost his mind—pulling himself back at the last instant as he started instinctively to break away and make his move. Burying his throbbing loins in the coverlet, he went on and on, until he felt the tightening of her body.

Recognizing the contraction for what it was, he pushed up on shaking arms and penetrated. She was tight but slick, the feel of her rocking his senses. He captured her face with his palms and kissed her as he drove deep, thrusting once, twice, before her spasms began—her body clenching round him, driving him to his own undeterrable climax. Danny tore his mouth away.

As release thundered through him, out of him, he was locked in a desperate strain above Savannah—his face turned to the ceiling, his hips cemented against hers. When it came to an end, he drew a ragged breath, his elbows relaxed, and he promptly collapsed.

Some time later he became aware of the rise and fall of Savannah's chest beneath him. Coming quickly alert, Danny gently withdrew. He was wide awake now—awake, fully satisfied, ready to take on the world . . . except for his concern for the woman beside him. He rolled to one side and propped himself up on an elbow.

"Good heavens," Savannah whispered, her eyes barely open. "Wherever did you learn how to do that?"

He smiled shakily. "Along the way."

"Is it like that every time?"

"Maybe not quite like that. That was pretty sensational."

"For you, too, then?"

"Of course for me, too." He reached out to run a finger along her cheek. "Couldn't you tell?"

"As you know, I'm not exactly experienced about these things."

"You're a natural," he said and was awarded a lazy smile. The feelings he had for her swelled within him. Danny settled his head on the pillow and studied her profile. Her eyes were completely closed now, the dark lashes dusting her cheeks.

"Come here a second," he said in a thick voice.

"Hmmm?" she responded without budging.

Danny reached out and turned to face him. The unforgettable eyes remained closed. Leaning over, he kissed her, his feelings continuing to escalate until he was flooded with them.

"I love you, Savannah," he whispered into her open mouth.

When she woke, Savannah wasn't sure if his whispered words had been part of a dream. She'd fallen asleep with Danny's lips on hers, and now she realized he was kissing her awake. Turning slightly against his lips, she began meeting the pressure of his tongue, a hand climbing to the back of his neck as though it were the most natural thing in the world.

Danny threw himself into it after that, settling his body full-length atop her, making love to her mouth, as he'd made love to all of her only hours before.

Savannah began to float on that newfound ethereal plane.

Eventually Danny put a rein on himself. With one last lingering press against her lips, he raised his head and propped himself above her.

"And how are *you* this morning?" he asked.

She stretched luxuriously, looked up, and gave him a delicious grin. "Wicked," she said.

"God, you're beautiful."

"You think so?" Her eyes were warm and shining.

"I know so."

Savannah reached up to brush the hair from his forehead. "I think you're beautiful, too. The most beautiful man—"

Danny couldn't help himself. Leaning down, he began kissing her anew and was almost caught up in it before he steeled himself.

"Lady," he said, backing off with a smile. "You're dangerous."

He climbed off the bed, and Savannah was suddenly aware of the morning light spilling into the room, and that Danny was fully dressed.

"What time is it?" she asked.

"A little past six."

Savannah sat up, dragging the bedsheet with her. "Six!" she said on a complaining note.

Danny tucked in his shirt as he grinned. "And you've never been so deserving of a late morning before."

Savannah answered his grin with one of her own. "You're the

one who's deserving," she said, and was amazed at the way she could joke with him about something so intimate. For heaven's sake! She was a completely different person!

Danny's hands came to rest on his hips, his grin fading. "I have to go, Savannah."

"Go?"

"The assignment. The hurricane. You know."

"Oh, that's right. I'd forgotten."

"I'll be back tomorrow."

"Yes, of course."

"Around suppertime."

"Okay."

Danny came to sit beside her on the bed. Her eyes were filled with a light that seemed to shine into his heart.

"I wish I didn't have to go."

She smiled. "I know."

Danny picked up a hand and planted a kiss in its palm.

"I'll be thinking about you," he said.

"And you can be certain I'll be thinking of you."

Danny chuckled and got to his feet. Looking at her sitting in the bed with nothing on but a sheet, he thought leaving was the most difficult undertaking he'd ever faced.

"I guess I'd better be going."

"You said that," Savannah reminded him with another smile. It seemed she couldn't keep the silly things off her face. Even the gloomy prospect of Danny's leaving couldn't dim the brightness within her. She felt like a candle, alight for the first time.

Shaking his head, Danny gave her a smile and crossed the room.

"Danny!" she called as he opened the door. When he turned, she added, "I'd like you back in one piece."

"Count on it," he returned in that deep voice of his. The door closed quietly behind him, and Savannah fell back on the pillows, her face dissolving once more into uncontrollable beaming.

She was still floating that afternoon when the doorbell rang.

"Why, hello, Mr. Cochrane," she greeted brightly. "What brings you to the Crossing?"

Moments later, her buoyance was shattered in a fell stroke.

"Mr. Cochrane, wait!" she said, catching up to him on his way to the door, unconsciously wringing her hands as he turned to face her. "You've been more than generous to Mother and me for a number of years. I know you have the right to do this, but . . . don't."

"It isn't up to me, Savannah. If it were, I'd carry the Crossing from now till doomsday."

She shook her head, the pain she felt showing in her eyes. "I don't understand."

"I'm under a great deal of pressure, Savannah."

"From *whom*?"

Ben turned away. "I'm sorry," he said as he walked out the door. "There's nothing I can do."

It was nearly dark when Rory pulled the Corvette up in front of the tall brick house. Six hours had passed since Ben Cochrane paid his little call on Savannah; that should be enough time for her to realize just how dire her situation was.

There were no lights on in the house, and when Savannah opened the door, she looked sufficiently distraught to suit his taste.

"Go away, Rory," she muttered and started to close the door on him. He stuck a quick foot inside.

"I've come to offer you a solution, Savannah."

"To what?"

"I've talked with Ben Cochrane."

It barely registered that she probably shouldn't let him in the house. Listlessly, Savannah allowed the door to swing open and walked into the parlor. Rory followed, pausing to turn on a lamp, enjoying the sight of Savannah's sagging shoulders as she continued to face away from him.

"You know, Savannah, until Papa had his stroke and I started analyzing his holdings, I had no idea how tremendously wealthy the McKennas are. I could pay off the mortgage on the Crossing without batting an eye."

Savannah spun around, a wild hope springing up within her. "Are you suggesting a loan?"

"No. I'm suggesting that you marry me."

The words resounded in her ears, deafening her, the concept momentarily blinding her. When her vision cleared, Savannah stared at him in wide-eyed disbelief.

"You must be insane!"

He laughed. "Is that a no?"

"What on earth makes you think I would marry you?"

"Lots of things. The Crossing . . . your mother . . . your pride. I can't picture you allowing yourself to be turned out on the streets, Savannah. What would you do? Where would you go?"

Finally accepting the fact that he was dead serious, Savannah felt the breath leave her body. "Why?" she asked a few moments later.

Rory shrugged. "My father married a Clancy. I have a hankering to link up with a King. Besides, I've always fancied you. You should remember that from high school."

She shuddered. Rory smiled as he stepped up and grabbed her chin, forcing her to look into his pale eyes.

"I told you I'd win in the end. I intend to possess you, Miss Savannah. To *own* you. No other man will ever have the right to touch you."

A sudden thought occurred to her. "Danny," she mumbled.

Rory released her with a shove, his smile broadening. "Can't you just see his face when he hears the happy news?"

"I haven't said I'll do it!"

"Oh, but I'm confident you will." Rory glanced at his watch. "Let's see, it's nearly nine. Sleep on it and give me a call at the house tomorrow morning. I'll expect your acceptance twelve hours from now. Nine o'clock sharp. And Savannah . . . don't be late. You'll learn I'm a bear to deal with when I'm kept waiting."

On his way out, he glanced around the parlor. "This place looks like hell. A lot of changes will have to be made."

Savannah followed speechlessly in his wake, finding her tongue just as he opened the front door.

"You're behind this, aren't you?" she asked woodenly. "The foreclosure was your idea."

"Why, Miss Savannah," he said with a grin, "whatever do you mean?"

The grin stayed in place until Rory screeched up the drive to his father's house and saw Clayton and Libby sitting at the tea table on the front porch.

"It's getting late," Libby commented as he came up the steps. "Where have you been?"

Rory looked from her to his brother and back again. "If you must know, I've been to the Crossing."

Libby's dark gaze flicked to Clayton.

"I'm feeling particularly high-spirited tonight," Rory added, drawing her eyes once more to himself. "Get in the house, woman."

"Sure, Sugar," Libby replied without missing a beat, and rose from the chair.

Dateline: September 12, 1:00 a.m.
At 8:05 p.m. Tuesday, Hurricane Zelda struck the South Carolina coast with winds of up to 125 mph. Despite concerted precautions by the Coast Guard, Red Cross, and local officials, early estimates of damage figured into the millions. Four hours after crossing onto land, the hurricane continued to pummel the coastline stretching from Pawleys Island to Myrtle Beach.

Electric sub-stations are knocked out, and miles of coast are without power. Beachfront structures are flooded, streets washed out, trees ripped from the ground. Radio communication from Myrtle Beach reports two piers out

Danny looked up with a start as a gust of wind hurled a clattering sign against the window of the Pawleys Island fire station. There was a chorus of screams from a group of refugees huddled around a lantern across the floor. Danny was camped out in a corner of the pitch black structure. Adjusting his flashlight so it shone across the laptop computer screen, he went on with the story. He'd waited as long as he could to be able to make the 2 a.m. deadline with the most up-to-date information.

Twenty minutes later, he'd just shipped it off when the fire chief hurried out of his office.

"Just got word a tree fell on that retirement home across the waterway!" he shrieked. "Any volunteers?"

There was a pregnant silence. Zelda shook the building and howled, taunting those who cringed within the meager shelter.

"Shit!" Danny muttered, and climbing to his feet, shrugged into his slicker.

Savannah paced the house, the hours slipping by at an uncanny speed. At 3 a.m. she made a pot of coffee. At daybreak, she slipped into her mother's room and peered down at the peaceful face, envying her the malady that afforded such peace.

Turning abruptly away, she walked to the phone in the hall, deriving small pleasure from rousing the McKenna household at dawn. A servant answered. Savannah waited as he went to get "the master," feeling sicker by the minute.

"Who is this?" Rory demanded irately.

"Like you said. You win."

There was a slight pause on the other end.

"Of course," he then replied.

Hearing the smile in his voice, Savannah dropped the receiver and hurried across the landing, barely making it to the bathroom before the vomiting began.

A couple of hours and a shower later, she felt up to facing the challenge of behaving with a semblance of normality. She stayed tuned to the radio most of the day, listening to coverage of Hurricane Zelda. That morning in *The Watch*, Danny's story had been brisk and to the point, but the horror of the hurricane had come through clearly. It was nerve-wracking to think of him in the midst of it. Still, her worries didn't hold a candle to the clammy sickness that swamped her at the idea of what she must tell him when he returned.

I'm doing it for Mother, she reminded herself. *For Daddy . . . for every King who ever lived here. I'm doing it because I'm the only one who can.*

There was something within her that simply could not allow the Crossing to be lost, not if there was a way to save it. And the way was Rory McKenna.

What a cruel jest of the gods, Savannah thought. But maybe this mess was no more than her just desserts, considering the way she'd railed at fate and destiny and everything holy the night of the senator's ball.

In the afternoon, the wind picked up. Savannah started out back to tie a tarp over the chicken coop and saw the sheet of notebook paper tacked on the kitchen door.

You must stay away from Rory!

A flash of fear pierced the lethargic dread that enveloped her. Savannah yanked the thing down and studied it. The handwriting was the same as on the last note, but she still had no idea who it belonged to.

"Stay away?" she muttered to the anonymous scrawl. "You have no idea how I'd love to."

Twisting the paper into uneven folds, she stuffed it in the back pocket of her shorts and headed across the patio.

Danny had worked most of the night at the stricken retirement home. Two residents had died, crushed to death when an uprooted cypress crashed into the building.

Sometime near dawn, Zelda had moved back out to sea. The

people of Pawleys Island couldn't help but rejoice, although everyone knew that when a hurricane retreated to the ocean, there was every chance she would rebuild.

When daylight arrived, Danny was drafted to help with the first round of reclamation on the island. He could hardly refuse, but as the hours ticked by, he'd done his utmost to keep abreast of the hurricane's status. As he feared, by afternoon Zelda's power had begun to escalate. Worse yet, she was traveling at a slow course up the coast. Finally breaking free of Pawleys, Danny leapt into the jeep and raced north.

Six o'clock rolled around. Zelda was once again designated a Category 4 threat, and if she decided to sweep inland, Kingsport was directly in her path.

By the time Danny reached the city limits, the news bulletins were frequent. Evacuation was underway as Zelda's influence was being felt along the shoreline—erratic tides washing under waterfront cottages, boats being ripped from marina moorings. After what he'd seen at Pawleys, he knew that was nothing compared to the full fury of the hurricane.

He sped through downtown Kingsport, more anxious than ever to get back to Savannah. It had been thirty-six hours since he left her. It felt like thirty-six days.

Chapter Thirteen

SAVANNAH piddled around the kitchen, filling her hands with trivial tasks, jumping at every outdoor noise. "Around suppertime," Danny had said. "I'll be back around suppertime."

Now time hung between the last hour of day and the first of evening. Outside the rain pounded like a muted drumroll. Inside, the old house was unnervingly still.

She checked the chicken, knowing full well it had another half hour to bake. The oven door banged shut in its unavoidable, halting way. She glared at the antiquated thing, smacked at it, and succeeded only in scorching her fingers. Spinning away to the sink, she thrust the offended hand under the faucet. As the water flowed, her pique drained away, leaving her to feel like a fool for taking out her frustrations on an oblivious kitchen appliance.

Turning off the water, she raised troubled eyes to the window. The dusk was a watery gray, the ground dark and sodden, the dirt drive at the side of the house, mud-orange. As she watched, the wind picked up and began tossing the rain at a new gusty pace. Outside, the old oak stood sturdy and unmoving. But beyond it, the tops of palms fluttered like windswept heads of hair. What had begun at dawn as a drizzle was turning into a storm.

Just then, Danny's jeep careened into view, sliding to a stop in the muddy drive. *Be calm*, she told herself. But when he threw open the door, she whirled with a start. He paused in the doorway, his frame silhouetted by rainy twilight as he swept the hood of a slicker from his head.

"Hello there," he said.

His voice sent shivers up her spine. Savannah's gaze raced over him. He looked tired and rumpled, unkempt, unshaven . . . and suddenly she knew. In the midst of her shock, she could say nothing. She attempted a smile, watching mutely as Danny shrugged out of the slicker and hung it on the peg by the door, transferring keys and wallet into its pockets.

It was amazing how the realization dawned. Out of the blue, all of a sudden, you looked at somebody and . . . *knew*. Savannah moved a hand to her diaphragm which felt suddenly hollow, then lower to her stomach, which was churning as though she'd just come off a roller coaster. She'd never felt so suddenly, violently ill—but then she'd never been in love before.

Years ago, she'd assumed she loved Clifford. Now she knew the notion for the sham it was. Love burned and chilled and shook you to the core. It was one of those things you couldn't possibly imagine until you felt it, but upon feeling it, there was absolutely no doubt of what had you in its clutches.

Danny pivoted and regarded her from the doorway. She had yet to say a word, returning his look with an unwaveringly pleasant expression that seemed forced. For two days, whenever there was a break in the frenzied action of the hurricane scene, Savannah had leapt into his mind like a cat, curling around his every thought until forced into the shadows by some new emergency. Now he was back, and she stood only yards away. With any other woman, he would have swaggered across the distance and taken her in his arms. But Savannah was not just any woman.

He started toward her at a casual pace, his boots leaving a trail of muddy footprints, his gaze roaming hungrily over her. The face was, as usual, devoid of makeup; the newly cropped hair stuck up in front, as if she'd swiped at her forehead and unknowingly left behind a tuft like the comb of a rooster. But it didn't matter about the hair or makeup. Her high patrician cheeks were rosy, her eyes like sapphires in a setting of lashes and brows so dark they drew contrast to her silvery blond hair. None of it required artifice.

She was wearing faded shorts and a T-shirt, but she could dress in a sack and still manage to look like royalty. There was an air of grandness about Savannah King, and the rush he felt just looking at her swelled his senses. Maybe he should tell her that the whole time he was driving back to the Crossing all he could think of was her.

"Zelda's about to cross into North Carolina waters," he said instead. "There's no telling when she might move inland again."

Savannah nodded. "I read your story in *The Watch* this morning."

A white smile appeared in the dark stubble. "I called in another one from down the coast. Deadlines were moved up so everyone could clear out of downtown before Zelda has a chance to strike."

He came to a stop before her and captured her eyes—his own probing, sparkling, affirming without words the intimate circumstances of the last time they were together. Savannah stood there uncertainly, searching for something to say. A blush crept up her neck as she was rocked with memories—touch, taste, smell, the way she'd lingered in bed the following morning, reluctant to get up and wash him from her skin. His gaze dropped to her mouth. In another few seconds, he'd be kissing her.

"Excuse me," she blurted. "I really must check the chicken." She made a beeline for the stove.

Danny followed, and as Savannah bent over to look inside the oven, he dropped familiar hands on her waist. Allowing the oven door to slam with a bang, she shot away like a scalded cat. Leaning against the wall, Danny watched her skitter about the room—from the stove to the refrigerator, the pantry, finally lighting at the hearth where she proceeded to flick a dust rag at the copper pans adorning the stone wall. It was the way she used to act when he touched her. He'd hoped they were beyond that.

"What's the matter with you, Savannah?" he grumbled. "You're flying around here like your pants are on fire."

She turned an impertinent butt in his direction. "As you can see, my pants—as you so colorfully put it—are not on fire."

"Well, something is!"

His gaze dropped to the pocket on the hip thrust impudently toward him.

"What's that?" he asked.

"What?"

Savannah barely had time to turn before he was snatching the mangled notebook paper from her pocket.

"Stay away from . . . *Rory*?"

The name came on a note of disbelief. She grabbed for the paper. He lifted it out of her reach.

"What the hell's going on, Savannah?"

His angry tone sparked a welcome feeling of belligerence. Anything was better than the knee-weakening dread that had nearly overpowered her. Savannah lifted her chin.

"The papers were served yesterday, Danny. The bank is fore-closing on the Crossing."

Danny searched her eyes, surprise and sympathy welling up to join a fast-forming sense of anxiety. Something was very wrong, something beyond the fate of the Crossing.

"Listen," he said. "I have a nest egg. Maybe not enough to solve the problem, but it will buy you some time."

Touched beyond measure, Savannah fended off the feeling. "Then what? Have them serve all over again? The difference being that you're minus your life savings? Thanks, Danny, but I can't do it."

He glanced to the floor, and as he looked away, Savannah studied him unguardedly, committing everything to memory as though it would never again be seen. Regret welled up until a bitter taste filled her mouth.

He raised his eyes. "What do you intend to do then?"

"R—" She cleared her throat and tried again. "Rory has agreed to buy the note."

Danny glanced at the note in his hand. Adrenaline pumped through his body. "McKenna? Why?"

"The Crossing backs up to the McKenna place. They've always wanted the property. You know that."

"I figured you'd rather let the bank have it than fork it over to Rory McKenna."

"I won't be forking it over. In essence, it will still be mine."

"I don't understand."

Savannah's gaze roamed his face. The love she felt made what she had to say all the more blasphemous.

"I'm going to marry him, Danny."

The sound of falling rain filled the silence.

"What?" he said, so quietly that the word was scarcely heard.

"It's the only way," Savannah responded, her voice beginning to shake. Her strength deserted her. She retreated to the bay window of the breakfast nook and stared into the rainy darkness.

Danny remained frozen near the pantry.

"Remember how it used to be, Danny?" she asked after a moment. "When we were both so young? I thought the world was mine for the taking. That was the way my parents made it seem. That was the way everyone made it seem. The Kings were rich, powerful, respected. I knew there were people less fortunate, but they seemed distant, far removed—like characters in a movie. You were one of them, Danny. People like you had your place; I had mine. You were born under an unlucky star. My star was the sun. There was nothing I couldn't have, nothing out of my reach."

She turned and faced him. "Now I know the truth. Nothing comes without a price."

"So," Danny said, forcing the breath from his lungs, "you're selling *yourself.*"

Savannah blinked, her momentary softness turning instantly hard. "I'm doing what I have to do. Nothing more. Nothing less."

He shook his head and gave her a scathing onceover that seemed to say she was disgusting. Savannah found it impossible to endure.

"I'd like to know why you think you can pass judgment!" she hurled. "I'm the one who struggled all this time! You don't have any stake in the Crossing at all!"

Danny moved toward her with a menacing scowl. "I think I have some stake. I grew up here, didn't I? All the time you were prissing around here like a princess who couldn't get her hands dirty, I was working my butt off around the pool, on the grounds, wherever your blasted mother decided she could use a field hand! I'd wager I've invested as much labor in this place as you have!"

"You drop in here after fifteen years and think you have some say-so?" she retorted. "Where were you when the going got tough? We both know that as soon as you were old enough to get yourself in real trouble, you took off like a scared jackrabbit!"

The confrontation dissolved into a yelling match. Danny attacked. Savannah retaliated with dreadful hurtful accusations, half of which she would never recall saying, none of which she meant. She was so miserable she was about to explode; she found that all she could do was lash out and hurt Danny as well.

"I absolutely forbid you—" he was bellowing.

"*Forbid* me?" Savannah broke in harshly. "What gives you the right to forbid me to do anything?"

The pain and rage were blinding. Danny could barely see, could hardly think. A treasured recollection flared into his mind's eye—Savannah naked, her eyes drifting, closing.

"What gives me the right?" he ground out. "I thought I

earned some rights the other night. I actually thought that meant something."

Thunder rumbled about the house. Savannah faltered. "It did—"

"Like hell it did! If it had, you wouldn't be marrying . . ."

Danny sputtered into silence, jerking his head around as if to shake the name out of it. "For God's sake, I can't even say it! How can you bear to *do* it?!"

"What do you expect me to do?" Savannah cried. "It's either marry him or lose the Crossing! I have no choice."

Night was falling, hastened by the murky influence of the approaching storm. In the short time since Danny arrived, the room had grown dim. In the glow that spilled through the window, Savannah could see that his face had gone pale and hard as stone.

Danny glanced down at the sheet of paper he continued to hold in his hand. Crumpling it into a tight ball, he threw it at her feet.

"You have a choice, all right," he pronounced. "You're simply making the one of a whore."

He turned on his heel, stalked out of the kitchen, and was instantly soaked. The rain was beginning to fall in ragged, windswept sheets. Bending against it, Danny zigzagged his way to the pool house.

He had to force his way in; honeysuckle and other vines had long since wound their way over the door. It would open, but only a few inches. Shielding his face from the downpour with one arm, he put up a shoulder and rammed the thing. After a few more tries it swung open with a clatter. Danny lunged in and, placing his body solidly behind the door, closed it against the gusting wind.

The pool house was shrouded in darkness, but seemingly sound. From memory, he made his way to the bar and pulled open a drawer, his fingers searching for and finding a book of matches. He struck one and opened the cabinet. The candles were still there. He lit one and moved into the main room, his eye drawn to the faded fishnets hanging on the walls.

"When people come over to swim, they come in here to change," echoed the little girl's voice.

Danny rubbed a hand across his stinging eyes and sank to the musty couch. She'd been all of seven years old the day she said that—just as devastating then as now.

"Savannah," he whispered, the sound mournful and low against the brewing storm outside.

Libby lit a cigarette and paced the length of the terrace room. At times she liked the grandiose gallery with its series of French doors and velvet drapes. But tonight the storm was a palpable presence hovering just outside those doors, winking at her with lightning, hemming her in with curtains of rain.

The servants had disappeared after supper, probably congregating in their quarters to monitor the latest bulletins on Hurricane Zelda. Despite the noise of the storm, there was an eerie quiet in the house—a ghostly stillness. Libby half-expected to see the shadow of her father rounding the corner, all dressed out in his butler livery, or maybe Mrs. McKenna drifting along the corridor in one of her pretty dresses, a bright scarf knotted about her throat. The notion brought the memory of that evening when she'd come out of a steamy bath and could have sworn she saw the dead woman stealing out of her bedroom.

Stubbing out the cigarette, Libby briskly exited the gallery. She had no wish to be alone with her ghosts. Anyone's company was preferable, even Rory's.

As she drew near the front of the house, she heard their voices. Both Rory and Clayton were in the game room. Libby started to walk in, but as she caught the gist of what Rory was saying, she stepped back and peeped furtively around the door.

"It took him years to pull off, but it's all right here," Rory announced, smacking some papers against his palm. "Not only did he arrange to ruin Jim King, but also he had the audacity to keep proof of how he did it! These papers here are just copies. Ten to one, he's got the originals stashed somewhere."

"That would b-be the kind of thing he'd keep. Like one of those t-trophies on that w-wall over there."

"I've already been through his deposit boxes and accounts. The only records I haven't examined are the ones down at *The Watch*. That's it!" Rory laughed. "I'd bet my life on it. The originals are down at the newspaper, sitting right inside the desk of the very man he stole it all from!"

"You d-don't have to s-sound so happy about it."

"You never did appreciate Papa's flair. I'll admit I had my own problems with the old man, but at least I understood him. Who else do you know who would mastermind the ruin of one of Kingsport's leading citizens, take him for everything he had, then hold onto proof of the fraud? I'd call that guts!"

"Or v-vanity."

Rory smacked the collection of documents once more in the palm of his hand. "If these papers had fallen into the wrong hands, Papa could have been arrested," he said slowly. "Even now, the right lawyer could cause an uproar—maybe even get everything returned to Jim King's heir . . . Savannah!"

Rory crossed to the fireplace and whipped a lighter out of his pocket. Setting the papers afire, he tossed them on the hearth and watched them burn. Stepping back a pace, he looked up at the portrait that hung over the mantel.

"We may have been cut from the same cloth, Papa, but I was always more shrewd. The originals will go the same route as soon as this damn storm lets up and I can get downtown."

Rory crossed to the bar and poured himself a drink. Turning again to the portrait, he raised his glass.

"I *will* do your tradition justice, however. As of today, I can promise that the McKenna takeover will be complete. Not only have I managed to gain control of Kings Crossing, but its stuck-up little mistress as well."

"What are you t-talking about?"

"You're about to get a new sister-in-law, Clayton. Here's to Miss Savannah, soon to be *Mrs.* McKenna."

Rory tossed down the drink and began refilling the glass. Clayton watched with wide-eyed alarm.

"B-but why would she m-marry you? She doesn't l-love you. She never even l-liked you."

"Love?" Rory sneered. "You're such a schoolboy, Clayton. Sometimes I wonder how the two of us sprang from the same pool of genes. It has nothing to do with love! I have something Savannah wants. I'm buying her, you idiot!"

Clayton sprang to his feet. "W-what do you w-want with her? She's not even your t-type."

Rory barked a short laugh. "Are you kidding? Thawing out that little iceberg will be the best time I've had in years . . . for a while anyway. Who knows? Maybe when I get bored with the new Mrs. McKenna, I'll give you a crack at her. Just like last time, eh, little brother?"

Rory laughed, and Clayton spun away. As he fled the room, Libby flattened herself behind the cover of the door. Her heart was beating so wildly, she wondered that Clayton didn't sense her presence. But he only shot past, darting across the foyer and up the stairs toward his chamber.

A crash of thunder shook the house. A gust of wind whistled round it.

"Damn hurricane," Rory muttered. "Tonight would be the night."

He moved back to the bar and poured another drink. Libby held her position, scarcely breathing, her mind reeling at what she'd heard. Big Ed had been the one to commit the initial crime, but Rory, too, was guilty. Tampering with evidence. Obstruction of justice. Maybe even accessory after the fact. A bloodthirsty D.A. like the one she'd known in Atlanta could nail him to the wall!

All the months of mascarading—of privately gagging each time Rory touched her—had finally paid off. Maybe she hadn't heard enough to destroy him altogether, but she could give him one hell of a bad time! A hard look came into Libby's eyes as the plan formed. She knew what she should do, what she *must* do as soon as she could escape unnoticed.

When Rory moved to the hearth and poked at the ashes of the destroyed documents, she made a stealthy break for the stairs. She couldn't risk leaving the house, not yet. Rory might stop by.

Libby closed the door of her room and checked her watch. Eight-thirty. She must wait. She simply must make herself wait.

Savannah had served supper to her mother but hadn't touched a morsel for herself. She had no idea where Danny had gone, and told herself she didn't care. Nonetheless, each time she passed a window at the side of the house, she confirmed that his jeep remained in the drive.

The downpour worsened, and she dashed about the upstairs rooms, placing pots here and there as the rain drove through the roof. There were a dozen leaks and as many aluminum receptacles singing out with every drip, each with its own tone so that the entire second story resounded with a metallic chorus.

"Plink! Plink! Plink!" sang the raindrops in a nearby pot.

Each tinny sound pierced her eardrums. Savannah fled across her bedroom, catching sight of herself as she passed the cheval mirror near the door. The image brought her up short. She still wasn't used to the missing hair.

"You just don't look like me at all!" she murmured.

Indeed, she was not the old Savannah—hadn't been for two days now, ever since Danny . . . She turned away from the mirror. It did no good to think of him. No good at all. Even so, when the phone rang at a little past nine, she leapt into the hallway, wondering with a brief, stupid thrill if it might be him.

"Hello?"

"Is Dan Sawyer there, please?"

Dan Sawyer? It was a female voice—a decidedly attractive silky voice. "No, I'm sorry. He isn't in at the moment."

"I see. And you are . . . ?"

A pang of annoyance stabbed Savannah. "This is Savannah King. Could I give him a message for you, Miss . . . ?"

"Kincaid. Carol Kincaid. Does the name mean anything to you?"

"No," Savannah answered rather sharply. "Should it?"

"I thought perhaps Dan might have mentioned me to you."

"No. I'm afraid *Dan* didn't."

There was a sigh on the other end of the line, and Savannah found herself increasingly irritated. "Look, Miss Kincaid, I don't mean to be rude, but we're in the midst of a terrible storm here. I have things to attend to. May I take a message for you?"

"Just tell Dan he was right about the connection."

"The *connection*?"

"Just tell him he was right. He'll know."

"Oh, I'll be sure to pass that along," Savannah commented with a caustic lilt. "If there's anything Dan likes to hear, it's that he's right. Is there anything else you'd like to tell him?"

"Loads," the woman replied. "Absolute loads. Unfortunately I don't think it would do me any good."

"I beg your pardon?" Savannah snapped.

"So. You're Savannah King." There was a throaty chuckle. "You sound just like he described—cool, polished, the proverbial lady of the manor. I can just picture you, languishing on the veranda swing, your long blond hair shifting in the breeze. You and I are exact opposites, Savannah. It's actually quite funny that we should have something so intimate in common. You see, I'm in love with Dan, too."

"*Miss* Kincaid!" Savannah sputtered. "Even if I were in love with Danny Sawyer, I certainly wouldn't condescend to discuss such a thing with a stranger—"

"What a waste," came the dry interruption.

There was a distinct click as the infuriating woman hung up.

Red-faced, Savannah stared at the receiver in her hand, then banged it down and stomped along the hall, her temper sizzling.

She'd been out for more than an hour, waiting and listening. Outside, the storm alternately moaned and shrieked. Within the great house, the halls had settled into silence. It was barely ten. Normally there would be a certain amount of bustle in the household. Tonight, however, all was still, the fearful anticipation of Hurricane Zelda having driven everyone behind the safety of closed doors.

Fools, *she thought.* Hurricanes never strike Kingsport. *She pulled on her gloves. It was time.*

She moved noiselessly out of the bedroom, glanced downstairs, and confirmed that it was deserted. Starting past the master chamber, she remembered the nurse had left some hours ago. Having been settled for the night, the big man was all alone in there.

She went in and found the room restfully dark. The sound of her steps was swallowed in thick carpet as she walked to the bed. His eyes were closed. Reaching to the bedside table, she flipped on the lamp and watched his eyelids flicker, lift, and fly wide.

"Hello, Ed," she said. "I've been waiting for this moment a long time."

The pale eyes darted wildly, up and down, side to side.

"What's the matter?" she taunted with a smile. "You look as though you'd seen a ghost. Oh, that's right . . . no more talking for you, no more moving." The smile vanished. "I couldn't have devised a more fitting imprisonment myself."

Reaching out, she brushed a lock of pale hair from his brow. "As for Rory, I have something completely different in mind. You see, I've been tracking him very carefully, laying first one snare, then another. Now it's time to spring the final trap."

She held up a gloved hand and revealed a brass button. "From the blazer he was wearing today. I've grown much stronger with the years, Ed. And more clever. This time, the victim will provide a fatal clue. Even you had your suspicions when Jane Wilson was killed. This time, no one will have a doubt that Rory is guilty.

"He's going to be charged with multiple murders, Ed. At the least, they'll lock him up for life. Maybe they'll even execute

*him. And you know the beauty of it all?" She laughed. "He
didn't do any of them."*

Ed's eyelids closed and trembled.

*"Now, now," she chided. "I should think you would admire
my methodology. After all, you inspired it. There are predators,
and there is prey. Isn't that what you always said?"*

*A tear seeped from between the man's fluttering lids and
slipped down his cheek.*

*"Good night, Ed," she said and turned off the bedside lamp.
"Sleep well."*

Danny made his way back to the main house through howling winds that made him think of Pawleys Island just an hour
before Zelda struck. Bursting into the kitchen, he circled the
ground floor and found Savannah coming down the stairs.

She was so glad to see him, wet and sopping and shedding a
puddle on the floor, that her feet almost flew to meet him. His
look of fury stopped the notion, however, and in the moment
that they stared at each other, Savannah resurrected her armor of
anger.

"I've been out at the pool house thinking," Danny announced. "And I've come to the realization you don't need a
tenant with McKenna picking up your tab for you. I ought to
pack my bags, get the hell out of here, and let you stew in your
own juice!"

"Then why don't you?"

"Damned if I know!"

Folding her arms across her chest, Savannah gave him an imperious look.

"You had a phone call a short while ago . . . *Dan.*"

"From who?"

"Whom."

"*Whom* then?!"

"Carol Kincaid. She said that you were right about 'the connection,' " Savannah snapped. "If that makes any sense at all."

A series of emotions washed over Danny—surprise, triumph,
and finally a tingling sense of impending danger.

"That tears it," he muttered, and lunging forward, grabbed
Savannah by the arms. "McKenna is a dangerous man! You're
not going to marry him, and that's that!"

Savannah twisted in his grip. "We've been over this already!

I remember your sentiments quite well! Something about a whore, wasn't it?"

"This goes beyond my personal feelings! You got a note warning you to stay away from him. Doesn't that tell you anything? There's a net closing around you, Savannah, and you're swimming right into the middle of it!"

"I can take care of myself, Danny!"

"Now there's a delusion of grandeur if ever I heard one!"

"It's none of your damn business!" she cried.

Danny clamped his teeth until his jaws ached.

"None of my damn business?" Danny repeated in a tight voice. "If you believe that, you're more deluded than I thought."

They glowered at each other while the silence grew into a tangible thing, a wall neither would make a move to scale. The racket of the storm pressed round them, resounding in the cavernous vestibule, joined suddenly by an insistent banging.

Jumping at the noise, Savannah irately wondered who on earth would come calling on such a night. Still, it gave her an excuse to turn her back on Danny. When she opened the door, a bedraggled Libby Parker brushed past, bringing a flurry of rain with her.

"What in the . . ." Savannah started, quickly closing the door only to watch the woman sashay across the foyer without so much as a backward glance.

Savannah fired a questioning look at Danny, but his expression remained grim. With a shrug, he turned and followed the redhead into the receiving room. Bringing up the rear, Savannah looked around his shoulder and saw Libby swing to a halt in the center of the room. She was quite a spectacle, wet and muddy, the streaks of grime thrown into relief against a low-cut black dress.

Savannah stopped within a few feet of her. "It's a beastly night," she commented. "How on earth did you get here?"

Libby rolled her hips. "How does it look like I got here?"

Savannah met the dark eyes, found a look as hard as nails, and matched it with one of her own. "Frankly, it looks as though you crawled. What do you want?"

Libby dropped the bomb. "Your father didn't simply lose *The River Watch* all those years ago. He was swindled out of it. Big Ed masterminded the whole thing. How do you like *that*?"

Outside, the storm wailed, its din filling the night, rattling the windows of the painfully silent parlor. Overhead, a telltale board creaked. Libby looked up. She knew whose chamber was directly overhead—eavesdropping, snobby old bitch! How many years had Ophelia King made her feel like dirt? Years when she was young and vulnerable, with no way to fight back?

"I said, 'How do you like *that*,' Mrs. High-And-Mighty King?" she shrieked at the ceiling. "The McKennas took your husband for all he was worth!"

Danny stepped forward. "Quiet down! What's this all about?"

"It's about *fraud*!" Libby snapped, swerving back to Savannah. "Rory found some papers in his daddy's desk at the house. That's all he's been doing ever since he took over, swooping through Big Ed's things like a hungry vulture. Tonight I overheard him talking to Clayton. It seems that, somehow or other, Big Ed managed to make your daddy lose everything—to take it all for himself and still come out smelling like a rose. Rory said if the papers fell into the wrong hands, they could make him give everything back to Jim King's heirs. To you, Savannah!"

Danny glanced aside to find Savannah transfixed, the incredible blue eyes widening until they seemed to swallow her face.

"It must turn your stomach," Libby went on. "I hear you were all set to marry Rory, and now you find out he was laughing about a plot that destroyed your father!"

Savannah's expression turned instantly alert. "He was laughing?"

"Hell, yes, the whole time he watched the papers go up in flames!"

"He burned them?!"

Libby smirked at her alarm. "They were only copies. He figures the originals are down at *The Watch* in your daddy's desk."

Savannah's fingers rose to her lips. "I can't believe it."

"Of course you can't believe it!" Libby snarled. "You're Savannah King. Nobody would dare do such a thing to you. Wake up, kid. Just because you're a King, just because you've been pampered every day of your life—"

"I have not been pampered!" Savannah retorted. "You've been away a long time, Libby. You have no idea what my life has been like!" Stepping forward, she spread reddened palms. "Do these look like the hands of a pampered woman?"

Libby's gaze rose from the work-worn hands to a faded

T-shirt the old Savannah wouldn't have been caught dead in. The tables had, indeed, been turned. But the fact failed to touch Libby; she was long beyond being touched.

"What am I supposed to do?" she asked bitingly. "Pity you? Sorry, Savannah. I've spent so many years hating you, I don't think I could give it up now."

"Cut it out!" Danny intervened. "You've burst in here, made all kinds of wild claims—"

"Wild, but true," Libby broke in, her eyes remaining on Savannah. "If you can beat Rory to the evidence, you could reclaim everything your daddy lost."

Everything returned? *The Watch?* The Crossing? Blinded by the brilliant possibility, Savannah fell into a blank stare.

Libby's expression turned sly. "Looks like I may be the messenger of your salvation, Miss Savannah. But maybe the papers are there, maybe not. Maybe Rory will get to them before you do."

"I have keys to *The Watch*," Danny put in sternly. "If the documents are there, we'll get them. Just as soon as this damn storm blows over."

"Let's go to *The Watch* now!" Savannah urged. "I'm sure the storm won't get any worse. Hurricanes never come in at Kingsport."

"We'll wait," Danny muttered.

"But we can't—"

"We'll *wait*, Savannah!" he roared.

"If *I* were you," Libby said, "*I* wouldn't be taking any chances."

"She's right—"

"There's a hurricane on the way!" Danny blasted. "Nobody's going downtown! Not McKenna, not me, and certainly not you!"

Libby regarded the two of them, faced-off as if to do battle, their expressions equally ferocious. They were well matched. But then she'd always thought so.

She laughed, the sound brittle and joyless. "Well, I wish I could stay and enjoy this little tête à tête of yours. It would be interesting to see who wins out. I need to get back to the McKennas' before I'm missed, but I simply couldn't resist the opportunity to share the news. I'm sure you understand."

Savannah turned away from Danny, unleashing her look of defiance on the redhead's receding back. "No! I don't understand. If it's true that you hate me, why have you told me all this?"

Libby glanced over her shoulder with a smile. The running makeup made the expression macabre.

"Isn't it obvious?" she said. "Because I hate Rory more."

Lightning flashed, the lights flickered, and thunder joined the keening wind. The woman in black turned, and in that instant Savannah glimpsed the friend who'd once been dear as a sister.

"Wait!" she cried. Libby halted. "Wait a while," Savannah added more calmly. "Stay here at the Crossing until the storm lets up."

When Libby turned, Savannah realized that all she'd seen in that passing moment was a spectre. The face was hard as granite, the smiling friend of yesteryear dead. Maybe they both were.

"I don't want to stay," Libby answered coldly. "Storm or no storm. You know, for years I wasn't good enough to feel at home in the Crossing. And now?" She threw a contemptuous look about the once-grand parlor. "Honey, *it* ain't good enough for *me*."

Then Libby Parker swept out as abruptly as she'd swept in, like some whirlwind part of the storm. The moment the door closed behind her, Savannah started for the kitchen.

Danny's arm shot out, his hand capturing her wrist. "And just where do you think *you're* going?"

"To get the car keys."

Danny caught the other wrist and held her before him. "You are not taking off on a wild-goose chase in the middle of a hurricane!"

"Let go of me! How do you know it's a wild-goose chase? What if those papers are there? What if I could get everything back?"

Danny clutched his hands to his chest, dragging her with them. "Good God, Savannah! Is there nothing more important than recovering the damnable King fortune? I'll take you downtown as soon as it's safe and not a minute before!"

She studied the tense set of his jaw, his brilliant eyes, and knew there was no reasoning with him. Affecting defeat, Savannah slumped in his grasp and looked away.

"That's better," Danny growled.

She refused to look at him. Finally he released her. Savannah wandered across the parlor, coming to rest at a faded chair some distance away. Danny's eyes bore into her stiff back, part of him longing to go after her, take her in his arms, tell her no one wanted it to be true more than he. If she could reclaim her father's property, there would be no need for a preposterous marriage. But another part of him continued to seethe.

"I'd like to be alone for a while," she said.

Danny nodded shortly. "I'll check the upstairs. I've seen a lot of damage done by Hurricane Zelda in the past couple of days."

Pausing at the doorway, he threw a dark look at her back. "There's more to it than just the hurricane, Savannah. A lot more. Maybe even life and death." She didn't look around, didn't make a move. After a moment of silence, Danny swept a frustrated hand through his hair and walked out.

She stood outside the parlor window, holding onto an old oak, cursing the storm, not for its fearsomeness, but because it blocked her view.

Danny and Savannah had words, and then he disappeared up the staircase. Moments later, Savannah darted out of the room.

She moved around the side of the house in time to see her quarry come out the back door. She hurried through the trees. She hadn't expected this, hadn't counted on Miss Savannah having the guts to come out in the storm.

The rain was torrential, the wind howling. She slipped in the mud as she hurried in the direction in which Savannah had been swallowed by the stormy darkness, arriving in time to see the lights of the old Cadillac convertible flash on.

Lunging through the cover of the storm, she ran for the car, her hand closing on the handle of the back door just as Savannah accelerated. The car lurched forward, dragging the slick handle out of her fingers.

Everything seemed to be against her. The wind gusted with gale force. The rain drove and stung. Within an instant of leaving the house, Savannah had been soaked. She'd struggled her way to the old Cadillac, raced out of the garage, but had gotten no farther than the front of the house when she had to slam on the brakes. A stripling had been ripped from the ground and driven into the courtyard gate so that it hung across the drive like a roadblock.

Ranting under her breath, Savannah shifted to park, got out and braved the savage storm once more, using the meager beam of headlights as she pulled and dragged at the stubborn tree. A punishing ten minutes crawled by as she fought at the wrought-iron gate. She was deafened, drenched, and certain that Danny would glance out a window any minute, see her in the glow of the headlights, and come charging out to haul her back inside.

Finally the tree came free. Savannah threw open the gate and trudged back to the car, slamming the door against the whipping rain. As she floored the accelerator and went spinning down the drive, all she could think was how that was just like Danny. Of all the times he should remember to close the gate!

The road was black as pitch, the noise of the storm a constant howl. Both helped to conceal the fact that she was not alone. Lightning bolted from the clouds, meeting nearby ground with a sizzle, outlining the passenger crouched on the floor in the back.

As Savannah drove dauntlessly toward town, her killer twisted a scarf into the unyielding form of a rope.

Danny made the rounds of countless windows. The house was on a promontory a safe distance from the coast, but one could never be too sure about a hurricane. The only room he left unchecked was Mrs. King's. Her door was locked as usual. He tapped politely.

"Mrs. King? You all right in there?"

No answer. Danny turned away. Savannah would have made sure her mother was okay. Hell, Mrs. King was probably better off than the lot of them—protected in a private world of garden parties and days gone by, a sunny world no storm could penetrate.

He completed his tour. Everything in the old house was secure. It had withstood a hundred years. It would probably stand up to a hundred more. His thoughts returned to Savannah and the mixture of shock and hope that had widened her eyes until they looked like the fixed ones of a doll.

How long had it been since he left her? Fifteen minutes? It seemed longer. He'd taken his time, needing a chance to simmer down. But if Rory McKenna were, in fact, The Strangler—and if the victims had all been, one way or another, his women—then Savannah could be next in line. The thought chilled him and made Danny hurry back downstairs.

"Listen, Savannah," he said as he strolled into the parlor. "Let's call a truce. I need to fill you in on something . . ." He halted as he looked at the chair where he'd left her. "Savan-nah?"

Silence. He walked into the kitchen. It was deserted. He moved back to the foyer.

"Savannah?" he called, a wave of fright slicing through him.

His legs began to move, and he vaulted up the stairs, knowing it was useless, knowing he'd just checked the windows in her room and that she'd been nowhere in sight. Her bedroom was empty. He took the stairs two at a time on the way down and sped onto the veranda. Rain swept across the porch, soaking him anew as he peered through the darkness. Lightning illuminated the courtyard, and he saw the gate standing open. The conclusion smashed into his brain. The damn, mule-headed woman . . .

Dashing back inside, Danny made a quick search for his keys, then realized quite suddenly that Savannah had taken them. Of course she'd taken them! The key to *The Watch* was one of them!

Bursting through the kitchen door, he was drenched in the few seconds it took to reach the jeep and leap inside. He ripped at the wires under the dash. Even in favorable conditions, hot-wiring an engine was not the easiest of tasks. And at the moment his fingers were jumping with a nervous energy he couldn't control. The nearby oak creaked noisily in the savage winds, emitting a loud crack as a limb gave way, banged against the house, and went toppling by the jeep toward the line of palms.

Danny didn't look up. His attention was riveted on the wires in his twitching fingers, though it registered that the storm had worsened drastically in the past hour. Its howling strength reminded him of the way things had been down the coast, and he knew this was no longer just a tropical storm. Zelda was coming.

He thought of the old legend. Anyone who'd grown up around Kingsport knew it. A full-blown hurricane had never struck the seaside town, which was purportedly protected by the ancient spirits of the Sapona Indians. So long as the King blood-line survived, Kingsport would remain unscathed.

Savannah was the last of the Kings. The hurricane was here. And though Danny was not a superstitious man, the hair on his arms was standing straight up.

Finally the engine chugged and caught. Rainwater streamed

down his face as he gripped the gearshift and hesitated, his gaze turning sharply up to the glowing windows of Mrs. King's chamber. He was leaving a crazy old woman alone in an isolated house in the middle of a hurricane. But Savannah was out there.

"Damn!" he yelled, and was soon speeding away from the Crossing.

Flying along the curving estate drive, the jeep was battered, yanked, and jolted. Danny thought of the tragedies he'd seen in the past two days, disasters wreaked by a mad hurricane called Zelda. His stomach went queasy with fear. Pushing the jeep to a hazardous speed, he kept sharp watch for any sign of Savannah's car—maybe turned over in a side ditch, smashed up against some tree, exploding in orange flames despite the deluge.

Danny smacked at the steering wheel. "No!" he yelled.

Pictures of Savannah whirled through his mind: less than an hour ago, standing so rigidly at the parlor chair . . . a few nights ago, lying in bed with afterglow in her eyes . . . fifteen years ago, her pretty face scarlet as she slapped him across the cheek . . . and so many times before that when he'd stared at her from a distance, his heart yearning. He fought to see as the images of Savannah went on and on, spinning behind his stinging eyes, like a time machine whirring him into the past.

Hurricane Zelda smashed into the cape, whipping the tide into frothing towers, hurling torrents through city streets, slapping buildings with gusts of over a hundred miles per hour.

Along the streets on the outskirts of town, palms bowed and bobbed. Flying debris smacked the car and bounced away while the wind tugged and pushed until the best Savannah could manage was a weaving course. Luckily there were no other cars on the road. No one else was fool enough to be out on such a night.

I must be mad, she thought, for she had no fear, only a deadly sense of purpose that blocked out everything else. After all these years, she had a chance at redemption. Her hands were locked on the steering wheel like claws as she strained to see through the flooded windshield and prayed—silently, fervently, over and over again. *Let it be. Please, God. Let it be.*

The car moved erratically into the city, past the commons, shaken by wind, pounded by rain. Slamming to a haphazard stop at the familiar building, Savannah leapt from the car and fished for Danny's keys as she lurched through the whipping rain to the front doors of *The Watch*. She knew them as well as those of her own home and let herself speedily inside. Like everything else in town, the newspaper building had been evacuated. It was like a tomb, dark and silent but for the squeak of her tennis shoes as she raced through the lobby and onto the unmoving escalator.

She climbed up four flights of darkness, and trotted to the publisher's office holding her side from the exertion. The door was unlocked. Rushing inside, Savannah flipped the light switch. Nothing happened. She looked stupidly into the dark room, taking deep heaving breaths that gradually slowed.

Outside, the storm was a shifting roar. Lightning struck and thunder cracked. She should have realized—the power was out! And she had no flashlight, not even a match.

Cursing herself, Savannah felt her way through the familiar room to her father's old desk. Her fingers slid along the polished surface and onto the handle of the file drawer. In the pressing darkness, she ran her palms over the collection of folders. How she was supposed to find the right one, she had no idea.

"Think," she muttered and, stepping closer, bumped against the trash can. One of those large metal things. She felt quickly inside and confirmed that it was empty. Without hesitation, she began removing the contents of the desk drawer, dumping the papers indiscriminately into the trash can. Either her salvation was there, or it wasn't.

Suddenly, above the rustling clatter, she heard something in the hall. She froze and in the new quiet she picked up the unmistakable clicking of footsteps. Savannah turned with a start and peered into the impenetrable darkness. The footsteps came closer . . . closer . . . stopped just outside the room. An eternity passed as she remained frozen—listening, barely breathing.

"Good evening, Miss Savannah."

Her heart leapt to her throat. "Who's there?"

There was a chuckle. "An old friend."

The voice was high and harsh and metallic, like the unnatural voice of a computer. Savannah knew she'd never heard it before. This was no friend. Fear washed over her, leaving her cold and clammy where the storm had failed.

"Did you find what you were looking for?"

"What?"

"I asked if you found the papers."

"I—I don't know . . . I—"

"You should have listened," the voice intervened. "You were warned to stay away from Rory."

"You sent me those notes?"

"No, but I know who did. You should have listened."

Lightning flickered through the room. Savannah caught fleeting sight of a female figure silhouetted in the doorway.

"I don't understand!" she cried. "What do you want?"

"I'm afraid it's your life, my dear."

The high-pitched voice grated like nails on a chalkboard. Silence hung in the room. When lightning flared once more, Savannah saw that the stranger had stepped inside.

Suddenly, instinctively, she dropped the files and bolted for the balcony. As soon as she unlatched the door, the forgotten storm snatched it out of her grasp. It banged crazily against the outer wall as she leapt outside, only to be sucked to the balcony edge by the ferocious wind.

The rain was torrential; the wind, a shifting gale. Savannah struggled against both, pushing away from the balcony, lunging for the door with the speed of sheer terror. The tower was the only part of the building with old-fashioned solid shutters that bolted on both sides. She grabbed the door, used all her strength to force it and the shutter closed. The bolt slammed into place just as she heard the banging begin on the other side.

Savannah spun away. She was cut off from the stranger for a moment. She was also cut off from further escape. The hurricane whipped about her, yanking at her clothes, threatening to pluck her from the precarious precipice four stories up. She found a handhold and flattened herself against the stone wall. Tears seeped from her eyes only to be swept up by the wind as time both crawled and flew—delayed by the terrifying storm, hastened by the insistent banging from nearby.

Five, ten, or maybe twenty minutes later, the shutter splintered open. Savannah cried out, but the sound was only thrown back at her. The hurricane was wild, ear-splitting. It was useless to try to say anything, to make any sense of the figure that moved threateningly toward her. Savannah was glued to the wall, unable to move, even to blink her eyes as they strained through the stormy darkness.

Two yards away . . . one yard . . . Lightning struck, and for a few blinding seconds the stranger was spotlighted as if on a

stage. With spiraling shock, Savannah saw that it was no
stranger . . . saw beyond the smeared lipstick and eyeshadow
that made the face look like a child's drawing . . . saw the familiar features that were, ironically, unknown. Suddenly she realized she was looking into the face of utter madness.

Darkness closed once more about them—the two of them
alone in the tower but for the fearful, binding presence of the
storm. Savannah began to sob. Rough stone bit into her clutching palms, drawing blood, failing to penetrate her hysteria. She
thought of jumping, but pictured the iron, spear-headed fence
surrounding the statue four stories below. Old Josiah King,
founder of the city, *The River Watch*, and the family line of
which she was the last. The legend flitted through her mind. As
long as Josiah's descendants lived, no hurricane would strike
Kingsport. And now Hurricane Zelda was thrashing the city for
all she was worth.

A moment later, lightning struck again. Through her tears,
Savannah saw arms reaching out to her . . . hands that held a
rope.

"No!" she screamed.

Danny skidded to a stop, his heart leaping as he saw Savannah's old car. Two of its doors were standing open. *Two!*

He flashed a searching look up the front of the building as he
vaulted out of the jeep. The place was dark, seemingly empty.
But he knew Savannah was upstairs in the publisher's office.
The thought that she'd made it through the hurricane did nothing to alleviate his panic. As he raced through front doors left
haphazardly open, the pit of his stomach churned with the intu-
itive certainty that she was in peril.

He was drenched. He galloped across the slick floor, and his
wet feet slipped out from under him. The tumble hardly broke
his stride before he was up again and moving, speeding onto the
escalator, cursing the four stories separating himself from the
woman who had been both the dream and torment of his life.

How many times had he vaulted up this infernal escalator because it moved too damned slowly? How many times?! Heaving for breath as he leapt onto the landing and started toward the
third floor, Danny fired a searching look above, gritted his teeth,
and made his cramping legs climb faster.

* * *

"Please!" Savannah cried.

The maniac lunged. Savannah's hands flew instinctively for the face, her fingers slipping, ripping the wig away.

"*No*, Clayton!" she shrieked, just before a lariat whipped round her neck.

"Clayton isn't here!" came the responding shriek.

Savannah clawed at her throat. The cord tightened. She was pinned to the stone wall by the weight of her assailant's body, as well as the driving force of the hurricane. And then, with eerie suddenness, the rain and wind ceased as a vacuous calm fell. *The eye of the storm.* Savannah stared with sudden clarity into the wild eyes above her.

"Clayton," she choked.

"I told you he isn't here. I overpowered him long ago. The most he could do was write you notes! Stay away! Stay away!" the painted face sneered. "But you didn't, did you, Miss Savannah? You're Rory's whore, just like all the others!"

The hands pulled. Savannah felt the noose bite into her flesh . . . and then Danny bounded onto the balcony. The pressure at her throat relented as her tormentor spun around.

"One move and she's dead!"

Danny stumbled to a halt. "Clayton?" he uttered in disbelief.

Drawing a strangled breath, Savannah drove an instinctive knee into his groin. Clayton's only response was to gasp and turn back to her, his expression more hideously frightening than ever.

Danny lunged a few steps, arms outstretched. "Clayton, wait! That's Savannah. Think! Remember all the times she took up for you? Remember when she pulled you out of the quickmud?" He babbled on, scared out of his mind. "She's been your friend a lot of years, Clayton. You don't want to do this."

Miraculously, as Savannah peered into the dark eyes, she saw a change—first of surprise, then of renewed determination.

"Go away!" rang the metallic voice.

"N-no!" Clayton's voice replied. "N-not Savannah!"

The hands fell. Savannah yanked at the scarf and drew racking breaths as Clayton backed away. She slumped down the wall, and Danny ran to her, dropping to his knees beside her.

"Are you all right?" he demanded fiercely.

"Yes," she rasped.

They turned in unison to peer across the balcony. In the tunneled center of the hurricane, starlight shone from the night sky, silvering the outline of the man in the pale floral dress. Clayton backed up against the ledge, gave the two of them a final look and, without a word, turned and threw himself over.

Savannah screamed, the sound splitting the stillness.

"Come on," Danny muttered. Dragging her to her feet, he kept a supporting arm around her as they moved to the balcony edge and looked over.

Four stories below, Clayton was impaled on the fence surrounding the statue of Josiah King. Danny looked swiftly away, pulling Savannah close as she began to sob. There was a stirring of wind, a few raindrops, and Zelda closed on them anew.

"Come on!" Danny yelled against the sudden noise.

Savannah squinted up within the shelter of his arm. "We can't just leave him down there!"

"What do you propose we do? Come *on*, dammit!"

Leaning into the wind, Danny drew her away from the edge of the balcony. They fought their way inside just as a gust of wind shoved through the broken shutters, shattering a window to their left with a loud crash. Glass sprayed across the room.

Danny dragged Savannah down, shielding as much of her as he could with his body. The wind whipped through the office. He pulled her up and started toward the door.

Savannah broke out of his arms. "Wait a minute!"

She bolted away before he knew what she was doing. Lightning struck, and Danny saw her at her father's old desk.

"Are you crazy?" he cried, running over and grabbing her by the arm. "Let's go!"

"The papers . . ."

"What?"

"I've got to get these files—"

"Leave them, Savannah!"

Grabbing up the weighty trash can, she glared through the darkness. "I came for these, Danny! And I mean to take them!"

Yanking the can out of her hands, he directed her out of the office and into the stairwell. The shaft on the interior of the building was black as ink. They felt their way down four flights. The hurricane continued to rage, Savannah knew, but the stairwell was eerily quiet. They stopped on the ground floor landing, and Danny set aside his burden with a disrespectful clatter.

"You stay here," he said and opened the side door.

"Where are you going?" Savannah shrilled.

"There's a maintenance closet just outside. Maybe there's a flashlight, a candle . . . something."

Savannah heard the door close. Inching her way to the trash basket, she sank to the floor beside it and covered her face with her hands. Her cheeks were streaming with both rain and tears. She wiped them away with a sniffle. Peering into the inky blackness, she saw Clayton, his mad eyes glaring at her from a frame of running eyeliner . . . and then his body, speared and hanging from the fence, his face pointed to the sky, his dress flapping around spread-eagled legs. Her eyes filled up again. Savannah swiped at them as she heard a noise at the door. It opened, and there was a shaft of light.

Danny swung the flashlight, halting when its beam fell on her face. Savannah squinted and cringed back against the wall.

"You're more lucky than you deserve," he accused. "I found a flashlight."

Stepping into the stairwell, he crouched to his knees and turned the light toward the ceiling.

"What are we going to do?" Savannah asked.

"For the moment we're going to sit here."

"What about Mother?"

Danny gave her a look of fury. "Don't you think it's a little late to think about her? The hurricane has shifted direction. We're going to wait it out. As soon as it's safe, we're going straight to the police."

"Wait it out? How long will that take?"

"I don't know, Savannah! Do I look like a damned psychic?"

Savannah's ragged nerves flared with anger. "I asked a simple question—"

"There's not a single damn thing about you that's simple!" Danny raged. "You almost got yourself killed tonight, not to mention me! And for what? A bunch of *papers*?!"

Their eyes met in the glow of the flashlight. Silence fell.

"If we're going to be here a while," Savannah said ultimately, "I'd like to use that."

"Shit!" Danny muttered and, handing over the flashlight, propped himself stiffly against the cement wall.

Shining the beam into the depths of the wastebasket, Savannah began sorting through the files. An hour later, when Danny took the flashlight and went out to check the condition of the storm, she had a stack of rejected files a foot high beside her.

She closed her eyes against the silent darkness. There was still a lot of material to be examined, but she was losing hope.

"Still going strong," Danny announced when he returned.

Taking his place against the wall, he made her ask once more for the use of the flashlight, just so it would give him occasion to deliver another scathing glare. Savannah's jaw set hard, and she went back to work with new determination.

At three o'clock Danny took another tour outside the stairwell. At four, Savannah's bleary eyes came suddenly alert.

"Oh, my God," she muttered, racing over page after page of records in a dog-eared file. "This is it! This is *it*, Danny!" she cried, looking up with jubilation.

"Congratulations," he returned shortly.

Savannah's expression fell, along with the hand holding the treasured documents.

"Can't you be happy for me?" she asked.

"Give me the flashlight," he demanded. Reaching out, he snatched it from her hand and turned curtly away.

"You know something, Savannah?" he said in parting. "Your priorities suck."

Shortly after five o'clock, September thirteenth, Zelda left Kingsport behind and roared inland. Danny drove Savannah to the police station in cold silence. The streets of the city were strewn with trees and debris, pieces of rooftops, and fragments of buildings. Some roads were entirely blocked, so they had to take detours. A lone siren sounded in the distance, soon joined by a chorus of others.

As they drove along, the light of dawn filtered over the desolate scene, glistening on the wet leaves of leaning palms, heralding a clear, cloud-free morning. Danny glanced in the rearview mirror. In the western sky behind him, he could see the edge of Zelda, like a dark blot on the horizon.

He pulled up in front of the police station with a grim expression. Generators had the place lit up like a neon sign, and clusters of chattering people were beginning to gather on the steps and in the lobby. Danny steered Savannah to Gilroy's office and found the lieutenant at his desk, unshaven and red-eyed. He looked as though he'd been there all night.

Leading Savannah inside, Danny closed the door behind him.

"Clayton McKenna is dead," he said.

It took a couple of hours to reconstruct the chilling events that had led to Clayton's suicide. It was after eight when Savannah began making her official statement. While she was thus occupied, Danny reviewed the infamous collection of papers that had driven her to *The River Watch*. Eventually she emerged from Gilroy's office.

"Do you think the phones are working?" she asked.

"No."

"I've got to go home. I've got to make sure Mother's all right."

"Take these to the D.A. first," Danny commanded briskly. Thrusting the file on her, he added, "I think you'll find these are everything you were hoping they would be. You can sue for fraud and ask for damages. Rory's attorney will probably cut a deal. You stand to get it all back, Savannah."

Leaning swiftly around the doorjamb, he called, "Hey, Gilroy! Do you think there's a black-and-white that could take her home?"

"I'll find one," the lieutenant replied.

Danny turned away. Savannah reached out and caught his arm.

"Where are you going?" She seemed forever to be asking him that question.

"I have a story to write," he replied.

He tugged at his arm. She held fast. He looked into her eyes, still furious. Savannah let go, and he stalked away.

Chapter Fourteen

September 15, 1991

SAVANNAH WOKE from a late sleep. She was still off schedule after the sleepless night of the hurricane. The Crossing had sustained relatively little damage, a path of roof tiles having been blown off the roof, a couple of trees uprooted. Her mother had fared better than anyone, having slept through the entire night of terror.

It was lunchtime when Dr. Crane showed up. Savannah poured iced tea, and they settled in the parlor. Two days had passed since Clayton McKenna's body was pulled off the fence at *The Watch*. Still, Savannah saw the sight quite clearly and feared that she would for years to come.

"We'll never know the full truth," Leo said, "but a few things seem clear. Clayton was out to get Rory, and through him, probably his father. Also, his madness was tied somehow to his mother's death. Maybe that's when it all began. MPD is generally rooted in trauma, something so traumatic that the individual simply can't face it."

"MPD?" Savannah questioned.

"Multiple personality disorder. It wasn't Clayton who attacked you that night at *The Watch*."

"Split personality."

"Exactly. The person who attacked you—and killed at least three women—could have been entirely unknown to Clayton. It's possible he wasn't cognizant of what the other personality was doing. Every case is different, but many MPD patients have proven amnestic to events experienced by the alternate personalities. Clayton probably had black-outs; he knew something was wrong. But it's possible he had no idea what was happening until the night you were attacked, Savannah. I'll wager Clayton's fondness for you was strong enough to bring him to the surface."

Savannah rubbed her forehead as she remembered. "His last words were, 'No. Not Savannah.' That was the only time he sounded like himself. The other voice was completely different from Clayton's. I didn't know who it was."

"Someone born of a tragedy," Leo theorized. "Someone strong who took over when Clayton crumbled, someone without a conscience to interfere with the carrying out of a lethal vendetta. I've often thought how like Margaret he was. Maybe Clayton had more of his father in him than I knew."

The two of them glanced aside as Danny came down the stairs and turned toward the kitchen without looking in their direction. Savannah's heart sank. His arms were loaded with baggage.

"That was quite a column in *The Watch* this morning," Leo said.

Savannah nodded, her gaze still turned in the direction in which Danny had disappeared. "He's extremely talented."

"He told the whole story," Leo went on. "Clayton's madness, Big Ed's treachery, Rory's calculation. But somehow the overwhelming feeling that came out was a deep-seated respect for Jim King."

"He always loved my father," Savannah murmured.

"He always loved *you*, too," Leo pointed out.

Savannah gave him a doleful look. "Maybe . . . once." Rising to her feet, she added, "Excuse me, Dr. Crane."

She went out the kitchen door and crossed the patio. The sky was a peaceful azure blue, making it difficult to believe that only two nights before it had roiled with the fury of Hurricane Zelda. Savannah paused beneath the Spanish moss in the shade of the old live oak, watching as Danny lowered the tailgate of the jeep.

"That was a beautiful piece in the paper today," she said in a calm voice that couldn't have been more contradictory to how she felt. "Somehow you managed to turn a sordid story of insanity and murder into a tribute."

"It was for your father," Danny replied shortly. "The eulogy I would have written twelve years ago if I'd been able."

She meandered down the patio steps. "By the way, you were right. The district attorney met with Rory's lawyer. They're of-

fering to return *The Watch* plus a cash settlement for lost profits
in the development of King's Club."

"Good for you," Danny grunted.

He hadn't yet looked at her, only began loading his bags into
the jeep as if he couldn't be away soon enough.

"So, you're leaving now?" she forced from a dry throat.

"I've done what I came here to do," he returned.

"*More* than what you came here to do."

Danny hesitated in the midst of lifting a duffel bag, then
hoisted it decisively.

"If you're talking about our little rendezvous a few nights
back, believe me, it was entirely my pleasure."

Savannah swallowed hard as the last of his things disappeared into the jeep. "The other night at the river, you said you
didn't necessarily have to leave."

Danny raised the tailgate and secured it. "A lot of things have
changed since that night at the river."

"Danny, please—"

She stopped as he held up a brisk hand, wordlessly commanding her into silence. He circled around to the driver's side.
She followed and tried another tack.

"*The Watch* could use an ace reporter like Buck Sawyer."

"You'll find someone else," he said, opening the door.

"Where are you headed?" Savannah asked in a dismal tone.

"Haven't decided yet. Probably back to *The Post*."

"*Why* are you leaving, Danny?"

He glanced over his shoulder. "*Why?*" he echoed with a short
laugh. She said nothing, only stared up at him with the deep
blue eyes that had been his undoing since boyhood. The old
yearning stirred; he forced it down.

"Don't be ridiculous," he added. "You know why."

"Because of me," she supplied quietly.

He shifted around and leaned back against the jeep. "You
know, Savannah, we grew up together, but I discovered something the other night. I don't *know* you. Maybe I never did."

"How can you say that? You know me better than anyone."

Danny shook his head. "I know some things. I know I've
loved you since I was a kid, and all you've ever done is take that
love for granted—treat it as if it were nothing more than your
due."

She opened her mouth.

"Let me finish," Danny said to stop her. "That's okay. I got used to that, but . . . I never suspected what's deep inside you, what drives you. I should have, I guess, but I didn't—even when you were about to auction yourself off to McKenna. It took the hurricane. That's when I realized there was nothing you wouldn't trade for the King fortune, the King name—not even your life!"

His voice had risen. It fell as he added, "Would to God you had half that much feeling for me."

"I *do* have—"

"What you have is the love of your life coming back to you—*The Watch*, the Crossing, the highfalutin social position. I hope you'll be very happy together. As for me, one day I intend to fall in love again with a woman who can love me back."

The thought of Carol Kincaid flashed to mind. "I could—"

"It's over, Savannah."

He started to climb in, and she grabbed his trailing hand, holding it within both of hers. "Don't go, Danny," she choked.

He turned slowly and found that her eyes were shining with unshed tears. His own filled with stinging moisture, though his face remained hard and tense.

"Or if you won't stay," Savannah whispered through shaking lips, "then take me with you."

The request hit Danny with the impact of a punch, startling him so that he yanked his hand out of her grasp. "What are you talking about, Savannah? You know damn well you'd never leave Kingsport, especially now that you've got everything you always wanted."

The tears spilled over. "I was wrong about what I always wanted. It doesn't mean anything."

"Don't play with me, woman! What the hell are you saying?"

"I'm saying . . ." she sniffled ". . . I'm saying I love you, Danny. I love you more than I thought it possible to love anything."

A fierce heat bolted like lightning through his body. Danny was stricken speechless. Around them came the sounds of the Crossing—the buzzing of bees, the twitter of birds, the faint stir of a late summer breeze.

"You'd go with me?" he questioned finally. "You'd leave it all behind?"

Tears continued to course down her cheeks, but once the declaration was out of her mouth, Savannah's trembling ceased. "I

wouldn't want to leave," she said. "But if it's the only way I can
be with you . . . I will."

Danny hung his head. The hope that seared through him was
a burning thing, pulling him inevitably toward her despite all
his firm resolutions to make Savannah King, once and for all, a
thing of the past. Slamming the jeep door, he stepped over and
took her face in his hands. His thumbs smoothed away the tears
as he stared into her eyes.

"You *mean* it?" he rumbled.

Savannah reached up around his neck, returning his seeking
look with one of serene, if tearful, assurance.

"Damn straight," replied the painfully proper Miss Savannah, and raised her mouth to his.

Rory McKenna was charged with accessory after the fact to
fraud, interference with business relations, and unfair and de-
ceptive trade practice. An outstanding indictment was issued
against Big Ed. Should his health improve, he faced similar
charges.

The trial date was set and a grand jury assembled. The papers
Savannah supplied were admitted as evidence, and in exchange
for immunity from prosecution, Ben Cochrane testified. But it
was the eyewitness testimony of Libby Parker that sealed
Rory's fate. He was convicted on all counts.

The day after the hurricane, the infamous Miss Parker had
moved out of the McKenna house and into the Ocean Forest
Hotel, where, it was reported, she took one of the most expensive suites. Gossip escalated to a frenzy when parcels and baggage began arriving from Atlanta, the coup de grace a black
Mercedes limousine.

On the late October day that Rory was sentenced, she made a
rare public appearance in the Brunswick County Courthouse.
The place was packed. A hum of whispering filled the air, a
good deal of it centering on the mysterious redhead dressed in a
black silk suit and matching cloche that must have cost thousands.

The whispering ceased when the judge entered. The convicted man was ordered to rise.

"Two years hard labor . . ."

As the sentence was announced, Libby rose from her place in
the third row. Rory whirled in an outburst of fury, his eyes
sweeping the courtroom and landing squarely on her. Arching a

brow, Libby blew him a kiss. Rory lunged in her direction. A flurry of gasps rose from the crowd as police officers sprang to restrain him.

Libby turned her back, and as she walked up the aisle, a hush fell on the courtroom. The most recognition she paid the staring eyes was a lift of the chin as she accelerated her pace. When the swinging door closed behind her, the courtroom came alive with a frenzy of chatter.

Savannah hurried out and caught up to her at the elevator. Libby glanced aside, and reaching up, pressed the "down" button with obvious impatience.

"Well," Savannah began. "It looks like Rory is getting what he deserves."

"Hardly what he deserves. But at least it's something."

"Thank you, Libby."

She turned enough to deliver a cutting look. "I didn't do it for *you*," she said. "And the name's Lilah. Lilah Parks."

The elevator arrived, and she stepped in without further word.

The next day Danny called from *The Watch* to report the latest. Libby Parker was packing up and moving out.

On the way to the Ocean Forest, Savannah wondered what she was going to say. The answer still hadn't come to her when she tapped at the open door of the posh suite and stepped inside to see Libby overseeing a group of bellboys. She glanced up as Savannah walked in, then turned briskly back to the luggage rack.

"That's the last of it, boys," she said, and proceeded to slap a series of bills into the series of hands. "See you downstairs."

The group rattled past Savannah. She kept her eyes on Libby. In contrast to the sober black in which she so often dressed, she was wearing a suit of vivid yellow. Topped with the flaming hair, she was an explosion of fall color.

"What are you doing here?" she asked carelessly, and moving to the nearby table, proceeded to light a cigarette.

"I came because . . . I was hoping we could get things settled between us."

Lilah expelled a rush of smoke. "Then you came for nothing."

"I don't understand—"

"You *couldn't* understand!" Lilah snapped.

Savannah held up a quick palm. "Please," she said. "We were best friends once. Can't you just tell me what happened?"

Lilah took a drag and strolled toward her. "You want to know the story? All right. Remember the New Year's Eve you gave me your emerald taffeta? We were sixteen. Rory raped me that night, and after that he took me whenever he wanted."

"No . . ."

"Yes! But that's nothing. When I left here, I was pregnant with his bastard. A little cash could have bought a discreet abortion from a qualified doctor, but I didn't have any cash. Remember?"

Savannah stared at her. "How could I remember? I never knew—"

"I was *butchered*, Savannah! I almost died, and all for the lack of your pocket money!"

"I don't understand," Savannah mumbled.

"I wrote you! I *begged* for your help!"

"No, I . . . I only got one letter from you. You said you'd write again when you got settled."

"I called you on the phone!" Lilah halted, Ophelia King's voice ringing in her memory's ear. "Your mother," she mumbled.

Savannah blinked, considered the explanation, and was struck by the rightness of it.

"Yes," she said in a hollow tone. "Probably so."

"I should have known, but it never occurred to me she would have intercepted the letters."

"I'm so sorry, Libby."

"I've told you before, the name is Lilah. Libby Parker died years ago, revived only for a brief performance here in Kingsport. I came back to get Rory McKenna, and I have."

"Why didn't you tell me?" Savannah asked. "Years ago you could have told me what Rory was doing."

Lilah chuckled sharply. "Tell *you*? The virgin princess?"

"I would have figured out a way to help. You were my friend!"

"I thought so once!"

The two of them exchanged a stormy look. Lilah was surprised to see tears come to Savannah's eyes, and suddenly something hard and unyielding within her crumbled. She drew a deep breath, a feeling of release spreading through her.

"I was very young," she said quietly. "Very ashamed."

"But it wasn't your fault."

"It wasn't yours either. I see that now."

Lilah reached up and placed a hand on Savannah's shoulder. Then she turned quickly away, stubbed out the cigarette, and picked up her purse. She hadn't said so in words, but Savannah knew. The hate was gone.

They rode down the elevator together and walked out into the mellow October sunshine. The extravagant Mercedes was parked at the curb.

"This car," Savannah commented with a sweeping look. "The clothes, the hotel . . . There are so many things I'd like to ask. You're a complete mystery, Lilah Parks."

"Part of my charm." Lilah opened the car door and tossed her purse inside.

"Where will you go?"

"I've got a nifty little penthouse down in Atlanta, but . . . I don't know. I feel like I've done the South. Maybe I'll take a spin up north. How about you?"

Savannah's brows rose. "What do you mean? Now that everything's coming back to me, you know I won't leave Kingsport."

"Even if Danny asked you?"

Color rushed to Savannah's cheeks. Lilah shook her head condemningly, though a whimsical grin pulled at her mouth.

"You're such a prude, Savannah King. I've known he was the one for you since we were nothing but kids."

Savannah's lips curved in a slow smile. "Yes, you have, haven't you? All right, then, I'll tell you. Yes, if Danny asked me, I'd follow him to the ends of the earth. Thankfully, it's not going to come to that. He's staying. We'll be putting the Crossing and *The Watch* back in shape together."

"So you got it all," Lilah murmured. "The brass ring, the whole works."

"Yes. I guess I did."

"Always kind of figured you would."

Savannah took another look at the car. "You don't seem to have done so badly either."

"I've got plenty of money, that's for sure," Lilah said with a smile. "Well, good-bye."

She offered a hand, but the two of them ended up in a hug.

"Let me hear from you some time," Savannah whispered.

"Sure," Lilah replied and climbed into the Mercedes.

As she drove away, she glanced in the rearview mirror and
saw that Savannah was waving, her fair hair shining in the sunlight. Lilah put up a hand adorned in an expensive driving glove
as a lump formed in her throat. She'd miss Savannah, for she
sensed she'd never lay eyes on her again. Savannah was part of
Kingsport, and Lilah knew she'd never return.

Speeding along the old highway on which she'd fled so many
years before, she slowed at the crossroads, put on a pair of dark
glasses, and turned north. Perhaps now that the shadow of Rory
had been lifted, she could find the sun. Perhaps somewhere out
there in the world, someday, she'd find the kind of happy life
Savannah would share with Danny.

Lilah smiled at the uncharacteristically romantic thought, the
expression remaining as Kingsport rolled mile after mile into
the past.

"Is this some sort of Halloween joke?" Ophelia shrilled.

Savannah glanced at Danny. Despite the shadows sifting
through the master bedroom, she saw telltale color rise to his
face.

"It's no joke, Mother," she said firmly.

"Don't be absurd," Ophelia scolded. "You can't get married.
You're a mere child."

"I'm a grown woman. Somewhere inside you, you must
know that."

"I know nothing of the sort." Ophelia's gaze swerved to
Danny. "Marriage? To *him*? Preposterous!"

Savannah reached out and took Danny's hand. "I love him,
Mother. And I intend to marry him as soon as he'll have me."

Ophelia folded her arms across her chest and looked back and
forth between the two of them. "Savannah Sawyer," she said,
voicing the name with obvious distaste. "Sounds rather like the
hiss of a snake, don't you think?"

Danny cocked his jaw and looked down at Savannah with
mounting irritation. A merry twinkle lit her eyes, and before he
knew what was happening, she'd thrown her arms about his
neck and was pulling him down to her. Savannah kissed him
fully, brazenly, chuckling into his mouth as she felt his lips
smile beneath hers.

They were married the following week in a private ceremony
at First Baptist Church. Dr. Crane acted as best man, Ophelia
King as matron of honor. Danny blew the horn of the old

Cadillac all the way back to the Crossing, drawing a smile even from his stodgy mother-in-law.

It was the first Saturday of November, the afternoon sun unseasonably warm. Leaving Ophelia and the doctor chatting in the parlor, Danny and Savannah strolled onto the patio hand in hand. The back lawns had been cut and seeded; the sunlight lay across the new green in a shining mantle.

"It looks almost like it used to, doesn't it?" Savannah sighed.

"Um-hmm." Danny looked down at her. She was wearing a lacy dress that reminded him of the kind of thing she used to wear as a girl. The spray of pink rosebuds pinned at her shoulder had been his contribution.

"Happy?" he said.

She looked up with a dazzling smile, raised her left hand, and flashed the wedding band. "What do you think?"

"I think you're the most beautiful bride I've ever had," he teased. Her expression dimmed. "What is it?" he asked.

"Only one thing could make me happier. I wish Daddy could have known. I think he always hoped we'd end up together."

Danny released her hand and stretched an arm around her shoulders. "Maybe he does know. Some people believe that's possible." Still, she looked a little sad. Danny cupped her chin. "I tell you what. We'll name our first son after him."

The smile reappeared. "He'd like that."

"Come on," Danny said. "Let's take a walk."

They strolled out onto the lawns, and when they were a fair distance from the house, he took her in his arms and kissed her. Like always, when she kissed him back, his blood caught fire.

"I want you, Mrs. Sawyer," he whispered.

"I want you, too," came the murmured reply.

"Right here. Right now." Taking Savannah's arms from around his neck, he shrugged out of his jacket and tossed it aside.

"Danny!" she said with an immediate blush. His tie followed the way of his jacket, and she stepped back. "You can't be serious!"

"Oh, *yes*." He grinned. "I'll show you just how serious in a minute."

Savannah continued to back away, a hand rising to her mouth as he stripped off his shoes and socks.

"Take off that pretty dress unless you want grass stains on it," he challenged and began unbuttoning his shirt.

"Danny Sawyer!" she chimed, her face as bright as her uncontrollable smile. "Mother and Dr. Crane are just inside. We are *not* going to—"

"Oh, yes, we *are*!" he announced, peeling off his shirt.

Savannah had backed off to a distance of several yards. Danny fixed her with a devilish look and started toward her.

"Ain't no boogers out tonight," he chanted. "Ain't no boogers out tonight."

In the spirit of the game, Savannah slipped out of her pumps and bolted toward the pines, chortling shrieks flying behind her, Danny in hot pursuit.

And once again, the stately grounds of Kings Crossing rang with their childlike laughter.